W9-BDL-222

Raymond C. Andrews, M.D.

MEDICAL GRAIL

A Novel

Books by Raymond C. Andrews, M.D.

The Life and Times of Benjamin Wiggins, MD
Medical Grail
How to Be a Patient and Live to Tell the Tale!
Driving the Great Western Trail in Arizona

All books are available as ebooks on Kindle. Printed versions are available from many online retailers and at the author's website:

www.medicalgrail.com.

Majette Publications First Edition 2011

www.medicalgrail.com
email: majettebooks@cox.net

Cover Design by Raymond C. Andrews, M.D.

EAN-13: 978-1456316082
ISBN-10: 1456316087

Acknowledgments

I wish to thank Frederica MacDonough for her support and encouragement. Without her patience, guidance, and practical suggestions, this book would never have been finished.

My deepest thanks also go to Peter H. Ventura, Atty. In addition to his word-by-word corrections of the text, he offered invaluable insight into the workings of the justice system.

I took the one less traveled by,
And that has made all the difference,

- Robert Frost, *The Road Not Taken*

To my Wife

Holy Grail

(in modern spirituality) a symbol of the spiritual wholeness that leads a person to union with the divine.

TheFreeDictionary by Farlex

Medical Grail

(in modern materialism) a symbol of material wealth that leads a medical professional to union with the devil.

Raymond Clifford Andrews, MD

I

Robert's shaking fingers grappled for the receiver of a phone he heard but could not see. It was dark and cold in that strange room. His clawed hand groped blindly for the rotary telephone. It scrabbled around, knocked an empty whiskey glass to the floor, and then found the jangling instrument. He rolled over on the lumpy mattress and put the receiver to his ear. He felt slightly dizzy.

"Pronto!" he slurred an Italian telephone hello. "Cris? *Pronto*." He was speaking to his dead wife. Again.

"Dr. Bascom? Dr. Robert Bascom?" a female voice stuttered, confused by his reply.

"Yesh. Sorry," the 35 year-old physician replied. "Yesh, dammit," he mumbled. His wife had died months earlier, yet he still talked to her. When he did so among friends, they gently reminded him that she was in "a better place." It angered him. Bascom did not consider a coffin in a tomb in Italy *a better place.*

He sat up, ran a shaky hand through his hair, and then squinted at his old army watch. It was between 0400 and 0600 hours. The dimly iridescent hands shimmered too much for him to be certain, but it made no difference. The phone call had interrupted a pleasant dream and had annoyed him.

"Who is this?" he asked as he blew the dust from his

nose.

"Donna Franklyn, sir. I'm a nurse at the hospital and I've a critical patient you need to see."

"Ms. Franklyn," he said as he rubbed an eye with the heel of his hand, "I don't start work till tomorrow morning. I don't even have staff privileges yet."

"Dr. Perkins says you can treat patients," she insisted. "There's no time to argue about this now. You can discuss it with Mr. Cohen in the morning if you like, sir. But I need you here immediately."

"What've you got?" he yawned.

"An unresponsive 25 year-old Mexican who's cut his arm to the bone," she replied. "His blood pressure is 50/0, pulse 32, and respirations 4. I put in a Foley catheter and he's got no urinary output."

"How much blood have you given him?" Bascom swung his legs over the side of the bed, cupped a hand in front of his nose and exhaled into it. The smell of stale alcohol bounced back at him. *If shock doesn't kill the guy, my breath sure will.*

He switched on the nightstand light. He had vowed to stop drinking the day he started work here in Whitney, but he could not resist pocketing the miniature Scotch bottles the hostess had offered him on the flight from Italy. He should have disconnected his phone before draining them and going off to sleep. Now he had to see a patient reeking of half-digested Scotch. Even if he was not drunk, being even a tiny bit under the influence violated his rigid standards of proper physician behavior. Robert Bascom knew he would chastise himself over this lapse for weeks – or until some other convenient, guilt-producing breach of protocol replaced it.

"No blood, just saline," the nurse replied.

"Don't you treat blood loss by replacing it?"

"Yes, but I need a doctor's order."

"Aren't there any physicians on duty in your ER?" he asked. Bascom's eyebrows furrowed with genuine concern.

"Dr. Perkins is here. But he's busy."

"Order six units of whole blood and three units of Hetastarch. I'm on my way." Robert hung up the phone and stood, holding onto the nightstand until the wooziness passed. He rubbed his fingers over the stubble on his cheek and thought about shaving, but there was no time. He donned the sweaty dress shirt he had worn on the plane, then fumbled with its buttons, all the while cursing those straight Scotch nightcaps.

Bascom smoothed the shirtfront over his flabby abdomen and stepped unsteadily into his jeans. He stood up and sucked in his stomach so he could button them. When he relaxed those muscles and breathed normally again, a doughnut of flab oozed over his belt line. *Disgusting.* In the six months since his wife's death, he had morphed from a trim marathon runner into a human pear. He had agreed to modernize Whitney's small hospital as a way of returning to the Bascom his colleagues respected and sometimes even feared. Unfortunately he would make his début appearance disguised as a street bum.

He pulled on a wool jacket and finger-combed his unkempt blond hair before exiting the house. It was November in the Arizona desert, and in comparison to the freezing temperatures in the Italian mountain town he had left the day before, the morning air here felt spring-like.

Bascom paused on the empty street to get his bearings. The taxicab driver on the way in from the Phoenix airport had told him the hospital was three blocks down and one over. But in which direction? He tried to freshen his breath with a mint spray he always carried with him, but the can was empty. He licked its nozzle. Maybe a leftover drop of the sickly sweet liquid would mask the stale Scotch. If any-one got too close he would breathe into his sleeve or hold his breath.

When will you realize her death wasn't your fault? Bascom tossed the empty can into a bin and hurried along the uneven sidewalk.

"But it is! You'll never live it down, Dr. Pain in the Ass Perfect," the familiar taunting voice in his head jeered. Bascom pulled up the collar of his jacket. He saw a sign and decided to hang a left.

"Basta!" he grumbled as he smacked the side of his head with his fist to silence the dissenting voice. He ran a few steps, then slowed to catch his breath and then ran again all the way to the hospital on Apache Lane. Before Cristina died he could have run the distance without working up a sweat. Now, as he burst through the ER doors, he was gasping for air and holding his chest like an old man with a heart attack.

A homely young woman in a white dress and blue sweater quickly rose from her chair as he approached the nursing station. He was wheezing.

"Are you in pain?" she asked, mistaking him for a patient.. A well-dressed man reading a newspaper in the corner of the nursing station glanced up, frowned, and then resumed his reading.

"No. Out of shape. I'm Dr. Bascom," he rasped. "A Ms. Franklyn called me in to see a patient."

"He's over there," the woman replied. He wheeled and saw two patients on opposite sides of the otherwise empty ward. One snored peacefully while a nurse and a young man in a blood-spattered uniform attended to the other. From where he stood, Bascom could see the patient was an unconscious, pale, cadaverous young Mexican. Walking toward the trio, he read the vital signs flickering on the battered EKG monitor next to the stretcher: heart rate 20, blood pressure 40/30.

"Hi," Bascom said, as he touched the Mexican's cheek with the back of his hand. The man's skin was cold and dry. Death was near. He clicked his tongue softly as he examined the gauze dressing over the man's elbow. It too was dry. And white.

He saw the nurse watching his shaky hand and quickly stuck it in his pocket. The woman was dark-haired, brown-eyed and probably in her early thirties. An American Sophia Loren – only prettier.

She pulled her granny glasses down onto the bridge of her nose, shook her head, and then pushed them back up and peered at the label on the bag of blood.

She knows, Bascom realized. A new shiver of old shame crept over him.

"Glad you got here," she said as she compared the bag's blood type label to the patient's wristband. "I'm Donna and this is Roberto, a paramedic from AZ-Amb," she explained, nodding to the emergency medical technician who was rhythmically compressing a rubber bag attached to a tube in the patient's mouth.

"I'm sorry I woke you. But this man needs your help."

"His vitals are incompatible with life," Bascom replied, pointing to the monitor. "It'll be impossible to save him. Has the other stuff arrived?"

"You mean the Hetastarch?"

"Yes. It treats shock by increasing plasma volume."

"I know what it does, Doctor," she replied with a half grin. *Haughty and contentious* came to mind. That was irritating. But then he knew an unshaven, flabby, half dressed doctor, smelling of stale alcohol was not conducive to inspiring staff confidence.

"I was just verifying your order," she said. "You mumbled it over the phone," she added, attaching the blood bag to a pole at the head of the stretcher.

"Refresh the vitals, please," he requested. Then he sighed and thought, *Mumbled? She did say, "mumbled." She knew damn well I was slurring my words.*

Donna hit a button on the monitor and the cuff hissed around the patient's arm. "Pulse 20, pressure 40/30," she said. "I've never seen vitals so low before."

"He's agonal. On the verge of death," Bascom replied. As he spoke, a pharmacist arrived with the Hetastarch. Donna took one of the plastic bags and hung it on the pole next to the blood.

"How did this happen, Roberto?" Bascom asked as the nurse plugged the tube from the bag to a needle in the man's arm. He cupped his hand discreetly over his mouth and breathed into it. That drop of breath freshener was not working. Bascom took a step back from the EMT.

"His ex-wife called 911 while he was breaking into her apartment. He probably cut his arm as he pulled it back through the broken glass door," Roberto replied, still squeezing the bag with his muscular hands. The patient's chest rose as air was forced into his lungs. "We found him in a pool of blood under a truck."

"How long ago?"

"Over an hour," the EMT replied. "We didn't know how long he had been there."

"He's past the 'Golden Hour,' the maximum time a body can survive in a state of shock before irreversible tissue death sets in. That dressing is bone-dry. It's not even pink," Bascom said, pointing to the gauze around the Mexican's arm. "The guy's out of blood."

"He wasn't before I changed it," the nurse interrupted. She straightened the tubing to increase the flow of the Hetastarch.

"What were his vitals when he arrived?"

"Pressure 80/50, pulse 140," Roberto replied.

"Why didn't you transfuse him then? You could have saved him," Bascom demanded. "This looks bad."

"Dr. Perkins was busy," Donna explained.

"Too busy to write an order for blood for a man who is dying right here in the ER?" Bascom fumed. "I find this hard to believe." He turned toward Dr. Perkins who stood behind the nursing desk. Perkins sensed his new colleague's anger. He snapped his newspaper tight and hid his face.

"Did you ask him to order blood for this patient, Ms. Franklyn?" he asked the nurse directly. He dug his right hand deeper into his pocket and impatiently drummed the fingers of his left on the stretcher's railing.

"Three times," she murmured. Her eyes narrowed to slits behind her granny glasses. "Each time he said he was too busy and to call you."

"Busy doing what?" he insisted.

"Reading the paper," she replied. "Dr. Perkins won't treat Mexicans or Indians if he can find a way not to, and he always finds a way not to."

Bascom had worked with bungling physicians and even corrupt physicians, but this was the first time he had ever worked with a killer physician. If what the nurse had said was true, Perkins was in Mengele's class. No more ethical than the German SS officer physician in the Nazi concentration camps. Mengele was known as the Angel of Death. Maybe Perkins didn't take pleasure in torturing his patients the way Mengele did – but he had flagrantly ignored the fate of a dying patient. Indeed he had stood by, watching from behind the goddamn local newspaper as the man bled to death. "I'll deal with him later," Bascom growled.

The nurse tilted her head, like a puppy trying to understand a new command. "Someone should've dealt with him a long time ago," she muttered.

"Excuse me?" Bascom said, as a blotch slowly appeared on the dry bandage. Light pink like dilute cherry soda, far from the dense red of blood.

"I said," the nurse repeated loudly, "the IVs are running fine, Doctor."

"Um. Do you have an arterial repair kit?"

"In the OR."

"Get it."

The nurse left the ER and Bascom undid the bandage and beamed the overhead light into the jagged gash above the man's elbow. Deep in the wound lay a severed artery from which oozed a dilute mixture of blood and Hetastarch. He crumpled a corner of the bandage, gently pressed it over the torn vessel and held it in place. Donna returned shortly with a blue bundle and placed it on the steel stand next to the stretcher.

"Put a finger on this," Bascom ordered before opening the surgical pack. He slipped on a pair of sterile latex gloves as the nurse read the monitor.

"His blood pressure is 40/0, Doctor," she said. "He's in shock."

"You mean he's *still* in shock," Bascom corrected. He picked up a clamp, held it over the wound and nodded. Donna removed the gauze. He reached in to clamp the artery, but it was no longer bleeding. The jagged tear in the artery's wall was dry.

"Measure his B/P again," he sighed, tossing the clamp onto the tray. It skidded noisily off the metal and landed silently on the blue towel. The nurse hit a button on the monitor. The blood pressure cuff hissed as it inflated around the man's arm. Bascom took a penlight from the technician's shirt pocket and flashed it into the patient's eyes.

"Zero," she said. "No pressure and no heartbeat." She looked up at Bascom. "Should we start CPR?"

"It's too late," Bascom replied as the monitor beeped. "You can turn that off. His pupils are fixed and dilated. He's dead. But he didn't need to be. I'm pronouncing him dead at 0730," he added, looking at his watch. "Is his family here?"

"No," Donna replied. "He's alone."

"Too bad you couldn't save this guy. Don't worry. You did what you could..." Bascom said, "...under the circumstances. Thanks. Good night," he added before returning to the nursing station.

He said *hi* to the woman behind the desk as he took the Mexican's chart from her. "Would you have the social worker tell his family?"

"Sure," she replied with a smile.

"Thanks. Where's Dr. Perkins?"

"He left a few minutes ago," she replied.

"Would you tell Mr. Cohen that I'll be in his office at 3 pm."

"I will," she said.

Bascom documented the events on the dead man's chart and left the ER. The thought of a bed, even a lumpy, dusty one, quickened his pace, and within minutes he entered a tan Santa Fe style house. He glanced up at its open-beamed ceilings, made his way between the hand-hewn chairs around the river rock fireplace, and slouched down the hall to the bedroom.

A queen-sized bed with a carved headboard and matching nightstands shared cramped space with a rugged pine armoire that boasted a full-length mirror. He paused to stare at his disheveled self. *Cristina would kill me if she saw me like this,* he thought. He also knew that if she were still alive, he would not be where he was, looking so scruffy.

He crouched down, opened a suitcase on the floor, removed her picture and traced her flowing blond hair with his finger. Cristina smiled seductively back at him from the antique silver frame. "I miss you, Cris," he whispered. "I did what I could. But it wasn't enough. Forgive me." He choked out the last word, set his dead wife's photograph askew on the nightstand, and collapsed on the bed.

II

The sun was well into the western sky when Bascom awoke on his first day in Whitney. The scene in the emergency room had dominated his dreams, and no matter how fast he ran to the hospital and no matter how much blood he poured into his young Mexican patient, the result remained the same: death. Or was it murder?

When he finally crawled out of bed, he felt as if he had run a marathon with his legs chained loosely together. He opened the windows in the house that had been abandoned for years before his arrival, and went to the bathroom to shave. He smeared a blue gel over his cheeks and chin and then put his razor to his face. His hand, once steady enough to pick a metal speck off an eye with a pin, shook. He nicked his chin. As he stuck a piece of toilet paper on the cut, he thought of Perkins, the doctor who had refused to treat a patient because of his race. He had never faced a similar situation during his 10 years as an emergency room director on the east coast, and he knew he could not ignore it.

He also knew his choices were few and flawed. He could call the police and the state medical society and accuse Perkins of… what? Murder? He shook his head and continued shaving. That never happened, not even in the movies. Doctors never violated their code of silence. It was far more powerful than the Mafia's *omertà*, and breaking it meant certain economic death. Plus he would have to rely on Nurse Franklyn's testimony. If she denied that Perkins had refused to order blood, instead saying a disheveled, drunken doctor had misunderstood her, Perkins would sue him for slander. And he would win, since no jury would ever believe a doctor in America would let a man die just because of his race.

He could book the next flight to Italy and let someone else deal with Perkins. There he could again spend his afternoons sipping wine in his *baita*, his comfy log home in the forest above Lizzano in Belvedere just outside of Bologna, until he saw double and could no longer stand, as he had done for the last six months. But he had accepted the job in Whitney to break that habit.

Bascom wiped the last of the shaving cream from his face. He could not ignore what he had witnessed a few hours earlier. Perkins had not shot or stabbed the Mexican, but withholding lifesaving care was, in his mind, murder. Even so, he was already ruing his decision to accept George Cohen's offer to improve conditions in his run-down hospital in the middle of Arizona's Sonoran desert. The administrator had hired him to solve a few "small problems," but Perkins was not a "small problem." He did not want to fight a battle he could not win. He would meet with Cohen, apologize for any inconvenience he might have caused him, and then return to Italy.

He showered, dressed in his signature sport shirt and jeans, donned his wool jacket, and checked his appearance in the mirror. When Cristina was alive, his jacket hung smartly from his tall, once muscular frame. Now the wrinkled garment draped over his shoulders and expanding belly like a half empty potato sack. *Pathetic!*

He left the house and felt the hot November sun bake

his back through the jacket as he walked to the hospital. He paused at its cracked walkway. In the moonlight, it appeared as an innocent shadow in a sea of twinkling stars, but the harsh Arizona sun mercilessly exposed the building as a squat, dingy box with cracks snaking across its weathered green stucco.

He wiped the sweat trickling down his aquiline nose onto his blond mustache and mumbled, "Lasciate ogni speranza, voi ch'entrate 'abandon all hope ye who enter here'." It was a line from Dante's *Divina Commedia* that came to mind each time he entered a hospital, any hospital.

As he stepped onto the meandering path between mesquite trees and south-pointing compass cacti, an old man stepped out of the hospital's glass entry and waved a white handkerchief, as if surrendering to an unseen enemy.

"In here," he yelled with a cracking voice. Bascom nodded and quickened his pace.

"Hi, Dr. Bishop," the man said as he entered the building. The bald man wore baggy pants and a stained jacket "I'm Dr. Wiggins. Pretty hot for this time of the year, eh?" He extended an arthritic hand and tilted his head so his gray eye could see around the strip of tape running diagonally across one lens of his glasses.

"My wool jacket makes it even hotter," he agreed, gently shaking the man's knobby hand. "My name is Bascom, not Bishop, and I'm pleased to meet you."

"Baggins. That's what I said. Say, where's your eye-talian accent?"

"I live in Italy, but I was born and raised in America," he laughed.

"Me too!" Wiggins giggled. "Where's your wife?"

"She died on the ides of March."

"Like Julius Caesar. I'm sorry to hear it," he replied, patting Bascom's shoulder. "I'm sure you miss her. Well, let's get on with it," he said as they entered a well-lit foyer. Scarred chairs lined its threadbare carpet and the sickly scent of oil of wintergreen wafted though the air.

"The vacant wards are down there," Wiggins indicated with a shaky finger.

"Vacant?" Bascom echoed curiously.

"Yep. Only the unlucky or uninformed come here," he replied as a blond, casually dressed man with a flattened boxer's nose exited an office down the hall. He was in his fifties and out of shape.

"Well, if it isn't Georgina Cohen!" Wiggins said irreverently as the man approached them.

"Thanks for the nice introduction, Dr. Wiggins," the man replied sarcastically before turning to Bascom. He offered a hand with scarred knuckles. "I'm George Cohen, the hospital administrator."

Bascom shook his rock-hard hand. "My pleasure," he answered with a smile.

"It's nice to meet you after all our phone calls, Doctor. Let's go to my office," he added as he turned down the hall.

"Bye, Dr. Blasely, and beware," Wiggins warned. "White man speak with forked tongue."

"He was eighty last month and is nuts," Cohen explained as they entered his small office. "We tolerate him because he doesn't make mistakes. He's old enough to, but he just doesn't. We'll force him into retirement when he does."

The administrator sat behind his desk and Bascom plopped on the worn couch in the rear of the room and rested his head on its greasy back.

"Why does he call you 'Georgina'?" he asked through a stifled yawn.

"We had a disagreement years ago," he replied vaguely. "Donna told me about the incident in the ER. I fired Dr. Perkins an hour ago and am sending a complaint to the medical board."

"I hear this wasn't the first patient he's mistreated, or murdered."

"We've had complaints about him in the past, but nothing this bad." Cohen frowned at the word "murder," and pinched his lower lip. "He's the medical society's problem now."

"Why wasn't he disciplined sooner?"

"He's a good moneymaker. He orders tons of tests and treatments, and refers the patients to the local docs. He's good for business."

"Hippocrates would lop off your head for that heretical statement," Bascom scowled.

Cohen frowned again before breaking into a smile. "I'm sure he would. Things here are too much even for me to stomach, and that's saying a lot. Graft is OK, after all, this is a hospital, but I do balk at 'murder,' as you crudely put it.

"Dr. Berkford, your buddy I met at a conference in San Diego, told me if you couldn't straighten out this place, no one could."

"I pay Lance 50 cents a compliment," Bascom laughed.

"Don't let me down, Doc. I need you," Cohen pleaded. "I'm sure Dr. Berkford wasn't exaggerating your worth.

"How's your house?"

"Musty and dusty, but its open-beamed ceilings remind me of my cabin in Italy."

"It is a nice old place from the last century. Been vacant since Emma Mullins died. I'll send over our cleaning crew as a welcoming present."

"Once a week?"

"Once, period."

"Better than nothing, but thanks," Bascom agreed.

"Now to business," Cohen continued. "According to our contract we'll reimburse your rent, the salaries of your office help, and guarantee a minimal monthly income for a year. You'll repay us with interest and legal expenses if you don't stay two years."

"Do I have to work in the ER or oversee your health clinics?"

"No. We have ER docs under contract. Physician assistants staff our clinics and send problem cases they can't handle to the local docs. We expect you to admit all your patients here and to use our laboratory and X-ray facilities for any outpatient testing."

"That's fair," Bascom agreed.

"Good. Our hospital has 45 beds and is shaped like a square doughnut," he said. He drew a quadrangle in the air and then poked its imaginary center with his finger.

"You said the daily census was five," Bascom interrupted.

"Sometimes fewer."

"How do you run this place with so few patients?"

"State and local tax revenues, our ER income, plus what we can get from the patients our doctors admit," the administrator explained. "That will improve now that you're here. In fact we're hiring two more nurses to help with the increased patient load."

Bascom was puzzled. "Where are these new patients coming from?"

"From you!" Cohen replied, pointing his finger at Bascom. "I figure if you admit two or three a day and keep them here four days, we'll fill up this hospital in no time."

"Wait a minute," Bascom said, jerking his head from the back of the couch. "You want me to straighten out this place, but you also want me to hospitalize people who don't need it just so you can improve your bottom line?"

"Why, yes. I thought you understood our tacit agreement," Cohen protested.

"Clearly I didn't." He tongued his upper teeth, producing a soft clicking sound. "But just so you know," he continued, "I only hospitalize patients I can't treat in their homes or in my office. And they're about as rare as a mosca bianca, a white fly."

"If you don't uphold our agreement," Cohen scolded, "you'll have to repay us with interest. It's your funeral." A sinister smile crept over his lips as he leaned back in his chair.

"What you're asking is unethical, and I won't do it. I came to tell you I was leaving, but all this has stirred my curiosity. I'll need to think about staying," Bascom said rising from the couch.

"I'll expect your answer within a week," Cohen nodded.

The men shook hands uneasily and Bascom left the office.

Ben was reading a memorandum tacked to the bulletin board in the hallway when the new physician exited the administrator's office. He waved, and Bascom walked up to him.

"Everything ok with Ms. Cohen?" he asked with a grin.

"I think you know the answer already, Dr. Wiggins. Maybe I'll see you again," he replied as he turned towards the exit.

Ben shrugged and limped down the hallway to see Evelyn as Bascom walked towards the exit.

Outside the hospital, he doffed his wool jacket and swung it over his shoulder as he walked a block in the blazing heat to the old office Cohen had agreed to let him use rent-free for a year. It was in worse repair than the hospital, and he hoped it did not smell of oil of wintergreen. "Robert

Bascom, MD, Family Practice," was inscribed in Gothic letters on a brass plaque fixed on the wall by its entrance. Numerous screw holes above and below it suggested many others had preceded it.

He pushed open the door and entered a large room where a few wooden straight-backed chairs with worn straw seats leaned on a table covered with dog-eared magazines. He entered a hallway to the left of the receptionist's window, leaned over the Dutch door barring entry to the small office, and knocked his knuckles on the jamb. An elderly woman cleaning her typewriter keys with a Q-Tip looked up from her task.

"Hi," he said cheerily.

"Oh, good afternoon. I didn't hear you come in. You must be Dr. Bascom," the thin woman replied, brushing her curly gray hair from her still pretty face. Her light blue eyes sparkled behind rimless glasses. "I'm Helen Sylva. Mr. Cohen hired me to be your secretary. It keeps me out of bars."

He laughed. "Do you hide that cross hanging from your neck before you go inside, or do you pull out a bible and try to convert their patrons?"

"Neither. Poor joke. I don't drink and never go into bars."

"You're forgiven. Do we have any patients today?"

"No, but Mr. Watts will be in tomorrow. Also Mr. Cohen phoned this morning and wants you to call him right away. It sounded urgent."

"I just came from his office," Bascom replied before continuing down the hallway. He glanced into two opposing patient cubicles, each identically equipped with a small desk and chair, an examining table, and an empty instrument cabinet. He peeked into the minimally furnished nursing station and then entered his small office, which contained a bookcase, a metal cabinet, a copy machine, two wooden chairs and a desk with a cracked leather top.

He returned to his secretary.

"What time will Mr. Watts arrive?" he asked the woman who was again cleaning her typewriter.

"10 o'clock," she replied. "Will you buy us a computer? This belongs in a museum."

"I'm a semi-Luddite, so I'll need to think about it. Is Cohen going to send someone to clean this place?"

"Later today, supposedly. We get one free cleaning and then it's up to us."

"I'll see you in the morning, Mrs. Sylva," he said before leaving the office.

III

That night Bascom tossed and turned on his lumpy mattress as he struggled with his options of staying in the desert or returning to Italy. Cohen had fired Perkins, making his decision easier, but he could not fill his hospital with healthy patients, tacit agreement or not.

Yet something, or someone, intrigued him about Whitney and just before dawn he decided to stay in town a few weeks longer. He realized he might eventually regret his decision, but for the moment, a battle was better than a bottle.

At 10 o'clock that morning, 40 year-old Jonathan Watts, wheezing and with his bib overalls pooled around his ankles, sat on the examination table in Bascom's office.

"I've got these painful bumps, Doc," the haggard farmer rasped as he pointed to the red circles on his shins. "I'm out of breath and my fever won't go 'way. Been sick two weeks now."

Bascom glanced at the irregularly shaped lesions. "They're called 'erythema nodosum,'" he explained.

"That sounds serious," the man asked, wide-eyed. "Am I gonna die? I sure feel like it."

"It's unlikely, but it'll be a year before you'll feel good again. You've got Valley Fever, a fungal disease named after the San Joaquin Valley in California. You'll need to get a few tests at the hospital so I can verify my diagnosis and monitor the course of your illness."

"Never!" the farmer retorted fiercely. He coughed spasmodically and then held his head for a few moments before continuing.

"Sorry. I feel crappy, but I won't go there. My wife went to that dump for belly pain and they kept her three days until her appendix bursted and she died. Helen promised me you'd take care of me here, but if you can't, I'm going to Phoenix."

"That's 60 miles away. There's no need to travel that far when we can do the tests here," Bascom explained. "And they're harmless."

"Won't happen. Will you help me or not?" the farmer wheezed.

"Yes, but I'll still need the tests."

"I'll get them in Phoenix," he replied firmly.

"As you wish," Bascom agreed.

He found a pad in the desk in the corner of the room and jotted down the names of the few tests he needed. He tore off the sheet and handed it to Mr. Watts. As the farmer dressed and went on his way, Bascom went to Helen's office.

"Thanks for warning me," he said sarcastically.

"I'm sorry," she replied, swallowing a bite of bagel. "I thought it'd be better if you heard firsthand what you'll be up against in this town. This office is like a motel; doctors check in, stay a week, and then are gone. Cohen has ordered so many signs, he gets a discount from the trophy shop. You'll be hearing more complaints like Jonathan's, and some are even worse."

"I can't wait," he said before returning to his office.

Bascom's reputation for keeping patients out of Whitney's hospital grew quickly among the gritty farmers and their impoverished migrant workers, and within weeks he was seeing twenty patients a day. He had to hire Frances Durio, a young divorcée, to assist him. On her first day she warned him the patient he was about to see had already refused to go to the hospital.

"She's the third patient today who'd like to torch the place," Bascom sighed. "What are they afraid of?"

"You'll find out soon enough," she shrugged. "You'll never get anyone to go there, but if you do and something bad happens, and it will, he'll judge you like he judges your colleagues in this town."

"Which is?" he asked as he turned the knob to the door to the examining room.

"My father would wash out my mouth with soap if I told you," she grinned.

"I already know then. My last patient told me." He laughed and entered the room where Mrs. Gonzales, an elderly, emaciated woman, was lying on the table, holding her knees to her chest and groaning. A woman caressing her forehead explained that her mother had been in pain for a month and had lost 15 pounds.

Bascom gently placed his hand on the woman's abdomen. Her scream troubled him less than what he knew would be her response to his request.

"Mrs. Gonzalez, I need to put you in the hospital."

"Not in Whitney!" she whimpered, shaking her head.

"You need treatment I can't offer in my office. You need to be in a hospital."

"No. They hate us Mexicans there. They let my nephew bleed to death in the ER after he cut his arm a few weeks ago," she replied defiantly. "I won't go."

"Mama," her daughter pleaded, clasping her thin hand in hers, "I think you can trust Dr. Bascom to make sure they take care of you right."

"If Dr. Grimes was here, he'd send me to Phoenix," the woman replied. She pulled her knees closer to her chest and groaned.

"Dr. Grimes saved my life when I was barely in my teens, Dr. Bascom," the daughter explained, wringing her callused hands. Waxy, scar-like lesions, the result of years in the fields picking fruit and vegetables under the brutal Arizona sun, covered her wrists and arms.

"I was bleeding from my vagina every couple of months," the woman continued, "and he told me I was getting cancer and took out my uterus to save my life. He gave us a discount for paying cash since we had no insurance. He's such a nice man, but he's away and my mom's pain got too bad for her to wait for him to return."

"My stomach hurts terrible," Mrs. Gonzalez interrupted, grimacing as she spoke. "I don't want to go to the hospital here, but if I do, will you promise you won't let them hurt me?"

"You have my word," he nodded.

"Okay," she said reluctantly.

"Good. Dress and go to the hospital. I'll meet you there later," he said before going to his secretary's office. She looked up from her computer when she heard his knuckles rap on her door jamb.

"Helen," he said, "tell the hospital we're sending over Mrs. Gonzalez, and have them call me as soon as she's admitted."

"OK," she replied, raising an eyebrow. "And good luck."

"I know what you're thinking, Mrs. Skeptic," he replied, "but I watched Joe Thompson operate the other day. He's a good surgeon and I'm sure he can fix anything she might have."

"You mean the 'Ass with the Golden Hands'?" she growled.

"You don't like him?"

Helen returned to her computer, ignoring his question. "Should I also call Mr. Cohen and give him the good news?" she asked. "He pesters me daily about why we're not admitting patients."

"No, he'll find out on his own," he replied before returning to his patients.

At 3 o'clock that afternoon, Bascom returned to Helen's office. "Any news about Mrs. Gonzalez?" he asked.

"No. Do you want me to call?"

"No thanks. I'll walk over. I need the exercise," he replied, patting his abdomen.

Minutes later he was in the admitting office talking to a plump young receptionist.

"Mrs. Gonzalez checked in three hours ago," the young woman replied. She smiled, showing a gap between her cracked front teeth.

"Three hours ago!" he exclaimed, pounding a fist on the countertop. "Didn't my secretary ask you to call me when she was admitted?"

The smile quickly drained from her face. "Yes, and I told the nurse," she answered.

"Where is she?"

The woman leaned forward and whispered, "In an empty patient room reading a romance novel and eating candy."

"Not the nurse, I mean Mrs. Gonzalez."

"Oh. She's in room 22."

Bascom walked around Cohen's nice square doughnut to room 22 where his patient was lying in bed, gently massaging her abdomen. A red light flashed on the wall above her bed.

"I want to go home," she said as he entered her room. "No one answers my calls. You promised you'd protect me."

"And I will, Mrs. Gonzalez, as soon as we complete your paperwork. I'm sure there's a reasonable explanation why no one has come in to see you," he said, taking her chart from its holder at the foot of her bed.

"I hope so," she murmured, slowly rocking back and forth.

As Bascom was completing his notes, an obese nurse in a uniform stretched far beyond its intended capacity appeared in the doorway. He quickly crossed the room and shuffled her back into the hall.

"Where have you been?" he demanded.

"Lunch," she replied glibly.

"Weren't you supposed to call me when Mrs. Gonzalez arrived?"

"I've been busy."

"How many other patients have you admitted today?"

"None."

"I'll speak to your supervisor about this."

"Go ahead," she replied defiantly. She turned and slogged down the hall, muttering what sounded like, "Fuck you."

Bascom was livid. He had never believed nurses should be subservient to a doctor's every whim, but he did expect them to treat him respectfully and his patients professionally.

"Mrs. Gonzalez," he said as he reentered her room, "I've ordered an IV and tomorrow we'll get a CT scan of your stomach. Now I'm going to talk with someone about your nurse." He jotted a note on a slip of paper and pressed it into her hand. "This is my private number. Call me when you need me, day or night."

He returned the chart to its rack and then went to the nursing supervisor's office. He knocked once on the open door before entering the cramped but tidy room.

"I've got a problem," he said to the woman behind a wooden desk. Evelyn Cooper, a prim, attractive, gray haired 60 year-old slipped off her glasses and placed them on her well-organized desktop.

"Please take a seat, Dr. Bascom," she offered politely, pointing to an old leather chair in front of her desk. "How can I help you?"

"I've just had a run-in with a surly nurse," he said angrily. "I don't like to complain, but we can't hope to improve patient care in this hospital if we let her do as she pleases.

"I would like an incident report on Mr. Cohen's desk tomorrow and a different nurse to care for my patient."

"Her again," she sighed wearily, tapping a manicured fingernail on her desk. "Unfortunately she can do as she pleases since she's Mr. Cohen's sister-in-law. I can't fire her, even though I've tried. If you'll write a complaint to Mr. Cohen, perhaps he'll listen to you."

"You've been through this before?" he asked.

"Sure. Normally she just hangs around the nurses' off-duty room, eating and watching TV. Another nurse must have asked her to cover for her. I'll find a different nurse to care for Mrs. Gonzalez."

"Thanks. I'll talk to Cohen tomorrow," he said before rising from the chair and leaving the office.

The next morning Bascom handed his complaint to the hospital administrator. George skimmed the letter and then dropped it into the trashcan beside his desk.

"There are things I can do, can't do, or won't do. This is

one I won't do. Besides you're in breach of contract, since one admission here was not what we had in mind when we hired you. The Board is deciding what action to take against you. You should have returned to Italy when you had the chance," he said firmly.

"You're right, George, I should have," Bascom replied before exiting the office.

When he arrived back in Mrs. Gonzalez' room, she was sitting in a chair, her red call light was flashing, and blood was backing into the plastic tubing in her arm.

"When did the IV run out?" he asked, avoiding her angry stare.

"An hour ago. I put on my call light, but no one came."

"I see," he said simply. He took a tissue from a box on the nightstand, folded it into a square, removed the needle, and pressed it on her vein.

"Did they scan your belly?"

"No," she replied. "My daughter wants you to transfer me to Phoenix."

"That sounds like a good idea. Hold your finger on this tissue until I get back," he ordered gently.

A lone technician was doing a crossword puzzle at his desk when Bascom entered the empty radiology department minutes later. "Why didn't Mrs. Gonzalez get her scan today?" he asked the dark haired youth with a chain tattoo encircling his right biceps.

"Sonics International won't replace our busted scanner tube unless we pay them with cashiers' checks," he answered without looking up from his crossword. "Regular checks from this dump bounce."

Bascom stopped to make a telephone call and to pick up a band-aid and a cotton ball from the nurses' station before returning to his patient. He was now certain Whitney Community Hospital was a cesspool, where everything wrong with medicine collected and rotted. He also knew the sediment would, by association, tarnish his name and reputation.

"Our scanner is down, Mrs. Gonzalez," he explained as he entered her room. He replaced the tissue with the cotton ball and band-aid. "So I'm transferring you to Phoenix where we can get your studies done immediately."

The woman let out a sigh of relief. "Thank you," she replied.

IV

A few days after transferring Mrs. Gonzalez to Phoenix, Bascom shaved with a steady hand, dressed in his finest jeans and went to a belated 'Welcome To Whitney" party in his honor at the home of the town's two surgeons. Joe Thompson, the older man, had made it clear when he invited him to the festivities that neither he nor his partner actually lived in the condominium, as it was small, run-down, and damaged their image as well-to-do surgeons. He described it as a "flophouse they used on the days they had to be in crappy Whitney each week."

The "flophouse" was a few blocks from Bascom's rental home and he walked the short distance as a storm loomed. Fine desert dust filled the air and lightning lit the skies as an increasing wind rustled leaves in the trees. In Italy their branches would be bare now, but Arizona's ash and mesquite were still in bloom.

Bascom turned into Thompson's gated compound. The gate, poultry fencing in a bent pipe frame, lay to the side of the road. The paint on the upper half of the guardhouse was peeling off in layers, but Spanish names and unfamiliar symbols had been freshly spray painted on its bottom half.

A hundred yards from the gate, Thompson's cactus green home sat among other drab and run-down dwellings. Fancy cars, out of place on a street lined with faded pick-up trucks and 20 year-old sedans, lined up in front of the house. Music streamed from its open windows.

As he entered the house, the aromas of tobacco and skunk, the latter not of animal origin, assaulted Bascom's nostrils. People, most of whom he had never met, stood shoulder to shoulder in the small living room. He was walking toward Ben Wiggins who was at a food table in the corner of the room when a well-dressed woman in her early thirties and reeking of alcohol, bumped into him.

"Dr. Basscombbe," she slurred, "I've been dyyying to meet you. At my place, later?"

"Much later," he smiled as he continued around her to Wiggins. The old man had piled so much food on his paper plate it was bending downwards. Bascom was certain that if he added the pickle he was trying to spear with a butter knife, the whole concoction would slide onto his multicolored jacket.

"Hi, Ben," he said cheerfully.

As the old doctor tilted his head to see around his taped eyeglass lens, his potato salad slipped off his plate and into the pickle bowl.

"Hi, Bonely. Do you get it yet?" he wondered.

"Get what, Ben?"

"Have you tried the meat loaf?"

"No. But it smells like something you might find in a barn." he replied, sniffing the air. He glanced at the doctor's tray, lightened by its recent loss but still tilting towards disaster, and added, "I'd pour mustard on those cocktail franks. It goes well with that jacket."

Wiggins smiled.

"Where's Joe Thompson?" Bascom asked.

"In the kitchen."

Ben put down his dish and followed Bascom to a door in the rear of the room. He stopped at the doorway, ten feet from the table where Thompson and Marty Nevins were sitting, since he knew they would never talk openly about anything in his presence.

Nevins, rolling a glass of beer between his hands, looked up as Bascom entered the room.

"Hi, Guys. Busy today?" Bascom asked as he dragged a chair from under the table.

"Usual stuff, Bob," 60 year-old Joe Thompson replied. He was as wide as the table, making his thin companion appear emaciated by comparison.

"I was at a private party in Phoenix," Nevins explained as he fingered his ratty beard. "Had to leave early to attend this bash in your honor. I hope you'll show your appreciation by sending me some patients."

Ben, standing to the side of the doorway, strained to hear their words over the din of the party-goers.

Bascom laughed. "I will. I'm glad you're here since I wanted to talk to you guys about the problems at our beloved Whitney Community Hospital."

"Which are?" Nevins leaned back in his chair and smiled mockingly.

"How about the farmer's wife who died of a ruptured appendix?" Bascom asked.

"It happens," Joe said as he combed a few gray hairs over his vast scalp.

"It isn't synonymous with death if the patient is already in the hospital," Bascom rebuked.

Joe speared a large French-fry with his knife and slid it into his gargantuan mouth. Nevins whistled. "I always wondered how a dinosaur ate," he exclaimed in awe.

"Anyway, because of this place's lousy reputation," Bascom continued, "I had to transfer the only patient that would stay in town."

"Status quo," Joe agreed with a nod of his huge head.

"Which is why we operate on most of our patients in Phoenix."

"Shouldn't we correct this situation?"

"Bob," Thompson explained, resting his knife on his plate, "others have tried and failed. If you think you can improve things here, maybe even convince Abe Grimes to stop performing hysterectomies on 16 year-olds, go right ahead, but I don't want to get involved."

"What?" Bascom barked, his eyes widening in disbelief. "Why would he do that?"

Son of a bitch has been doing it for years, Ben thought. *I couldn't stop him and I doubt you can.*

"To cure their irregular periods," Joe said.

"That's outrageous! All girls have that problem at that age," Bascom countered angrily. "They become regular as they get older."

"Everyone knows that," Joe continued after sipping his coffee, "but Abe tells them they need surgery because they might develop cancer if they don't get their uteri and ovaries removed. Instant sterility, but only if they have cash. If not, he tells them the problem might disappear so he'll look like a genius when their cycles stabilize on their own, and sends them home."

"The guy should have his license pulled," Bascom bristled, thinking back to Mrs. Gonzalez' daughter. *She didn't have cancer as Grimes told her she 'might' have. She was just another victim of the bad medicine that had its epicenter in the Sonoran Desert.*

"An old crusader called in the state to stop him and paid the price for violating our code of silence," Nevins interrupted.

We could have stopped him if you cowards had stood up with me. A young man holding a bottle of beer interrupted Ben's thoughts. "Dr. Wiggins, how are you?" he asked. Startled, Ben looked up at the intruder.

"Ok. Do I know you?" he wondered.

"You should. I'm a laboratory technician at the hospital." He frowned, obviously upset the old man did not remember him.

"Oh, right," Ben apologized. "I didn't recognize you in the fog." *Now get lost; I need to hear what's going on in the kitchen.*

"And how are you?"

"I'm fine. We don't get many orders from you anymore."

"I didn't know you had ever gotten many orders from me. Most patients don't need all those newfangled tests you people do," he said. *Now PLEEZE, go away.*

"Guess you're right, Doc. Well, it's nice to see you're up and around."

"As long as I can stand and pee in the morning, I'll have a good day. And so far I can!"

The young man walked away, shaking his head as Ben moved nearer the doorway.

"Anyway, I won't stop the guy because I need him," Nevins continued. "He treats almost every insured patient in this town, and his referrals are worth plenty." He drained the beer and put the empty glass on the table. "Tastes better warm," he explained as he wiped his mouth on his sleeve.

"Bob, we did strike once," Thomson said, reaching across the table to patronizingly pat his colleague's arm. "Nothing came of it, except Cohen fired a contract doc who went bankrupt repaying his advances, legal fees and interest. Whitnians didn't give a damn that we had gone out on a limb for them. They just went to Phoenix for care while we sat home and lost money.

"Striking will put only you in the line of fire. Cohen won't touch us because without the bones we throw him, no pun intended, this place would sink. Besides, my business is doing fine, and I like things just as they are."

"Joe, how would you like your mother to get the care these people get?" Bascom asked.

"She'd never come here, so don't try to play on my sympathies," he scolded, holding his palms up to silence Bascom.

"Then how about replacing Evelyn Cooper?" Bascom asked. "We need someone who can fire Cohen's deadbeat relatives, and she can't."

Try it and see what happens to you! Ben silently warned his new colleague.

Thompson stabbed his meat loaf a few times and then dropped his napkin over it. "Not a good idea. Cohen wanted to fire Evelyn when she tried to dump his sister-in-law, and again after she ratted on Grimes, but Wiggins forced him to back down. Now they insult each other mercilessly.

"Ben and Evelyn are lovers," he said in a loud whisper. "She's a fine-looking woman for her age, but I doubt he can still get it up."

"Fat bastard! You should know what I can do!" Ben grumbled loud enough to get the attention of people standing nearby. He hoped Thompson had not heard him.

"Ev's a good supervisor and an excellent nurse," Nevins added, patting his moth-eaten beard. "She tries to improve conditions here, but Cohen undermines her authority, and he'll do the same to her replacement. Firing her won't change anything."

"But getting decent nursing care is…," Bascom protested.

"I don't care what the nurses do," Nevins interrupted with a shrug.

"Why did you become a doctor, Marty?"

"To get rich. It's the new Hippocratic Oath. 'Don't do surgery unto others unless they pay in cash in advance 'cause their insurance companies cut fees.'"

Bascom's anger bubbled like acid on limestone. "You're an inspiration, Marty," he said ironically.

"Joe," he asked the fat surgeon who had lifted the corner of his napkin and was peering at the meat loaf as if to see if it were moving, "you said you lost money during the strike, but how do you make any in this town?"

"We do minor surgery in our office, you know, hernias, plastics, wound care, biopsies on our lesser quality citizens. We operate in Phoenix on our rich, insured patients several times a week. Plus we get referrals from the ER," he replied.

"Is that the new definition of the 'quality of human life' - surgery in Phoenix instead of Whitney?" Bascom scowled. "But as to referrals from the ER, I've gotten only a few."

"I'll bet they were uninsured migrants, right?" Nevins snickered and rubbed a finger over his lower lip.

"How did you guess?"

"It wasn't a guess. Ed Hunter, our friendly ER chief, skims the insured patients to his office and to his friends; sends the uninsured really sick to Phoenix; and sends the uninsured not-so-sick to you."

"That's a conflict of interest," Bascom said angrily. "Plus it's a violation of EMTALA, the Emergency Medical Treatment and Active Labor Act, to transfer patients to another hospital just because they don't have insurance."

"Sure, but our population is mostly illegal Mexicans, Filipinos, and Indians who aren't going to pay. So why not let someone else take the loss?"

"That's BS," Bascom said irately as he ran a hand through his hair, stopping to scratch a spot behind his ear. It was what he did when he was angry or peeved.

"Maybe, but Hunter pretends the cases are too difficult for him to handle. So PUH has to take them."

"So much for the law," Bascom replied bitingly.

"Do I detect a touch of irony, Bob?" Thompson asked, looking down his nose at him.

"Irony? Hell no! Try anger or sarcasm. Did you expect me to compliment Hunter on his professional morals and unbridled concern for his patients?" Bascom replied. "What's your take in this referral scam?"

"It's not a scam. Hunter doesn't want surgical patients, and sends us the gallbladders, broken bones and the like. Ninety percent of the people here are poor, but the remaining 10 percent are rich, well-insured farmers and businessmen. Those we take to Phoenix, since they won't set foot in WCH. We toss Cohen the workman's comp cases and the rare paying illegal. It keeps him happy."

"I can't believe this," Bascom said, shaking his head. He picked up a plastic knife from the table and twisted it between his hands. It snapped in two and he tossed the pieces into the middle of the table.

"You won't get referrals from anyone unless you play the game," Joe warned, shaking his finger.

"By the way," Marty interrupted. "I spoke to Hunter about the guy with the cut arm that Perkins let die because he was caring for a man with a heart attack. The medical board reviewed the case and decided he needed a psychiatric evaluation to see if he hates Mexicans."

"Perkins was reading a newspaper at the nursing station the entire time I was there," Bascom said angrily. "There were two patients in the ER that night, and he let mine bleed to death while his slept peacefully. Now you tell me all this murderer needs is a psyche consult?"

"Yup. And since the board feels he can work, he's back

in the ER until he gets it."

"This is intolerable," Bascom replied angrily. "Since you won't straighten out this place, I'll call in EMTALA, Medicare, the TV and the press."

Whoa! Ben thought. *Now we're getting somewhere. Ev might be right about this guy, if they don't drive him into the desert and kill him.*

"Don't do that!" Thompson pleaded. The color drained from his face. "The fines would put the hospital out of business and I'd have to work in Phoenix. Competition is tough there!"

"Then correct the abuses," Bascom replied heatedly. "Sit on Cohen until he listens."

"I'll make sure Perkins doesn't get any more work," Joe pleaded. "Please don't call in the thugs from EMTALA!"

"I can't promise I won't," Bascom replied acerbically as his beeper sounded its coded alarm. He read its message and stood from his chair. "I'd love to continue this stimulating conversation, but I'm wanted in the ER. Thanks for the lovely party. I feel so enlightened now that I understand you true concern for the people of this town, I may just skip and whistle all the way to the hospital."

Ben turned from the doorway as Bascom brushed by him. The young physician fought his way out of the smoke filled and still crowded living room, and walked to the ER where a clerk directed him to Victor Forest. The frail 67-year old man was lying on a gurney next to his green, home oxygen tank. Donna Franklyn was slipping a catheter into his dusky blue forearm while a diminutive nurse measured his blood pressure.

"Hi, Donna," he said to the dark-haired nurse. "How's our patient?"

"Sick, Dr. Bascom," she replied, her brown eyes sparkling behind her granny glasses. "Victor's got severe lung disease and hates us."

"Why?"

"He's supposed to get four liters of oxygen a minute, but last time he was here someone gave him fifteen and shut down his breathing. It almost killed him."

"He's got good reason to hate this place. Have you ordered blood gases?"

"The tech is on her way."

"Good. Miss, er, Ruiz," Bascom said to the second nurse as he read the metal name tag over her breast, "keep the oxygen at no more than four liters a minute."

"Jes," she replied with a heavy accent.

"Four liters, not fourteen," he repeated firmly. "Do you understand?"

"Jes."

"How are you, Mr. Forest?" he asked, turning to his patient. Victor opened his eyes and feebly moved a blue finger. Bascom listened to his chest with his stethoscope, wrote orders on a chart, handed it to Donna, and then went to the waiting room where Victor's overweight wife was wringing a blue handkerchief through her plump fingers.

"Tell me he'll be all right, Doctor," the gray-haired woman pleaded as he approached her.

"I can't do that just yet. Victor is very ill and will need to stay in the hospital," he said softly.

"Not here!" the woman exclaimed, wide-eyed. Two Mexicans sitting on old benches against a wall of the small room looked curiously at them.

"He's too unstable to transfer, Mrs. Forest," Bascom replied, turning his back to the inquisition. "He could die before he reached another hospital."

"Victor didn't want to come here," she said, shaking her head, "but the ambulance driver said he had to."

"The law requires him to bring patients to the nearest

hospital," he explained patiently. "I promise you your husband will get the best of care."

"You'd have to walk on water to make me believe that," she said.

"I do," he replied with a laugh, "but only when it rains. I'll personally watch over him while he's here."

"You'd better," the woman replied skeptically.

They returned to the ER and explained their decision to Victor whose quivering lips mouthed "good-bye" to his lifelong mate before he closed his eyes.

Donna had gone to the intensive care unit while he was speaking with Victor's wife. Bascom felt uneasy about leaving Nurse Ruiz alone with his patient, but he had to review the man's chest X-ray.

"I need to go to radiology, Miss Ruiz," he said. "Keep the oxygen at four liters per minute. Four, not fourteen. Do you understand me?"

"Jes," she replied vacantly.

"I'll tell our son," Mrs. Forest added as she rummaged through her purse for her cellphone. "You'll hear from him if anything goes wrong. He's a lawyer in LA."

"I'm sure we'll have a lot to talk about if he does." Bascom turned to the nurse and said, "I'll be right back Miss Ruiz," before he and Victor's wife left the area.

When Bascom returned to the ER fifteen minutes later, he heard a loud whistling sound escaping from under the mask on Victor's face and raced to his stretcher. The nurse inexplicably had set the oxygen flow to fourteen liters and the man was no longer breathing. He ripped off the mask, grabbed an endotracheal tube from the cart near the stretcher, inserted it into Victor's windpipe, and attached it to an Ambu bag so he could pump air into his lungs.

Bascom rhythmically squeezed the bag while a livid

Mrs. Forest and the nurse quickly pushed Victor's stretcher to the intensive care unit. Donna was at the nursing station and rose from her chair when she heard the stretcher crash through the unit's double doors.

They positioned Victor's stretcher in the slot next to the nursing station. Bascom could feel Mrs. Forest's glare on his back as he attached the respirator to her husband's endotracheal tube. The machine was old and he had difficulty adjusting it.

After he and Donna finished attaching life-support systems to the gravely ill man, Bascom turned to Mrs. Forest and advised her Victor might not survive the night.

"I hope you're wrong," she threatened. She picked up her husband's hand and tenderly squeezed it as Bascom and Donna walked to the nursing station.

"Third world hospitals are better than this one," he grumbled to the tall, vivacious woman after they sat at the desk.

"This place wrote the manual on how to screw up care. I didn't want to leave Victor, but I had to help with Dr. Thompson's patient," Donna apologized, nodding to the woman in the bed next to Victor's.

"Ruiz is in the country illegally and I don't think she has a license. I complained to Cohen, but he warned me to keep my nose out of hospital business.

"I need to get back to the ER before she kills any more of my patients," she concluded. "Good luck with Victor's wife. The Forest's have a nasty reputation that goes way back. I hear they were train robbers and killers in the 1800s. Don't let her gray hair and chubbiness mislead you."

Victor succumbed early the next morning, and his exhausted wife sobbed softly by his side as Bascom removed his endotracheal tube.

"I'm sorry, Mrs. Forest," he said as he wrapped it in a towel and placed it on the stand next to the bed. "Victor was extremely ill; there was nothing I could do for him."

"You people killed him, as Victor predicted you would," she sobbed. "I shouldn't have listened to you! Now leave me alone with my husband."

Bascom returned to the nursing station to write a note on Victor's chart. A few minutes later Mrs. Forest approached him. "I'm going to sue you and this lousy hospital," she growled. "You haven't heard the last of me, believe me!"

"I'm sorry," was all he could say as she stormed out of the unit.

"Porco giuda, I've had enough!" he mumbled as he lay on his couch an hour later. "Doctors let patients die because they're Mexican, unlicensed nurses can't understand English, and lazy, fat ones do nothing. Not even Charles Dickens could have invented a setting like this.

"I'll call EMTALA, Medicare and Medicaid later this morning," he told his scuffed loafers, "and to hell with Thompson and Cohen!"

V

It was late afternoon and Bascom had just fallen asleep when his telephone jolted him awake. He had tried to see patients in his office after Victor's death, but a migraine headache had forced him to return home and to crawl into bed.

"Hello, and please don't shout." he warned the caller. Any noise louder than a whisper worsened his nausea and relentless pain.

"Migraine again?" Lance Berkford wondered. He and Bascom had met in medical school and had worked together in an emergency room on the east coast. Bascom had been Lance's chief. Because of their uncanny ability to save even the most severely injured patients, everyone I the ER called them the "Trauma Twins." The one they could not save was the most important person in Bascom's life. He could still feel Lance's hand on his shoulder and hear his words as he held his battered wife in his arms: "She's gone, Bobby."

"The usual headache. What's up?" Bascom replied. He sat on the side of the bed and rested his forehead on his palm.

"I just wanted to know how your job is."

"It sucks. Patients drop like flies around this dump and no one gives a damn, as long as they pay their bills first."

"Cohen never told me things were that bad," Lance clucked. "I'm sorry. It seemed like a good way for you to get back on your feet."

"In theory it was. I have a two-year contract, but repayment will be a bitch if I don't last that long. And I probably won't." Bascom yawned. "I'll never forget the horrible problems we faced after we formed the union during our residency, and I don't look forward to a similar battle against these bozos. But they are screwing these patients, and I don't like it."

"Oh, oh! Trouble ahead! DQS! Don Quixote in Scrubs is back in action again!"

"Lance! Ow!" Bascom barked. He was close to vomiting.

"What's wrong, Bob?"

"Worst hcadachc I'vc cvcr had."

"WHAT?"

"Sorry. It's not the worst," he quickly corrected.

"Are you sure it's not an aneurysm? Your father died of one."

"It's just my usual migraine."

"I hope so," Lance said.

Bascom stuck his feet into the sheepskin slippers Cris had given him as a Christmas present years earlier. He wiggled his toes and one peeked teasingly through the torn stitching. He covered it with his other foot. *Gotcha!*

"How are you doing?" Bascom asked. He lay back on the bed and put a pillow over his eyes to shield them from the light.

"Great. I've got your old job as ER director. Every time administration denies one of my requests, I tell them you're coming back. It scares the hell out of them, and they give me what I want."

"I wish I had that power here. When are you coming to

visit?"

"Not for a while, but I'll bring Rachael Polgreen with me when I do."

"Rachael? I thought you didn't date beautiful women." The pain was intense and worsening. *Perhaps it is an aneurysm.*

"I put a bag over her head when we're in the sack."

"Ha, ha!" Bascom grimaced. He squeezed his temples between his thumb and finger, but it had no effect on the throbbing which he was sure would reach explosive force and scatter his brain around his still musty bedroom.

"Lance, it's been great talking with you, but I need to pick up a car."

"A Rolls?" he laughed.

"Sure. A Rolls," Bascom replied sarcastically. "I'd never own one even if I could afford it. My secretary has a friend at a Ford dealership, and he's got a used SUV in good shape. Can I call you back?"

"You'd damn well better! If I don't hear from you in 24 hours, I'll be on a plane out there."

"I'll live," Bascom said before hanging up. He went to the bathroom and swallowed two aspirins from a bottle in the medicine chest. He showered and dressed, then walked to the car dealership. An hour later, with the paperwork completed and his headache in remission, he drove his red Explorer to Joe Thompson's office.

After Victor's unnecessary death he had decided to call in government watchdogs to examine the hospital's workings, but he would give Thompson a last chance to help him resolve its problems.

An elderly woman behind a kneehole desk looked up as he entered the surgeon's waiting room. "May I help you?" she asked, removing her glasses and letting them hang from a gold chain on her sagging bosom.

"I'm Dr. Bascom," he answered with a quick smile.

"Oh, nice to meet you. Doctor will be with you shortly."

He walked around the room, pausing occasionally to examine the diplomas hanging on the walls. The largest parchment stated Thompson had graduated from Johns Hopkins University thirty years earlier. Another testified to his outstanding surgical performance at Bellevue Hospital in New York City.

With these credentials, why is he in this dumpy town?

A door opened and Joe, arms outstretched and a smile on his wide face, waddled toward him. "Come in, my friend," he said, energetically clasping Bascom's shoulder with his huge hand. He led him into his spacious office and offered him a chair in front of a massive desk. As Joe lumbered to the oversized captain's chair behind it, Bascom scanned the tomes and memorabilia in the antique bookcases lining the walls of the room.

"What can I do for you today, Bob?" he asked as he lowered his huge frame into the chair. It groaned before falling silent.

"My patient died last night in the nosocomio," he replied wearily.

"I know. Another nursing screw-up," he said, pulling on his deformed right ear. Its lobe was pushed up into itself, leaving a small dimple in its wake. "The news upset me too.

"Our anesthesiologist quit because he hasn't been paid in a month," he grumbled, "and Cohen replaced him with a nurse who speaks an undetermined language. We're out of supplies, and I had to operate in Phoenix five times this week instead of three."

"Life's a bitch," Bascom replied coldly. "Did you know Ruiz is here illegally and does not have a license?"

"Wouldn't surprise me. This state is full of illegals, and many have first-rate forged documents," he replied, shrugging his massive shoulders. His chair squealed and creaked ominously.

"Furniture isn't as strong as it was years ago," Joe grumbled. "Chair whimpers like a whipped dog every time I sit in it." He took a gold cigarette case from his pocket and placed it on the desk. "I need to quit," he explained, tapping the case, "but I'm afraid it might stimulate my appetite. Quite a dilemma, don't you think? Do I save my lungs or my belly?"

"When your clothes don't fit anymore, buy a Damascan Jubba," Bascom snickered. "Of course the NSA might mistake you for a terrorist with an atomic bomb strapped to you belly if you wander too close to a government building, but that's the risk you face."

"You do have a talent for flattering people," Joe replied, stung by the unkind reference. "You aren't an Asperger's, are you?"

"Why do you ask?" Bascom replied, amused by the question.

"Because you seem bright and are a royal pain in the ass."

"It takes more than that to qualify for Asperger's. Thanks for asking, since it would put me in the same class as Einstein, Bill Gates, and other geniuses, but I'm not an Asperger's."

"Did you talk to Cohen about this nurse?" Joe wondered.

"Why bother? He knows if she's illegal; he hired her," Bascom replied. "How many more patients need to die in that hellhole because nurses aren't nurses and can't speak English?"

Bascom spied a photograph of a young woman in running shorts and string top on a shelf in the bookcase. She looked familiar.

"If you doubt they're nurses, check their licenses before you entrust your patients to them," Thompson suggested.

"You mean the forged ones you just mentioned? Mind if I look at that picture?" he asked. He rose from his chair without waiting for permission, went to the bookcase, and picked up the photo. "To Joe, with all my love, Helen," was scrawled across the bottom.

"Is this my secretary?" Bascom asked, studying the picture.

"Yes. She had just won an Olympic bronze medal for the 10,000 meters," Thompson explained.

Bascom replaced the picture on the shelf and returned to his chair. "Interesting bit of history. Anyway Victor should have died on his terms, not ours. We need to boycott the hospital. We could provide urgent care in our offices and send everything else to Phoenix until Cohen corrects the problems." Bascom leaned back in his chair and rubbed a fist in his palm.

"I won't strike. You work in your office," Joe answered as he turned the gold cigarette case in his hands, "but I work in a hospital operating room. I lose money if we strike; you don't. And besides, it didn't work last time."

"You're already driving to Phoenix every day, so how can it hurt? If WCH can't meet its responsibilities, it should close," Bascom griped.

"Strike then, Dr. Asperger," Thompson snickered. "I'll even paint the sandwich sign you can wear while pacing up and down in front of the hospital. How about, 'The End is Near,' on the front, and 'Kiss My Ass,' on the back?"

"Thanks for your understanding, Joe," Bascom replied sarcastically. "I won't subject my patients to any more risks and I will change the way people do business around here, with or without your help."

"I'd suggest you wait until Abe Grimes' party next month before you cut off your balls. He's been in town forever. If you can convince him to stand with you, the others might follow. Personally I'd give you better odds on your running down a Cheetah in the African Savannah."

"A guy who performs hysterectomies on teenagers isn't a stalwart of the medical community," Bascom replied, rising from his chair.

"No, but it might be worth getting at least one person on your side."

"Thanks," he replied as he left the office.

Helen was working at her computer as he passed her desk minutes later. "Still a runner?" he wondered.

"What? Why no, not anymore," she stammered. "How did you find out?"

He realized too late that he had entered a minefield. "I saw your picture in Joe Thompson's office."

Helen paled. "What else did that shit have to say about me?"

"Nothing. Gotta run," he said continuing down the hallway as his secretary mumbled obscenities he did not know existed in the English language.

VI

On a starry spring night six months after his arrival in Arizona's Sonoran desert, Bascom parked his red SUV behind Mercedes, Jaguars, and a beat-up old Buick, in the semicircular driveway of Abe Grime's rambling Tudor mansion. The white, half-timbered home would have gone unnoticed in Beverly Hills, but among Whitney's dust-cloaked shacks, some bound with bailing wire and duct tape, it was an imposing medieval castle.

He had stopped admitting patients to the hospital following Victor's death. Cohen, who had repeatedly ordered him to respect their agreement, had given him an ultimatum; admit patients or repay his advances with interest and vacate his office. Two weeks earlier the threatening phone calls ended. Bascom had no idea why, but he would not admit healthy patients to the hospital, and he had no intention of leaving his office unless it collapsed over him. And he feared it would on days when relentless winds blew sand through the cracks around the windows and doors and onto hapless patients sitting in its path.

"It's time to see if I'm faster than Thompson's cheetah," he muttered as he straightened his corduroy jacket and climbed the steps to the hand-carved mahogany doors of the manor. The invitation specified formal wear, which Bascom interpreted as meaning anything that covered tattoos and nipple rings. Even though he had neither, he felt his jeans, sport shirt and wool jacket fulfilled his host's requirements for admission to the party.

A strain from Bach's *Toccata and Fugue in D Minor* followed his tap on the button by the side of the door. Seconds later, Abe Grimes, a tall man in his early 70s with white hair and a deeply lined face, opened the door. His thin, bloodless lips curved into a permanent scowl, but his voice was pleasant.

"Robert, welcome," he said warmly. He invited Bascom into a vast hall and then led him into a crowded ballroom.

"Eat hearty," he said, pointing to the cornucopia of refreshments on the tables along a wall covered with pictures of desperadoes from a century earlier.

A group of chattering, bejeweled soubrettes in brocade dresses sniffed at his plebeian dress as he passed them on his way to the bar. Ben Wiggins, his head tilted back, was standing at the far end, trying to slip a slice of pink salmon down his gullet. Wine was dribbling down his tuxedo pants from the tilted glass he held waist high.

"Hello, Ben," Bascom said, slapping him gently on the shoulder. "Enjoying the party?"

"Er, yes," the startled doctor answered. As he straightened up, the lox smacked against his forehead and he stopped pouring wine down his pants.

"Oh, it's you, Bristol. Do you get it yet?" the old man asked. He put his glass on the bar, picked up a napkin and dabbed it on his forehead.

"Get what?"

"Did you come alone?"

"Yes."

"Too bad. You need a friend. Love lubricates all body parts," he said, pointing across the room to Evelyn. The nurse, in an elegant white sleeveless gown with a strand of black pearls around her neck, was dozing in a Victorian chair. "How I love that woman. She stirs me to savagery," he growled softly. He rubbed the napkin on the wine stain on his pants, leaving white particles in its wake, and left the bar.

Abe Grimes approached Bascom as Wiggins tottered towards Evelyn. "The old fool is proof we need euthanasia to rid the world of trash," he said coldly before sipping his whiskey from a cut crystal glass.

"Are you enjoying yourself, Bob?"

"I was until now," he responded curtly, irritated by the callous remark.

"I hear you lost Victor. I couldn't have saved him either. But even without him, you'll soon be earning enough to get a Mercedes and some new clothes," he sneered, glancing at Bascom's casual clothes. "By the way, I know why you're here – and I won't strike. The hospital is fine as it is. Good luck in your next job, if you don't settle down and follow our rules," he added over his shoulder as he left to rejoin his foppish guests.

"Testa di cazzo! Scratch a tux; get shit under your nails," Bascom fumed while walking over to Joe Thompson. The fat man was sitting on two barstools and stuffing handfuls of peanuts into his cavernous mouth.

"I just spoke with Grimes, Joe," he said before ordering a diet drink from the bartender. "You were right. He won't strike. He needs a lesson in manners though. He's a biased prick who would sell his mother into slavery for five bucks."

"Two bucks would be enough," Joe laughed. "He'd exhume his grandmother and force her into prostitution for five. Anyway, I have good news, although with your crusader's attitude, I'm sure it'll be only a temporary reprieve."

He raised his champagne glass to his mouth, spilling a drop on his vest.

"Taking lessons from Dr. Wiggins?" Bascom quipped as Joe wiped off the liquid with a cocktail napkin. He sipped his soda while the surgeon scooped up another handful of salted peanuts from an ornate silver plate, popped them into his mouth, and wiped his fingers on his crumpled napkin.

"The Board sold the hospital," he mumbled, spitting fragments of the salted nuts onto the bar.

"How do you know?" Bascom asked.

"A bunch of government agencies stormed the place, and they had to put it up for sale because they couldn't pay the fines. Would you know anything about that?"

"Would it surprise you if I did?"

"No. Only you would have the balls to follow through where others have only threatened. You lucked out though. If some members hadn't welcomed the investigation, you would have become another obnoxious Whitnian who got 'lost in the desert.'" Joe gulped down the last of his champagne and let out a sonorous belch.

"Can I have a refill, in a bigger glass?" he asked the bartender as he pushed the empty glass across the bar. The man shook his head as if to ask, "How about a trough?"

"From what I hear," Thompson continued, "the Feds are fining the hospital $200,000 for letting the Mexican bleed to death. They fined Perkins $125,000 and put him on a lifetime suspension for the same reason. Plus they billed the hospital another $100k for hiring an unlicensed nurse, who just happened to be Victor Forest's nurse.

"The Board sold WCH for a song to a guy from San Francisco."

"That's great news!" Bascom exclaimed, rolling his glass between his hands. *But is it? Il diavolo che conosci è meglio di quello sconosciuto, 'the devil you know is better than the one you don't.'*

He would have preferred Cohen and the Board make the changes, and not an unknown San Franciscan who might make the situation even worse than it already was.

"What do you mean by 'temporary reprieve'?" he wondered.

"If the new owner makes a mistake, according to your antiquated morality, Dr. Asperger, you'll be all over him. But if you do, from the rumors I hear about this guy, you'll end a squashed bug on the system's windshield. He's a major prick that does not tolerate insubordination. Makes Cohen look like a gay Boy Scout."

"Optimism isn't you're forte, is it, Joe?" Bascom asked, shaking his head at the bartender's silent offer to refill his glass.

"No, Bobby boy. Realism is. You're a misguided idealist playing in the wrong league. You were lucky this time, but if you don't change your interfering ways, you'll learn hard lessons about how this system works. Davidson is the one to teach them to you. Unless he's mellowed into a devout churchgoer."

"That's all that's lacking in this conservative hellhole; someone who preaches faith and morals but rapes sheep for a hobby. I'm optimistic about Davidson, but if he isn't what I hope he is, I'll still uphold the ethics of the profession, no matter what the consequences," Bascom stated before leaving to find Cohen.

He stopped the administrator as he was leaving with a purloined bottle of champagne under his arm.

"Did you sell the hospital, George?" he asked excitedly.

"We'll know in a couple of weeks. The Board has decided to give you a temporary reprieve until then," he answered before exiting into a mellow evening.

Temporary reprieve. It was a catchy phrase, but hearing it twice in two minutes from two different characters was not coincidental. Bascom mulled over his conspiracy theory as he made a last round of the food tables, wrapping and stuffing delicacies into his pockets before quietly slipping from the party.

He tried to read a medical journal as he lay in bed that night, but the thought of the impending hospital sale elbowed the dry facts from his mind. He put it aside and slept until his telephone roused him at 2 a.m.

"You've got a patient," the clerk said brightly.

"One of mine?" he asked groggily.

"No. It's one Dr. Hunter won't admit because he's uninsured."

"I'm on my way," he said as he rolled out of bed.

Ten minutes later Bascom entered the busy ER and walked to its gray-haired chief standing by a patient that was bleeding from a small cut in his forehead.

"Hi, Ed. It looks like you've got a busy night," he said, fanning a hand around the ward.

"It makes it go by faster," Hunter smiled.

"Got a minute?"

"Sure," he said, turning from his patient.

"Why are the few referrals you send me always uninsured?" Bascom asked. Hunter's smile quickly disappeared.

"Coincidence," he explained lamely.

"Could it be because you send the insured patients to your office and don't want the rest?"

"Listen, Bascom," he replied angrily, "what I do here is my business. Now if you'll excuse me," he huffed before turning back to his patient. Bascom sighed and went to see his patient.

"Hi, Mr. Dodd," he said, pulling a curtain around the 45 year-old man's stretcher. "I'm Dr. Bascom. What brings you in tonight?"

"When I flopped naked on a chair, a Coke bottle accidentally went up my ass," the thin man whispered, massaging his abdomen. A woman on a nearby stretcher laughed.

"I see," Bascom replied, frowning at the invisible intrusion. He was no longer surprised or scandalized by anything a patient told him. His only lament was that the oddest cases always arrived in ER the middle of the night.

He donned a rubber glove from the stand next to the stretcher, greased a finger with K-y jelly, and had his patient pull down his pants and roll on his side.

"This might be uncomfortable," he warned as slipped his finger into the patient's rectum. The man moaned as Bascom scratched the smooth end of the bottle with his fingertip. He could not coax it back out.

"Mr. Dodd," he explained as he pulled off the glove, "I'm going to call in someone who can remove this." He dropped the glove into the bio-hazard trashcan on the way to the nursing station and dialed the phone on the desk. A sleepy voice answered.

"Joe," Bascom said, "I need you in the ER. Now."

"Can't you send the patient to Phoenix?" Thompson asked hopefully.

"Nope. Your buddy here could have, but I can't."

"I'll be over."

The disheveled surgeon lumbered into the ER thirty minutes later and joined Bascom at the patient's stretcher. After positioning Mr. Dodd on his side and donning a latex glove, Joe said, "Bob, push in and down on his abdomen when I tell you."

Thompson inserted a lubricated finger into the man's rectum and he moaned like a love struck coyote. The woman on the next stretcher howled with laughter.

"Push," the surgeon said, rotating his meaty finger in the patient's rectum. "More, more," he urged. "One more push, and, ah, finally," he said as he held up the curved glass bottle.

"Mr. Dodd, I'd suggest you drink Coke from a can from now on. G'night," he cautioned before leaving the cubicle with Bascom. He pulled his glove over the bottle and deposited them both in a trashcan.

"Are we through?" he asked tiredly.

"I guess not everything goes better with Coke," Bascom quipped as they walked to the office with the patient's chart.

Thompson groaned.

"Write a note and I'll take care of the rest," Bascom said, handing the chart to his colleague before they sat in the worn chairs. "Thanks for coming."

"Like I had a choice," Thompson grumbled.

"That was an interesting party tonight," Bascom said.

"Bunch of rich phonies, but you never know when you'll need them," Joe replied as he scribbled his report across the page.

"Or when they'll screw you. How did Grimes get so rich?"

"It'll piss you off, but he invents diseases and phony treatments to keep his patients coming back. They're creative and convincing enough to have earned him almost $1,00,000 last year, at least according to rumor."

"How much?" Bascom gasped.

"I know it sounds incredible, but it's true. Here," he said, handing the chart to Bascom. "Good night."

Bascom added his own notes, discharged the patient

and returned home. He sat on his bed holding Cristina's photograph and traced her blond hair with his finger. "Buona notte, tesoro," he said, before replacing the photo on the nightstand. "Mi manchi e t'amo moltissimo, 'I miss and love you very much'."

The rising sun brightened his room as he pulled the covers over his head.

VII

After weeks of speculation about the identity of Whitney Hospital's mysterious new owner, its staff met the San Franciscan at noon on Friday the 13th of May. The nattily dressed, short, balding man in his mid-fifties was talking to George Cohen when Bascom entered the boardroom. A few of his colleagues sat around a large oak table reading the contents of the manila folders that were in front of each chair. He greeted them as he made his way to the duo in the rear of the room.

"Dr. Bascom," the administrator gushed, "this is Dr. Simon Davidson, our new owner." As the men were shaking hands, Ben Wiggins slipped quietly into a chair in the rear of the room.

Cohen usually wore wrinkled slacks and a psychedelic sport shirt he never tucked into his pants, but today he sported a pinstriped suit, a dark tie and a starched white shirt. He fidgeted in his new clothes.

"I'm pleased to meet you," Bascom said politely. He studied his new owner for a few moments before twitching his nostrils at the man's overpowering Musk cologne.

"I'm pleased to meet you, Doctor," the dapper figure replied. He frowned at Bascom's jeans and sport shirt before fanning his hands down and away from his shoulders to show how a respectable physician should dress. In his case it was a tailored, three-piece pinstriped suit and a platinum and black tie pinned with a dazzling diamond to a Birdseye white checked shirt. Gold links flashed from his shirt cuffs, one of which was caught under a gold Rolex watch. Bascom thought his thin-soled, perfectly shined Italian shoes completed the image of a ruthless king who would walk on his prostrate subjects to keep from muddying them.

"Hum, Bascom, Bascom," he mumbled as he buttoned and unbuttoned his jacket, "I've heard that name somewhere. Yes, now I remember," he exclaimed wide-eyed. "You are the doctor who complained to the government about conditions here."

"I am," Bascom agreed.

"You'll not do that again," Davidson warned. He reprimanded Bascom with a wagging a finger, as if he were a wayward schoolboy. "I will buck no insolence from you or anyone else on my staff. You will work with me to turn this hospital into an excellent institution, and you will do so without unwanted publicity, or you will leave. Am I clear?"

"You'll have no trouble from me as long as patient welfare and economically accessible care remain our primary concerns," Bascom answered coolly.

Davidson knitted his black eyebrows into a thick band. "The economic viability of this hospital is my concern, not yours," he warned in a voice that attracted the attention pf everyone in the room except Joe Thompson. The giant was snoring softly in his chair.

"I'm sure it is," Bascom replied uneasily. He excused himself and joined Donna Franklyn at the table. Her tight blouse and jeans accented her perfect shape and attracted the attention of every male, and one or two females, in the room.

"You think he's a nice guy?" she asked, closing the

folder in front of her.

"As nice as Dracula," he replied, sitting beside her.

"Then you'll hate this even more, Doc," she said, tapping a polished nail on the folder in front of her.

"I love surprises," he grinned, reaching for a folder.

"Before you read this and ruin your day, I'm having a dinner party at my house in a week. Would you like to join us?"

"There is nothing I'd like to do more, Donna, but I've rented a condo in Puerto Peñasco that week to do some fishing. How about a rain check?"

"Sure," she smiled.

"Thanks."

Bascom opened his folder. "Dr. Simon Davidson's Rules and Regulations for Physicians in the Modern World," was typed in boldface across the top of its single document.

The first was, "Physicians shall not wear sports shirts, jeans, or sneakers while on duty." He smiled.

He closed the folder and pushed it away. He realized Cohen had described him to Davidson before the meeting, since no one else in the hospital dressed as he did. They had to have also discussed his "temporary reprieve." Davidson had guessed he would be a threat to his plans for Whitney, had singled him out, and was already preparing for the kill.

"'L'abito non fa il Monaco,' Donna," Bascom said. "Clothes don't make the man." He would never exchange his wardrobe for a suit whose pinstripes reminded him of elitist prison garb.

After the last straggler arrived, Cohen and Davidson went to the end of the table where someone had aligned a water pitcher, glasses, pen and notepad with military precision. George tapped his pen against a glass and announced,

"I'd like you to meet our hospital's new owner, Dr. Simon Davidson."

A halfhearted applause followed as Davidson stretched to his full Napoleonic height and bowed slightly, as if granting an audience to a group of peons working in his garden.

"In case you're wondering, I am a doctor, but I haven't practiced for a decade and am now in hospital management," he said, scanning his audience. He frowned at Joe Thompson who was snoring in his chair, a victim of his Pickwickian girth.

"Harrumph. If I may have your attention, Dr. Thompson," he said, impatiently tapping his pen on the table. The surgeon awoke with a start and rubbed his eyes with his meaty paws.

"Thank you," Davidson said. "New equipment is on its way. Should any of you have special needs, Mr. Cohen will take care of them immediately. Also, we'll advertise in all the media for competent nurses." He extended a hand and George placed a glass of water in it. He sipped it, handed it back, and then pulled his jacket sleeves back to one centimeter above his shirt cuffs.

"Any comments?" he asked. The man was smiling, but his tone suggested there was no need for any. Bascom raised his hand.

"Yes, Doctor?"

"I have two. First, Evelyn Cooper should have the authority to discipline the nurses under her. And that must include her right to fire those she considers unfit to practice. Now she can't and our patients receive poor care as a result."

"Write that down, George," Davidson interrupted. The administrator nodded and scribbled dutifully on his pad.

"Next suggestion."

"Ed Hunter refers all the paying patients from the ER to his own clinic and sends the indigent to me. I don't mind caring for them, but it's a conflict of interest and I think he should run either the ER or his clinic, but not both."

"Thank you, Doctor," Davidson replied. "I'll look into your requests. Any other comments?" When he received none, he said perfunctorily, "Thank you for coming. All dismissed."

Bascom had expected him to paraphrase John F Kennedy's presidential acceptance speech, "Ask not what Whitney Community Hospital can do for you, but what you can do for …me," but the pinstriped general simply turned on his heels and exited the room with Cohen stepping gently on his shadow.

Bascom wrote his name on his folder and left it on the table before leaving the boardroom.

As he walked down the hospital corridor, he bumped into a disheveled Ben Wiggins exiting Evelyn Cooper's office. The old man was smiling as he straightened his polka dot tie.

"Hello, Ben. You and Evelyn having fun?" he asked mischievously.

"None of your dang business, Blofeld!" Wiggins replied with a wink.

"You missed the meeting," Bascom chided.

"You were just too caught up with Davidson to notice. I was there, but I'm too old to waste my time with a pissant," he answered as he waddled down the hall. He pulled a handkerchief from his pocket and rubbed it over his bald pate.

"Watch out for the static electricity," Bascom warned.

"Do you get it yet?" Ben yelled back.

"Get what?" he asked. But the old doctor had already turned the corner and did not answer.

VIII

A few weeks after meeting the hospital's new owner and self-appointed caliph of the medical harem in Whitney, Bascom moved his practice to a 100-year old brick building six blocks from the hospital on a day when it was 112 degrees in the shade. The only sign of life in the desert town, apart from Bascom who was moving furniture into a U-Haul truck in his shorts and a sweaty T-shirt, was a lone Mexican mowing a lawn. The teenager wore a sweatshirt with the hood up and a towel wrapped around his neck.

To Cohen's chagrin, Bascom had continued sending his seriously ill patients to Phoenix University Hospital after Victor's death, and would continue to do so until he knew with certainty they would be safe in Whitney's hospital. The administrator had called him after Davidson's meeting to tell him he had not seen any of his patients in a long while. He had hoped Bascom would again admit them to WCH, especially since Dr. Davidson had agreed to honor his contract even though he had not.

Bascom had promised he would think about the request, but had sensed serious problems were looming between him and Davidson. In fact he was so convinced the new owner would bring more problems than solutions to the medical crisis in Whitney that he had moved on his own rather than face eviction later.

What concerned him more than eviction was repayment of the $50,000 he had already received from the hospital. That amount would double over the next six months, and unless he practiced in the hospital for two-years, which now seemed unlikely, he would have to repay it all with interest. It was a serious concern since he was not a businessman-physician. It would take him a lifetime to pay off his debt.

To the casual observer, Bascom was prospering in the little town. His waiting room was always full, but since he never charged the destitute, never performed laboratory studies or procedures "just to be sure," and never had patients return "just to see how they were doing," his income, in reality, was modest. Even with Cohen's supplementary checks, he still had to juggle his monthly payment schedules.

At a staff meeting shortly after his move, the staff elected Bascom emergency room director. Even though he knew no one else wanted the position, he happily accepted the position. He would not have to work in the ER, but he would have to resolve its day-to-day problems and evaluate the quality of care patients received there.

He had spent most of his time in the emergency room during his residency in family practice, and rather than open an office after completing his training, he accepted a position as director of a local emergency room. He would be returning to the environment he loved, and he eagerly looked forward to it.

In the middle of July, two months after Davidson's takeover of the hospital and a day after he returned from a dermatology conference in San Diego, Bascom bumped into Donna Franklin in the hallway of WCH.

"Have you heard?" the beautiful nurse asked, tapping a

manicured finger against his chest.

"Heard what?" he asked. A man pushing his cleaning cart was coming up rapidly behind her. He grabbed her shoulders to move her out of the way, and she stumbled into him.

"Excuse me," she said unrepentantly before adjusting her uniform. "Davidson fired Hunter and brought in docs from San Francisco to run the ER."

"Why he didn't tell me?" Bascom asked, scratching his head. "As its director, he should have. How are they?"

"One is ok, the other orders twice as many tests as Hunter did, and he was no slouch. I think he's incompetent, and I told Cohen. He said docs always order unnecessary studies 'just to be safe,' and to keep my nose out of hospital business."

"Greedy fools," he mumbled, rubbing his hand through his hair. "'Just to be safe' is an excuse doctors use to justify the unnecessary examinations they order on unsuspecting patients. A history and physical are all a competent doc needs to arrive at a diagnosis he can confirm with a laboratory test," he explained.

"Besides, ordering 'all the tests' is misleading, since doctors order the same ones no matter what their patient's symptoms. They're useless in rare or unusual diseases. To make matters worse, naive patients who believe the more tests doctor orders, the more competent he is, unwittingly encourage the practice.

"Well, Donna, it's been great bumping into you," he said. "And excuse the pun." She laughed.

"Anytime, Robert." She winked before hurrying down the hall, "I have to get back to the ER."

Bascom was leaving the ER ten minutes later when two Emergency Medical Technicians pushing a stretcher, forced him against a wall.

"Bad auto accident, Doc," one shouted over his shoulder as he brushed by him. "He's yours."

He raced behind them into the trauma room and helped lift Carl Price onto the operating table. He remembered the muscular teenager's quick wit and shy smile when he performed a sports physical on him in his office two days earlier. Now he was comatose with a bloodied bandage wrapped around his head and a splintered bone protruded from a gash in his left thigh.

Bascom's mind morphed the youth into the crushed and bloodied body of his dying wife. His head swirled and his knees buckled as they did when the only woman he had ever loved died in his arms.

Donna's voice pulled him back from his incubus. "Dr. Bascom, are you ok?" she asked, gently taking his arm.

"Er, yes. I'm fine," he mumbled, shaking the horror from his head. "Code blue," he yelled. As he tore open the boy's shirt, Ben entered the room and limped to a corner where he could unobtrusively observe the scene.

"Donna," Bascom ordered, pointing to a puffy area around a needle in the boy's arm, "pull that infiltrated IV and start another."

"Right," she said. She opened a drawer on the crash cart and picked up a cellophane covered box and a bag of clear fluid.

"Jane," he ordered another nurse as he straightened the boy's legs, "cut off these pants and cover that bone with saline soaked towels."

"Ok," the black woman replied.

Bascom went to Carl's head as Joe Thompson lumbered into the room. "He needs an endotracheal tube, Joe. With this head injury he might not be breathing much longer."

As the giant surgeon prepared to intubate the 16 year-old, Bascom shined a flashlight onto his pupils. They narrowed and he breathed a sigh of relief. The boy's brain had not started swelling. There was still hope.

"B/P is 60/40 and I can't feel a pulse!" a nurse yelled.

"I'm in," Donna said as she attached a bag of saline to the catheter she had just inserted into a vein.

"Run it wide open, Donna," he ordered, "and start another. He's in shock and he needs fluids now!"

Linda Stevens, a pediatrician, had already sliced through the skin in the opposite arm with a scalpel and was probing it with a curved clamp.

"I've got a vein here," she yelled. She inserted a catheter into it, drew blood into its syringe, and handed it to a laboratory technician.

"Four units of universal blood, Larry," she ordered. "I need a bag of Ringer's, someone."

"Would you prefer Hetastarch?" Donna asked.

"What's that?" Stevens asked.

"Hang it," Bascom ordered.

"Right." Donna said as she ran to a cabinet where Ben was standing to retrieve the solution. "This guy is dynamite," she said. "If he can't save this boy, no one can."

Ben nodded. "He is cool under fire," he agreed.

Bascom checked the monitor. The spikes marching across the screen were flattening into an unwavering horizontal line. He knew the boy's brain was swelling, shutting down its vital centers. Unless he could stop it immediately, Carl would die in minutes.

"Where do you want me, Bob?" Marty Nevins asked as he burst onto the scene in bloody OR scrubs.

"CPR, Marty, he's flat-lining. Donna, hang 100 grams of Mannitol," he ordered. "And Joe, double the rate on the respirator. It might reverse the cerebral edema. Quickly! We're losing him!"

Nevins went to the boy's side and began pumping on his chest. "An amp of adrenaline!" he yelled. A nurse injected the contents of a syringe into the IV tubing as the surgeon continued his chest compressions.

Ted Steele, a family doctor, arrived, looked to Bascom who pointed to Carl's fractured legs, and went to the foot of the table. He removed the blood-soaked towel covering the gaping leg wound, gasped at the jagged end of the shattered femur pointing at him, and replaced the towel.

Bascom reexamined Carl's eyes; his right pupil was now larger than his left and not narrowing in response to the light.

Airway, Bleeding, Circulation. All were under control, yet despite his team's concerted efforts, the straight line on the EKG monitor continued unbroken.

Carl was dead.

With a choked voice, Bascom said, "That's enough. I'll handle it from here."

The death of any patient, especially one so young and vibrant, always weighed heavily on him. He never felt he had the power to decide who would live or die, but was sure if a patient died under his care, it was because of something he forgot to do, or worse, had done wrong.

He sighed deeply before asking Donna to make the boy presentable to visitors, and then trudged to the waiting room where Martha Price was wailing hysterically despite her husband's efforts to calm her.

"Martha," he said, "I'm so…"

"Dr. Bascom!" Donna shouted from the trauma room.

"I'll be right back," he said, and raced to the nurse's side.

"Look!" she demanded, pointing to the peaked pattern on the monitor. "He's alive!"

Bascom put his stethoscope to the boy's chest and

heard a heartbeat. Incredibly Carl was alive!

He wrote orders on the boy's chart and then went to the nursing station to call the Phoenix University Hospital to tell them he was transferring the boy by helicopter.

"Well, Donna," he said, returning to his patient, "miracles do happen."

"Your presence didn't hurt, either." She smiled as she adjusted Carl's IV.

"Somebody's presence anyway," Bascom replied before returning to the boy's parents to give them the good news. Their son's recovery would be long and perilous, but he was alive.

He brought them into the trauma room and left them with their son before retreating with Donna to the charting room. As he was documenting the events, a young, muscular male in a spotless white jacket poked his head in the door, mumbled, "excuse me," and disappeared.

"Who was that?"

"Dr. Evans, Davidson's 'prodigy' from San Francisco."

"Just coming on duty?" he wondered, returning to his report.

"He's been here all morning."

"He wasn't at the code."

"Typical. Remember I told you one of our new doctors was ordering too many studies and might be incompetent?"

"Sure."

"That's him. To protect himself from patients' germs, he wears a mask and stands three feet away from them. After he asks where it hurts, no matter what the answer, he orders all the tests he can think of. He carries a list of all the laboratory tests we can run here and checks it regularly.

"What irks me is that a patient will tell me he didn't black out in an accident, but Evans will write on the chart that he did, then order a head CT. He orders three or four a day.

"Blood also nauseates him, so when he heard the EMTs bringing in Carl, he ran out the back door."

"Are you serious?" Bascom asked incredulously, dropping his pen on the chart.

"You bet," she replied. "The guy's useless. He should have become a radiologist – they never touch patients! But he can't read X-rays worth a damn either. He wouldn't even make a good autopsy specimen. He's rotten inside."

Bascom whistled softly. An ER physician who refused to touch a patient was incompetent under the best conditions; under the worst, criminally negligent. This time Evans had been fortunate there were other doctors on duty, but he shuddered to think what would have happened he had been alone in the hospital when Carl arrived. He had no idea if Davidson knew his new employee was inept, although even as a nonpracticing physician he should have. As the ER director with responsibility for what happened there, he needed to clarify the situation.

He completed his charting and searched out Dr. Evans. The masked physician was standing four feet away from his patient, a foot further than Donna had described, scribbling on a chart.

"Hi. I'm Dr. Bascom. I'd like to speak with you," he said politely.

"About what?" he grunted arrogantly through his mask. Taut muscles bulged under his white jacket as he pulled the chart to his chest and turned to his inquisitor.

"In private."

"Here's fine," Evans replied cockily.

"Where were you during the code?"

"On Nature's Call. What's it to you?" he answered menacingly.

"I need to know what goes on here."

"Simon told me to ignore you. You got a problem, talk to him," he replied coldly, returning to his patient.

"Fine, but next time you answer 'Nature's Call,' wipe when you're done; you're smelling up my ER," Bascom replied before going to recheck Carl.

The boy's vital signs were stronger, but would his brain survive its injury without leaving him crippled or blind? Hippocrates cautioned physicians in his *Aphorisms* to "never underestimate a minor head injury nor overestimate a severe one." Time would tell if the ancient Greek physician's belief would prove true in Carl's case.

Thirty minutes later medical technicians loaded the boy into their ambulance to take him to the airport for the helicopter flight to Phoenix. Bascom went to his office.

"Maybe your source exaggerated the facts, Bob," Joe Thompson said over the phone that evening. He was crunching food and his words were difficult to decipher. "I haven't heard anything bad about Evans. He sends me patients all the time."

"I never would have guessed," Bascom replied sarcastically. "You do well with our ER docs. Did you see him at the code?"

"No."

"He was on duty and should have been there. Besides, the person who told me he's incompetent knows firsthand he's a bum."

"Ok, calm down. I'll talk with him. Who's your mole?"

"None of your business. Just let me know what he says as soon as possible, Ok?"

"Sure."

"Thanks," Bascom said as he hung up the phone. *I doubt you will, but if I hound your fat ass enough maybe on day you'll begin to act like a physician.*

He went to bed, bemoaning the fact that Whitney's patients now received not only bad care, but also costly and unnecessary laboratory studies. He rued having called in the government to evaluate the hospital since it had brought Simon Davidson and Albert Evans into Whitney.

He wondered what else was in-store for the desert town.

IX

"This is a dangerous part of town," Donna warned Bascom as he skirted an overturned trashcan in a narrow, garbage-strewn alley. It was early evening and the peaceful orange sky belied the storm that had just passed through town. Fine particles of sand had covered everything in the path of the tempest, leaving the decayed houses surreal in their tan drapery.

"A gang mugged Fran's uncle right there during a fake emergency call." His nurse pointed to the "MS 13," spray-painted on the cinder block wall, the signature of one of the world's most vicious gangs. Its feared tribe members ruled Whitney's back alleys.

"If I didn't know Maria, I would have told her to call an ambulance rather than risk getting stabbed like he did," she said, cuddling the sack of medical supplies on her lap.

"Her daughter and son-in-law died in a car accident last year, leaving their two boys for her to raise. Sad. I became friends with the family after that.

"These people are dirt-poor," she added, "which is why Pedro refused to go to the ER. I told her I'd bring over the best doc in town."

"Good to know I'm a bit better than Perkins and Evans," Bascom replied.

"A bit cynical, Doctor?"

"It's my best trait."

"I doubt it. Thanks for doing this, even though Pedro is not your patient."

Bascom shrugged. "I can't ignore a call for help from anyone. It's odd they attacked Fran's uncle though. The bad guys usually leave us alone since we have to take care of them after they get stabbed."

He pulled up in front of a rusty gate and they descended from the truck, he carrying his medical bag and Donna toting her sack. She pushed open the gate and they walked to the house through a weed-infested garden dotted with broken toys.

Paint of various colors and layers peeled off planking that curved out from the walls of the tiny home. A screen covering a cracked window was split down the middle, as if someone had cut it with a knife.

As they approached, an elderly Mexican woman opened the door.

"Oh Donna," Maria cried, hugging her, "It's Pedro's heart again. Please hurry, Doctor," she added, stepping aside to let him pass.

Bascom entered a small room that was dimly lit by a bare bulb hanging from the ceiling. A spiral of sticky flypaper covered with carcasses of insects hung next to it. Two shy, half-naked children sitting on a shabby couch looked away as he passed them. In the bedroom an emaciated old man lay on a thin mattress on the floor. He knelt next to him and lifted the tattered blanket off his frail body.

"How's your pain, Pedro?" he asked as he picked up the man's wrist to feel his pulse. It was irregular and weak, an ominous sign.

"Bad. He runs to my neck and arm," he croaked. A smile broke the creases of his leathery cheeks but there was sadness in his sunken eyes.

Bascom took a pressure cuff from his bag, wrapped it around his patient's arm, and pumped its bulb a few times. "One-ten over seventy," he said while deflating it. "Are you allergic to anything, Pedro?" The man shook his head.

"Donna," he ordered, "give him an aspirin to chew and swallow, start a saline drip, and give him 4 mg. of morphine IV. Pedro," he said turning to the old man, "you need to be in the hospital."

"No," he protested, shaking his head, "they'll kill me, then take my house and throw my family on the street. They did it to my friend. But you'll help me? Please? I can pay."

"I'll help you. And you can pay me when you get my bill," Bascom replied, squeezing the old man's hand.

Donna started the IV and injected the morphine into the tubing. The drug would quell the pain within minutes, but since most deaths occur during the first hours after a heart attack, Bascom made the only decision his conscience would allow. "I'll be back," he said before going into the yard. He called the Phoenix University Hospital on his cellphone and asked the ER physician to admit Pedro to their coronary care unit.

"Does he have insurance?" the attending wondered.

"It's unlawful to ask that question, so I'll pretend I didn't hear it. If you refuse to accept him," Bascom chided gently, "we and EMTALA will discuss the future of your hospital."

"I'm sure we can find a bed," the doctor replied quickly, "and we'll get him on Arizona Health Care besides."

"Good. We'll be there soon," Bascom said. He then dialed 911 and asked the operator to send an ambulance before reentering the house.

"Ok," he explained to the concerned faces around the

mattress, "Pedro's going to Phoenix by ambulance."

"No money," the man protested weakly. His wife knelt by his side and took his hand.

"Can't you help us here?" she pleaded.

"Pedro will get free care."

"Really?" Maria asked doubtfully.

"Really," he replied. "I'll ride with him in the ambulance and Donna will follow with you and the children in my car."

The woman shook her head, seemingly unconvinced by Bascom's promise. Her grandchildren hugged her legs, hiding their faces in the folds of her worn dress, and she rested her hands on their heads.

"We'll stay with relatives in Phoenix while Pedro is in the hospital," she said.

"Fine," Bascom nodded. "I'll drop you off there."

The ambulance arrived and within minutes its EMTs had lifted Pedro onto a stretcher and then into their vehicle. Bascom sat on a stool next to him and watched as Donna helped Maria and the boys into his SUV.

They departed together, but the ambulance, with its blaring sirens and flashing lights, was soon far ahead. Bascom was talking to Jesus, a young EMT with a Pancho Villa mustache, when Pedro squeezed his arm and then went limp. Bascom glanced at his heart monitor; bizarre shapes raced across its small screen. The old man's heart was quivering erratically and he would die in minutes if it did not return to a regular rhythm.

Bascom began pumping on Pedro's chest from his cramped position as the EMT charged his defibrillator.

"Ready, Jesus?" he asked without looking up.

"Charged at 200," he replied, placing the paddles on Pedro's chest.

"Shock!" Bascom ordered. He leaned back from the

stretcher. The paddles popped and the monitor went blank, but the lethal arrhythmia returned when it lit up moments later.

"Shock again!" Jesus' recharged paddles popped but the fatal arrhythmia persisted.

"Shock at 360." The EMT turned a dial on his defibrillator and replaced the paddles on Pedro's chest.

"Clear!"

"Go!" Bascom replied. The machine popped, but still there was no change. Pedro could not survive three minutes without oxygen and half had already passed.

"Should I give him amiodarone, Doc?"

"Intubate him first," Bascom ordered as he restarted the chest compressions. The waves on the monitor were half as large as they were seconds earlier. Death was near.

"Right," thc EMT said, taking a curved tube from a drawer behind him.

"Ready?"

"Yes!" Bascom fixed Pedro's throat between his fingers, making it easy for Jesus to insert the tube into his windpipe.

"Done," the EMT said as he attached the tube to a respirator fixed to the ceiling of the ambulance. The machine hissed air into the Mexican's lungs.

"Record time!" Bascom glanced at the monitor; Pedro's heart waves were now almost a flat line. He shook his head. "Give an amp of adrenaline and shock again," he ordered.

The EMT emptied a syringe into the IV tubing and picked up the paddles. "Clear?" he asked, placing them on Pedro's chest.

"Clear," Bascom replied. The paddles fired but to no avail.

"Give the amiodarone," he ordered.

The EMT emptied another syringe into the IV tubing

and within seconds, larger waves appeared on the monitor.

"We're getting a response, Jesus. Shock again."

The EMT's paddles popped and the screen darkened. When it relit, there were regular waves flowing across it.

"Wow! You sure earned your fee, Doc," the EMT beamed.

"We couldn't buy a cup of coffee with it," Bascom replied as the ambulance bounced off a curb in front of the hospital. "This must have been the fastest trip to Phoenix in the history of ambulance lore."

"We've done better," Jesus replied as his driver opened the rear doors.

The men offloaded the stretcher and pushed it into the hospital.

As soon as Pedro arrived in the ER, his heart stopped again. Within seconds a team of specialists rushed to his stretcher but despite their efforts, could not restart it.

The ER doctor walked over to Bascom. "I'm sorry," he said grimly.

"You did your best. His wife will want to see him when she arrives."

"She'll have all the time she needs," he replied before excusing himself to attend to another patient.

Bascom went outside and awaited his SUV. When it pulled up in front of him, he opened the passenger door, took Maria's hands in his and said, "I'm sorry, Maria. Pedro died. Please accept my sympathies."

"Not my Pedro!" she cried, covering her face with her hands.

Donna hugged her friend. "My church will take care of you, Maria," she said through her own tears.

Bascom led the crying woman into the ER, waited as she wailed good-bye to her lifelong companion, and then walked her back to the SUV and helped her into the vehicle. Donna was in the backseat hugging the boys as he slipped into the driver's seat.

After leaving Maria and the children at her sister's home, he and Donna drove in silence until they turned off the highway into Whitney. Burned-out houses still lined the exit, a dismal memorial – or was it a warning? - to a farm workers' unsuccessful strike for better wages years earlier.

"What good is a hospital if people are afraid they'll be killed or bankrupted within its walls?" Bascom asked as he pulled up in front of his office. "They might as well be brothels, then people wouldn't feel bad about paying for the screwing they know they're going to get."

Donna laughed. "Are you being cynical again?"

"I told you it's my best trait," he replied tiredly. "Pedro is only the latest victim of medical hypocrisy in this country. Fifty million citizens have to live with their diseases, or die from them as Pedro did, because the system is broken. It's a disgrace. I wish I had never become a doctor."

"I'm grateful you did," she replied.

"Anyway, you're a great nurse and it's always a pleasure to work with you."

"Likewise," she said, giving him a kiss on the cheek before exiting the SUV. She climbed into her yellow Jeep, started the engine and drove away.

Bascom watched her taillights disappear into the distance before driving home.

X

After passing the night lying on his couch and griping to his feet about Pedro's death, Bascom drank two cups of coffee and drove to the hospital. He knew the Mexican farm worker might not have survived his heart attack even if he treated him in Whitney's hospital, but he also knew the rear of a careening ambulance was not ideal place to revive a failing heart.

He had hoped Dr. Davidson would make WCH a decent place for Whitney's populace to get care, but based on Pedro's fears and the stack of bills from disgruntled patients Helen had left on his desk, he realized the San Franciscan had intended to squeeze Whitnians between the spikes of his Iron Maiden until he had bled their last coin out of them.

He parked his SUV in front of the hospital and, bills in hand, stormed up the cracked path and through its entrance. He followed the nauseating stench of oil of wintergreen to Marty Nevins' office. The surgeon was sitting behind his desk, dabbing the smelly liquid on a bald spot in his beard. Instead of his usual cardigan, sport shirt and slacks, he wore a pinstriped suit, white shirt and dark cravat tied in a huge knot an inch below his collar.

Nevins dropped the cotton ball in his ashtray as Bascom entered his office. "Hi ya, Pilgrim," he said, snarling a poor imitation of John Wayne. "Can I buy ya a drink?"

"Oil of wintergreen will not regrow your ratty beard, so spare us the nauseating smell, Duke," Bascom replied, briefly holding his nose. "This place stinks bad enough as it is. We need to talk about what's been going on here lately."

"I avoid politics, Bob," he said as he screwed the cap back on the bottle. "It's in the Hippocratic Oath. 'The modern physician shall not stick his nose into hospital business, even if his patients' lives and fortunes are at stake, because it could lower his income.'"

"Sounds more like the Hypocritic Oath to me. Do you know the cost of some tests has increased 200 percent since Davidson took over?" Bascom asked, dropping the bills on the desk.

The surgeon quickly made the sign of the cross over them as if they were chartaceous vampires. "I don't wanna know 'cause I don't get no respect," he said, changing his accent.

"When you decide you'd like some, call me. And what's with the new suit? Going to a funeral?" Bascom asked before leaving the room.

Linda Stevens bumped into him in the hallway, pardoned herself and then ran into her office. He followed the red-haired pediatrician into her book-filled cubicle and leaned against a wall as she sat in a high-backed chair in the corner of the room. She pulled her legs up under her and gazed out the window.

"Got a problem I can help with, Linda?" Bascom asked.

"Yeah," she grunted. "Shoot Davidson for me."

He laughed. "Call James Bond. I'm not licensed to kill. What'd he do?"

"He closed down peds to open a drunk tank."

"That's absurd!"

"According to Cohen," she continued, absentmindedly spinning a diamond ring on her left hand, "insured drunks pay, migrants' kids don't. He says the hospital isn't licensed for pediatrics anyway."

"Were his pupils responding to light?" He understood why Davidson would want to eliminate unprofitable services, but to deny care to children for that reason was abominable, and in the case of a life-threatening emergency, illegal.

"I'm not in the mood for cute remarks, Bob," she replied, looking up at him. "If I can't admit my kids here, I'm moving my practice to Phoenix. My patients will follow me."

"A few of the wealthier families might," he replied, running his hand through his long blond hair, "but no mother would drive 120 miles round-trip just because her kid has a runny nose or needs a vaccination. She'll go to your replacement and forget your name in a week. We'll straighten this out, Linda. Just don't make any rash decisions, Ok?"

She nodded and Bascom left her office, bumping into Betty Perez, an overweight ER nurse.

"God, what a day," she said, blowing a strand of hair from her chubby face with a stream of air from crooked lips.

"What's your problem?" he wondered.

"Dr. Davidson just opened a walk-in clinic next to the ER and I haven't been able to sit for more than thirty seconds." She was a good nurse, but sitting was what she did best.

"A clinic?" Bascom echoed in disbelief.

"Yep. For patients that don't have their own doctors, he says. But everyone we treat gets a compulsory follow-up appointment there.

"Gotta go. Patients are piling up," she said as she waddled off to the emergency room.

Wiggly lines, harbingers of a migraine headache, began encircling his field of vision as Ted Steele approached him. The family practice physician was bouncing on his heels and moving his head like a bobblehead doll. He, like Marty Nevins, was wearing a dark suit, tie and shiny wing-tipped shoes.

What is it with these suits? Are there alien controlled pods in the attic?

"Got something for you, Bob," the chief-of-staff sang out, waving a document in his thin hand.

"A tithe on my earnings?"

"The proposal for the clinic Dr. Davidson just opened."

"He opens the clinic and <u>then</u> proposes it?"

"Yes," Ted said, shrugging his scrawny shoulders.

"Don't you think this is conflict of interest?"

"I don't know." He shrugged his shoulders again.

"Did you forget Hunter skimmed off all the insured patients and left the charity cases for us?" he asked, irritated by the man's apathy. His head was pounding and he had difficulty focusing. His headache was more severe than usual.

"He sent me many insured patients."

"Lucky you," Bascom replied sarcastically. "Davidson will not be sending you any, and he'll be keeping yours besides. And you think it's ok, even if the cost of care to our patients will double?"

"Dr. Davidson promised would return my patients to me for follow-up," Steele said before slithering down the hall.

Bascom watched in disgust as the messenger disappeared around a corner of Cohen's, now Davidson's, square doughnut. It reminded him of Nietzsche's scribbling a century earlier: "A letter is an unannounced visit and the postman is the intermediary of impolite surprises."

He went to the OR dressing room where Joe Thompson was changing into street clothes. "Simon says it's his hospital," the obese surgeon roared, "and he said if we don't like his changes, we're free to leave. The clinic doesn't affect me since I don't have any patients to lose. Docs refer them to me for surgery and I send them back after I've finished with them."

"Always the altruist, eh, Joe?" Bascom replied. "Simple Simon, rotten pie man. He's more devious than simple. Have you checked into his ER crew as I asked?"

The giant surgeon took a white shirt from his open locker. A photo of old-time bodybuilder Charles Atlas was taped inside the door. "No," he replied as he donned it, "but our radiologist says his business has tripled since Evans arrived in town. Almost every X-ray he orders is normal."

"We need to talk," Bascom said, rubbing his temples. "Come to dinner tomorrow night. I'll make some tortelloni or tortellini and a nice secondo. Bring your wife."

Joe licked his lips. "What's the difference between them?"

"Tortellini are small and filled with meat. Tortelloni are large and filled with cheese."

"How about both?" Joe wondered, smacking his fat lips.

"How about tortellini and Spaghetti-Os, or tortelloni and Spaghetti-Os?"

He laughed. "I'll take the big ones. Give the Spaghetti-Os to Cohen."

"I eat at seven, so be on time."

Bascom would not let the San Franciscan pillage the community as he saw fit, but he needed allies to stop him. Even though Joe would never do anything to imperil his income, he still hoped to convince the fat surgeon to stand with him against the professional bandit.

Helen was jotting a name in the appointment book, when he arrived back in his office. He rapped a ditty on the ledge of her Dutch door.

"Anything interesting?" he asked as he pried a splinter out of the knuckle of his middle finger.

"Yes. Mrs. Gonzalez called to tell us she survived her surgery and is home and well."

"I need to sand down this shelf," he said, gently rubbing his hand over it. "What did they find wrong with her?"

"She doesn't know. Says her doctors didn't speak any of her languages."

"Which are?"

"English, Spanish, and Filipino."

"She needs to learn Medicalese," Bascom laughed. "Why does she speak Filipino?"

"Her first husband was Filipino. Anyway we've nothing to do this afternoon. Fran has a stitch removal and a blood pressure check tomorrow," she replied, looking up from her desk. "According to the Bascom Billing System," she continued, "tomorrow, at least until the phone starts ringing off the hook, we earn nothing."

"The cost of the surgery includes stitch removal, but I might charge for the B/P check."

"More than the $9.50 for the skin tumor you removed?" she chided.

"That was what the guy earned in three hour's work," Bascom explained. "It took me ten minutes to do the surgery. If people have to pay $40 just to know what their pressure is, they'll stop coming in. Then I'll have to treat them for heart attacks and strokes.

"Is Fran still here?" he asked.

"She's in back."

He went to the nursing station where his young nurse was replacing the plastic cover on her blood-testing machine. Her hair was slightly mussed and she looked tired.

"What happened to my usually perfectly groomed nurse?" he asked.

"Last night was Tuesday," she smiled.

"It was Monday," Bascom corrected.

"If I say it was Tuesday, it was Tuesday," she insisted.

"So be it. Have you figured out why our test results are wrong, Fran?" he asked. He walked to the counter and turned off the water dripping into the sink.

"Outdated reagents," she replied. "You don't run enough tests to use them up before they expire."

"Maybe we can buy them in smaller quantities."

"I'll check. By the way, Dr. Thompson called. He said to tell you his wife can't come, but he promised to eat her share so you won't feel offended."

"It's nice how he sacrifices himself for others."

"He's much better at sacrificing others," she added with an arched eyebrow.

"Like whom?"

"Like Helen," she whispered. She closed the door. "Fat boy couldn't afford med school, so he convinced the hospital Board that if they'd pay for his education, he'd practice here. After he returned he and Helen became inseparable until he dumped her for a millionaire farmer's daughter. Ironically the guy died broke and Joe never saw a dime of the money he hoped his wife would inherit and he could spend."

"So that's why he's stuck in this town," Bascom said.

"I heard about the changes in the hospital," Fran continued as she dropped the outdated reagents into the garbage bin. "What do you think about them?"

"Your father would wash out my mouth with soap if I

told you," he laughed, remembering her comment on her first day at work. "I invited Thompson to dinner to convince him to help me reverse some of them."

"Don't trust him, Doc, you'll regret it," she warned.

"Sometimes people hide their good qualities, Fran. You just have to bring them to the surface."

"All his fat will make it a slippery job," she giggled. "Just don't believe his promises!"

"I'll remember," Bascom replied. He left the nursing station and went to his desk to check the mail. After shredding the offer to buy a beautiful time-share bungalow in the Brazilian rain forest, he went home.

That evening he rolled a *sfoglia,* a sheet of pasta, on the butcher-block table in his kitchen. He cut it into squares as Cris had taught him, filled them with ricotta cheese, then folded them into triangles, wrapping their corners around his little finger to form *L'Ombelico di Venere* 'Venus' Bellybutton' and lined them up on a towel to dry. He then prepared the *pomodori in forno* and *cotolette alla bolognese*, covered them with aluminum foil, and put them in the refrigerator.

"Now I need a coup de grâce to end Joe's insensitive behavior," Bascom mumbled. He went into the bedroom, pulled his suitcase from the top of the armoire, placed it on the bed and opened it. His collection of Stan Getz, John Coltrane, Bach, and Rachmaninoff CDs was sitting on top of a pack of yellowed love letters. It reminded him of the nights in front of the fireplace with Cris in their *baita*. He could still hear the music playing softly in the background while they read snippets of their favorite books to each other. It also reminded him of Beethoven's "Fűr Eliza," which he had been listening to it in his office the night she died.

He pushed them aside and picked up a print by Renato Guttuso, an Italian expressionist painter. It was a fake Cris had bought from a street vendor outside the porticoed entrance to the *Archiginnasio*, a 16th Century university building in Bologna's medieval hub. He thought of hanging it in the bedroom, but dropped it back into the suitcase. There were already too many events in his daily life that sparked memories of Cristina, and he did not need another.

Rummaging through the suitcase, he came across a brown envelope containing two ticket stubs from *Rigoletto*, an opera they had seen at La Scala in Milan when he was still a medical student. They were in the top row of the balcony, so high up that Cris had lamented she needed binoculars just to see the floor of the opera house. They laughed about it in bed later that night before turning to more pleasurable matters. He stuck them back in the envelope and dropped it onto Guttuso's print.

Wrapped in towels in the corner of the green bag, under old, leather bound copies of *The Aphorisms of Hippocrates* and Sir Thomas Browne's *Religio Medici*, were gifts a wealthy politician had given him for pulling his son out of a crevice along the ski trail at the *Corno della Scala*. One was a small black glass bottle of Armando Manni's Tuscan olive oil, *Per me*. At $350 a liter, it was the world's most expensive vegetable oil. Critics had compared its purity to a fine wine and renowned chefs offered it to their most favored guests.

He placed it on the bed and unwrapped Pedroni's balsamic vinegar and its handblown glass dropper. The company had produced only 100 bottles of the 50-year-old complex and viscous condiment named *Caesar*, in honor of its founder. Its cut glass container was as small as Manni's, but ten times more costly. It had arrived at his door in a carved wooden box, with a book and a signed lot number card.

Pedroni's book explained that 900 years ago vintners in Modena gave balsamic vinegar as a mark of favor to those of importance. Although mistakenly considered wine vinegar, it is made from sweet white Trebbiano grape pressings boiled down to dark syrup and then placed into oaken kegs along with a vinegar "mother." Over decades it is decanted into ever-smaller kegs of ash, chestnut, juniper and other fine woods that progressively add character to it as the moisture evaporates, further thickening the vinegar and concentrating its flavor.

The bottle came with its own dropper since only a few drops could dress a salad.

Bascom replaced his suitcase on the armoire and brought the expensive condiments into the kitchen. He put them on the table in the breakfast nook and then went to the garage for lumber and cinder blocks. He dragged them into the kitchen and built a makeshift bench he hoped would be strong enough to support Whitney's fat surgeon.

While lying in bed later that evening, he took Cristina's picture from the nightstand and stood it on his chest.

Well, Cris, I hope tomorrow's meal will get to Thompson's heart and not just his stomach. The people of this dusty town face challenges you couldn't begin to imagine, and I need fat boy to help bring some relief into their lives.

He fell into a troubled sleep with his wife's picture still wrapped in his arms.

XI

The neurosurgeon from Phoenix called Bascom at home early the next morning to tell him that Carl Price was still comatose but stable, and he was transferring him back to Whitney. Bascom had reluctantly agreed to admit the boy to the custodial care unit of Davidson's hospital because his parents were tiring of the long, daily trip to Phoenix. He would need nursing care until he awoke, but Bascom could not forget Nurse Ruiz. Her incompetence had caused Victor Forest's premature death, and he was afraid Carl might meet a similar end if a nurse like her cared for him.

As he rolled out of bed, Cris' picture frame cracked under him. "I'll fix your spirit tomorrow," he apologized as he picked up the pieces and placed them on his nightstand. "I wish I could have fixed your body a year ago."

As he showered, he thought of ways to persuade Joe Thompson to help him fight Davidson's onerous changes at WCH. Apart from erecting a huge bronze statue in his honor on the hospital's front lawn, or offering him free *tortellini* for life, nothing came to mind. All Joe's interests were rectangular and green and fit into his wallet; he would never give them up just to save a farm worker from bad care or a lifetime of debt.

The Shadwells were waiting for him when he arrived

in his office at 9 o'clock. Rose, a tiny woman with tired eyes and gray hair, was standing next to her husband, a wizened man lying on the table and coughing spasmodically. After catching his breath, he rasped, "I've got lung cancer, hip pain, bad headaches, and can't see anything on my left side."

"Bill threatened me with a knife, Doctor," Rose added as she rested her tiny hand on his chest, "and he accused me of adultery. I'm 60 years-old and should be so lucky," she lamented. Her pale lips trembled. "He's always been gentle and loving. I don't understand why he's behaving so badly now." Tears were a word away, and Bascom covered her hand with his.

"Mrs. Shadwell," he replied gently, "Bill's symptoms and his anger are due to the spread of the cancer to his brain. If you wish, I can admit him to the hospital while we search for a solution to your problem."

The Shadwells agreed and Bascom admitted Bill to the chronic care ward that afternoon. Carl arrived by ambulance at the same time, and he admitted him to an adjoining room. The boy was comatose, had a respirator connected to his tracheotomy tube, and his leg was in a cast. Recovery was still months away.

Joe lumbered into Bascom's home at 7 o'clock that evening, sniffed the air, and followed the scent into the kitchen.

"This is what I call 'aroma,'" he said before storming to the table like a bull elephant chasing a female in heat.

He sat on the makeshift bench and stuffed an end of his napkin into his collar. Even though Bascom had used the stoutest wood he could find, the bench sagged under the huge surgeon's weight.

"Bring it on!" he said, smacking his lips.

"Would you like a glass for your wine, or would you prefer to just knock the neck off the bottle and drink it straight down?" Bascom asked bemusedly as he uncorked a bottle of Lambrusco.

"I'll take a glass, but leave the bottle right here," Joe ordered, pawing the table next to his plate.

"Um, ah, damn this is good," he repeated as he gulped down every tortelloni, all the vegetables and meat, and an entire loaf of French bread in 10 minutes. As he was reaching for the salad bowl, Bascom went to the living room to answer his phone. When he returned, the bottle of Armando Manni's olive oil was lying empty on its side and the fat surgeon was pounding the heel of the bottle of Pedroni's *Caesar* to force the last drop of the rare, costly balsamic vinegar onto his salad.

"Couldn't you afford a bigger bottle of vinegar?" He raised it to his eye, peered into its narrow neck, and then rolled it over to its counterpart.

"Damn it, Joe," Bascom growled, "that's...." His voice trailed and he shook his head. He was angry with Thompson, but more so with himself. He should have known the buffoon could never appreciate the rare and savory condiments.

He picked up the glass carcasses and the unused dropper, all now irrevocably linked to the most beautiful and the ugliest events in his life, and placed them in the cabinet over the sink. He would decide whether to keep them as mementos of heaven or of hell, but not today.

As Bascom closed the cabinet, Joe pushed his huge frame from the table, knocking the board off its cinder block support. "That was good," he griped, "but I'm still hungry. I'll stop at McDonald's for a few hamburgers on the way home."

He plodded into the living room and plopped into Bascom's favorite chair. It moaned as the fat surgeon's huge derrière forced apart its hand carved arms. He rubbed a sausage-sized finger across his teeth and then looked at it. He moved it towards his mouth as if her were going to lick the green speck on its tip, but instead flicked it off with his thumb.

"I have news," he stated. His chair creaked ominously. "Davidson fired the housekeeping crew today and replaced it with a couple of illegal immigrants at a fraction of the cost."

Bascom leaned back on his couch and interlaced his fingers behind his head. "This has to stop, Joe," he grumbled. "With reasonable increases Davidson could earn a 15 percent return on his investment, but he's out to triple his take in record time.

"Our poor live in hovels or abandoned railroad cars and bust their butts in 100-degree heat for subminimum wage. If they go to his hospital, they're indebted for life."

"We ship them to Phoenix for hospitalization, remember?" Joe interrupted. "Davidson won't let us to order test on a patient who can't pay. He believes uninsured people don't need laboratory studies.'"

"That's illegal and unethical," Bascom protested. He knew from the moment they met that Davidson was a fraud, but he had no idea how devious and dishonest the man could be.

"Sure," Joe agreed, "but the docs at the hospitals in Phoenix and Tucson know we have limited services here. Evans has a list of exotic diagnoses needing advanced care we can't provide here. They have to take his transfers. Cohen gets nasty letters since some of the diseases are no longer known by the names Evans uses – when was the last time anyone had 'dropsy'? - but no one can prove he's dumping patients. All they can say is that he's incompetent.

"My name isn't on the transfers and they don't affect my bank deposits, so I don't care what they say about him."

"It's incredible how you condone ethics violations just so you won't lose a dime," Bascom rebutted.

"I don't condone them, Bob," he corrected, "I just don't get involved."

"That's worse."

Bascom rested his hands on his abdomen and slowly spun his thumbs around each other. "It really doesn't bother you that the people in this town are getting over tested by Evans and overcharged by Davidson?"

"According to you Evans orders unnecessary studies," the surgeon explained, "and you're right." He took a gold case from his inside jacket pocket and extracted a filter cigarette. "But therapy is opinion. There are dozens of ways of arriving at a diagnosis, and dozens of opinions on how to treat a disease. If you accused him publicly, Davidson would pay some doc to agree Evans needs all the tests he orders. He'd probably even swear he would order more just to make Evans' excesses appear reasonable. Then he'd sue your ass for libel and win, and you know it.

"I already warned you. Davidson is tough. Don't mess with him or his stooges."

Thompson tapped the cigarette on the case before lighting it. Bascom knew of doctors who had justifiably accused colleagues of incompetence and were sued, just as the fat man had warned. He did not understand how a crook could successfully sue someone for calling him what he was, but this was America, and suing was as American as apple pie.

"Were you ever poor, Joe?" he wondered, slurring his words as he often did at the onset of a migraine headache.

"My parents were dirt-poor," he replied, blowing a smoke ring into the air. It shimmered overhead, grew larger, thinner, and then faded away.

"Did they have problems paying the rent or putting food on the table?"

"Sure. Times were tough back then. We ate meat and potatoes without the meat."

"How much worse would it have been if you had to skip even the potatoes because a corrupt administrator or an unethical doctor had deliberately padded your hospital bill?"

"We went to Ben Wiggins when I was a kid. He rarely charged us. Even gave us free medication," Thompson said lamely.

"Damn it, Joe, Stop making excuses! Simon Davidson is no Ben Wiggins!" Bascom growled. He raised his hands to the sides of his head ans slowly massaged his temples. "A family in this town doesn't eat in a day what you just gobbled up in 15 minutes. It's thanks to them you'll be farting in silk for the rest of your life while they dress their kids in burlap. And you don't care? Don't you owe them something? Like making sure they're treated competently and billed honestly?"

Joe shrugged his indifference, blew another smoke ring in the air, watched it float away. "You won't let WCH or its incompetent doctors rape your patients, myself excluded of course, but how can you stop them, Dr. Asperger?"

"Damn you Thompson!" Bascom shouted, pounding his fist on the coffee table. "I don't have Asperger's!" He took a deep, sighing breath and asked in a near whisper, "When will you grow up? I don't know how to stop Davidson, but I know where to start."

"Where?"

"With Cohen. Call him and demand a meeting with Davidson."

"Why?"

"To complain about the rip-offs and to learn if he has any other plans to screw this town."

"I'll try, but now I need to go since I have surgery in Phoenix early tomorrow. I won't call you 'Dr. Asperger' again," he promised. Bascom nodded. The chair creaked and wobbled as he pushed on its arms to lift his bulk from it.

"Thanks for the meal," he added as he waddled to the door. "Maybe we can do it again some time."

"Only if you earn it," he replied as Thompson exited into the night.

Joe telephoned Bascom in his office the next day. "I just spoke with Cohen. He said Dr. Davidson wouldn't waste his time flying down for a meeting with us, so I told him we'll strike if he doesn't."

"Strike? Why the change of heart?"

"Perhaps it was the promise of more tortelloni. Are there any left?"

"You ate the leftovers."

"Too bad. Anyway I thought about what you said on my way to McDonald's last night. You're right; we can't let Davidson and Evans rip off our patients."

"Who is 'we'?"

"Me and Linda Stevens. She said she'd strike, even though her pediatric department is now a drunk tank. I made it sound like the entire staff is ready to walk."

"That's great! I'm proud of you. When will our 'owner' be down?"

"Tomorrow evening at eight. Cohen invited us to a potluck dinner in the cafeteria at seven."

"Ask the staff to be there early so we can discuss a plan."

"Will do," he replied.

As Bascom hung up, he remembered Fran's warnings: "Don't trust him. Don't believe him!"

XII

At 7:05 the next evening Ben Wiggins and Bascom stood shoulder to shoulder at the food counter in the Whitney Community Hospital cafeteria. Cohen had offered a buffet dinner to those attending the meeting with his boss. Bascom caught a whiff of the smells emanating from under the sneeze guard and wished he had brought along a food-taster.

"Do you get it yet, Bolton?" Ben asked as he tried to drop a gob of overcooked spaghetti onto his plate. It stuck to the spoon and he pried it loose with a fork.

"Get what, Ben?" Bascom asked, pouring oil on his wilted salad.

"Davidson's a bad character," the old man said as he slopped a red sauce onto his spaghetti, adding a few spots to his *pois* jacket. "Are you sure you want to take him on?"

"No, but I can't ignore what's happening here. Besides, Thompson promised he'd speak out against the changes, so I won't be alone."

Ben tilted his head to see around his taped eyeglass lens. "You'd have better luck praying for a blizzard in the desert then relying on that man," he warned. "Don't trust him." *Don't ever trust him. No one in town does, including your poor secretary. She's a good woman, but because of him, everyone thinks she's a whore.*

"Any suggestions then?" They picked up their trays and walked to a table to the right of the makeshift podium.

"If Davidson beats you, which is likely since he's got most of us in his pocket, your 'holier than thou' colleagues will divide your practice and destroy your reputation," Ben explained as they set down their trays.

"If you can't face that, agree with everything he says, apologize profusely for wasting his time, and promise never to upset him again."

"Are you in his pocket too?" Bascom asked as they sat down.

"Maybe, maybe not," he replied mysteriously. "But if you have to ask, you don't know much about me."

At exactly 8 o'clock, Simon Davidson preceded Cohen and his staff of pinstriped physicians into the cafeteria. Bascom wondered if his colleagues were coming from a private meeting held elsewhere in the hospital. Davidson strode directly to the podium as his disciples sat at the tables. Donna Franklyn, stunning in formfitting jeans and blouse joined two nurses at a rear table.

Davidson tapped his gold ring on the metal podium. "I am here for one reason, and one reason only," he said angrily. "I cannot ignore intimidating threats. Mr. Cohen tells me you intend to strike if I don't reverse my recent changes. I warn you that I'll fire anyone who does, and replace him before he's cleaned out his desk, understood?"

Some nodded and others blanched as the fiery San Franciscan scanned his audience. When he focused on Ben, the old man held him in a steely gaze until he cleared his throat and looked away.

"Who called this meeting, since it couldn't have been Dr. Thompson as he made it appear?" he demanded.

"I did," Bascom said. He leaned back in his chair and

watched Thompson pull on his deformed earlobe. It was then he realized his coworkers had not come to the meeting because Joe had asked them, but because Davidson had ordered them to attend. Old Ben was right. Their new owner had them in his pocket and could squeeze them whenever he wanted. He had come to Whitney to draw a deeper, clearer line in the sand – the one Bascom had already crossed.

"Who else but you?" Davidson sneered. "Why did you drag me down here?"

"I missed your company," he replied mordantly. A tap of Davidson's ring on the metal podium quickly stifled a laugh from a far table. "But seriously, your price increases are causing our poor to go without care."

"I don't tell you how much to charge your patients, and you'll not tell me how much to charge mine, understood?" he responded coldly.

"Our farm workers can't afford your prices. Most earn minimum wage, if they're lucky, and have difficulty feeding their kids."

"If my prices are too high, they can go elsewhere."

"They're too illiterate to know their alternatives."

"I said it's not my problem! Is there something in that phrase you don't understand?" Davidson asked, glancing at his gold watch. "I've a plane to catch. Are there any other questions before I leave?"

"I have one more," Bascom offered.

"Yes, Doctor!" he sighed while impatiently drumming his fingers on the podium. "Be brief!"

"Your new clinic is a conflict of interest."

"Since it's for patients who don't have their own doctors, it stays," Davidson replied. "Anything else?"

"That's blatantly untrue," Bascom replied heatedly. "Every patient who goes through your ER gets an appointment to your clinic. You're stealing our patients and over-charging them twice, once in your ER and then again in your clinic."

"Are you calling me a liar, Doctor?" Davidson's voice trembled with rage.

"Sure. Didn't your mommy teach you that a person who tells lies is a liar?" he replied coolly. The audience gasped. Bascom was prodding an angry lion with the tip of an unloaded rifle, and he knew his colleagues were waiting for Davidson to leap up and claw him to death. Out of the corner of his eye, he saw Ben cross his arms and smile.

"The clinic stays. Do you have anything else to say?"

"Sei un ignorante, puzzolente testa di cazzo."

"I don't speak Greek. What does that mean?"

You're an ignorant, smelly, dickhead. "We love you," Bascom replied sinisterly.

"Christ," Thompson uttered under his breath.

"Did I hear you say you're quitting, Dr. Thompson?" Davidson queried with a raised eyebrow.

"I didn't say anything, Boss. I mean, Dr. Davidson," he replied sheepishly. He fingered his dimpled earlobe.

"Harrumph! Good night!" Davidson said before storming out of the room with Cohen following dutifully behind.

"I hope there's sand in their K-Y jelly tonight," Wiggins said with a swish of a limp wrist as the duo disappeared from view. Everyone laughed and Bascom patted Ben on the shoulder. He felt the old man, crazy or not, had become an ally. Maybe his only ally.

He walked to the makeshift bar to get a drink, and Donna joined him moments later.

"Nice guy, eh?" she asked rhetorically. She ran her finger along the back of his hand and Bascom felt a shock run up his arm. It caught him by surprise, since only Cris' touch had ever done that to him.

"I've met worse," he said, rubbing the spot as if it were a burn.

"I've got better Scotch at my place," she murmured.

"Let's go," he said softly.

They walked to their cars in the parking lot. He followed her yellow Jeep to a quiet street in north Whitney, parked in front of her gingerbread house with its grated doors and windows, and walked with her to the front door.

Donna keyed two locks, opened the door, and flipped a wall switch. Lamps on old mahogany tables flanking a cream leather couch bathed the small parlor in soft light.

"Have a seat," she said before crossing the room and turning on her stereo. John Coltrane's melodic rendition of "What's New?" filled the air. "My father was a saxophonist," she explained, turning down the volume, "and Jazz was the only music I heard in our house while growing up. All I get on the radio here is Country and Western. It runs through me like cod liver oil."

"I agree," he laughed. He sat on the couch and picked up a photograph of Donna riding a huge palomino horse. "Coltrane is one of my favorites also," he said, "but some of his work is painful, like *Interstellar Space*. I've never been able to listen to it in its entirety."

"But his ballads are sooo erotic," she cooed. "He and Stan Getz are my favorites."

"Do you ride much?" he asked, replacing the photograph on the table.

"As often as I can. Do you?"

"Once. I fell off the beast and vowed never to ride again."

"Too bad. Maybe if we ride together you'll have better luck."

"I doubt it."

"What can I get you to drink?" Donna asked, walking

to the dry bar in the corner of the room.

"Scotch, straight up."

"Not Ovaltine?" she laughed. It was throaty and sensuous, like Cristina's when she wanted special attention.

"Do I look that 'goody-two-shoes'?" he wondered.

"You tell me," she replied, filling two glasses with Scotch. She walked over and handed him one before sitting next to him.

"Cheers," she said, holding up her glass.

"Cin Cin," he replied, clinking his glass to hers.

"So tell me. Did you come to the desert as penance for your sins?" She sipped her drink and then placed the glass on the table on her side of the couch before turning off the light. "It was blinding me," she said.

"You must have eyes behind your head," he chided.

She laughed. "I need them to work at WCH."

"A bulletproof vest would be a good idea also. To answer your question, a friend of mine thought the change would do me good, so I came," he replied sullenly. "I won't need to repent later for my sins though. This place is purgatory and hell combined." He put his glass on the coffee table.

"If you stayed under the radar, it might not be so bad. And you'll never make money if you keep treating your patients for free," she said, moving closer to him. She reached behind him and pressed her breast against his arm as she turned off the light on his side of the couch.

"That was blinding me too," she explained. "I have sensitive eyes. Besides, Coltrane sounds better in the dark, don't you think?"

Her Shalimar perfume was inebriating. He leaned back and closed his eyes as she ran her finger down the side of his neck. His skin tingled under her touch. Bascom had not felt so at peace in over a year.

Donna brushed his lips with hers then led him to the bedroom. Seconds later Bascom had her pinned against the wall, his thigh pressed between hers. He kissed her hard and she moaned softly.

He fumbled the buttons of her blouse, tearing loose the last. Donna purred as he lifted her bra and ran his tongue slowly, teasingly around her erect nipple.

Zipping down his pants, she whispered, "Wow," and led him to the bed by his erection and then pulled off her jeans and panties. He fell on top of her, quickly entered her, pumped furiously for a minute, and then groaned, "oh, Christ," before collapsing by her side. He lay with his head on her breast until his breathing slowed, and then murmured, "I'm sorry, D. It's been a while. I'm not in shape to run marathons."

"How about a few sprints then?" she giggled as she ran her fingers through his hair.

"Sure, just give me a minute," he replied, tracing her nipple with his finger. He felt it grow erect in the semi-darkness.

"Tell me about yourself," he said.

"There isn't much to tell," she replied. "I was born, raised, and schooled in New York City, and at 26 I married my high school sweetheart. Six months later he dropped dead from a heart attack. That was ten years ago. Since then I've been working ERs and avoiding wolves who couldn't think past my boobs."

"Oops. Does that include me?" he asked, squeezing her breast.

"No. Even though you looked like a bum the night we met in the ER, you intrigued me and I wanted to know more about you. That hasn't been easy. I have to beat off everyone else at WCH but you, and I was beginning to wonder if you were gay or a male impersonator," she laughed.

"Easy with the compliments, please," Bascom replied. "They make my head swell."

"Which one?" she asked, rising to see his groin.

"All good things come to women with patience," he replied.

"Oh, all right," she pouted, falling back on the bed.

"As much as I'd rather not, I have to leave, Donna," he said. He rose from the bed and stepped into his pants. "I've something important to do tomorrow. Guess that sounds like, 'slam, bam, thank you ma'am,' but it ain't. I'll call you soon."

"So you want me to stop dating Davidson then?" she replied, watching him button his shirt.

"What?" he shouted before a smile crept across her lips. He laughed. "If you don't, we'll have a reenactment of Benito Mussolini and Clara Petacci's final moments right here in Whitney."

He kissed her on the lips and then he was gone.

Early the next morning Bascom invited Dave Olsen, the Hospital District Board's lawyer, to breakfast.

"Rough night," Dave said as he forked the yolks of his eggs at the local greasy spoon. "I gotta get married so I can cut down on my sex life." Olsen was a good-looking, 35 year-old tennis ace whose successful law practice had earned him a Porsche and a wardrobe of expensive clothes. The rumor around town was that few women, married or single, dark-skinned or light, could resist his advances.

"You're breaking my heart," Bascom replied, unimpressed by his plight. "We have serious problems at the hospital, Dave, and I need your help."

He explained the situation and the lawyer listened, brushing crumbs from his mustache after each bite of his toast.

"It doesn't sound good," Dave agreed after Bascom had finished his monologue. "Can you write a rebuttal to Davidson's clinic proposal?" He wiped his mouth with a napkin.

"Sure."

"Get it to me tomorrow and have your colleagues in my office Monday night at eight."

Bascom agreed, paid the bill, and they went their separate ways.

Joe Thompson, Ted Steele, Linda Stevens, and Abe Grimes, were talking together when Bascom arrived late for the conclave in Olsen's office. Ben Wiggins, working on a crossword puzzle in a corner, waved him into a chair next to his as the lawyer began speaking.

"I haven't finished my investigation," Dave explained, shuffling a few papers on his desk, "but I've learned Davidson buys distressed hospitals for a song and then brings in his own docs, raises prices and dumps unprofitable services, as he's doing here. He makes big bucks when he sells them, although there are lawsuits against him because he falsifies his profits, and much of the hospital's outstanding debt is not collectible."

"I'll bet he's a pinstriped Martian and needs all the radiation his X-ray department can produce to keep his batteries charged," Wiggins giggled. After several similar comments Linda took him by the hand and ushered him from the room.

When she returned after a long delay, she explained Evelyn was asleep in her car and she could not wake her to open the door. The others laughed but it puzzled Bascom since this was the second time the nurse had fallen asleep under unusual circumstances.

"The Board controls the hospital's purse, which, contrary to a statement my predecessor once made, I believe is still being filled with tax dollars," Olsen continued after the laughter died down. "According to the terms of the sale, Davidson can tap into it any time he wants."

"They're taxing the citizens of this town to support a private hospital?" Bascom asked incredulously. "It's preposterous!"

Olsen shrugged. "The Board expects him to provide services to locals with the money, even though he's not doing it. There's a meeting next week in City Hall. He'll be there and I'll convince the media to attend. The community might like to know what's going on here."

"I'll be there too," Bascom answered as he rose from his chair.

Thompson mumbled a sarcastic comment he did not understand, but as banter did not interest him at the moment, he said goodnight and went home.

XIII

The next morning Bascom sat in his breakfast nook listening to his coffeepot perk on the gas stove. In 36 hours he would accuse Dr. Simon Davidson of unethical business practices, and he feared the consequences. He knew the hospital owner would not beat his breast and beg forgiveness from the town fathers. He was too proud and cocky for that. He would play the victim and then quietly plan his revenge. What that would be, Bascom did not know. What he did know was that he wished he were back in Lizzano sipping wine and listening to one of Stan Getz' CDs in front of the fireplace in his comfortable *baita*.

As his thoughts drifted back to that small cabin on the hillside, he could hear Lance laughing as he did when they charged windmills together years earlier.

Bascom stood from the breakfast nook, turned off the stove, and then drove to the hospital. His two patients in the chronic care ward were less than Cohen had ordered him to admit, but as the hospital's patient population had grown from five to forty-five since Davidson's takeover, the administrator had stopped pestering him. Nothing had changed to justify the nine-fold increase in admissions except the new owner's arrival in Whitney. He preferred not to know more.

He parked his SUV in the lot in front of the ER and entered the hospital. He sniffed Marty Nevins' oil of wintergreen as he passed through its main wing to the chronic care ward. Rose was caressing her husband's skeletonized hand when he entered their room.

"How are you two today?" he asked. He need not have. The physical and psychological toll of Rose's long vigil by her dying husband's bedside had carved dark lines around her tired eyes and lips.

"We're fine, Doctor," she said, running a hand through her unkempt gray hair. "Bill and I have just been reminiscing about a trip to Mexico years ago. I reminded him of a beautiful doll I bought; he reminded me of the diarrhea he caught. Isn't it curious what we remember?"

"I've always found it so," he laughed. They both knew a tragedy he could not prevent would soon overshadow those happy memories.

"Are you in pain, Bill?" he asked as he rested his hand on the man's wasted shoulder. He could feel the irregularities in the bone as if there was only a sheet of plastic wrap between it and his hand.

"Not yet, Doc," he answered weakly, twisting his head to the voice.

"Can I do anything for you?"

"Yes. The nurses don't come when I call them and the place is filthy," Rose complained bitterly, pointing to the overflowing wastebasket at the bedside.

Some things never change. "I'll check on that and get back to you." Bascom gave her arm a fraternal squeeze. "You're a strong woman, Rose, but call me when you feel overwhelmed. I don't want to have to admit you here for exhaustion."

"Oh, sure," she replied with a crooked grin. "I can see you admitting me to this dump for such a phony reason."

"Call day or night," he urged before leaving to visit

Carl in the next room.

Martha Price was sitting in a chair with her feet up on the bed rail. She was reading a newspaper to her comatose son when Bascom knocked on the door.

"The place is a pigpen!" she complained as he entered the room. "Look at that mess," she insisted, wagging her finger at the overflowing wastebasket by the door. "Plus, I ring for help but no one comes."

"That's an old story, Martha. I'll be right back," Bascom went to the nursing station where a young woman was shouting into a telephone.

"I need you NOW, Dr. Grimes," she demanded, tapping her foot impatiently. She listened with knitted eyebrows. "Are you deaf? Get off that golf course and get in here NOW or the next hole will be in your head!"

She slammed down the phone and rubbed her forehead before noticing Bascom standing in front of her.

"Follow me," she ordered. They hurried down the hallway and into a room where an elderly woman was coughing blood into a handkerchief. An old man holding her shoulders moved aside to let Bascom place his stethoscope on her back.

"How much fluid have you given her?" He folded his instrument and put it back in his pocket. He could hear the air bubbling through her fluid-filled lungs without it.

"Seven liters of saline," the nurse replied. "I said it was too much, but Dr. Grimes insisted. He wanted her rehydrated in a hurry since she'd had vomiting and diarrhea for two days."

"She's drowning. Turn off that IV," he ordered. He shifted the woman so her legs dangled over the side of the bed. "She needs a pressure mask and cuffs on her arms and legs."

The nurse took a mask from her cart and strapped it to

the woman's face, and then grabbed four blood pressure cuffs, two large and two small, from the cart's bottom drawer.

"Does she have any allergies?"

"No," she replied.

"Give her 4 mg. of morphine and 40 mg. of Lasix, IV," he said. She dropped the cuffs on the bed and searched for the medications in her cart as Bascom put his hand on the old man's arm.

"Once the water's out of her lungs she'll be as good as new," he explained reassuringly.

"We're married sixty years, Doc," he replied through twitching lips. "I couldn't live without her."

The nurse cracked the top off a vial and sucked its contents into a syringe.

"Put in a catheter also," he ordered as she injected the medication into a port in the IV line. "She'll be peeing up a storm soon."

Within thirty minutes the woman was breathing easily and Bascom and the nurse returned to her station.

"Thanks," she said as she handed Bascom the woman's chart. "I didn't know what to do."

"You did fine. My patients tell me you never answer their calls and their rooms are a mess," he said, watching her face from the corner of his eye.

"I know, and I'm sorry. Mr. Cohen laid off most of our aides and housekeepers as part of his 'New Vision Plan,'" she replied, flushing at the criticism. "He says I should be able to do everything, even clean the bathrooms. But I can't and I won't. I'm returning to my old job in Phoenix University Hospital tomorrow. Patients are at serious risk here, and Davidson can't pay me enough to chance losing my license."

"Is it like this throughout the hospital?" he wondered

as he jotted a note on the woman's chart.

"Yes. There is a mass exodus in progress. Everyone hates it here," she explained. "Making money has become more important than saving human lives in this dump."

Three call lights flashed on the board in front of her, and she shut them off with a shrug. "I guess I'll need to round on everyone again," she frowned. "I'm upset when patients attack me as soon as I enter their rooms. They don't understand I'm alone and can't respond as quickly as they'd like."

"Our loss is Phoenix's gain. Good luck," Bascom sympathized. He handed her the chart and returned to Carl's room where his mother was still reading the newspaper to her expressionless son.

"You'll have to put up with the inconveniences, Martha," he apologized as he approached the bed. "You've got a good nurse; she's just overwhelmed with work."

"Too bad." She put down the paper. "I've been speaking with other disgruntled patients and we're forming a PADD coalition, 'Patients Against Davidson's Dirt.'"

"That'll be fun to see," he laughed before turning to Carl. It had been months since the accident and the boy was still comatose. He was no longer on the respirator and his leg was no longer in a cast, but he still depended on others for all his needs.

Bascom was listening to his chest when Jonas entered the room. His hair had turned gray and he had lost a significant amount of weight since his son's accident, but he had remained steadfastly optimistic that his son would wake up and play football again.

"How's my boy, Doc?" he asked. He walked to the head of the bed and brushed a lock of hair from his son's forehead.

"His lungs are clear and his heart is strong," Bascom

replied. "He just needs to wake up. Have faith. Miracles do happen."

"Miracles?" Jonas replied.

"You'll have to ask Her," he said, pointing to the ceiling. "They're not in my job description."

Jonas laughed. "Maybe not, but can you get someone to clean this room? It's an outrage."

"I just explained the situation to Martha. You can air your gripes at the Board meeting tomorrow night if you want."

"I'll be there!" Jonas exclaimed. "You can bet on it."

"And I'll bring a bag of trash to throw at the board members," Martha added. "Bunch of useless bastards," she grumbled. "All bought and paid for by that con artist Davidson."

"I'm glad you're not opinionated, Martha," Bascom laughed. "Come to the show, but leave the garbage here."

During a lull in his office later that morning, he telephoned Evelyn Cooper. Her falling asleep at odd times and her sometimes erratic gait concerned him. He thought they might be early symptoms of a serious disease, and asked her to drop by his office when she had a free moment.

She arrived that afternoon and was fidgeting in a yellow paper gown on his examining table when he entered her room. He pulled the chair from under his desk and straddled it in front of her.

"Thanks for coming, Ev," he said.

"I'm glad you called. I wanted to talk to someone about my symptoms. I don't trust any of the other doctors in this town and I didn't want to tell Ben, since I didn't want to worry him," she replied, twisting her paper belt around her finger. "The truth is, I do stumble and tire easily. Ben has asked me about it, but I pretend it's menopause. I know it isn't."

"For how long?"

"A few months, I guess. It's hard to be sure since the symptoms are subtle, plus I have days when I feel strong and fit. I thought they were due to stress and would disappear after my forced retirement from the hospital, but they haven't."

"I'm sorry about that, Ev," he apologized. "You're a good nurse, but Cohen was blocking you from doing your job. I wanted Davidson to give you more power, but he fired you instead."

"It was time to leave," she said matter-of-factly. "Ben has been embarrassingly generous since I retired, so everything worked out for the best."

"I'm glad you're not upset with me."

"Let's not mention it again. Do you think my symptoms are serious?"

"Let me examine you before I give you my opinion," he said, rising from his chair.

Evelyn studied Bascom as he examined her. He was meticulous but discreet, a demanding but gentle man whose hands transmitted warmth, courage, and optimism. She felt safe and secure, as she did when Ben treated the burns and broken bones her husband had inflicted on her years earlier. She knew he would find the cause of her illness, if indeed she were ill, and cure it.

After his examination he returned to his desk. "You seem to be in perfect health," he said as he wrote his notes. "Maybe it was job stress."

"Then I won't worry," she said, relieved by the good news.

"Ev, can I ask you a question?"

"Sure," she replied.

"Why does Ben wear an old spotted jacket and taped

eyeglasses?"

"It's a costume for his act," she laughed. "They make him seem crazy, but he's far from it. Years ago his son hurt his back and became addicted to the painkillers Dr. Grimes prescribed for him," she explained. "Ben asked him to stop, but the boy convinced his mother otherwise, and she got Abe to continue prescribing them."

She paused and looked Bascom in the eye. "Don't mention this to anyone, you hear? This is a sensitive issue with Ben; he doesn't share his personal life with outsiders, and he'd be upset if he found out I was telling you this."

"Ev, everything anyone tells me in this office is confidential," he replied, rubbing his chin. "And that includes what you tell me today."

"Good. Anyway," she continued, "one morning Ben found his son dead in bed. He was holding Grimes' empty bottle of pills in one hand and an empty bottle of whiskey in the other. I heard he was so enraged he wanted to kill Abe. He didn't, of course, but he did divorce his wife. He hasn't spoken to either of them since, or tries not to.

"Ben's been fed up with our local doctors for a long time, but he's too old to fight them anymore. His spotted jacket and taped eyeglasses, his 'wackiness,' as he calls it, keep his 'failed colleagues' at arm's length. He's crazy like a fox, and it's fun watching him. I never know what he'll come up with next.

"He cares deeply about those patients who still seek him out. Despite his colleagues' vicious attempts to force him out of business, he has a better practice than anyone could imagine, although it has dwindled over the past years."

"E' più unico che raro – he's more singular than rare," Bascom said, standing from his chair.

"That's Ben. But he's doting and would fret if he

thought something was wrong with me. So please...."

Bascom held up a hand. "No need to mention it again. I promise you I won't talk to him without your permission. Call me if your symptoms return, Ev," Bascom said before leaving the room.

Bascom was reading his mail a few hours later when Abe Grimes burst into his office and slammed a chart onto his desk.

"Goddamn thieving prick!" the old doctor growled. His angry eyes were mere slits in his bloated, red face.

"That's friendly," Bascom said sarcastically. He dropped the letter and picked up the yellow folder.

"You stole that patient from me, Doctor," the white-haired physician said heatedly, pointing to the chart.

"I never 'stole' her," Bascom replied after reading the name and tossing the chart back on his desk. "I didn't know she had left your so-called care. I treated her since she was drowning, thanks to you, after you refused to come in off the golf course to do it yourself."

"Bullshit," Grimes shouted. "If you steal another patient from me, I'll turn you in to the medical society's ethics committee."

"I'd get that flabby ass of yours into a pair of steel shorts first," Bascom challenged. "And if you perform one more hysterectomy on a 15 year-old, I will cut your balls off. Then you won't need the steel shorts."

"Harrumph," Grimes grumbled. He stormed out of the room, slamming the door behind him.

Fran rushed into the office after he left. "What was that all about?" she asked.

"Peterpause," Bascom laughed. "I'll be in at sunrise to prepare for the Board meeting tomorrow night," he added as he left his office.

"Remember what I told you about Thompson," she warned as he disappeared into the hallway.

XIV

The October sun softened the asphalt of Whitney's pot-holed streets on the morning of the District Board meeting, and Joe Thompson left his footprints, large as a baby di-nosaur's, in the soft tar on the way to the hospital. Bascom and Donna, whom Thompson had repeatedly but unsuc-cessfully tried to verify was Bascom's mole, had accused Davidson's protégé, Dr. Albert Evans, of incompetence and corruption. He was on his way to investigate the charges.

He already knew Evans was incompetent since he had misdiagnosed and over studied many of the patients he had sent him from the emergency room. Until now he had not wanted to confront the bodybuilder *eccellente* but physician *abissale* about his abuses, since the man had a bad temper. His goal that morning was not quixotic, as he had often re-ferred to Bascom's seemingly endless battle against the hospital. It was self-serving. Bascom had promised him free tortelloni for life if he investigated Evans, and he grinned knowing he could point to the tracks of his size 14 EEE shoes in the macadam to convince his obnoxious col-league he had fulfilled his duty as a competent and con-cerned physician.

He was certain a brief, simple, non-confrontational chat with Evans about the weather would guarantee him a great Italian meal at least once a week. His mouth watered in anticipation.

The elephantine surgeon was sweating heavily when he arrived in the ER, and he loosened his tie as he lumbered over to Evans. The handsome physician, holding a chart in his muscular arms, was talking through surgical masks to a patient three feet in front of him. Donna Franklyn, alluring even in her dowdy nurse's uniform, was measuring the man's blood pressure with a new automated machine. For years he had tried to date her but she had ignored his offers until the day he cornered her in the drug room and showed her tickets to a Diamondbacks baseball game. When she coldly asked him where his wife's ticket was, he smiled sheepishly and never bothered her again.

"Hi, Albert. How are you today?" Thompson asked, wiping the sweat from his brow with the back of his beefy hand.

"Not bad," he replied coolly. Evans' masks, an outer blue one and an inner yellow one, slightly muffled his words.

"You wanted to talk to me about the number of tests I order?" he asked as he lifted his masks from his face and let their elastics snap them onto his forehead. His words seemed friendly, but the way he said them was subtly harsh and threatening. It made Thompson tremble.

"Not me. Bob Bascom thinks you're ordering too many studies," he replied nervously, "and he asked me to check. I told him you're doing a splendid job," he added, pandering to the man. "With all the cases you send me, I'd know if something was wrong. And I can assure you, there isn't. They're all perfect. You do fine work."

"I'm glad you agree, Joe," Evans responded coldly. "I order only what I need to do this job real good."

"I agree. But Bob…"

"We'll be in my office, Donna," Evans interrupted,

handing her the chart. He led Thompson to a small room in the rear of the ER.

"Bob feels being too safe doesn't warrant all the studies you order," Joe apologized after Evans had locked the door. He had just realized his mission could cost him untold sums of money if Evans stopped sending him patients. To avoid that catastrophe he needed to smooth his ruffled ego. *How do you placate a gorilla?* he wondered.

"Did you know Dr. Davidson is bringing in another surgeon?" the ER doctor asked sinisterly. He pushed aside a pile of comic books and sat on the corner of his desk.

"That's ridiculous!" Joe spluttered as he took his gold cigarette case from his pocket. "There's not enough work now."

"No smoking here, Thompson," Evans ordered.

"Sorry, Dr. Evans, you're right. I smoke too much anyway," the obese surgeon replied meekly. He quickly slipped the case back into his pocket.

"I know there isn't enough work for three surgeons. It would be plenty for one if us all us ER docs referred all our cases to him. But he has to be ready to take a bullet for Simon."

"I understand," Thompson responded meekly. He was sweating profusely and his damp shirt stuck to his chest. He fanned his face with a Superman comic book he lifted from the desk.

"I'll convince Bascom you're performing superbly and carefully, Dr. Evans," he groveled, "and that it only seems you order lots of tests because you're so thorough. We don't want lawsuits because you're not being thorough, do we now?

"Would that be enough, Dr. Evans?"

"Yes," the muscle-bound doctor agreed. "I know Simon will be very appreciative if I tell him he'll have the full support of Whitney's top surgeon at the meeting tonight."

"Tell Dr. Davidson not to worry. I won't let him down," he promised, returning the comic book to the desk.

"Good, and I'll tell him to hold off on that new surgeon for a couple of days," he replied. "Remember though, we'll be watching and listening."

Evans popped the masks back on his face and left the office. He flexed an arm and palpated its taut bicep as he returned to his patient.

“The bastard has a way of making his point,” Thompson said as he plodded back through the sweltering heat and melting macadam to his office. He was careful not to destroy his earlier footprints.

Sorry, Bascom, but it's your ass or mine, and I have more to lose. Have a nice trip back to Italy, Dr. Asperger. You're a nuisance and don't belong here anyway. I'll eat Spaghetti-Os.

"You look like you've been through a wringer, Dr. Thompson," his secretary commented as he passed her desk minutes later.

"It's hot out," he answered, fanning his face with his hand. "I don't wish to speak with Dr. Bascom today for any reason, Mrs. Farnsworth. Do you understand?"

"I understand," she replied as he disappeared into his inner office.

XV

By 3 o'clock that afternoon, Bascom had called Thompson's office four times to hear the results of his meeting with Evans. Each time his secretary had used an implausible excuse about why she could not pass him though to his colleague. As he was hanging up after his last try, now certain the reason Thompson was refusing to speak with him was far different from the ones offered by Mrs. Farnsworth, Helen staggered into his office.

"Someone insists on seeing you," the curly, gray-haired woman giggled before running from the room.

Seconds later Ben Wiggins, in a spotless sport shirt, pants and jacket, appeared in the doorway. He was puffing and carrying a large cardboard box.

"Hi, Bittle," Ben said. "Do you get it yet?" The old man, usually slow and deliberate in his movements because of his arthritic hip, bounced energetically across the room. His metamorphosis to a vibrant, stylish Romeo was astounding.

"Get what, Ben? Why do you always ask me that question?"

"Notice anything different about me?" he asked as he placed the box on the desk. Grinning from ear to ear, he pushed out his chest like a teenage athlete trying to impress a cheerleader. Bascom presumed he was referring to his new toupee. Apart from being too low on his brow, it was also two inches off center.

"New glasses?" Bascom replied, stifling a laugh. "Well yes, those too. Ev was tired of looking at the taped lens," he replied. He adjusted the thin gold frames on his nose. "They make me look dignified, don't you think?"

"Absolutely."

"Too bad I can't see out of the damn things. Notice anything else?" he asked, pointing to his toupee.

"There are no spots on your clothes," Bascom replied, deliberately ignoring the hint.

"Also Evelyn's doing. But, no, no, darn it! Look!" he ordered, performing a perky pirouette and tapping his head. "It's the hairpiece. She said it would make me look years younger. She placed it on me herself, but I adjusted it after I left the house."

"Wow!" Bascom responded excitedly. Ben wagged his head this way and that to grant him a 360-degree view of what resembled a road-killed animal dusted with talcum powder. "I've never seen a lovelier toupee! Its uniqueness defies definition."

"I'll bet," he laughed. "I'm retiring and am sending you my patients. They're old and need looking after by someone who won't kill them. But the exciting news is that Ev and I are getting married next week and we want you to be my best man," he beamed.

"I'd be honored, Ben," he said. *If this is what true love does to a man, Cris and I must have just been friends.*

"That's great!" Ben exclaimed. "No gifts, though. Just bring yourself and a guest, if you like.

"Now I want to show you the retirement gift Cohen sent Ev," he said, extracting an old bowling trophy from his cardboard box. He carefully handed it to Bascom as if the tarnished brass object were of fine crystal and would break if not delicately and carefully transferred from one admirer to another.

The female figure crouched on the base of the odd accolade with one bent knee ahead of the other. Her right hand was thrust backwards and the other extended forward, palm up, as if she were going to release a bowling ball. In place of the ball was a tiny thermometer, an extension of her middle finger that left little doubt about the true offensive purpose of the gift. "To Evelyn: In Appreciation of All Your Years of Dedication to WCH," was inscribed on its scratched brass plaque.

"I'm sure the administration feels this way towards certain other members of the staff also," Bascom mused as he returned the grotesque prize to his friend. *It makes no difference what you do in this world. As long as you agree with those who run it, they'll praise you. Cross them and obscenities such as this will be the least of your punishment.*

Wiggins carefully replaced the statue in its box and cross-locked its lid. "The wedding is at ten o'clock in North Park on the 10th day of the 10th month. Don't be late," he warned before picking up the box and leaving the room.

"He's something, isn't he?" Helen asked when she reentered the office, still giggling.

"One of a kind. Evelyn and Ben are the perfect odd couple."

"You won't find better people in this town. He was born here," she explained, leaning on the corner of his desk, "but Evelyn arrived 40 years ago with her husband and infant son, Ronald. Ben treated her for a broken arm shortly after that, and a while later for a black eye. When she appeared with a burn on her chest, he knew her husband was abusing her. She denied it, as many co-dependent women do, but eventually confessed to him her husband drank and beat her regularly. He offered to help her resolve the problem, but she felt his bad behavior was the result of her inadequacies and resisted his offers.

"She finally left him after he broke their son's nose. She was destitute and Ben bought them a house and paid her way through nursing school. After she graduated with honors, he got her a job in the hospital. Even though he was divorced and they dated openly, she wasn't, he wouldn't live with her unless they got married. Odd behavior in today's world, but that's Ben.

"Her husband died last year, which everyone applauded even though it was unchristian to do so, and now they'll be married," Helen concluded.

"Good for them," Bascom replied.

"I'm certain they'll be happy," she added before returning to her office.

Bascom called Thompson for the fifth time and his secretary again deflected his call. He hung up in quiet despair and went home.

He can't have turned against me; he has no reason.

He pulled into his driveway. The idealist in him wanted to believe there was a valid reason Thompson would not answer his calls; the realist knew he had already betrayed him.

XVI

Tonight's the night! Bascom thought as he drove to City Hall. He would confront Davidson at the District Hospital meeting, but he doubted he could convince him to lower his scandalous but not illegal hospital charges. Evans, however, was a different problem. As much as he would have liked to, he would not mention him during the war of words he knew would ensue between him and his boss. The emergency room doctor was unquestionably incompetent, but Bascom knew public criticism, with or without documented proof, would result in a lawsuit.

So why attend this meeting? All I need to do is to warn the town of the danger and expense awaiting them in Davidson's ER, and to admit my patients elsewhere. The result would be the same but the stress would be less.

Bascom pulled to the curb a block from City Hall, shifted his truck into park, and rested his forehead on his steering wheel. *Cris would make me turn around and go home. She knew when to fight and when to walk away, and she would not fight this battle*

But Cris was not there. He would challenge Davidson alone. The working poor in Whitney faced hunger and privations his rival could never understand, and while he hoped he was wrong, he believed he was the only one who cared enough to defend them.

Unfortunately, from his experience with Lance fighting the abuses in their hospital years earlier, he also knew the town's illiterate citizens would not understand what he was doing for them and might one day turn against him. Still he felt he had to defend them.

He shifted the SUV back into gear and drove to the City Hall parking lot with Lance's taunting laugh in his ear: *DQS, DQS, Don Quixote in Scrubs, la-la-la-la.*

The three-story glass and steel town hall was an expensive monstrosity a few commissioners thought would revitalize Main Street, however the narrow series of potholes lined by decrepit 60 year-old stores and shops remained abandoned, as Whitnians preferred to shop in a mall a few miles down the highway. Across from it was a garbage-strewn park a wealthy Mexican family had dedicated to the town's children. Its rusting merry-go-round and a lone swing seat hanging by a chain suggested none had played there in ages.

Bascom parked behind the building, entered through its back door, and made his way to its faux Greek amphitheater. On its stage were a glass-topped table with a microphone in front of each chair, and a podium of carved cherry wood. Plastic Doric columns lined its beige walls, and banks of plush velvet seats climbed the conch to the ceiling in the rear of the room.

Jonas and Martha Price sat in the third row next to a handful of people he had never seen before. Each was young and neatly dressed, except for a lad with a bright orange Mohawk haircut and earrings, and balanced notebooks and tape recorders on their laps.

Donna and a female companion sat a few rows behind them, and he nodded to her before going to the building's entrance to wait for Joe Thompson.

As he stood on the stoop that mild October evening,

dozens of mostly friendly people filed past him, including his secretary and Rose Shadwell. The latter tiredly climbed the steps, pulled twice on his jacket sleeve, and ordered, "Give 'em hell, Doc. They deserve it," before other denizens of the town swept her into the building.

At 6:55 p.m. a black limousine pulled up to the curb and Simon Davidson and George Cohen exited. They trotted up the steps, a general with his briefcase-carrying aide in tow, and paused in front of Bascom. Davidson sniffed the air as if he had just passed an outhouse and then entered the building.

Moments later Joe Thompson huffed up the stairs, mumbled, "Don't go in there. Davidson's out to castrate you," and quickly entered the hall.

If Thompson knows Davidson's plans, then he has to be part of them. Bascom followed the fat surgeon into the room and sat next to him in the front row. Joe immediately moved two seats to his right and looked away, symbolically dissociating himself from his colleague.

Davidson, seated at the table with Cohen and six members of the Board, noticed the rebuff and smiled sinisterly. A rap from Dave Olsen's gavel called the meeting to order. The natty lawyer, cleanly shaven except for his Wyatt Earp mustache, wore an expensive jacket and slacks. "Before we discuss other business," he said, "we need to discuss some serious problems in the hospital. Dr. Bascom, would you present your concerns?"

"Thank you, Mr. Olsen," Bascom responded, standing from his seat. Davidson, like an impatient executioner waiting for the condemned man to say his last words, tapped a finger on the table.

"First," Bascom said in a voice he hoped would mask his terror of public speaking, "the new alcohol rehabilitation program has eliminated our pediatric unit. Rehabilitation is not an emergency, but a child's illness can be. Rushing him off to Phoenix for care because he can't get it here is illegal and will eventually have fatal results."

Cohen raised his hand but Olsen prevented him from speaking. "Not now, George. Please continue, Doctor," he ordered.

"Next the 200 percent increase in hospital charges adds to the misery of our farm workers who have trouble feeding their families. These people may seem unimportant to some," Bascom said, glowering at Davidson, "but they comprise 80 percent of the population in this town. They give us fair service, and we should give them fairly priced, competent medical care in return.

"Then there is the reduced nursing staff, which has resulted in inadequate patient care, and the firing and rehiring of the cleaning staff under a different name with fewer workers at lower pay, resulting in an unclean hospital."

Olsen twirled the end of his Wyatt Earp mustache, and Bascom wondered if he held a Buntline Special under the table, the lawman's legendary if not journalistically fabricated Colt Peacemaker revolver with its extra long barrel.

"Last," he said, "the new clinic and its compulsory referral policy is in conflict with the private practitioners in town and is unnecessarily expensive for our patients. As a result, Dr. Davidson overcharges them twice, first in his ER, and then in his clinic." He thought of describing Evans' unethical policy of inventing symptoms and diseases and then ordering tests to show they did not exist, but again decided against it.

"That's all for the moment," he said as he resumed his seat.

"Thank you. Now, Mr. Cohen, your comments," Olsen said, inviting him to the podium.

"I have something to say first," Davidson interrupted,

jumping from his chair. He buttoned his silk jacket and stormed the podium like a Marine attacking an enemy fox-hole.

"I object strenuously to what is happening here tonight. This is not the place to air hospital linen," he protested, pounding his fist on the podium. His face was livid and his voice trembled with rage. "The alcohol rehab program is not jeopardizing pediatric care, and I feel this, this, doctor's assessment of it," he said, waging finger at his accuser, "is nothing more than a cynical attempt to downgrade an important new service.

"Mr. Cohen has received many inquiries from Whitnians who demand it, but I can't tell you who they are since their names are confidential."

Olsen twirled the end of his mustache and smiled at Bascom as if to say, "you found the right button. He'll hang himself."

"We have changed laboratories," Davidson sputtered, "a unanimous decision by all our doctors, however, I cannot control their charges. Now George," he said, waving a hand behind his head as if he were brushing away a buzzing mosquito, "continue." He spun and returned to his seat as his administrator walked to the podium.

Bascom was unsure if he had stuttered his last word, but his snarl and tone revealed his inner rage. As for the "unanimous decision," he was unaware of the change of laboratories and suspected that "blood money," he smiled at the unintentional pun, was the reason for the switch.

"Dr. Bascom's right about the housekeepers," Cohen explained sheepishly, "but we're good, honest people. When we learned the new company was paying its employees less, we voluntarily gave it more money, despite its objections, to bring wages back up to previous levels."

Shrieks of laughter erupted in the back of the auditorium and it took several loud raps of Olsen's gavel to stifle them.

"As for peds," the administrator proceeded unperturbed by the outburst, "it's true we've opened a rehabilitation unit in its place, but the hospital isn't licensed for pediatrics. Even so, we're still accepting children."

"You refused to admit one of mine yesterday," Bascom interrupted. Davidson compressed his lips into an angry line.

"Excuse me?" Cohen asked uncertainly.

"I said you refused to admit one of my critically ill kids yesterday, George," Bascom repeated loudly. "Your policy put his life at risk. I had to intubate him in the ambulance on the way to Phoenix after Dr. Evans refused to treat him in your ER. That will result in another visit from the boys at EMTALA. I'm sure you remember them, since they fined you heavily once before for letting a patient of mine die in your hospital.

"Evans didn't recognize the emergency, and he and your hospital are lucky the boy didn't die."

"This attack comes at a very poor time. Whitney's hospital has just emerged from a dramatic financial crisis," Davidson lamented as he returned to the podium. He pushed Cohen out of the way, and the administrator drifted back to his seat.

"To answer another of Dr. Bascom's complaints, the clinic is an internal issue, having n-nothing to do with the quality of care."

"But it may be a conflict of interest, Dr. Davidson," Olsen replied. "Dr. Bascom?" he asked, turning to the physician, "do you have anything to add?"

"The quality of Dr. Davidson's responses to the issues is the same as the quality of care he offers at WCH." There was another shriek of laughter and applause from the audience. Olsen let it run its course as Davidson fumed.

"Would anybody else like to comment?" he asked after the ruckus had died down.

"I would," a man yelled from the rear of the room. "How about the chapel our society furnished and which you dismantled with the pediatric ward, Mr. Davidson?"

A drunken voice chimed in, "Yeah, Davidson, you queer bastard, what about the fucking chapel?"

Olsen furiously pounded his gavel on its block. "Gentlemen, please. I will not allow abusive language at this meeting. Any further outbursts and I will clear the room."

Cohen stood and raised his arms in a selfless attempt to draw the fiery attention from Davidson to him. "I'm planning a new area for the chapel," he said, "and when it's installed in its new location, people will use it more than they did before."

Cohen's odd reply resulted in bedlam as Olsen's gavel thumped vainly to restore order.

"I would like to say something," Rose Shadwell said, standing from her seat in the second row. The crowd quieted as the woman straightened her skirt. "I'm a retired nurse and my husband is a cancer patient at WCH. Despite what I have heard here tonight, I can assure you the rooms are filthy, the care is the worst I've seen anywhere, and I hope you never have to send family members to that place unless you care of them yourself or want to collect their life insurance." Her comments brought renewed laughter, which this time quieted quickly with a rap from Olsen's gavel.

"If you care about our community," she continued, wagging an accusing finger at the Board, "you'll straighten out that hospital or shut it down."

"Mrs., Mrs....?"

"Shadwell. Rose Shadwell."

"Mrs. Shadwell," Olsen inquired gently, "why did you come here tonight instead of complaining to the hospital administration?"

"I have complained, repeatedly," she replied, "but they ignored me. Where else should I go? You're my last resort. If you can't help me, I'm transferring my husband to another hospital."

"I agree," Jonas Price interrupted, rising from his seat. "The place is a pigsty. My wife cleans my son's room and she's getting tired of it. And the nurses don't answer our calls either."

"If Davidson doesn't clean up his hospital," Martha threatened from her seat, "I'm going to have Dr. Bascom transfer my son back to Phoenix. I won't spend my money in a dump with poor services." A long applause followed as Jonas kissed his wife on the head and sat down.

"I agree there's a long way to go," Davidson replied from the podium. His features had softened and the hostility was gone from his voice, but he was staring intensely at Thompson. Bascom squirmed.

"I know some of you might find it hard to believe" he continued, "but WCH is a far better hospital now than it ever was. We have, I have… er, I'm sensitive to what I've heard tonight. I've suffered the same frustrations with friends in the finest hospitals in the country, but that is no excuse. I assure you I will review the hospital's problems, but not in public under hostile conditions."

"Dr. Davidson?" Helen asked from the middle of the auditorium.

"Yes," he replied, flicking a hand as if shooing her away.

"If these people's complaints are valid, will you correct the problems?"

"No," he replied sternly.

A silence fell across the room; Bascom was beginning to feel victorious when his opponent addressed his obese colleague.

"Dr. Thompson," Davidson asked sinisterly, "would you care to comment on Dr. Bascom's allegations?"

"I disagree with everything he said, and the nurses are ok," he mumbled.

"You mean the unlicensed nurse whose incompetence resulted in the death of my patient in the ER is ok, Joe?" Bascom blurted in disbelief. A hush fell over the room as the amorphous surgeon put a hand to the side of his face as if it were a horse blinder.

That's it, Joe? The nurses are ok? THE NURSES ARE OK? T-H-E I-N-C-O-M-P-E-T-E-N-T, U-N-L-I-C-E-N-S-E-D N-U-R-S-E-S A-R-E O-K?

The executioner had released the trapdoor, dropping Bascom into a void where the tug of a rope would abruptly halt his free fall.

Lance had often referred to him as "Don Quixote in Scrubs," because of his rebellious nature. But the Don of Spanish literature had a loyal ally. Not only was this Panzona bolting in the heat of battle, he was taking his sword and his horse Ronzinante with him.

Olsen rapped his gavel. "The purpose of this meeting was to consolidate agreements between the hospital and the district," he said. "Before we do, I urge the Board, as its legal adviser, to study these matters. I believe they could risk our position with the state licensing board and the various insurance companies who pay the bills that keep us in business."

The members agreed and without seconding the motion or taking a vote, adjourned the meeting. Davidson exited the room in a huff with Cohen tailing him as Bascom rose and turned to Helen who was walking down the aisle.

"Nice try, Bob," she said, resting a consoling hand on his arm. "He is a seedy fat bastard." She was too gracious to add, "I told you so, Lummox."

"G'night, Helen. I'll see you in the morning," he said before leaving the meeting.

Donna was leaning against his SUV when he arrived in the parking lot.

"Looking for some fun, stranger?" she asked.

"I've already been screwed tonight. But thanks," he laughed.

"You did great in there, Robby. No one else in this town would have stood up to Davidson."

"I shouldn't have either. I'm a slow learner."

"No, just idealistic. Are you sure you don't want company? You shouldn't be alone tonight."

"No thanks, D. I'll be fine."

"Ok. Call if you need me."

"I will," he said before kissing her. They hugged briefly and then Bascom climbed into his SUV and drove home.

He entered his house, slamming the door hard enough to bounce the pictures on the walls, and went to the kitchen. He tossed his keys onto the butcher-block table and poured himself a tall Scotch from the emergency bottle he kept over the sink. He gulped it down, refilled the glass to the brim, and went to the living room. He lay down on the couch, drained his glass a second time, and closed his eyes.

"Sticks and stones may break your bones, but names will never hurt you," was a popular ditty he remembered from his childhood. But Thompson's names had hurt him, much more than the sticks and stones ever could. He knew he should have trusted his instincts and not gone to the meeting.

Eventually the alcohol clouded his mind and he fell

into a fitful sleep mumbling Helen's words: "Seedy bastard."

A few days later Helen yelled into the hallway, "Newspapers." He picked them up from her desk and brought them to his private office.

"Hospital Accused of not Serving Patients," the Whitney *Times* shouted. The headline in the Phoenix *Globe* stated, "Hospital's Self-Serving Secrets Exposed."

He was engrossed in the articles when Helen told him the Board's attorney was on the telephone.

"Yes, Dave," he said, feeling better than he had in a while.

"Bob, I'm sending over a letter Davidson's sending to the *Times*. It's a corker."

"I can't wait to read it."

"I'm sure," he replied ironically before hanging up.

A short while later Olsen's pretty secretary stood in front of his desk, offering the missive in a hand with rings on every digit. "Present from Dave," she said cheerfully.

"Thanks," he replied. He eagerly tore open the envelope as she left the office.

> "Dear Mr. Olsen: (the letter began)
>
> "The *Times* says you are investigating the accusations made against the hospital on October 4th.
>
> "I welcome this, since the attack was personal and unrelated to the care the hospital provides. Although the citizens of Whitney can voice their complaints before the Hospital Board, it should be in a more civilized manner than what occurred at the meeting.

"I assure you I will not ignore attacks that could destroy the hospital's excellent reputation and its demonstrated ability to render service.

"Very truly yours,
"Simon Davidson, MD"

Bascom's reply to the *Times* was brief:

"I sincerely hope Dr. Davidson will provide a quality hospital to the community at a price it can afford."

Two days later Davidson's letter appeared above his own on the *Times*' editorial page. Immediately below his was one from a mother entitled, "Best Hospital in the State." According to the woman, her daughter had just spent a month at WCH and had found the place spotless, the food excellent, and the prices much cheaper than in Phoenix. So cheap in fact, that she could afford a two-week vacation in Hawaii with the money she saved by going to Dr. Davidson's institution instead of University Hospital in Phoenix.

"Extraterrestrial life does exist on Earth," he mumbled as he dropped the newspaper into the trashcan by his desk.

XVII

On the morning of Evelyn and Ben's wedding, Bascom took his 1845 leather bound copy of *Religio Medici,* 'The Religion of a Doctor,' by Sir Thomas Browne, Kt. MD., from his suitcase of Italian treasures and gift wrapped it. He and Cristina had discovered the small volume, which he had read and enjoyed several times, in a bookstore behind Bologna's *Duomo* during one of their exploratory treks through the ancient city.

Dr. Browne's philosophy was simple; he encouraged man to follow his own religious beliefs and to honor his creator by examining his handiwork. Bascom felt Ben was the only physician in Whitney who would understand and appreciate the book, and he would lend it to him permanently since the old man had firmly refused a wedding gift.

At 9:45 a.m. on October 10th, a beautiful, sunny, warm day without a cloud in the sky, Bascom, in his best jeans, sport shirt and corduroy jacket, drove to the park on the north side of town. He had thought Ben would celebrate his marriage in quiet surroundings, but traveling carnival pitched on the site surprised him.

He parked his SUV at the end of a row of old pick-up trucks and walked across the weed-infested field to the entrance. Ignoring the beckoning fragrance of grilled sausage and the chattering barkers in clown suits, he headed towards the merry-go-round where Ben, in a spotless tuxedo, was standing next to Evelyn and two men. His powdered toupee leaned precariously to one side and only his bent ear kept it from becoming an epaulet.

"Hi, Bapple. Do you get it yet?" he yelled over the cacophony of children's voices.

"Get WHAT?" Bascom shouted back, his hands encircling his mouth like a fleshy megaphone. Ben's question frustrated him. The old man asked him the same question every time they met, but would never explain what he meant.

"I'm glad you could make it," he said, shaking Bascom's hand. As he pushed his toupee back on his head, Evelyn, radiant in a blue dress and purple hair, stopped spinning a white plastic band on her left ring finger.

"Dr. Bascom, I'd like you to meet my son, Ronald," she said, introducing the man by her side. Fit and in his forties, only his crooked nose, which according to Helen was a "gift" from his father, marred his good looks. His suit was finely tailored suit and he wore his Breitling aviator's watch over his shirt cuff, as did Gianni Agnelli, the deceased heir to the Italian automobile dynasty.

"I'm honored to meet you," he said, shaking Bascom's hand. "My parents speak fondly of you."

"It's my pleasure, Ronald."

"And this is Father Hartnet," Evelyn added. The rotund priest smiled and daintily shook the tips of Bascom's fingers.

"Let's go, kids," Ben ordered. "God can wait, but I can't. The pill lasts only four hours, and Ev and I have fun things to do before it peters out. I mean stops working." Evelyn blushed and coyly kissed him on the cheek.

"Behave, Ben," she whispered.

"I am," he whispered back.

The merry-go-round slowed to a halt and Ben scooted the entourage onto it as if he were herding chickens into a coop. "Evelyn and I will ride the middle horses," he explained. "Mine goes up and down but hers doesn't, so we'll have to allow for that when I place the ring on her finger."

"The ring?" Bascom asked. "Where is it, Ben?"

"It's there, tied to a big brass one, Bascue," he replied, pointing to a notched wooden beam extending from a pole near the edge of the ride.

"You'll mount the bounding steed next to Evelyn's and grab it as we go by. You miss it and we don't get married."

"Father," the old physician ordered as Bascom laughed, "you'll sit backwards on the lion in front of us, and Ronald, you're in the flying turtle behind your mom. Are we ready?" The group agreed and Bascom mounted his vertically mobile palomino, the priest, his lion, and Ronald slid into his turtle's shell.

Ben signaled the carney with a circular movement of his arm. "I planned this trip to marital bliss with the engineer of this contraption," he said proudly. The man in grease-stained overalls rolled his eyes and leaned on his lever. As the ride slowly began turning, the wooden animals sprang to life.

"We're off!" Ben exclaimed as curious onlookers lined the ride's circumference. The merry-go-round picked up speed, carnival music plinked, and within moments Bascom's horse was bobbing up and down, Ronald's turtle was lurching forward, rising, then falling backwards, Father Hartnet was flipping through his bible on his lion, and old Ben was whipping his bucking wooden charger with one hand and holding Evelyn's with the other.

"Dearly beloved we gather here," the priest began in a shrill voice as Bascom, intent on retrieving the brass ring, lunged towards the wooden arm. His horse dove at the last second and he missed it. The crowd booed.

"Come on, Bottle!' Wiggins chided, interrupting the priest's droll litany. "Get that ring!"

"I will, Ben," he replied, "hold your horses. I'll get it the next time 'round."

"... today to join this couple in holy matrimony," the priest continued dully. He raised his arm to get everyone's attention, but all eyes were on Bascom, who failed a second time to snatch the ring.

The crowd booed even louder this time.

Ronald, now a light shade of green and lurching piteously to and fro in his turtle, feebly announced he was about to leave his breakfast in its shell. Bascom ignored his plight since he had a more important job to do. As he again prepared to snatch the ring that was fast approaching, the priest muttered, "Let him come (burp) forward. 'Scuse me."

The music roared as Bascom's wooden stallion reared on its third approach to the brass ring. "Go! Go! Go!" the crowd chanted as he stood on the saddle's outer stirrup and rested his knee on the horse's back. "Bury me with Custer! No! With Marilyn Monroe," he yelled as he stretched for the ring.

"Get it, Blarney!" Ben yelled.

Bascom's foot slipped from the stirrup and he swung out towards the crowd as he was slipping his finger through the ring. "I'm falling, Ben!" he yelled.

"Do you, Evelyn, take this man?" the priest droned, oblivious to Bascom's heroic efforts.

"Ohh!" people yelled as they scattered from the path of the falling doctor. Ben's toupee fell onto Evelyn's lap as he grabbed Bascom's coattails, almost toppling off his own horse during his heroic rescue. As he pulled Bascom back into his saddle, Ronald's turtle lurched sideways and his color changed from green to gray. He covered his mouth, only temporarily preventing the inevitable.

"Hooray, Bolton," Ben shouted, sitting back in his saddle. "You got it!" He took his toupee from Evelyn's outstretched hand and stuck it on his head as Bascom untied a hue princess cut diamond in a platinum engagement ring from its bronze casing and held it up for all to see. The crowd cheered as Bascom watched Evelyn's eyes widen in joyful surprise.

"I do," Evelyn grinned to the priest who was still droning on as if he performed similar ceremonies every day.

"Give it over, Basket," Ben yelled. Bascom handed him the ring and then held his hands to the sides of his head and spun them 90 degrees, hoping Ben would understand and straighten his hairpiece.

"And do you, Benjamin, take Evelyn to be your lawfully wedded wife?"

"I wouldn't have any other," Wiggins said proudly as he placed the ring on her finger. He winked at Bascom before adjusting his toupee.

"I now pronounce you man and (burp) wife."

Ben leaned over and kissed Evelyn. "I love you, Ev," he said, "and I always will. You're the best thing that's ever happened to me."

Evelyn cried as she wrapped her arms about her husband's neck. "I love you too, Ben," she replied. "You're a great man and I'm ecstatic we're finally married."

They kissed and the crowd roared its deafening approval. The Carney yelled, "Yahoo, Cowboy!" pulled on his lever and the merry-go-round slowed to a stop. The newlyweds dismounted their tethered hoses while Bascom pried Ronald's white-knuckled hands from the turtle's shell and helped him from the beast. Ben handed the Carney a bill from his wallet, and then, like a victorious boxer, raised his stretched arms, fists clenched, to the crowd that was clapping and wishing him good luck and happiness.

"Now then," he said as he led his guests to a nearby hot dog stand, "it's time for lunch. With or without mustard?" Bascom and Father Hartnet opted for mustard and sauerkraut on the foot-long wieners, but Ronald, now a lighter though still remarkable shade of green, declined the offer.

"Thanks for coming, Biscuit," Wiggins said to Bascom. "It wouldn't have been the same without you."

"I wouldn't have missed it for the world. By the way, I'd like you to have this," he said, taking Browne's small book from his jacket pocket. "It's a loan, not a gift."

Ben took it and gave his friend a hug. "Thanks," he said as he slipped it into his tuxedo pocket. "I'll open it later."

"Good luck," Bascom mumbled after taking a bite from his hot dog. He walked over to Evelyn while washing his lips with his tongue.

"I'm happy for you, Ev," he said. He tossed the rancid wiener into a bin before putting his arm through hers and leading her from the crowd.

"How are you feeling?" he asked, studying her drawn face. Ben perked up at the question. "She says she's OK, but, damnation, something is wrong! I knew it!" he murmured as he moved closer to eavesdrop on their conversation.

"I still stumble, Robert, but I'll be all right. I just need to rest more," she replied, holding up her hand and twisting it. Under the sparkling diamond was a thin white plastic band.

"What's that?" Bascom asked, pointing to the band.

"My engagement ring," she laughed. "We were shopping in Safeway when Ben asked me to marry him. He didn't have a ring, so he unscrewed the cap on a coffee creamer container, pulled off the tab and slipped it onto my finger. When he got down on his knee to propose, the store manager thought he was having a stroke and called 911."

"I wish I could have been there," Bascom laughed. "Ben looks happier than I've ever seen him." He eyed her purple hair.

"I love that man more than I can say, Robert. He's the reason I'm alive today. And Ben did it," she said, answering his unspoken question about her coiffure. "He said gray hair made me look old, so he dyed it himself. I'm just glad it didn't turn out pink. I hate old women with pink hair. He felt so bad when he saw the result, he offered to dye his toupee a matching color, but I told him it wasn't necessary."

"Gosh, Ev, you're not old," he laughed again. "But no tattoos and no body-piercing, OK? Can you imagine what wrinkled tattoos on an 80 year-old lady must be like?"

"No, and I'd rather not. Yuck!" she smiled. "No tattoos and no piercings, I promise."

They hugged as Ben called out, "It's time to see Ev's wedding gift, everybody."

He led the group to a new red Lexus SC convertible with tan leather interior parked in the far end of the parking area. A huge sign clipped to a giant gold bow on its trunk read, "I love you, Ev. Ben."

Like the teenager who spray-paints his amorous message on bridge over a busy highway, the old man wanted the world to know Evelyn was the love of his life.

XVIII

A few days after the wedding, Bascom invited Donna to dinner at *Il Pappagallo* 'the Parrot,' in Phoenix. That night, dressed in his usual sport coat and jeans, he knocked on her cottage door.

Donna opened it and his jaw dropped. She was even more beautiful than his mental image of her. Her auburn hair framed her angelic face and designer lenses on her perky nose accented her brown, soul-piercing eyes. The jade necklace on her silk blouse rolled sensuously over her full breasts while her short skirt displayed her shapely legs to erotic perfection.

"Flattery, even silent flattery, will get you everywhere," she grinned.

"Someday you'll be on a postage stamp honoring the most beautiful woman in the world," he replied.

"I'll repay that compliment later tonight," she purred. She closed the door and they walked arm in arm to the SUV.

The Parrot, a newly opened restaurant in a high-end strip mall on the outskirts of the city, was small but cozy. Its faux columns and plaster statuary were a tacky copy of its famous counterpart in Bologna's historic center, but its food was genuine b*olognese*. Bascom had eaten there when he needed a respite from Whitney's drive-through restaurants, and had promised its jovial owner he would return.

"Ben tornato, Dottore," the middle-aged man said when he saw them. He was short, plump, and spoke with an accent that came from an area far south of Bologna. "Welcome back. This time you have a beautiful woman with you."

Donna smiled at the compliment.

"It's good to see you again, Marcello," he replied, shaking his hand. "I told Donna you serve the only authentic bolognese food in Arizona, and she's eager to taste it

"You are too kind, *Dottore*. I'll prepare a meal that will be better than anything you've eaten anywhere in Italy. Please follow me."

They went to a table in the corner of the room where a young man in a white shirt, black vest and apron was waiting. He seated them and handed them leather bound menus.

"Cosa posso portarvi da bere, Signori?" the curly-haired waiter asked after seating them. "What can I bring you to drink?"

"Una bottiglia di San Pellegrino gassata 'San Pellegrino sparkling water'."

"Water only, *Dottore*?" the young man asked. "We have just received a shipment of Barolo wine from Piemonte, and it's excellent."

"Barolo is my favorite wine," he said. "But we'll have water, *grazie*."

"Would you like an antipasto?"

"Not tonight. What's your special?"

"*Lasagna verde*. It's delicious."

"Good. We'll have it, plus a rucola salad and a selection of grilled meats."

"Subito, Dottore," he said before walking to the kitchen.

"Spinach added to the dough makes green lasagna a

specialty," Bascom explained. "Since I couldn't speak Italian when I first arrived in the old city, I ordered it whenever I could afford to eat out until I learned what the other foods on the menu were.

"Sorry you missed the wedding," he added, caressing her hand.

"I would have been there had I not missed my flight from New York. But I heard about it from a friend. She still laughs every time she thinks about your clumsy attempts to snare Evelyn's ring," she replied.

"It was a memorable event. Ben is nuts, but madly in love."

"Madly in love but not nuts, although he likes to make people think he is. When I first got to town a nurse told me he was a walking textbook, and she was right. I hear he was a firebrand in his early years, a crusader who cut down bad docs with impunity. I can tell you he still terrifies our doctors, even if they pretend he doesn't.

"Anyway I hate weddings. They make me bawl my eyes out. I don't know why. Must be some love-hate thing, but it happens every time."

"Odd," Bascom replied. "So how was your day?"

"Wonderful," she grunted. "Two patients died, and one was only 18. I had a fight with a doc who thought he knew it all. He would have too, had he also known he's an idiot. Then I had to take a cold shower since my boiler broke, and I hate cold showers. I'm so hyper I could strangle Godzilla with my bare hands.

"Anything else you'd like to know?" she asked.

"Had I not seen it," he said, "I wouldn't have believed it."

"Seen what?" she snorted.

"You're beautiful when you're angry," he replied, running a finger over her neatly trimmed nails. She had painted a gold design on a red background each one.

"Robby, that's not fair. I earned the right to be angry," she said. Her frown turned into a smile.

"And you're even more beautiful when you smile," he added.

The waiter brought the sparkling water, filled their glasses, and placed the bottle in the center of the table before leaving.

"By the way, I read the letters to the editor in the Whitney rag. Any news from Davidson?" she asked as she sipped her water.

"No, but you can be sure he's plotting his revenge."

"I'm glad you spoke up at the meeting. Maybe you did some good."

"Words are useless weapons against greed," he said as he spun his glass by its stem. "In fact money is the basic problem in medicine today. We waste billions on unnecessary tests; incompetent or dishonest doctors steal more. All this would stop if we did away with insurance and each patient paid his own bill. Reasonable charges would have to replace the outrageous ones we're seeing now because then no one could afford to pay the latter.

"The HMOs are crooks themselves. There's one in California that pays each of its top three executives $12 million a year! Can you imagine how many requests for care it must reject to pay those bozos their $36 million?" he asked as he placed his glass on the table. He flicked his finger against his glass a few times, causing bubbles to rise to the surface and pop with a tiny spray.

"And talk about scams!" he continued distractedly. "If you want to raise the price of a piece of cheap plastic from 5 cents to $50, just say it's for 'medical use.'

"Basta! We shouldn't be talking about medicine now. It'll ruin our appetites."

The waiter arrived with their green lasagna, ground Romano cheese onto them, and then left again.

"Tell me about Florence," she said as she cut a corner off her pasta. "I hear it's a tourist trap."

Bascom smiled. "Every city in Italy is a tourist trap, but they are still beautiful. You just need to know how to avoid the scams."

"When we go, will you show me how?" she asked.

"Who said we were going?" he replied before forking a slice of lasagna into his mouth.

"Aren't we?"

Bascom smiled. "These lasagne are really delicious," he said.

After finishing the grilled sausage and steak, and too full to taste the exotic desserts, Bascom paid the bill and they left the restaurant.

They walked down the quiet, tree-lined street outside the mall holding hands, stopping occasionally to hug and kiss in the shadows.

The *lasagna verde* had stirred Bascom's memories of his student years, and during the long drive back to Whitney, he described his dizzying climb up the 498 rickety and irregularly spaced stairs to the top of the *Torre degli Asinelli*. The 320 feet tall tower, built in the 12th Century by the noble Asinelli family, stands 50 yards from the original *Pappagallo* restaurant in the heart of the city known as *Felsinea* to the Etruscans. The promised prize at the top was a view of the Alps and the Adriatic Sea, but the furthest he could see that overcast day was the roof of his orange apartment building a few miles away.

He parked in front of Donna's home and they walked with linked arms to her door. She opened it and asked mischievously, "Would you like to come in for a nightcap?"

"Yes, I would," he said, stepping into the foyer.

XIX

Well before Helen told him someone wanted to see him, before the pile of patients' hospital bills sitting on his desk grew taller than his coffee cup, and even before the Board had decided if the new clinic conflicted with its best interests, Bascom had been searching for a way to expose Davidson's billing schemes to the townspeople. The hospital owner had told the Board his doctors had unanimously chosen his new laboratory, but Bascom knew nothing of the decision and he needed to know what exactly had occurred between Davidson and his new laboratory.

As fortune would have it, a week after the Wiggins' wedding the answer arrived in his office with Rupert Hayward, a representative of Mansfield Laboratories. The congenial, prematurely balding youth had sold Bascom several inexpensive used machines for his mini-laboratory. They had become friends and had enjoyed occasional lunches together.

"Good-bye?" Bascom echoed in amazement after their handshake. "Why, Rup?"

"Lavabo Labs has taken over at the hospital and I'm going to sell boats in Washington with my father," the young man replied. He sat in front of the desk, took a bent cigarette from his jacket pocket and stuck it between his lips. He had quit smoking to silence Bascom's constant harangue about the evils of nicotine, but he could not break the mechanics of the habit. Several times a day he would pull out a cigarette, take a puff, blow an imaginary smoke ring, flick off a nonexistent ash, and return it to his pocket. Strands of tobacco would fall from its paper casing each time he performed the ritual, and by the end of the day the cigarette would become so ragged and bent it, looked like he was sucking a strand of overcooked fettuccine.

"What do you know about them?" Rupert asked. He blew a faux smoke ring before returning the cigarette to his pocket.

"I've never even heard of them," Bascom answered, settling in his chair.

Rupert snapped the brass locks of his briefcase, pulled out a newspaper clipping and handed it over the desk. "Then read this," he ordered.

The Wall Street Journal article described kick-backs from laboratories to doctors amounting to $2 billion of the $20 billion they earned yearly. One company, Appletree Clinical Research Laboratories in San Francisco, Davidson's hometown, had paid $2,900,000 in commissions to doctors in an eight-month period. The government had also accused it of buying a 17th Century Italian painting for an ex-physician now in hospital administration, for fraudulently processing blood specimens for another laboratory, and for defrauding Blue Cross and Medicaid.

"Interesting," he said, pushing the clipping back across his desk, "but what does Appletree have to do with Lavabo?"

"They're the same company. It changes its name after each indictment."

"WHAT!" Bascom exclaimed, bolting upright in his chair. "How do you know?"

"It's my job, or it was. Right now the lab is under federal investigation under both names," he said.

"Does our lab chief know about this?"

"Probably not since Dr. Volkers is too honest to get involved with crooks," Rupert, said shaking his head.

"That's a relief. Who's the Lavabo rep in this area?"

"Leslie Kirwan, one of the finest pieces of ass you'll ever meet," he said, licking his lips. Rupert rummaged again through his briefcase and pulled out a calling card.

"This is her number. She shares her shapely wares privately in motels in case her smile alone doesn't convince you to use her lab."

Bascom felt a cyclopean cacodemon claw into his body, a devil intent on rummaging through his every ligament and muscle in search of the quintessential reason for his stubborn adherence to a self-appointed task. He wished he would find it, strike off its figurative head and impale it on a spike in WCH's parking lot.

"Thanks for the info, Rup," Bascom said, standing from his chair. "I'm sorry you're leaving, but I wish you luck in your new venture."

"My family is a major supplier of fishing gear in Seattle and has been after me for years to work with them. I don't like the rain that much, but it's better than the desert dust that clogs my sinuses.

"Come up when you want to do some fishing," he concluded.

"I'll do that," Bascom said before they shook hands and his friend left. Helen entered the office moments later.

"Problems?" she inquired, picking up a pencil stub with a broken point from his desk.

"Naturally," he said, handing her the card. "Ask Miss Kirwan to stop by."

"Right, Boss," she replied. She tossed the pencil into the wastepaper basket, but quickly retrieved it. "We can't afford to waste supplies. I'll try to sharpen this one more time," she said before taking the card and returning to her office. Seconds later Bascom heard the pencil sharpener grind, a sorrowful "darn!" and then the pencil hitting an empty metal can.

The next day Leslie Kirwan, a pretty, well-endowed redhead in her late twenties arrived in Bascom's office with a briefcase full of what he was certain would be good news for the right people. *It's too small to contain a painting, but a check for kickbacks would fit easily.*

"Good day, Miss Kirwan," he said cheerfully. "How are you?"

"I'm fine, Doctor. How did you hear of us?" she asked with a smile only an orthodontist could have created. Her silk shift barely covered a body so perfect, it had to have been designed in a laboratory based on the PET scan of some randy male's brain.

"Your reputation is well-known in the business, Miss Kirwan."

"Call me Leslie," she beamed, smoothing her unwrinkled blouse.

And you call me Doctor. "Well, Leslie, tell me about your company," he insisted as she sat on the edge of her chair. He knew she never would tell all, but he would accept any information that would expose Davidson's latest scheme.

"We supply everything you need," she explained, aiming her perky breasts at him as if they were ray guns ready to disintegrate any resistance on his part. "We pick up your specimens daily and fax you the results within 24 hours."

"How are your prices?" *And point those things elsewhere. If they explode, I'll never get the silicone off my clothes.*

"Unbeatable. We have three lists," she explained, taking a few brochures from her briefcase. She held them fan-like and pointed to each as she described them, "one for Medicaid, one for your cash paying patients, and one for your insured patients."

Ding! You lose, but thanks for playing. The law requires you to charge each patient the same price for the same services, no matter his ability to pay.

"May I see them?" he asked innocently.

"Certainly," she answered, handing them over. "I can begin servicing you tomorrow."

"I'm sure you can, Leslie, I'm sure you can," he said ironically as he flipped though the lists.

"The sooner we start, the sooner you'll begin receiving your commission checks."

"How much would they be for?"

"Twenty-five percent of our stated fees."

"Sounds enticing. I'll call you in a few days."

"Great," she cooed, again smoothing her silk blouse as she stood. "Would you like my home number?"

"No," he replied firmly. Leslie wrote it on her card and placed it on Bascom's desk before leaving. He was reviewing her price lists when Fran popped her head in the door.

"You still alive, Doc?" the pretty nurse asked with a grin. "No chest pains from performing uncommon exertion? Friction burns on your cheeks."

"Jealous?" he asked with mock chagrin.

"Nope," she replied, her eyes sparkling behind tinted glasses. "I just don't want a Jezebel to lead my doctor down the path to perdition."

"I feel so safe when you protect me from me," he laughed. "What do you want?"

"You've got a patient in two."

Bascom dropped the brochures on his desk before

walking to room two and taking the chart from the rack on the door. Henry Lord, a mentally retarded 12-year-old who grunted loudly or softly depending on his needs, was coughing fitfully when he entered the room.

"Hello, Mr. Lord," he stated. "How are you and Henry today?"

"I'm fine, but Henry ain't," he said in a huff. "I took him to the ER t'other day, and they did all these here tests, but he's still coughing." Bascom glanced through the wad of laboratory slips the man handed him.

"Wow!" he exclaimed when he realized what serendipity had bestowed on him. "Do you have the bill for these?"

"Sure. It's in there," he replied heatedly, pointing to the papers. "I gave Hank's AHCCCS card to the ER clerk, but they still want me to pay the bill. I ain't got no money, Doc. I can't pay this."

"You won't have to. I'll handle it," he replied, placing the documents on his small desk.

Bascom then examined Henry, and after suggesting an inexpensive over-the-counter remedy for his simple cold and sending him home, ran to his desk to compare Henry's bill to the lists Leslie had left him. Her laboratory was charging the boy $119.80. Not only did the price differ from that specified in her three brochures, it was higher than the highest of the three.

After his last patient left that afternoon, Bascom took the bill to Harrison Volkers, the hospital pathologist. When he entered his laboratory, the thin, 50 year-old doctor whose face bore the scars of a battle against acne, was peering into a microscope.

"Welcome, friend. Have a seat," he said heartily, pulling a stool from under the bench. "I'm just checking a tumor from a patient with blood pressure crises. Steele diagnosed a pheochromocytoma and Thompson removed it, just like in a real hospital. Take a look," he said excitedly, pointing to the second set of objectives on his microscope.

Bascom peered into the eyepieces as Harrison described the histology of the lesion.

After his crash course in rare diseases, Bascom handed him Henry's bill. "Those charges aren't on any of Lavabo's lists," he said.

"I don't doubt it," Harrison reflected grimly, scanning the document. "Davidson's got his own lists for everything. I'll check and get back to you."

After running a mile that evening, as he had been doing for weeks to return to his form when Cristina was alive, Bascom soaked his sore muscles in a warm bath until the water cooled, forcing him from the tub. He was drying off when his phone rang.

"I can't figure out how many price lists Lavabo has," Harrison said. "Henry's bill was for $119.80. Your list says $50.85, mine says $60, and they billed state for $200, even though its reimbursement rate is $40."

"Can you do anything about this?"

"You bet. Either Davidson drops this lab or I call in state investigators. Lavabo has been fined before, but he hasn't yet. I presume he'd rather avoid that distinction."

"That's great," Bascom said. "Oh, by the way, have you heard anything about kickbacks or free paintings?"

"Nobody has offered me anything, except Miss Kirwan. I'm a vegetarian so I turned down her offer," he laughed. "I'll take care of this bill; Mr. Lord is off the hook."

"I wish I were as efficient as you are, Harrison. Thanks."

Bascom had decided not to attend the end of October

District Board' emergency meeting called to resolve its conflicts with Davidson, since he felt another shouting match would be unproductive. But on the morning after the meeting he called Dave Olsen to learn the Board's decision. According to his secretary, he was recovering from an all night interview with a red-haired reporter. She would have her boss call him as soon as possible.

He was in bed reading a book on medieval architecture when his phone rang that evening. *Finally recovered, eh, Olsen?* He picked up the receiver, but the gravelly voice was not the lawyer's.

"Hi, Bob, how are you?" Thompson asked. He had not spoken to the obese surgeon since he betrayed him at the first Board meeting, and his anger quickly welled.

"I was doing fine until you called," he grunted.

"Davidson's pissed."

"That makcs my day. Why?"

"Harrison made him get rid of Lavabo Labs and the Board made him close down his clinic since it was a conflict of interest and ran up patient bills."

"Aw, shucks," Bascom replied sarcastically. "If I caused any of that, I don't apologize."

"He told me he intends to run you out of town."

"Won't happen. What else did the spiffy dwarf say?"

"Lots. But I warned him not to make any more changes without consulting the staff first."

"Did you threaten to sit on him if he did?"

"Like I said," he replied, "he wants you out of town."

"I will decide when I'll leave here, not him. Capisci, testa di cazzo 'understand, dickhead'?"

"He demands a meeting with you."

"He'll have to bend on one knee and kiss my dic.., er, ring."

"He's sending someone from San Francisco to talk to

you."

"I'm shaking all over," Bascom said, slamming the receiver into its cradle.

XX

Bascom was on the phone with Dave Olsen two days after the Board meeting when Ben knocked on his office door. The old man's wig was askew and he had a wild look in his eye. "Mind if I come in?" he grinned as he entered the room. Bascom waved him into a chair in front of his desk.

"I won't meet Davidson's representative without a witness, Dave," he continued. "Cohen and that fat bastard Thompson will deny what they say, or change what I say, to suit their boss at any meeting not monitored by the UN."

He listened a moment and then replied, "Then I won't go," and hung up.

"What's up, Ben?" he asked. He leaned back in his chair and put his feet up on the corner of his desk.

"You're really battling that hospital," he replied.

"Every morning I promise myself I'll stop, but something always pulls me back into the fray by noon. I need a prescription for Soma, the euphoria-producing drug Huxley described in his *Brave New World*."

"It doesn't work, and you're right not to meet those people alone," he continued, shaking his head. "Wear a wire if you do. You can easily hide a tape recorder under your jacket."

"Would you come with me?" Bascom asked.

"Nope, I don't have your courage or foolhardiness. Besides, I'll be dead when you go to trial."

"Trial?" he repeated. "What trial?"

"Yours is a clash between morality and capitalism, and capitalism always wins. To you medicine is a 'poor mistress'; to Davidson she's a 'wealthy whore.' If you don't kowtow to him, he'll sue you and order his doctors to devour your practice and to destroy your reputation. And believe me, they'll comply just to get rid of you. Doctors don't want competent colleagues looking over their shoulders.

"This meeting, if you decide to go, will be your last chance to repent before your indoctrination into manhood."

Ben leaned back in his chair and locked his fingers behind his head. His gray eyes silently challenged Bascom. "Well, whippersnapper, what are you made of?" they seemed to ask.

"I stopped by to thank you for being my best man," he continued, unlocking his fingers and leaning forward in his chair. "But Ev and I were disappointed you came alone. We were sure you'd bring Donna."

"What made you think I might?"

"I saw you two leave the cafeteria together after our meeting with Davidson. You looked like a perfect match. It's obvious she adores you."

Bascom nodded. "She wanted to come but missed her flight and arrived home long after it was over," he explained.

"Right," Ben replied, "she told us about her trip back east. If you intend to fight WCH, you'll need someone tough, understanding, smart, and especially loyal, at your side. Donna is that person. I always rated her the best nurse in the hospital. Except for Ev, of course."

"Of course," Bascom laughed. "I'm sure she is too, but that much dependence on her could lead to a long-term relationship. I'm not ready for that yet. I don't need support; I need someone to convince me to drop this mess."

"You'd never do that, no matter who tried to convince you."

"What makes you so sure?"

"I know your type. You'd rather die than walk away from Davidson. Anyway thanks for this gem," he said, taking the *Religio Medici* from his pocket and tapping its cover. "I loved it. It reminded me of the old days of medicine. Where did you find it?"

"In an old bookstore behind the Cathedral of San Petronio in Bologna. Cris and I enjoyed exploring the dustiest, dingiest looking shops we could find on our trips throughout Italy, and we often uncovered treasures not even the shop owners remembered having."

"Cris was your wife?" Ben asked. Bascom nodded and studied his feet on the desk.

"You never talk about her."

"I know," he sighed.

"She must have been quite a woman," Ben offered as he straightened his wig.

"She was. We met in a head-on collision while skiing at the Corno della Scala in Italy," Bascom said, leaning over to close a desk drawer that was open a quarter of an inch. "In a restaurant that night in Lizzano in Belvedere, her hometown down the hill from the slopes, she told me she was a nurse at the Sant'Orsola hospital in Bologna where I was doing my internship. A week later she called me to help her convince a professor to stop using a medication she was certain was killing one of her patients.

"Suggesting a demigod made a mistake is enough to get you blackballed in Italy if you're a doctor. If you're a nurse, well, let's not get too graphic," he continued, rubbing his neck.

"I was just an intern," Bascom explained slowly, "and in no position to help her, but I knew she was right. When I couldn't convince the professor either, I pulled the IV out of the patient's arm right in front of him. You would not believe the ruckus it caused. They wanted to toss us off the staff. When the truth came out, the professor dropped his complaint to avoid further embarrassment. From that time on we were inseparable."

"I can see why you loved her," Ben nodded.

"We had a few wonderful years together when a few lifetimes wouldn't have been enough," he said as a tear appeared in the corner of his eye. "Sorry," he said, wiping it away with a finger. "Desert dust gets into everything."

"It's worse when it covers your sheets," Ben laughed. "It makes sleeping in the nude feel like you're lying on the beach. And it's worse if you're floundering around on them. How did she die?"

"A truck ran over her the night before we were to return to Italy. I had accepted the job as her hometown's doctor," Bascom replied as the scene came alive in his mind. It was as painful now as it was then.

"I was in my office in the ER listening to Beethoven's "Fűr Eliza" and talking to Lance Berkford," Bascom related, "when they called her code. She was in cardiac arrest when we got to her, and died minutes later in my arms.

"We brought her back to Italy for burial," he continued, again wiping an eye with his finger, "and I opened my practice in Lizzano as we had planned. Waste of time. I couldn't go on without her, and because of a bad habit I picked up after her death, closed my office a couple of months later."

"Did you blame yourself for her death?" Ben asked, scratching his chin.

Bascom took a handkerchief from his pocket and blew

his nose. "I still do," he said as he refolded the cloth. "She asked me to shop for the special dinner she was preparing for us. I was busy and told her to go herself. Had I gone shopping for her that night, she'd be alive today. Knowing I caused her death, or that I couldn't save her, will haunt me forever."

"Could anyone have saved her?" Wiggins wondered. His voice was soft, cuddly, inviting. The old physician was coaxing Bascom's demon to the surface.

"No." His lower lip trembled. "No one could."

Ben massaged one knobby hand with the other. "You didn't cause Cris' death," he said, "and, since no one could have saved her, you shouldn't blame yourself for it. Most of all, you shouldn't allow her death to cause yours.

"My son James died of an overdose of pain pills years ago," he continued thoughtfully. "Abe Grimes prescribed them for my wife and she gave them to our son. I ordered them to stop, but they continued behind my back.

"I made her life a hell after he died, and when she couldn't take it any longer, she left. Everyone in town thinks I threw her out of the house, but that's not true.

"He was a rational adult with a bad habit that killed him," he continued, looking at Bascom, "but we were all to blame for his death. Me for not noticing his addiction; Grimes who prescribes narcotics to keep his patients happy and his bank account well into the black; his mother for pampering him; and James himself for voluntarily taking a lethal dose of the drug and washing it down with alcohol.

"We suffer when our loved ones die, but we shouldn't punish ourselves or others for their misdeeds or faults."

Ben rested his chin on his fists. "After James died, I developed a bad habit, just like yours," he continued, raising an eyebrow. Bascom saw the old man smile and winced when he realized his past drinking problem was no longer a secret. "But as I was sliding into the abyss," Ben continued, "Evelyn grabbed my hand and refused to let go. She saw something in me I didn't and still don't, but I'm grateful to her. Had I died when I wanted to, I would have missed the happiest part of my life."

"I've already lived the happiest part of mine," Bascom interrupted.

"We'll see, we'll see. Well, I've got a date with my beautiful wife," he said as he rose and walked to the door. "We're going to Phoenix for dinner, a play, and a night in a hotel on a sand free mattress.

"Bye," he added before tilting his wig to one side and disappearing into the hallway.

XXI

It was an overcast day in mid November when Bascom trod the same cracked cement path to the hospital that he had for the first time a year earlier. This time scaffolding surrounded the decrepit building, and Mexican workers in yellow safety helmets and gray overalls were laying tiles on its roof and refinishing its facade.

He had reluctantly agreed to meet Davidson's emissary after several cajoling phone calls from Thompson, but was ambivalent about his decision. Dave Olsen had quit his post with the Board to accept a lucrative position as a pinstriped in-house counsel for Davidson. Without him Bascom would be entering the lion's den without a reliable witness to testify in court if Davidson should decide to sue him.

Yet he needed to know what punishment his foe would inflict on him if he continued interfering in his affairs. Since he had every intention of doing so, knowing the risks was essential.

Evelyn had once told him Ben had continued to meet with his colleagues to keep an eye on them; he thought that a wise decision. That and the tape recorder Ben had suggested he carry in his jacket pocket were the forces pushing him toward the hospital's twin glass doors.

He entered the building and sniffed the air. *Davidson hasn't eliminated Nevins' oil of wintergreen yet,* he thought as he walked down the hallway. Joe Thompson, in a pin-striped suit and rocking on his heels like a lumpy tethered balloon, was waiting for him outside Cohen's office. The fat man offered his hand, but pulled it back nervously when Bascom ignored it.

"Have you seen George?" he asked the ceiling.

"Whose side are you on this time, Joe?"

"On the side of truth, as always. You know I want nothing but the best for the citizens of this town. Er, maybe he's inside, Bob," he said uneasily before lumbering into the office.

Seconds later George Cohen appeared in the doorway, buttoning a new suede jacket. He was clean-shaven and perfumed, but dark patches under his eyes and white streaks in his once blond hair suggested stress had infiltrated his once easy job.

"I'm glad you could come, Doctor," he said loudly enough for anyone in his office to hear. Then he whispered, "I'm sorry about this, Bob, but Dr. Davidson has ordered us to get rid of you. If we succeed, fat boy will get the directorship of the cardiovascular and orthopedic departments Davidson intends to open in a few months, and my salary will double.

"I've never told anyone before, but I have a disabled child and an ex-wife in LA to support. I can't afford to lose this job. I don't agree with a lot that's happening here; in fact Some of Dr. Davidson's ideas are way over the top, but I need this job and can't fight him.

"I won't help you in there, but I won't hurt you either. As a friend I suggest you drop this fight before it gets messy, and it will, I assure you," he concluded. Bascom nodded and followed Cohen into the office where an elderly man standing in the middle of the room was waiting to greet him.

"Dr. Bascom?" he questioned sternly. "I'm Henry Rutledge. I'm pleased to meet you." Dark eyes flanked the bridge of his wide nose, giving him an Asian appearance, but his narrow, comb-like mustache was akin to that of a long-deceased dictator from Western Europe. To Bascom he looked like trouble from whichever geological direction you approached him.

"Same here," Bascom agreed. Rutledge shook his hand and then sat imperiously in a leather chair facing a new black velvet sofa. Cohen and Thompson sat in wicker chairs on his flanks. Bascom sat on the sofa, facing the lopsided inquisition.

"Dr. Davidson wants you to know he is unhappy with your exposure of matters he adamantly feels should remain private," the emissary declared. He swept his index finger and thumb down the sides of his jaw to his pointed chin like an irate father considering the punishment to impose on his wayward, poorly dressed child. Bascom opened his jacket so his tape recorder could capture Rutledge's every word.

"He demands you end the displays you have been staging or face severe consequences."

"Save your threats for someone who depends upon your hospital to make a living, like Thompson," Bascom replied, nodding to the obese surgeon who was rolling his tilted head back on his fat neck as if searching for a UFO on the ceiling. "Your boss thought it would be easy to economically rape this community, but I won't let him get away with it."

"What!" he sputtered. "Are you intimating Dr. Davidson is dishonest?"

"I'm not 'intimating,' anything. 'Davidson' and 'honest' don't belong in the same sentence. The man is a crook."

"You could face severe legal repercussions for that remark," Rutledge retorted. "I'd suggest you mind your insulting dialog."

"And you yours," Bascom replied. He leaned back and banged the soles of his penny loafers together. "If you want to discuss the problems Davidson has created for this community, fine. But if you're trying to intimidate me, you're wasting my time and yours."

Rutledge spluttered and Thompson and Cohen leaned away from him as if he were a stick of dynamite ready to explode.

"And your boss isn't the only bad apple here. For months I've received nothing but complaints about the unnecessary studies Evans orders in the ER and their outrageous costs," Bascom continued. "To make matters worse, his lackey is so incompetent, he can't arrive at a diagnosis even with all the tests he orders. Someday he'll kill a patient, and I will happily testify for the plaintiff."

"It's none of your business how Dr. Davidson runs his hospital!" Rutledge scolded, shaking his finger at Bascom. Thompson extracted his gold cigarette case from his pocket, but Rutledge covered it with his hand and he quickly replaced it.

"Oh, but it is. It most certainly is," Bascom corrected, running a hand through his hair. "Anything and everything that has to do with my patients' health and economic welfare is my business, from the time I first see them until their tests are run, their diagnoses confirmed, and their therapy completed. And that especially includes everything that happens to them in this death trap."

"But," Rutledge interrupted.

Bascom held up a hand to stop him. "Let me finish. Suppose you call me at 3:00 a.m. because your child is ill," he said, pausing to let the emissary create the scene in his mind.

"And suppose," he continued as Rutledge nodded, "I tell you to go to the ER because I can't help you for whatever reason. You refuse, but I insist, assuring you he'll get proper care.

"You reluctantly go because you trust me and know I would never tell you to do something that could endanger your child.

"Got the picture so far, Mr. Rutledge?" Bascom wondered.

"Continue," he said.

"Fine. So two days later you storm into my office and yell, 'they killed my little boy in that ER! How could you send me there when everyone knows how dangerous that place is?'

"As the father of that dead child, Mr. Rutledge, how would you like to hear me tell you: 'I knew that ER doc would eventually kill someone, but if I didn't send you to the hospital, Dr. Davidson would have been angry with me. I'm sorry your child is dead, but I had no choice'?"

Rutledge scratched his cheek.

"A less dramatic scenario is also unacceptable as far as I'm concerned," Bascom continued. He interlocked his fingers behind his head. "Suppose you are a farm worker earning $1,000 a month and the hospital charges you $4,000 to diagnose your son's constipation. Would you choose to buy food for your family or would you pay the inflated hospital bill? And if you chose the former, what would you do when the hospital takes your *tugurio* 'hovel' to settle your bill?

"Mr. Rutledge," he concluded, "I want to be clear about this. My patients will always come before any contract, and Dr. Thompson knows that's true."

Rutledge turned a questioning eye to the obese surgeon fidgeting in his chair. "You're being too hard on Dr. Davidson, Bob," he replied weakly. "He's a nice guy. You shouldn't criticize him so much."

"How many shekels did you get for your greasy soul this time, Joe?" Bascom asked angrily. Thompson reddened and fell silent.

"Doctor," Rutledge asked, "what would you do if Dr. Davidson were to authorize an investigation into your allegations and then, whether its results give them validity or not, decided not to correct the situation to your satisfaction?"

Bascom leaned forward to make certain his tape recorder picked up his every word. "I'd consider our contract void and leave the hospital," he declared.

"I think that would be acceptable with Dr. Davidson," Rutledge agreed.

Speak into the microphone, Rutledge.

"You are agreeing to let me cancel my contract, without penalty of any type, if an investigation proves me right, Davidson does nothing to correct the situation, and I resign from the hospital?" he asked.

"I am."

"Dr. Davidson specifically authorized you to make such an offer?"

"He did, however, you must agree to stop persecuting him and his hospital."

"How about if the committee whitewashes the investigation?"

"You mean if it doesn't consider your complaints to be valid?"

"That's what I just said."

"I'm sure Dr. Davidson will be happy to let you resign in that case also."

"So I can resign without penalty in either case. That's fair, but there is one more thing. My September and October rents are overdue and I'd like a check for them this week."

"I'll talk with Dr. Davidson about that," Rutledge replied. "Oh, I almost forgot. He's replacing you with Dr. Evans as ER Chief."

"No, he's not," Bascom retorted. "Hospital bylaws specify a physician can hold office only after being on staff eight months, and Evans has a few months to go. I'd suggest he use them to study medicine while he's waiting for his promotion. Modern medical books are full of pictures, and I'll send the crayons so he can color them."

Rutledge recoiled at the criticism of Davidson's chosen aide, but quickly regained his composure. "I'll relay your messages to Dr. Davidson," he said, standing from his chair. They shook hands and Bascom left the office. As he walked down the hallway leading to the hospital's exit, he turned off the tape recorder.

In his office that afternoon, Bascom took the tape recorder from his pocket and turned it on. Nothing happened. He cursed as he replaced the batteries, rewound the tape and played it back. The last recorded words were Joe Thompson's. "On the side of truth, as always," he said.

Three days later, in the middle of his lunch hour, Helen announced with unconcealed disgust that Thompson wanted to see him.

"Frisk him for a weapon before you let him in," Bascom said as he bit into his turkey sandwich.

"I'll have to don my rubber gloves first," she replied wryly as she left the office.

When his uninvited guest appeared in the doorway in a wrinkled pinstriped suit, Bascom wrapped his sandwich and put it aside.

"What's on your mind?" he asked coldly.

"Hi, Bob," Thompson said lightly, as if they still were the best of friends. He took a sheet of paper from a folder and handed it to Bascom. "*Ad Hoc* Committee for Study of ER Care at Whitney Community Hospital," was typed in boldface across its top.

"Three of us will review all Evans' work for September and October," he explained. "Rutledge asked Davidson to order it."

"Have you talked with anyone else about this?"

"Yeah, and everyone agrees the ER has problems."

"You're just now realizing a well known fact? Donna tells me horror stories all the time."

Thompson perked up when he heard Donna's name, then shrugged. His jacket slipped backwards, releasing a nauseating stench of nervous perspiration. "She would know, wouldn't she?" he said as he pulled it back. "Well, I gotta be going," he added before nervously retrieving the document and exiting the office.

As Thompson disappeared into the hallway, Bascom received a call from the hospital; Bill Shadwell was having difficulty breathing.

"I put him on oxygen and ordered a chest X-ray," the nurse said. "Do you want me to do anything else?"

"No, I'm on my way," he said, tossing his sandwich in the trash. He pocketed his stethoscope and left for the hospital.

Rose Shadwell was pacing outside her husband's room when he arrived, and her sad eyes described the desperate situation awaiting him. When they entered the room, they saw a well-dressed man wearing a turban standing by Bill's bedside. He turned to them.

"Who are you and what are you doing here?" Bascom demanded.

"I'm Dr. Sahri, an oncologist from San Francisco. I'm

treating Mr. Shadwell's cancer."

"Under whose orders?"

"Dr. Davidson told me to treat his cancer patients when I come down once a month."

"Mr. Shadwell is not Dr. Davidson's patient, he's mine," Bascom said harshly.

"Er, well."

"You wouldn't be here because you're behind on your alimony payments and need some quick cash, would you?" he demanded.

"There's no need to be offensive," he pleaded with a weak smile.

"You have no idea how offensive I can get, Dr. Sahri, but you'll find out if you're still in this room thirty seconds from now. And if you ever touch another patient of mine without my permission, or if you dare to send these people a bill, I'll have your license. Do you understand?"

"Yes," he said, banging his knee on the bedpost as he scurried sideways from the room to avoid contact with Mrs. Shadwell.

"I'm sorry, Rose," he said.

"It's always something, Doc," she replied, clucking her tongue. "I'm glad you're here to help us."

Bascom went over to Bill who was now totally blind and crippled from a fracture that had sheared through the metastatic tumor in his pelvis. He could hear the oxygen hiss into his face mask and then bubble through his fluid-filled lungs.

"Hello, Bill," he said.

"Dr. Bascom, I'd like you to meet Bill's mother," Rose interrupted as an elderly woman entered the room. She was blotting her tears with a yellow handkerchief.

"Hello, Mrs. Shadwell. I'm sorry," he said. She had watched her son grow from an infant dependent on her, to a man of strength, and finally to a corrupt specter. He felt her pain as well as his own, since neither could help her dying son. He explained the uselessness of further therapy and then left for the radiology department to review Bill's X-ray.

Art Compton was exiting a procedure room when he arrived. The elderly radiologist worked mornings in Whitney and afternoons in Phoenix as part of a group that serviced hospitals in several cities. His deformed, arthritic hands prevented him from performing the once-intricate studies he enjoyed, and he now spent his time now performing barium enemas, interpreting routine X-rays, and CT scans, when the unit was not down for repairs.

"Hi, Art," Bascom said, "do you have Shadwell's X-ray?"

"It's on the desk," he volunteered, arching his back. Bascom took the X-ray from a two-foot tall pile and pushed it under the clips of a lighted view box. The black and white film showed a large tumor invading Bill's lungs and ribs, giving the latter a moth-eaten appearance.

"Have you seen Thompson recently?" he asked, returning the X-ray to the pile.

"Yeah," Art nodded. He hung his heavy lead apron on a rack, exchanging it for an old tweed jacket with leather-patched elbows. "He mentioned an investigation into the habits of our ER docs," he said, donning the jacket.

"I've been meaning to talk to you about them."

"Why? You know the problems."

"I've heard rumors; firsthand information would be better."

"That's from the ER in the past twenty-four hours," he griped, pointing a knobby finger at the pile of films on his desk. "It's three times higher than it ever was before Evans came to town." He clawed through it with his deformed hands and clumsily extracted a stack of films.

"These X-rays are all on one patient," he explained, fumbling them under the clips on the view boxes. "What do you see?"

"Nothing abnormal," Bascom replied after studying each of the ten X-rays.

"Right. Now look at this," he said, placing one more on the view box before taking a briar pipe from a jacket pocket.

"The radius and the ulna have hairline fractures."

"Right again. This patient came in last night after an automobile accident. Evans ordered all the X-rays he could think of and then admitted her 'just to be safe,' even though she didn't need it. He ignored her complaint of pain since he missed the cracks and thought she had just bruised her arm.

"Marty Nevins saw the fractures this morning and put a cast on her arm."

"Is this an isolated incident?"

"Hell, no!" he answered, jabbing the stem of the unlit pipe in the air. "Thanks to Evans, where I once found six problems in ten X-rays, now I find one in twenty, and it's usually one he misses. It's an absurd waste of technology and money."

"Will you tell the members of the committee that?"

"If they ask me, sure."

"Do you know what contract he has with the hospital?"

"He gets a big salary plus a share of the income from the tests he orders; the more he runs, the more he earns."

"Thanks, Art," Bascom said as he returned to his office.

He was reviewing charts late that afternoon when Jonas Price burst into his *Piccola Repubblica,* 'Little Republic,' as he called his inner sanctum. Helen had chided him when he told her about the christening, asking if he intended to design a flag and a coat of arms before stretching barbed wire around the building. He told her it seemed like a good idea.

"Carl's awake!" Jonas exclaimed joyously. "While one of the nurses was leaning over him, he opened his eyes and asked, 'Where am I?' Can you imagine the look on her face?"

Bascom could not, and accompanied Jonas to the hospital. Martha was smothering Carl in kisses when they entered his room. He went to the foot of the bed, gently squeezed the boy's toe, and said simply, "Welcome back, Carl."

"Who are you?" the boy wondered, cocking his head to the side.

"He's Dr. Bascom, don't you remember him? He saved your life," his mother explained proudly.

"I was only one of many who helped you save your own life," he corrected before examining the boy. The stiffness in Carl's right arm and leg indicated brain damage, and considering the time that had elapsed since the accident, it would be permanent.

"Tomorrow we'll begin physical therapy," he said after finishing his examination.

"Will he be as good as he was before the accident?" Martha wondered.

"I don't know, but the sooner we start the PT, the sooner he'll get home," he replied.

"That's wonderful news," Martha yelled. She grabbed Bascom and kissed his cheeks.

"Wow. I'm glad I didn't tell you he'd be running track in two days," he laughed. He shook Jonah's hand, said, "see you tomorrow," and left the room. On his way out he noticed the overflowing garbage can in the corner.

Some things never change.

He was leaving the building when a nurse called him on his cell phone to tell him Bill Shadwell had died. He returned to the man's bedside and sympathized briefly with Rose and Bill's mother before heading for home.

XXII

Joe Thompson arrived unexpectedly in Bascom's office on the chilly December morning Dr. Davidson had chosen for his *ad hoc* meeting. Helen made him sit in the empty waiting room for an hour before admitting him to the inner office. As a woman scorned, she enjoyed pecking at the fat man's fragile ego whenever she could.

"I haven't reviewed the charts yet," Joe apologized to the rebel in his *Piccola Repubblica*. "But I will."

"Isn't the meeting in an hour?" Bascom asked as he leaned back and put his feet up on the corner of his desk.

"Yup."

"How many charts are you supposed to review?"

"Seven hundred."

"So you'll review them after the meeting?"

Thompson began to sweat and ran his finger under his tight collar. "No. I'll finish before it starts," he said lamely. "John Cody will review the records for November, so we'll evaluate three months of Evans' work. We had a meeting the other day and we agreed to close him down if we uncover more than simple deviations from proper procedure."

"I can see the halo over your head from here," Bascom replied sarcastically. "Who's John Cody?"

"An OB doc who moved to Phoenix," he answered nervously. "He volunteered because he needs referrals. He didn't do well here and I hear he's not doing any better there."

"So you're going to review 700 charts in an hour, and an inept obstetrician who knows nothing about emergency medicine and who can't find his ass with both hands and a flashlight is going to report on 700 more.

"You're pathetic," Bascom hollered. "Get the hell out of my office!"

Thompson quickly turned and left. As Bascom watched the obese surgeon bounce off the doorway before disappearing into the hallway, he was certain the committee would whitewash the investigation.

Twenty minutes later he drove to the hospital and parked in front of its entrance. Its once cracked green stucco was now desert sand tan, and wavy orange tiles covered its roof. "At least Davidson has made one positive contribution to this place," he murmured, striding up the new flagstone walkway.

At the glass entry he bumped into a furious Donna Franklyn dressed in street clothes.

"Off duty, D?" he asked the nurse. Angry, knitted eyebrows and pursed lips disfigured her usually radiant face.

"Hell no! Cohen fired me!" she fumed.

"Why?"

"Davidson found out I was your informant about his bozo in the ER."

"It had to be that bastard Thompson!" he said angrily, smacking his forehead with the heel of his hand. "I unintentionally mentioned you to him and he reported you to Davidson. I'm sorry."

"Don't be," she answered, putting a hand on his arm. "I was quitting anyway and just wanted the satisfaction of resigning. I start in the Phoenix University Hospital ER in a few days. My only regret is I'll miss working with you. Call me on my cell until I get a landline, will you?"

"Ok," he replied.

She kissed him on the lips before continuing on her way.

The usual stench of oil of wintergreen engulfed him as he stopped in the hallway to speak to Linda Stevens. The pediatrician was standing in the middle of her gutted unit watching workers install a new nurses' station.

"Missing it, Linda?" he asked the red-haired doctor.

"Simon is redoing the department for me." She blushed and her cheeks turned more crimson than her hair.

"I thought his drunk tank had taken it over."

"He's moved it to another area," she replied vaguely before walking away.

Cohen was right when he said he lost money taking care of uninsured, impoverished children. So why did he reopen the pediatric unit?

He continued down the corridor to the radiology department where Art Compton was reviewing a huge pile of X-rays. Instead of a tweed jacket with its leather-patched elbows, he wore a pinstriped suit and white shirt. In the middle of his blue tie was a golden "D" adorned with a wreath and crown in Emperor Napoleon style. His had shined his shoes and had plastered neatly in place the few hairs on his scalp.

"How's business, Art?" he asked.

"Fine," he replied without his usual smile.

"You know Davidson's committee meets today?"

"Yeah," he said, rubbing a knobby hand over an X-ray he was reviewing. "I spoke with Cohen earlier."

"What did you tell him?"

"Evans orders more X-rays than any competent doctor would."

Compton was lying; Bascom could hear it in his voice

and it troubled him. *Cospirazione*! Was now certain that Joe, who would not review the charts, Linda, who again had her pediatric unit, and Compton, who was lying about what he told George Cohen, were all part of a conspiracy to get him out of the hospital.

"And George replied?" he asked.

"'Thanks.'" Compton said as he clumsily pulled the X-rays from the view boxes and piled them on his cluttered desk. "He just said, 'thanks.'"

"Did Thompson or any of the others on the committee talk to you?"

"Nope."

"Interesting."

Bascom left for the laboratory. The Suit-Monkey had visited Compton, and he wondered what Harrison Volkers would be wearing.

Once a quiet room hidden in the bowels of the hospital, the laboratory was now a beehive. Harried technicians scurried about while Harrison, in his wrinkled lab coat, flashy sport shirt and corduroy pants, peered intently into his microscope. He looked up when Bascom called his name.

"Hi, Bob," he replied tiredly. "Welcome to the Whitney Zoo."

"I'll say! I've never seen this place so busy."

"All 45 beds in the hospital are full, but we're running tests as if we had 100 patients. This place must hold the record for the highest percentage of healthy patients and normal tests in the state. What can I do for you?"

"Have any of the *ad hoc* members talked to you?"

"Only Cohen. I hear Davidson has turned the screws; his guys get you out of his hair or he gets them. My friend," he said concernedly, "get ready for some big-time grief."

"I expected as much," Bascom replied. He stuck his hands in his pockets and leaned back against the workbench. "I'd like to say I'm used to it since I've been in a situation like this before, but I'm not. It wasn't pleasant then and won't be now."

He left the laboratory and walked to the boardroom. Davidson had orchestrated a perfect *opera buffa,* 'comic opera.' Cohen, if anything remained of the spark of integrity he showed before the meeting with Rutledge, could damage Davidson's hope for a perfect scenario. He could never change the finale, however, since his co-panelists would outnumber him by three to one.

When Bascom entered the boardroom, Ted Steele was sitting at the head of the polished oak table. Joe Thompson and George Cohen sat facing John Cody, the incompetent obstetrician, and Linda Stevens. Bascom sat next to Linda.

"As you know," Steele said gravely after a brief period of polite but uncomfortable socializing, "Dr. Davidson has asked us to examine Dr. Bascom's allegations of over-utilization of services, physician incompetence, and over-charging in our ER.

"After a careful and thorough review of Dr. Evans' charts and patient billings, I find no truth to any of those charges," he said, brushing a speck of lint off his jacket's lapel. "In fact," he continued, avoiding Bascom's glare, "the records from September 1st to the 20th are perfectly correct and the billing is right with one minor exception."

Bascom's fingers whitened around his pencil.

"I questioned why Dr. Evans ordered tests for lupus on a man with a rash," Steele continued, referring to a yellow sheet of paper. "As every medical student knows, lupus never presents as a purplish, itchy rash in the groin of a healthy male athlete. The tests, including X-rays, blood and urine cultures, were all negative and, of course, the man had jock-itch."

Bascom's pencil snapped like the blast of a Derringer,

but no one looked in his direction.

"Dr. Stevens," Steele smiled, "would you present your findings?"

"All these records are fine," she said, patting her pile of charts. "I found no unnecessary studies or overcharging."

"Good," Steele said. "Dr. Thompson?"

Joe tugged at his misshapen right earlobe. "Everything's ok," he said softly.

"Thompson," Bascom growled, "you.... Nothing. Excuse the interruption."

John Cody's feminine voice cut through the awkward silence. "Everything's ok for November," he said. "Good, competent work."

Bascom could not know if their responses were a result of incompetence, promises of riches by Davidson, lack of concern about the welfare of their patients, or all three. It made no difference to him since no excuse could counterbalance their mockery of the profession he held sacred.

He lifted several charts from Linda's pile and as he skimmed through them, asked, "have any of you spoken with Dr. Compton or Dr. Volkers about these problems?"

"I spoke with Dr. Compton," Cohen answered with utmost seriousness. "He showed me a pile of X-rays Dr. Evans had ordered on a 4 year-old boy who had fallen off his tricycle. The request said the boy had not hurt his arm and the studies were 'just to be sure there was no fracture.'

"Dr. Compton stressed that Dr. Evans was just being thorough, but he suggested a simple X-ray of the entire arm, instead of X-rays of the shoulder, humerus, elbow, forearm, wrist, and hand, as well as the same X-rays on the other arm for comparison, could have saved a few bucks."

Bascom rubbed a finger back and forth across his closed lips. "Has anybody else spoken with Dr. Compton?" he asked after digesting Cohen's statement.

Joe raised an arm. "I spoke with both Art and Harrison," he said. "They told me everything is fine."

Lies have short legs, Bascom thought as he listened to the fat man, and *pance enormi* "huge bellies."

He rapped his knuckles on the table. "You people are full of crap," he exclaimed. "Excluding George, none of you spoke with anybody other than the pinstriped dwarf in San Francisco to get your orders. My dear pseudoillustrious colleagues, these four charts," he made a show of counting them, "were on Linda's pile, which you heard her say are flawless. The first," he slid it across the table to Cohen, "belongs to a woman with cystitis. For those of you who don't understand medical terminology, it means she burns when she pees, and she pees all the time. Evans X-rayed her spine but didn't order a urine analysis or prescribe medication. She left with the same disease she came in with.

"This," he said, tossing it after the first, "is a 5 year-old boy with pinworms which his mother said she saw squiggling in his stool. Evans ordered a chest X-ray and a blood panel, but never checked his stool and never killed the worms.

"Next, revered colleagues," he continued, his voice trembling with anger, "is a patient who got a skull X-ray for his nose injury. I'm sure you paradigms of the profession know you can't diagnose a broken nose on a skull X-ray because the techniques are too different. If this patient did have a fracture, he never learned about it from this hospital. Moreover, he was exposed to unnecessary radiation and charged more than he would have been had Evans correctly evaluated his injury.

"This last one belongs to a 15 year-old girl who was upset because a dirty old man made an indecent proposal to her. She got a chest X-ray and an electrocardiogram." He tossed the last two charts across the table to join their comrades in a haphazard pile and then scrutinized his colleagues one by one; under his harsh gaze, each avoided his harsh gaze, preferring to examine an invisible artifact on the table in front of him.

"Four patients, four cases of malpractice. Evans is batting 100 percent, but I don't envy his record," he continued. "Covering up his incompetence is terrible dues to pay for membership in Davidson's club."

As Bascom quickly rose from the table, his chair crashed to the floor. "As far as I'm concerned, this farce is adjourned," he growled before leaving the room and slamming the door behind him.

Once in the hallway he thought, *Compton! Is he or is Cohen lying about Evans?* He raced to radiology department, but Art was no longer there.

"When did he leave?" Bascom asked the technician who was jamming X-rays into an overloaded filing cabinet.

"After you did this morning. Never said why," the genial youth said, stepping down from his kick stool.

Bascom leaned against a desk. "Have you noticed an increase in X-rays since the new ER doctors arrived?"

"Sure," the lad answered. "They X-ray everything, especially Evans. I used to get time and a half to sleep before they came along. Now I'm up all night. The X-rays are almost all normal, but it wouldn't make any difference if they weren't," he sniggered. "Evans couldn't find a fracture on an X-ray if there was an arrow pointing to it. We have to recall most of his patients because his readings are wrong."

"Could you pull his X-rays from September 1 to November 30 for me?"

"It'll be a big pile. Do you think you can stop him?"

"Probably not, but it's worth a try. Call me at home when they're ready."

"Ok, Doc" the technician replied. "But don't quit.

Evans and Davidson might not like you, but all the techs do. No one is respected more in this place than you are."

"I doubt Davidson would agree with that statement, but thanks," he said. "Oh, by the way. Is there any politicking between Dr. Compton and Davidson?"

"I'm not sure what you mean by 'politicking,' Doc, but his group is renegotiating its contract with the hospital."

"Thanks again," Bascom replied before leaving the department.

XXIII

The *ad hoc* committee had adjudicated Evans and Davidson innocent of over use and over pricing of laboratory studies, but Bascom knew they were not. Since his colleagues had deliberately covered up a situation that directly harmed the citizens of Whitney, he realized he could no longer rely on them to help him correct the hospital's myriad problems. Even so, he remained optimistic that after his own review of the X-rays, and with the help of governmental watchdogs, he could stop the abuses.

When he answered his telephone the night after the meeting, he was sure it was the technician telling him Evans' films were in a pile that reached the ceiling, waiting for him to review them.

"Bascom here," he said excitedly.

"I can't get your X-rays," the technician replied immediately.

"Why not?"

"You get them, I get fired."

"Who threatened you?"

"I can't help you," he said simply before hanging up.

Bascom slammed at his receiver in its cradle and went into his kitchen. He rinsed a glass from a sink of dirty dishes, filled it with Scotch, and went into his living room. He lit the mesquite logs in his river rock fireplace and then plopped on the couch and put his feet on the coffee table.

The Hippocratic Oath has become an ignoble group protective treaty, he thought as he sipped his drink and watched the yellow and orange flames prance excitedly over the logs.

He closed his eyes and rested his head on the back of the couch. As the warmth of the fire and euphoric effect of the alcohol united to pry open the rusty gates to his childhood memories, he saw himself seated at a table in his high school library, a pimply-faced, rumpled hair teenager poring over Jim Flexner's, *Doctors on Horseback.*

Were his glowing tales about Benjamin Rush, William Beaumont, and Crawford W. Long all lies?

He had not believed they were when he had read the book decades earlier; in fact he was so impressed by his heroes' devotion to medicine, he had vowed to emulate their standards of excellence. Now, in an attempt to take a step towards that goal by simply asking his colleagues to treat patients competently, respectfully, and honestly, he had found himself derided like a leper in a beauty pageant.

Bascom realized his reading and Jesuit education had not prepared him for the realities of this world, and his last fear before the glass fell from his hand and he lapsed into a tormented asleep was that Dr. Davidson's pinstriped crows were going to peck him to death. He knew he could not stop them.

The next morning Bascom transferred Carl Price to a newly arrived physician in town. Since he had decided to resign from the staff, he could no longer care for the boy in the hospital. Martha disagreed with his decision and promised to have Jonas convince him to change his mind.

He was commenting on the cover-up in censurable Italian phrases as he passed Helen's office ten minutes later.

She brought him hot coffee in his favorite cup decorated with Christmas scenes and, sensing his ill humor, put it on his desk and quietly returned to her office.

As he sipped the fragrant brew, he wrote a letter and then called Helen into his *Piccola Repubblica*.

"Please type this for me," he told her, offering the scrap of paper.

She stared at it for a moment before turning it upside down and then sideways. "What language is this?" she grinned.

"Very funny," he said with feigned irritation. "It says, 'Dear Doctor Davidson: From this date, December 5th, I am resigning from WCH because of ethical concerns. I trust you will notify the appropriate departments. Sincerely, blah, blah, blah.' It must go out today."

"Don't do this, Dr. Blah," she pleaded with a weak smile. "You'll need to repay everything the hospital advanced you, and you'll cut off your referrals," she continued. "We'll starve. It happened to Ben Wiggins, but since he was the best doctor in town, he survived."

"You mean I'm not the best?" Bascom replied with feigned indignation.

"Most patients think you are, but even more judge their doctors by the smoke they blow up...somewhere," she replied. Her weak smile did not mask her apprehension.

"Dear boss, until you give them what they want and not what you think or know they need, they'll never appreciate you. Besides, Ben was a multimillionaire and didn't need the money from his practice. You do."

"So they screwed Ben also, eh? Donna told me he lopped off heads with impunity." A void surrounded by wiggly lines appeared in his field of vision, and Helen became headless. Another migraine was beginning.

"She wasn't here to see what was going on. I was, and

it was horrible. When Ben reported Grimes to the state medical society because of the hysterectomies he performed on teenagers, all the other docs with their dirty little consciences thought they were next and tore him apart in the press and in their offices. Gently of course, to avoid lawsuits. None of their accusations or slurs was true, but they raised doubts in the minds of the townspeople. Most transferred to other doctors, and their exodus almost put him out of business.

"Even though we rarely spoke at the time, I asked fat Thompson to help Ben. A word from him would have gone a long way. He laughed in my face. Said he didn't want to lose referrals because he backed a loser, and just stood by and watched.

"Ben was the best doc this town had ever had until you came along. He practiced out of passion, not profit, as you do. And he was too much of an idealist, too naïve to understand how fickle people can be, exactly like you. When the situation had worsened to the point where he was seeing only a couple of patients a day, he started drinking heavily, which I pray you don't do. Adding that to his depression following his son's death, we thought he might commit suicide. Thank god for Evelyn. Had she not been there for him, he probably would have."

Helen sighed and again held up Bascom's note to the light. "Are you sure this is in English?" she asked.

Bascom looked to the door to his office. The hole in his vision hid it from view, *scotoma scintillante* the Italians called it, but it let him see Helen from the corner of his eye.

"Squirting lemon juice on it won't work either," he grimaced. "So Ben's the silent knight! He told me about his son's death because of the drugs Abe prescribed. No wonder those two don't get along."

"They hate each other with a passion. The hospital

took Grimes' side in the state investigation," she said, folding the paper and putting it in her pocket. "It would have cut its own financial throat had it not. After a 10-minute investigation, the inspectors turned up one case where they thought surgery might have been unnecessary, but decided the patient hadn't been harmed. They dropped the investigation, and Ben lost his battle.

"Grimes never forgave him and tried to fire Evelyn, since she was the one who told Ben about the hysterectomies."

And so the pattern repeats itself; Cohen had fired Donna for telling me about Evans.

"I once thought medicine was a noble profession," he commented, "but I was wrong! Anyway, referrals from our patients will keep us alive."

"Don't count on it," she contradicted, vehemently shaking her head. "You're about to find out what this town is like, especially when Davidson lambastes you in the newspapers about the money you'll owe him."

"I already know what this town is like, but there won't be a problem with Davidson. Rutledge and I agreed I'd resign if I didn't like the committee's report, and that's what I'm doing. I won't have to repay a dime." *I would feel better about that agreement if my tape recorder hadn't died.*

"Dream on," Helen chided. "When are you going to start listening to reason?"

"Boy, I thought my mother was tough, but compared to you she was a pussy cat," Bascom replied. He rubbed his chin between his first two fingers, feeling the stubble he missing while shaving that morning. "I also want you to post copies of that letter around the office."

"Is that really necessary?" she asked in an angry but subdued tone.

"Yes, Miss Hyde," Bascom answered. "Now you can

go back to being Secretary Jekyll. And have Phoenix U send us the forms to apply for hospital privileges. We'll admit our patients there."

"Right, Boss."

"One more question. Where is Fran today?"

"She's always late after Tuesday nights."

"Last night was Thursday."

"Not for her. It was a running joke that she always had sex with her husband on Tuesdays. They're divorced now, but he still stops over to her place to revive his spirit. She calls those days 'Tuesdays.' I don't know what they do, but she's exhausted the next day," she explained before returning to her office.

That evening, after the last patient and his staff had left the building, Bascom phoned Donna. Her phone rang a long time before she answered it and yelled, "Don't hang up!" He listened to blaring strains of Coltrane's "Giant Steps" before she came back on the line.

"Sorry," she said. "I was in the shower. Who is this?"

"Bascom."

"Robby! Hi! What's up?"

"I wanted to apologize again for getting you fired."

"Don't let it worry you. How are you?"

"I quit today," he said. He leaned back and put his feet up on the desk.

"You did what?" she asked.

"Quit. The committee's investigation was a whitewash, so I quit."

"I'm not sure you should have."

"Why not?"

"Because instead of disarming the bandits, you'll now be ducking their bullets. And you'll never know when or from which direction they'll arrive. Had you stayed on staff, you could have at least kept an eye on them."

As Evelyn told me Ben had done. "I never thought of it that way, Donna," he replied, scratching his head. "But it's too late now."

"I can't blame you," she replied. "I left because I couldn't take that ER anymore either. If you don't know already, Evans and his buddies are stealing your patients. Before they leave they give them a list of the other providers in town and, after trashing you, insist they go to one of them for follow-up. I tried to redirect a few, but Evans caught me. I guess that's one of the reasons they fired me."

"And we know Thompson is the other. They have a knack for firing competent employees and keeping the trash in that dump."

"Be careful, Robby. They're a mean bunch," Donna warned. "How about a home cooked meal and a shoulder to lean on. I learned to boil water at an early age and can make a pot of it on a moment's notice. It's good for cooking hot dogs or delivering babies."

Bascom laughed. "I'm not interested in either, but I can make tortellini. How about Saturday night?"

"I'll be waiting."

Bascom was locking his office door ten minutes later when Jonas Price tapped him on the shoulder. "Martha told me you've transferred Carl to another doctor," he rued. "You can't. I won't let anybody touch my boy without your supervision."

"His physical therapy has been going well over the last couple of weeks. He'll do fine without me," he replied, putting his key in his pocket. "Dr. Kuhn will do a good job caring for him. But Carl is like a son to me. If my help means that much to you, take him home. I'll stop by your place every day to see him until I'm satisfied I'm not needed any longer."

"We'll always need you. Tell me what do I have to do."

"Sign him out of the hospital and I'll make the arrangements for outpatient therapy."

"Whew! I feel much better now. How do I do that?"

"Ask the nurse to do it. She'll try to scare you with a list of things that'll happen to Carl the minute you take him home, but he'll be fine, I promise you. If they give you a hard time, let me know," Bascom grinned. "Then I'll have one final talk with Davidson."

"I think I can handle it," Jonas laughed.

"Good," he replied. He pulled on the doorknob to make sure it was locked before adding, "now let's go home. I have some running to do."

XXIV

Meteorologists were reporting a January blizzard in New York, but in the warm Arizona desert, where a sweat-shirt and shorts were all Bascom wore to keep warm, birds chirped in the budding mesquite trees and flowers bloomed. Neither fauna nor flora knew the worst was yet to come.

A month had passed since his resignation from the hospital, and although Cohen had not demanded repayment of what he had paid him to leave his heavenly mountaintop for the infernal desert, his colleagues were busy stealing his patients, as Ben Wiggins had predicted and Donna had confirmed. His income, never spectacular even when his office teemed with patients, was falling and he was having trouble paying his bills. Despite the crisis, of which Helen reminded him several times a day, he remained optimistic his patients would return to him when they understood what he was doing for them.

He was walking to his office on that balmy January morning when he saw Linda Stevens and Marty Nevins walking towards him. The pinstriped surgeon opened his mouth as if to speak, but Linda pulled him into the street before he could utter a word. They darted across the road, forcing a pick-up truck to swerve to avoid them, and continued without looking back.

As Bascom continued to his office, he recalled the

tragic story of Ignaz Semmelweis, a Hungarian obstetrician teaching in the Allgemeines Krankenhaus in Vienna in 1847. Childbed fever was killing an alarming number of women giving birth in his hospital, and after careful investigation, he discovered students were performing autopsies and then delivering babies without washing their hands. He had them rinse them in chloride of lime after they left the cadavers, and the mortality rate dropped from 11 to 1 percent.

Semmelweis described his findings in *The Etiology, the Concept, and the Prophylaxis of Childbed Fever,* a copy of which Bascom kept on a shelf alongside other leather-bound tomes in the library in his *baita*. Unfortunately the obstetrician also launched a scathing attack against leading doctors who disagreed with his findings. They considered his affront to their unscientific posturing unpardonable, and their condemnation of his work resulted in his breakdown and death in a mental institution.

To his chagrin, Bascom was learning the medical community had not improved its behavior in the intervening years, and would still eagerly destroy any member who disparaged its invented reputation or decreased its income.

Ben and Evelyn were waiting for him when he arrived in his office. The unsmiling nurse, with downcast eyes and interlocked fingers on her lap, wore a yellow paper gown and sat primly on the examination table. Ben was standing next to her. He was pale with the eyes of a child asking his father if he could save his pet gerbil an automobile had just been run over.

"Well, dear friends," he inquired gaily in an attempt to lighten the oppressive atmosphere, "what brings you in today?"

"I think there's something wrong with Ev," Ben said, resting a shaking hand on his consort's shoulder. "She isn't as lively as usual."

Bascom pulled his chair from under his desk and straddled it. "What's wrong, Ev?" he asked.

"My muscles ache and I've lost 10 pounds since the wedding," she said softly. "Walking is a chore and I can't drive my new car because I don't have the strength to push the pedals anymore."

Bascom asked her several questions and then examined her. The woman's general examination was normal, but the wasting away of her leg muscles alarmed him. He helped her from the table and asked her to stand on her toes. Despite her best effort, she could not lift her heel more than a fraction of an inch before falling back against the table. After her second failed attempt, the two men lifted her onto it.

When she settled down, Bascom opened a safety pin and gently touched its point to her ankle.

"Ouch," Evelyn said, pulling away.

"Sorry," he apologized before going to his desk to jot notes on her chart. "I'm finished tormenting you."

"Well, what do you think? Is it serious?" Wiggins asked softly, wringing his knobby hands.

"It's too early to be certain," Bascom replied, turning to his friends. "Minor diseases sometimes mimic major ones. Suppose we check for them before we jump to worrisome conclusions?"

"So you don't think it's serious?" Evelyn asked, tightening her gown around her thin waist.

"Maybe not," he replied gently. But he already knew it was.

"Botsum's right," Wiggins reveled. "You'll be fine, honey, and the lab tests will agree."

Bascom suspected the old physician knew the diagnosis and was simply bolstering his wife's spirits, but he could not be sure. The possibility of a remission of the illness existed, and he preferred to wait to see if Evelyn's symptoms worsened before naming her disease.

He drew her blood, told her he would contact her with the results, and excused himself so she could dress.

As he exited the room, Helen was in the hallway, holding a stack of hospital bills she had collected from disgruntled patients.

"More unwanted information?" he asked, taking them from her.

"I'm only the messenger, but since you've got an hour before your next patient, I thought you might like some interesting reading," she replied.

He took the bills into his office, put his feet up on his desk, skimmed through them, and decided the time had come to warn his patients and the entire town that a trip to the ER for anything except a life-threatening emergency was foolhardy.

He typed the article on his computer and had Helen mail copies of it to the Phoenix *Globe*, to the Governor, to the Arizona Health Care Cost Containment System, to the Medical Association, and to Medicare fraud investigators.

XXV

"I can't do this, Donna, believe me."

"You can, Robby," shc insistcd. "Oncc you'rc in thc saddle, it'll come back to you."

"I rode once," he protested, "and I almost broke my fool neck."

"Big baby," she taunted. "Remember when I said you'd have better luck if we rode together."

"No."

"It was at my house."

"The first night at your house? I remember being in the saddle that night," Bascom said wryly, "but horses had nothing to do with it."

"I hope you last a bit longer this time," she laughed before humming the theme from *High Noon*.

The SUV groaned and shook as it traveled over the washboard road leading to a small ranch a few miles south of Whitney. When they arrived, an old cowboy with a large abdomen and bowed legs was standing in front of his trailer home. He waved as they pulled up in a cloud of dust.

"Ready?" Donna asked.

"Ready as I'll never be," Bascom responded anxiously. "Let's go then," she ordered. They exited the SUV and Donna ran to the cowboy and gave him a hug.

"Welcome back," he said. "It's been a while."

"I've been busy," she replied as Bascom walked up to them.

"Nat," she said, "this is Dr. Bascom. He wants to ride Tuffy."

The cowboy studied Bascom's sport jacket and penny loafers while rubbing a gnarled finger over his lips. "'City slicker' don't come close to describin' you," he said. "I'm not sure Tuffy is for you."

"He's been on a horse before, he just dresses funny," she assured him.

"Ok," he said reluctantly. "We can get an ambulance here in a few minutes."

He led them to a corral where a bay horse was standing by the rail and a huge palomino stallion was chewing hay in its center. The gelding whinnied as Donna wrapped her arms around his neck and kissed the white star on his forehead. He rested his head on her shoulder until she broke away.

"This is 'Killer,'" she said. "He sounds like a bad guy, but he's gentle as a lamb. He used to be a racehorse. Tuffy, over there," she pointed to the palomino, "used to work rodeos until he got too old. Now he just eats Nat out of house and home."

The horse looked up, snorted, and then returned to his lunch.

"Did you see the terror in his eyes," Bascom said. "Listen, I think I hear his knees knocking."

"Those are your knees, Robby," Donna laughed. She entered the corral, slipped a halter over Tuffy's head, and led him to the hitching rail.

"See how gentle he is," she said, patting the beast's massive neck.

"With those huge feet he'd make a perfect tractor for a Tibetan farmer."

Nat saddled the horse and he held his head while Bascom jammed a loafer into a stirrup. After he tried unsuccessfully three times to mount the gigantic horse, Nat whispered, "t'other side, Doc."

"I was just checking to see if you were alert," he replied. He passed widely behind the animal and mounted from the other side as Donna tittered like a schoolgirl.

After Nat turned him loose, Bascom pulled hard on Tuffy's reins and kicked him in the flanks.

"Ok, Thunderbolt," he commanded, "mush!"

"The brakes or the gas, Doc," Nat suggested. "Not both."

Bascom released the reins and kicked Tuffy hard in the flanks. This time he snorted and walked over to Killer.

The great, small screen heroes of the past rode smooth as silk in their saddles, but Bascom, despite his determination, bounced in his as he trotted behind Donna and Killer to Frazier Wash. A dense chaparral of false lilac and manzanita trees, whose frosted gray green leaves seemed spray painted on tight-barked purplish stems, lined its sandy banks. A flock of vultures, rising from a hidden lunch, glided overhead.

"I love this area, Robby. It always makes me want to canoodle after a hard ride."

"Just the thought is stimulating," he replied, "I mean the canoodling. This horse doesn't lope."

"Oh yes he does," she insisted. She tossed a leg over her saddle, slid to the ground, and walked to Tuffy. With her back to Bascom, she pulled a piece of paper from her pocket and held it to the rebel's roving eye, moving an index finger sternly from the paper to his nose.

"Capito?" she asked firmly. Tuffy whinnied.

"He'll lope now," Donna said with an air of mystery. She mounted Killer and yelled, "*Go*!"

Killer flew towards the horizon as Tuffy reared up, flashed his hooves in the air, and took up the challenge. Bascom hung onto the saddle horn while one foot frantically searched for a stirrup.

Tuffy thundered past Donna as Bascom struggled to pull himself upright in the saddle. The steed roared down the wash, sand and rock flying from his golden hooves, for half a mile before slowing to a walk with sweat foaming on his massive neck and chest. Donna caught up with them moments later.

"I told you he'd lope," she crowed.

"Damnation!" Robert exclaimed. "What did you show him?"

She pulled a wrinkled photo from her pocket. "This," she grinned, handing him a picture of a hamburger.

XXVI

The inhabitants of the desert town on Route 85 to Mexico responded with mixed reaction to Bascom's expose' of the inner workings of their local hospital in the Phoenix *Globe*. His patients loved it and many of them called his office to tell him so. Davidson and Cohen were less enthusiastic and would soon tell him how much they disliked his literary skills.

A few weeks after his article appeared in the press, a certified letter arrived for Bascom at the post office. He waited on a long line in the stifling hot room until a sweaty clerk had him sign a receipt before handing him the letter. He hoped it held a check for his back rent.

He exited the post office banging the long envelope on the palm of his hand as he walked to the curb. He sat on a wooden bench and tore open the envelope.

"Dear Doctor Bascom: (the letter began)

"Whitney Community Hospital has referred your recent request for what you consider 'back rent' to this office for reply. Rather than the Hospital being indebted to you for your alleged rent, because of your resignation from the medical staff, among other matters, you are now obligated to repay all funds previously advanced to you under your agreement with the Hospital.

"Said amount of $98,975.20 is now due and payable in full.

"We hope to settle this matter amicably, and that you and the Administration can agree on payment terms for the amount you owe, without further involvement of our office.

"Sincerely,
"William North, Atty."

Bascom crumpled the letter in his fist. *So this is the way we tear up our agreement and go our separate ways, eh, Rutledge?* But he knew he had brought Davidson's wrath upon himself. His lawyer's letter was not a response to his request for back rent; it was a reprimand for his expose' in the *Globe*.

He and Rutledge had agreed he would leave the hospital if the *ad hoc* committee had seconded his allegations and Davidson refused to correct the situation or if the committee had disagreed with his complaints. As part of the bargain, he had agreed to stop harassing Davidson. He had broken that promise by writing his expose'. North's letter was the San Franciscan's first step before filing a lawsuit against him, and it was exactly what Ben Wiggins had predicted he would do.

He drove home and penciled a response to North on a scrap of paper on his butcher-block kitchen table and then went to the bathroom to wash up. As the water ran in the sink, he studied his face in the mirror. His unkempt blond hair was now almost shoulder length and curled at his neck and his tired eyes sunk into black circles under his furrowed brow.

His emotional toil had made him old before his time.

Walk away from this suicide mission while you still can, before you end up like Semmelweis, chained to a wall and beaten to death by guards you pissed off.

As he stuck his head under faucet and poured a pine-scented shampoo onto his hair, he remembered a line from Robert Frost's famous poem, *The Road Not Taken*: "I took the one less traveled by, / And that has made all the difference."

Bascom understood why his road was "less traveled." Who would want to walk down a lonely road with signs pinned to his back that said: "ostracized," "pariah," or "recluse"?

He remembered the first was pinned on him when he and Lance had unionized the house staff in their hospital years ago. It was unheard at the time, since doctors never struck, even if it were to force their hospitals to improve the way it treated their patients.

His colleagues at the time had called him, "DQS – Don Quixote in Scrubs." He felt it insulting, but had accepted the title with dignified resignation. His present dilemma was worse. If his colleagues continued their assault on his reputation, he would soon earn the worst title he could imagine: bankrupt loser.

Taking the one less traveled has made all the difference, Mr. Frost, but it's not the one I'd hoped for. Now tell me how to get off it.

He dried his hair and hung the wet towel on the rack by the sink.

Evelyn, ever more morose over her disabling, slowly progressive disease, arrived in his office in a wheelchair the next day. Ben had attached red crepe streamers to its handles, had interwove colored strips through its spokes, and had clipped playing cards onto the fender so they clicked against the spokes of the wheel as it turned. He pushed her into the examining room with the pomp of a toreador entering a bullring.

"Hello, dear people," Bascom said as he entered the room a minute later. He pulled his chair from under his desk and straddled it in front of Evelyn. "How are you today?"

"We're fine, Batson," Ben said, adjusting his toupee. "Do you get it yet?"

"Get what, Ben?" *If he doesn't stop asking me that question, I'll wring his scrawny neck. And my name is Bascom. B-A-S-C-O-M!*

"Fran told us the laboratory tests were all normal."

"I apologize for not calling you myself, but she's conscientious and wanted you to know right away."

"I'm glad she did," Ben replied. "Waiting for test results can be nerve-wracking."

"You're right. Sometimes we forget how much our patients worry about them, since they always presume the worst.

"How do you feel today, Evelyn?" he asked, turning to the wan woman in the wheelchair.

"Better," she said wearily. "I'm stronger and not as tired as usual, but I don't have the energy to walk today. I wish I could regain some weight. All my clothes hang like sacks."

"It's good to hear you're feeling better," Bascom smiled. But he knew Evelyn could not be stronger and too weak to walk at the same time. She was fighting her disease with optimism, an effective weapon against the relentless destruction of her nervous system. It was a far better and safer therapy than anything he could offer her.

"I think so too, Beetle," Ben added. "Do we need to do

anything else?"

"Just make sure Ev eats a balanced diet and exercises as often as she can. It'll do more for her than all the pills in the world. And schedule monthly appointments, even more frequent if you like, until we solve this problem."

Bascom rose and rested his hand on Evelyn's shoulder. "We'll beat this together, Ev. Call whenever you need me."

"We will, thanks. Vroom, Vroom!" Ben said as he revved up the wheelchair and screeched out of the room with the cards clicking a brisk staccato against its spokes.

As Bascom was updating her chart, Helen told him Dr. Frank was calling from Phoenix. He went to his office phone, spoke briefly to the physician, and agreed to meet him that same afternoon.

Douglas Frank was chairman of the Health and Consumer Affairs Board in Phoenix, and as soon as Bascom arrived in his office in an old building in the center of the city, his nurse showed him into the doctor's private office.

"Welcome," Dr. Frank wheezed. He was short of breath and spoke slowly. "Can I offer you something to drink?"

"No, thanks," he replied. Frank nodded and his nurse left the room, softly closing the door behind her.

"Have a seat," he wheezed, pointing to a Chippendale chair in front of his antique desk. "Your newspaper article about ERs was interesting. Has anyone contacted you about it?"

"A few patients did. The hospital owner went through the roof, the Governor and the Arizona Health Care Cost Containment System didn't, and the Arizona Medical Association said 'thanks but no thanks.' Medicare said it was interested, but not today."

"Typical responses from bungling Republican politicians. Poor care and overcharging are rampant in this coun-try," he scowled. "We've formed a committee to control the problem here before the government takes over and screws up everything.

"Would you like to testify at our next meeting?"

"Sure," Bascom answered excitedly.

"It's in a couple of weeks." Frank handed him a card. "Call the secretary of HCAB for details. You'll have to ex-cuse me now; I have an appointment with my cardiologist."

XXVII

Lightning flashed in a black sky as Bascom drove into the parking lot at St. Paul's Hospital in Phoenix two weeks later. A torrential rain was arriving from the southeast, and he wished he were home listening to the soft music of Stan Getz in front of a cozy fire.

He entered the old facility and meandered though its high-ceilinged corridors until he found the domed conference room. Art Compton was at an *hors d'oeuvres* laden table in the corner of the room talking to a young woman with a microphone protruding like a lone antler from the side of her head. Bascom walked up to the arthritic radiologist and tapped on his shoulder.

"Well, whom do we find here?" he asked sarcastically.

"Hi, Bob," Compton coughed, choking on a cracker. "I heard you were coming tonight."

"Wow! And you came anyway. I'm surprised. At Davidson's meeting George said you didn't tell him Evans ordered unnecessary X-rays. Who was lying?"

"I, er, he, he must have misunderstood."

"I'm sure. Is your new contract with Davidson as you wanted?"

"I gotta do something," he replied sheepishly before leaving the room.

Bascom sampled as many of the *hors d'oeuvres* as possible before a gavel rapped behind him.

"Everyone to their seats, please," the middle-aged, obese chairperson ordered from the large table in the center of the room.

"I'm Marvin Adelsohn," he explained, removing an unlit cigar from his dusky lips and placing it in an ashtray after the attendees took their places. "I'm acting chairman tonight because Dr. Frank died of a heart attack three days ago."

After the shock of the momentous news passed, he turned to the black, muscular individual sitting next to Bascom and said, "Dr. Norman Jefferies, welcome. How are things in the ER at our University Hospital?"

"Fine, Marvin. That's sad news about Doug. I wish he were here," he replied in a derisive east coast accent. It was obvious he and Adelsohn were not friends.

The chairman shrugged and turned to his casually dressed guest.

"And you are Dr. Bascom, I presume?" he asked.

"Yes."

"Dr. Frank showed me your article. I'm interested in hearing your comments."

"Thank you, Dr. Adelsohn," Bascom replied, clasping his hands on the table. "I wrote it to warn my patients that doctors in Whitney's ER routinely order studies unrelated to their diseases, and that our hospital charges 10 times more for those tests than you do here at St. Paul's. The sad result is a child's simple ear infection can cost $700 and chest pain can cost $20,000, making care impossibly expensive for our farm workers."

Adelsohn tapped his cigar with his finger. "I'm sure you understand that because of 'defensive medicine,' we run all the tests we can," he explained. "I always order precautionary studies on my patients to avoid lawsuits in this litigious world. And I'm sure you understand that what hospitals charge is their business, not ours."

"Dr. Adelsohn," Bascom countered, "lawyers don't file malpractice suits because doctors don't perform enough tests. They sue doctors who misdiagnose or mistreat their clients, no matter how many tests they order.

"'Running all the tests,' especially when they aren't relevant to the patient's disease or when a doctor misinterprets their results, is foolish and wasteful."

"You're entitled to your opinion, Doctor, but I disagree with it," he replied coldly with a rap of his gavel.

"What do you think about all this, Norm?"

"I agree with Dr. Bascom," he replied. "Too many doctors, in and out of the ER, order excessively. The situation is disgusting and worsening."

"I disagree with you too," Adelsohn said with a louder rap of his gavel. "Well, let's take a break," he added, looking to the buffet table.

"There are only a few *hors d'oeuvres* left, so I'll give you 15 minutes to finish them and then we need to discuss important business."

Twenty minutes later Adelsohn recalled the meeting to order. After a few minutes, Bascom realized he was no longer needed or wanted and left the room. Norm Jefferies followed closely on his heels.

"Thanks for the help," he said as they walked down the hallway together.

"Those who count in this world don't want to here the truth," Jefferies replied bitterly. "Many reasons why, but none are ethical."

"I figured as much, but came anyway. Do you know Albert Evans?"

"Unfortunately I do," he sneered. "He was one of my residents until I threw him out of my program. He runs a million tests, can't interpret any of their results, and hasn't a clue how to treat the occasional disease or injury he diagnoses correctly. I think he finished his training in a small hospital in San Francisco."

"That's interesting," Bascom replied. "The guy who bought our hospital, Davidson, is from there."

"Simon Davidson?"

"Yes."

"He makes Evans look brilliant. They pulled his license 10 years ago. I heard he buys up hospitals and makes lots of money when he resells them."

"I wish he were out of the hospital business too," Bascom added ruefully. "As long as the Adelsohns of the world run the clean-up programs, we'll never get rid of roaches like Evans and Davidson."

"It's all about money," Jefferies shrugged, "The tons we spend don't guarantee the sick will get competent care, just expensive care. The Davidsons of the world get rich by manipulating the system.

"There are good doctors who can work in this broken system, but many are discouraging their children from going to medical school," he said, shaking his head.

"Yet we need to continue to correct the problems," Bascom replied. "By the way, do you know Donna Franklyn?"

"Best and toughest nurse we've ever had. When she gives an order, nurses and doctors follow it."

"She gave me that impression when we first met."

"I know. She told me about that episode with the Mexican. She compares everyone here to you. Her favorite line is, 'if Bob Bascom were here, he'd kick your butt for doing that.' You must be damn good. My assistant director is leaving soon. Why not join us? I could use you."

"Perhaps. I have to resolve a few problems in Whitney

first," Bascom replied.

"Let me know. Anyway I'm sure we'll be seeing each other again," Jefferies said, "since we're involved in something that's attracting much public interest."

"I'm sure we will too."

"The New Yorker in me loves a fight," he added. "If you ever need my help, give me a call."

"I will," Bascom replied.

After a handshake, the physicians went their separate ways.

XXVIII

"Could you do me a favor?" Helen asked Bascom on March 15th. It was payday and he looked up from the check he was signing. His gray-haired secretary was in the doorway next to a thin, neatly dressed man in his late twenties. Their facial features were almost identical.

"What?"

"Phillip, has a sore throat and fever," she said. "Would you please take a look at him?"

"Sure. How bad is it?" he asked, walking over to the young man.

"An't swallow," he gurgled.

"Come with me."

Bascom led him into an examining room and had him sit on the table. He took a tongue depressor from the shelf above it and gently inserted it into the young man's mouth.

"That's exciting," he said as he shined his penlight onto swollen, pus-filled tonsils. He tossed the blade into the trashcan and took his otoscope from the shelf.

"Let's look at your ears now," he said. As he turned Phillip's head to the left, goose bumps appeared on his arms. His right earlobe was tucked up into itself. It was identical to Joe Thompson's.

This is the fat man's son!

"It's simple tonsillitis," he said as he replaced the otoscope in its charging base. "Penicillin should solve the problem, if you're not allergic to it."

"Not," Phillip mumbled.

"Do you prefer a shot or tablets?"

"Taglets."

"I you can't swallow them, come back for the shot."

Phillip nodded.

Bascom wrote a prescription and offered it to the lad, but Helen grabbed it.

"Phil," she ordered, "go home and rest. I'll pick this up at the drugstore and will be along soon."

"Anks," he smiled before leaving the office.

"You know, don't you?" she asked when they were alone.

"Yes."

"Joe was the 'Prince of the Town,'" she explained, tearing the wrinkled paper from the examination table. She balled it up and deposited it in the trashcan.

"I loved Joe until he left me for Carol." she continued. "A year after they married, he told me he intended to leave her. We met secretly a few times and I got pregnant. It was wrong, but I was young and believed his lies. All that bastard ever does is lie.

"Joe denied he was the father, of course, and I raised Phillip on my own. He never paid me a cent of child support and it was tough at times. What made it more unbearable was the title a few members of my church gave me."

"What does Phillip do?"

"He's a scientist at Scripps."

"Wow! He's obviously intelligent or he wouldn't be there. Stop beating up on yourself for a mistake you made as a girl; you've made the best of a bad situation and raised a fine young man," Bascom replied. "Be proud of him and be grateful he's better than his father."

"I am," she replied. She rose from the table, gave him a quick hug and left the office, wiping her eyes along the way.

Bascom replaced the paper on the examining table before writing a note on Phillip's chart. It was then he noticed the date: March 15th, the ides of March. The date Julius Caesar was assassinated at the foot of Pompey's statue in the temple of Venus in Rome in 44 B.C. It was also the date on which his beloved Cristina had died two years earlier.

I still miss you, Cris.

He wrote "no charge" on the slip clipped to the front of the chart. He stuck his pen in his shirt pocket and brought Phillip's record to Helen for filing.

"No charge?" she asked.

"No."

"He's got insurance."

"I don't charge friends or immediate families of friends," he shrugged. "It's a rule I'll never change."

"Too bad our suppliers aren't as generous," Helen replied. "Ev's in room two. She looks bad, so smile when you go in."

"I will," Bascom replied. He drew happy lines on the sides of his mouth with his fingers as he turned down the hallway.

"Ev!" he exclaimed gaily, entering her room. "Nice to see you. How do you feel today?"

"I can't walk," the frail figure replied from her festooned wheelchair. "Thank goodness I have Ben." The old man rested his knobby hand on her shoulder and she rubbed her fingers over his.

"Let's see how you're doing today," Bascom said as he knelt in front of Evelyn to examine her legs.

He felt her sorrowful eyes boring into him as he palpated her calf muscles. He knew she was trying to decide if he knew she was worsening as fast as she knew she was.

"Do you need to run any more tests?" she muttered. The diffuse twitching and increased withering of her legs answered her question. Bascom knew she was dying and no test could change that.

"Not today, Evelyn," he responded evenly.

"Do you know the diagnosis yet, Bob?" Wiggins stammered. Bascom ignored his friend's question. He would have told Evelyn, but she had not asked him. He was certain Ben already knew the diagnosis, since he was too astute a physician not to have known. He would give him time to accept Evelyn's fate.

"Just make sure Ev eats a balanced diet and exercises," he replied. "Even a few minutes a day will keep her joints limber."

"There are no miracle pills?" Evelyn asked.

"None that won't harm you. *Primum non nocere* 'first do no harm' is one of my rules. I don't want your cure to be worse than your disease."

"I believe that too," Ben agreed. "We'll wait a while longer, won't we, honey?" he asked before kissing her on the cheek. "You'll get better. This is just a bad virus. We won't let it get us down."

"If you say so, darling," she replied through quivering lips.

"See you again next month, Bimbo," Ben said as he yelled, "Ole!" and pushed the wheelchair out of the room. As he wrote a note on her chart, he rued her evaluations had deteriorated into a mere recording of the agonizingly slow demise of a friend about whom he cared deeply. He vowed he would be at her side when she died, but he dreaded the moment.

XXIX

Bascom sat alone in his office reviewing his monthly statistics on a gloomy, quiet afternoon when not one patient had called for an appointment. His work had been decreasing steadily since his resignation from the hospital, and it was no longer rare for him to pass an entire morning doing Italian crosswords at his desk, or an afternoon puttering in his garden.

His loyal patients referred their friends and relatives to him, but they were few and often poor. He treated many of them for free. Helen had tried to convince him to charge a small fee to help cover his overhead, but he would not hear of it.

"I've never charged the impoverished," he would shrug whenever she suggested it. "I can't charge them now simply to arrive at some arbitrary income."

"But maybe a test or something extra on those that can pay?"

"No," Bascom insisted, shaking his head. "I make my living by charging my patients only what they need to get well. I don't need to 'run all the tests' to make certain my diagnosis is correct."

"True, but nobody in this town has charged $5 for an office visit since Taft was president," she chided.

Several days later Tom Whitethroat was sitting on the examining table breathing into an oxygen mask when Bascom entered the room. The 58 year-old half-Indian had suffered from repeated attacks of asthma and pneumonia over the years and his deeply scarred lungs struggled to keep him alive.

"Hi, Doc," he said between gasps. "I got... problem... hospital."

"I'm not sure I want to hear it, Tom," Bascom said as he prepared an inhalant to clear the man's asthma. He attached the canister to the mask on his patient's face and then sat at his desk.

"Since you're determined to tell me, be brief."

"... minute," he said as he nosily inhaled the medication. He took several deep breaths and then smiled as his asthma started to clear. "Thanks, Doc," he said. "You're a lifesaver.

"I spoke with a tech at WCH about the lung studies you suggested," he explained slowly. "He wanted a written order. When I told him you were my doc, he said he'd call Abe Grimes for the ok. The tests cost $495, so I called St. Paul's in Phoenix. They wanted $45! Can you believe it?"

"You would have surprised me if you told me WCH was cheaper," Bascom replied.

"I'm glad I listened to you," Tom continued, his voice muffled by the mask. "You're the reason I'm still alive. Last year Dr. Grimes told me I had two months to live and asked me to make sure I paid my bill before then."

"You'll be fine," he laughed. "I won't let you die until after you pay my bill. So take all the time you need. You may leave when you've finished your treatment. Do you have enough medication?"

"I could use another inhaler."

"Ask Fran for one. I think I have a few free samples

left."

He returned to his office where Helen sitting in a chair holding a letter. "Mrs. Reyes wants to know if she should sign this, Bob," she said handing it to him.

He sat behind his desk and unfolded the missive.

"Dear Parents, (it began)

"To better serve you and your family, Whitney Hospital is setting up a 'Treatment Permission for Minors Program.' This is to obtain your permission to treat your child during an emergency.

"By law the ER doctor needs consent before treating a minor during an emergency. Without it a delay would be unavoidable while the hospital searches for a parent or legal guardian. This could have serious consequences for your child.

"Participation in this program will let us treat him in an emergency.

"Sincerely,
"George Cohen."

"Damn these lying people!" Bascom said, tossing the letter onto his desk. "The law guarantees care in a true emergency, Helen. The ER doc doesn't need to contact anyone before he can save a life. They're simply frightening parents into signing a document that will allow them to treat a runny nose, with blood tests, X-rays and anything else they can think of, without the parent's prior consent or even knowledge of what they're doing to his child.

"Why is the almighty dollar so important that they have to frighten people to get it?" He ran a hand through his hair before interlocking it with its mate on his abdomen.

"There's more," she said.

"I can't wait," he grumbled.

"WCH was on the Spanish station this morning warning parents their children could die if they didn't sign up."

"Damn!" he growled before mumbling a few uncomplimentary Italian phrases. Helen covered her ears and quickly left the office.

As he pondered the first two complaints for the day, Fran told him Mr. Purcell was waiting to see him in surgery. When they entered his room, the 50 year-old was lying on the table with his foot propped up on a cushion. He said, "hi," then lamented about the ER and handed a wad of bills to Bascom, including one for a urinalysis they had never performed, "unless they got it out of my arm," he griped.

Bascom reviewed them and realized the hospital had discovered a billing loophole. Doctors ordered blood panels because a machine can perform twelve tests more economically than a technician can perform one. Plus it's faster than writing the names of each of the twelve tests on an order sheet. This means a sugar level will diagnose diabetes, but since a panel costs the same as the single test, a doctor can evaluate his patient's kidneys and liver for free. It was one of the few bargains left in medicine.

Evans had ordered a blood panel, but the hospital, charging each test individually, had billed Mr. Purcell $300 instead of $25.

"Why did you go to the ER?" Bascom asked, returning the papers to his patient.

"To have that thingy in my heel removed," he replied. "I couldn't walk."

"Is that why Dr. Evans ordered all these tests?"

"Yes. He said he was the best doctor in town because

he was so thorough."

"He could order every test in the world, and it wouldn't make...." Bascom shook his head. He had been warning his patients for months about the ER, but they continued going there for problems he could easily treat in his office.

"I'd ask for a refund for the urinalysis they never did," Bascom suggested as he examined the wart.

"I will," the patient replied. "I should have listened to you, but I thought your newspaper article was an exaggeration. Now I know it wasn't. I won't go back there unless I have a real emergency."

"Have you ever had one of these before?" Bascom asked, scraping his fingernail over the top of the cauliflower-like lesion buried in the skin.

"No."

"It's a plantar wart," he explained as he took the anesthetic filled syringe Fran was offering him. "It's a nuisance, but nothing more.

"Do you have any allergies?"

"Only to needles," the man winced.

"Then this is the worst part," he said as he injected the anesthetic into the wart. He withdrew the needle and waited for the drug to take effect before selecting a curette from his instrument stand.

"You'd get a painful scar if I cut this out, but you won't if I just scoop it out of its nest," he said, inserting the instrument into the wart. With several quick twists of his wrist, he deftly removed the growth and put it on a towel on his instrument stand. He pressed a square of gauze over the blood welling up from the wound.

"Are you ok, Mr. Purcell?"

"I hardly felt a thing."

"Good. Fran," he said, "dress this and tell Mr. Purcell how to care for his wound." She put a finger on a corner of the gauze, allowing Bascom to remove his.

"There's no need to return unless you have a problem. Any questions?" The patient shook his head and Bascom stormed to the telephone in his office.

"You thought this war was over, Davidson?" he said as he dialed the State Comptroller's Office in Phoenix. "We're not even close to signing a peace treaty."

A man answered the phone, and for fifteen minutes Bascom described the scalping that occurred daily at the institution on Apache Lane.

"I can't help you, Doctor," the man replied. "The hospital can charge what it wants for its services."

"Do its ER doctors have the right to order tests that have nothing at all to do with the patient's disease, and then bill the state for them at an inflated cost?"

"I'm sorry, I still can't help you," he repeated.

"And I'm sorry I wasted your time," Bascom said irately. He slammed the receiver into its nest and called Helen into his office.

"Take a letter, please," he ordered.

"I'm ready, Boss," she replied, pulling a pad from her pocket.

He dictated a letter to the Joint Commission for Hospital Accreditation and told her to mail it with a copy of the "Treatment Permission for Minors Program" proposal. Then, from the bottom drawer of his desk, he took out a new folder labeled "Ripley's Believe It or Not, Medical Division, Whitney, Arizona," and handed it to her.

"Add copies to this file," he ordered.

Next he wrote an article to the Phoenix *Globe* and Whitney *Times* warning patients about Davidson's new billing protocols and price lists. He was reviewing the article when Fran appeared in his doorway.

"Patient, Bob," she said with a sinister grin. "She'll

make up for the bad news you received today, I promise."

"Um. I'll bet," he replied unenthusiastically. He rose from his chair and walked to her room. A middle-aged woman holding her shoe in her hand smiled at him when he entered.

"What is your problem, Mrs. Voight?"

"I stepped on a tack and came in for a tetanus shot," she explained, offering her shoe to him. He examined the quaintly perfumed article and noted the tack had slightly pushed up but not penetrated the shoe's inner surface. He then examined her foot.

"Mrs. Smith," he said, "the tack never entered your foot."

"Oh, I know, Doctor!" she exclaimed, aghast at the thought. "But my mother told me to get a tetanus shot whenever I stepped on a rusty nail."

He smiled at the thought of vaccinating the shoe, but just explained the meaning of the phrase and sent her on her way without charging for the visit.

XXX

A week after writing to the Joint Commission seeking its opinion on WCH's illegal "Treatment Permission for Minors Program," Bascom sat at his desk and read its short, maddening response: "We can't comment on the ethics or legality of the Permission Card."

"Isn't anyone responsible for anything anymore?" he wondered. He jammed the missive back into its envelope and called the Commission's office in Phoenix.

"Mr. Fry," he told the voice on the other end of the line, "WCH wants to run kids through its expensive mill and not have to worry about their parents' complaints when they get the bill."

"You're right, they are."

"So what are you going to do about it?"

"Nothing."

"Isn't it your responsibility to keep hospitals in line?"

"Talk to your medical society."

"What does it have to do with this?"

"Sorry."

"Does everybody in this world wear a pinstriped suit?" Bascom shouted as he slammed down the phone. Helen rushed into his office.

"What's wrong now?" she asked, puzzled by the outburst.

"Nothing a permanent return to Italy wouldn't cure," he replied, angrily banging his fist on his desk. "Davidson invents a scam a day and I can't stop any of them."

"Give it up, Bob," Helen pleaded. "This crusade has aged you ten years in two. I can't stand to see you so nervous and irritable. I wasn't happy when you resigned from the hospital, but I accepted it because I thought it would make you feel better. I was wrong; you're worse now than ever."

"Thanks, for your concern, Mum, but I'd like to be alone," he answered crisply, ignoring her admonition as a stubborn child would his mother's warning that a sharp stick could put out your eye.

Helen returned to her office and he read the rest of the responses to his exposé of medical swindles. NBC wrote, "no thanks." *New West Magazine* said the same but more succinctly.

"What a country," he complained, tossing the replies in the trash. "A movie star's sex life makes the front page of every newspaper in the union, yet corrupt hospitals and unfit doctors are screwing millions of patients a year, and that doesn't get a line of print."

Helen knocked on his door as he was massaging his temples.

"Want to talk to a reporter?" she asked cautiously.

"No," he replied. He had no wish to talk to anyone, especially a reporter since he instinctively distrusted them, but Davidson's lawyer's request for $100,000 hung over him like a Guillotine and he was curious to know if it was the reason for the interview.

"He's local," she insisted.

"Show him in."

She stepped back from the doorway, allowing an underweight, pimply-faced young man to enter the office. His

Mohawk haircut consisted of a series of blue tepees standing in a line down the middle of his scalp. Two silver earrings pierced his right earlobe and the tail of a lightning bolt tattoo stretched from his shirt collar to his left ear.

"I'm Charles Flemming from the Whitney *Times*," he stated politely, standing in front of the desk, "and I'd like to ask you some questions."

"As long as they're not personal," Bascom replied. "Have a seat."

Flemming placed his camera on the floor and straightened a listing tepee to vertical before sitting in front of the desk. He took a spiral pad from his hip pocket.

"Haven't I seen you someplace before," Bascom asked.

"At the hospital board meeting. Dave Olsen asked me to come and to bring some friends," he agreed. "That was quite a show you put on."

"It wasn't a show," Bascom replied heatedly.

"Sorry," Flemming said. "I meant that in a good sense. You had them flubbing lines like the poor actors they are. I spoke with Mr. Cohen about his billing codes you described in your article," he continued, thumbing through his notes. "He told me, 'it's possible we overpriced some services, but we're correcting that.'

"He explained the lung studies cost more here because his equipment allows for more comprehensive testing than at other hospitals, and because it's a private institution not supported by government subsidies other hospitals use to keep prices down."

"Baloney," Bascom interrupted. "I can diagnose most lung problems with a spirogram and a blood gas. Performing a full battery of tests on every patient who breathes funny benefits only WCH, which <u>is</u> supported in large part by local tax dollars. Besides, St. Paul's in Phoenix is private and it charges 1/10th what Davidson does. WCH breaks down its blood panels into individual tests so it can bill $300 instead of the $30 it advertises."

"Is that illegal?" Charlie asked, scribbling on his pad.

"Is 'bait and switch' illegal?"

"I guess so. Anything else, Doc?" he asked, looking up from his notes.

"Unfortunately, there is," he said, pushing the Joint Commission's letter and Cohen's "Treatment Permission" letter across his desk.

Flemming skimmed them. "Can I have these?"

"You may borrow them. I'll fine you 25 cents a day if you don't return them in two weeks."

"No problem," he said, slipping them into his pocket. "Thanks for the interview," he added before picking up his camera and exiting the office.

Several days later Flemming's article appeared on the front page of the *Times*, and Bascom summarized it to Helen after dropping the newspaper on her cluttered desk. "George says he'll treat any patient needing emergency care without a consent form, and he'll charge for a panel as a panel. Think he'll keep his word?"

"Yes and no," she replied. "He'll bury the 'Permission for Treatment' scam now that you've exposed it, but I wouldn't bet on the other. People don't understand the mysteries of creative billing, and even if they did, they'd never have the courage to do anything about it."

"You're right," Bascom laughed. "Many of today's high school graduates read at a 5th grade level and would never understand what Davidson is doing to them. Their ignorance is compost for evangelistic politicians and insurance companies.

"When this country disappears like the Holy Roman Empire did two thousand years ago," he added wryly, "the tattooed, body-pierced masses who were too ignorant to know how corrupt their leaders were, will scratch their beer bellies and wonder what happened."

"You think it could be worse than it is now?" she asked as she went to the filing cabinet behind her desk.

"Sure. Have our patients call Charlie the next time they want to complain to someone about their scalping on Apache Lane. He's better than I at keeping WCH on the straight and narrow, and I need a rest from the fray."

"A withdrawal would be nicer," she demurred, pulling a chart and returning to her desk. "I'd love to work for the old Dr. Bascom again."

Two weeks later Flemming reappeared in Bascom's office. The tepees of his Mohawk were neatly aligned one behind the other, but he needed a shave and looked tired.

"Listen to this," he said excitedly. "A mother took her son to WCH because of stomach pains. She complained to my girlfriend about her bill, and I went to investigate. They kept him there for three hours, did four X-rays and seven blood tests before they arrived at the diagnosis.

"Know what it was?"

"Constipation?"

"Wow! Did you guess or did you already hear about the case?" he asked with a raised eyebrow.

"You wouldn't be here if it were appendicitis," Bascom shrugged.

"You're right!" he agreed. "Anyway, they got a bill for $1,328.75, which included $50 for a single Ex-Lax pill and $510.75 for blood tests. Cohen admitted his billing office was still itemizing panels when he saw it had charged the teen $294.50 for a blood panel that should have cost $30, and he promised to reimburse the family. But he said he will not give refunds to prior patients who had itemized panels, since it was a recent administrative decision to change billing procedures."

"Typical BS," Bascom interrupted.

"I agree. He also jumped on the 'just to be safe' bandwagon."

"How?"

"He said, 'an ER doctor has to be thorough since he is usually unfamiliar with the patient's medical history.'"

"All he has to do is to talk to the patient and he'll get all the information he needs. More BS."

"And it's waist deep. Do you have any comments for the *Times*?" Charlie asked, resting his pencil on his pad.

"Sure. A doctor who needs three hours, four X-rays, and seven blood tests to diagnose constipation should return to medical school. If he's that dumb, it shouldn't have admitted him in the first place."

"Ok," Flemming said, scribbling on his pad. "By the way," he added before speeding out the door, "the boy is Tony Ricardo. One of your patients."

Bascom interlocked his fingers behind his head and leaned back in his chair. Tony had no insurance and a single, unemployed father. His family was an example of one of the fictional cases he had presented to Henry Rutledge months earlier. At least the boy survived his "care."

Flemming published his report the next day under the banner "$1,328.75 to diagnose constipation," and included Bascom's inflammatory remarks about his colleague's incompetence.

Bascom laughed as he read the article. “I never believed he'd print that,” he said as he clipped it from the paper and added it to his Ripley's File.

XXXI

Bascom often lamented that he passed much of his day trying to convince patients that cocaine is not Vitamin C, and that alcohol and tobacco were not food supplements. His iterated warnings were usually unsuccessful and he eventually had to agree with Tiberius, a Roman Emperor who mocked those who, after age thirty, still needed counsel about what was good or bad for their bodies.

Curing disease made his tribulations bearable. Today, however, he would have preferred to face all his vexations at once rather than the singular one awaiting him in his office.

As soon as he entered Evelyn Wiggins' room that afternoon, Ben nudged him back into the hallway and closed the door behind them. He was not wearing his toupee and his ready smile was gone.

"Listen, Bob," he said, putting his arm on Bascom's shoulder and turning him from the door. "Ev's symptoms remind me of Lou Gehrig's disease. What do you think?"

"You're right, Ben," he answered sympathetically. "I'm sorry. Have you told her yet?"

"No, I wanted to speak to you first," he replied dejectedly.

"I'll tell her. It's my job."

Ben looked sorrowfully at his friend, then put his head

on his shoulder and wept. Bascom led him into his office and closed the door. "You need to be strong for Ev's sake; she needs you now more than ever," he said, facing the old physician.

Ben pulled a handkerchief from his pocket and blew his nose. "I love her so much," he said through his sobs. "She's my Queen. It was all so wonderful but so short. It just isn't fair."

"Life never is, Ben, but perhaps a miracle drug will come along, or the disease will go into remission as it sometimes does. She won't die tomorrow or even next year, so think positively."

"I'll try," he replied, taking a deep breath and rubbing his eyes with the heels of his hands. "Money's no object, Bob. I can cover the cost of any treatment, no matter how expensive it might be. If you discover something, you'll let me know, won't you?" he pleaded.

"Anything that'll decrease her suffering will help. It's killing me to see her like this."

"I'll call you immediately, but we do have old drugs to make her comfortable."

"Good. Now let's go see my Ev," he said, regaining his composure. "I miss her already."

They reentered the examining room and Ben limped to his wife's side. He took her hand and pressed it between his. Bascom pulled his chair from under his desk and straddled it.

"How are you, Evelyn?" he asked the sad figure in the wheelchair. He need not have asked. Glancing at her hands, he could see the hollows had deepened between the bones where muscles once were, and he knew her disease was progressing more rapidly than he had expected.

"I overheard you two in the hallway," she replied. She put her other hand on Ben's and massaged it with her thumb. "What's Gehrig's disease?"

"It's called amyotrophic lateral sclerosis or ALS," he explained. "It was named after Lou Gehrig, a Yankee baseball player who had it years ago. It's a neurological disease of unknown cause, characterized by weakness, muscle wasting, and quivering. There are no tests for it, so we base the diagnosis on its classic symptoms and signs.

"About 30,000 Americans have it, Ev. It starts with problems in dexterity or gait and slowly progresses to severe weakness. Your bladder and bowel, sensory functions, and intellectual abilities will remain unaffected."

"Is there a cure?" she hoped.

"No," Bascom replied, shaking his head. "There's a new drug that allegedly controls some of the symptoms, but I've seen no documented positive effects from its use and it doesn't halt the progression of the disease."

"Can I try it?"

"Sure, but it can cause weakness, nausea, dizziness, elevation of liver enzymes, and a decrease in white blood cells. I'm sure we'll find other problems with it as more patients use it. It could make you significantly worse."

"Bob's right, honey," Ben added. "The bad effects of a drug don't show until it's been around for a while. So who knows what else it can do?"

"Oh, Ben," Ev pleaded, her eyes wide with hope, "there's no guarantee I'll get any of them. I want to try it."

Bascom disliked refusing a drug popularized by the media since patients sometimes interpreted his reluctance to give them what they wanted as incompetence or obstructionism. He knew the pharmaceutical industry used misleading advertising and invented diseases just to sell its products, but disgruntled patients were not interested in his explanations. They usually stomped out of his office and went to a more understanding colleague.

"Unfortunately Ben's right, Ev," Bascom explained. "The literature is full of examples of new drugs killing or maiming patients before they're pulled off the market.

"But you and Ben decide if it's worth the gamble," he explained, crossing his arms over the back of his chair. "If you feel the benefits outweigh the risks, I'll prescribe it for you."

Evelyn looked to Ben, her eyes begging him to let her try it, no matter what the risks.

"Remissions occur spontaneously in this disease," Bascom continued, "making it impossible to know if this or any other medication does any good at all. It's absurd, but the only way we can know if it'll prolong your life is to clone you and treat one of you with it and the other with a placebo. Then we see which of you does better.

"Proper diet and exercise are more important to your health than any of these drugs. And even though it's too soon to be concerned, you might think about a feeding tube, since you could eventually develop problems swallowing."

"No," Evelyn replied firmly. "I intend to die on my own terms. There will be no feeding tube, and that's final."

"And so it shall be, but you can change you mind."

"How long do you think I have?" she asked as she lifted Ben's hand to her face and rubbed his bent finger across her lips.

"I don't know. Steven Hawking, the brilliant English physicist, has lived with it for more than 40 years. But consider each day a gift. Do the things you've been putting off for a 'better time.' That time is now."

"We'll do what you say, Bob" Ben agreed. He stepped behind Ev and revved up her wheelchair. "Vroom, vroom," he uttered. "I'll call you about the drug, and I'll write to Professor Hawking to hear if he has any tips for us.

"Ev," he continued, kissing her hair, "I promise you I

won't let this take you from me." She nodded, but her eyes had dulled once again.

Bascom moved his chair and opened the door to let Ben wheel Evelyn out of the room. After they were gone, he wrote a note on her record and then waited until his composure returned before going to see his next patient.

A few days after Evelyn's visit, Bascom entered his home as his telephone was ringing. He picked up the receiver and sat on the couch.

"Robby, tell me it isn't so," Donna said quickly.

"It isn't so."

"Does Evelyn have ALS?"

"Where did you hear that?" he asked. The question disturbed him since he would not tolerate leaks of patient information from his office.

"From one of Ben's friends."

"You'll have to ask Ev, Donna," Bascom replied, relieved by her answer. "I can't talk to you about her since she's my patient."

"Ok," she answered. "Then if someone did have it, how long would that someone have to live?"

"I don't know. It's an odd disease that can kill in months, years, or decades, although if you're 60 when you're diagnosed with it, you don't have many decades left anyway."

"I hope she doesn't have it. We worked together for years and she's a great person. The news hit me like a knife in the gut."

"I know how you feel. How are you doing?"

"Great. Norm Jefferies told me just yesterday he met you a few months ago. He wants you as his assistant."

"I told him I couldn't accept until I finish my work here. The guy sure is opinionated."

"And you aren't?" she laughed. "You should come on staff. You'd be great together. Like black and white saddle shoes."

"Donna!" Bascom laughed, "that's not 'pc.'"

"Maybe not, but it's true," she insisted.

"I'd love to work with you again, since you're cooler than I in an emergency and can read my mind, but I can't leave Whitney right now."

"No one's 'cooler' than you in an emergency, Robbie. What time will you be up for dinner tomorrow night? Then we'll see if you can read my mind," she teased.

"I already know what's on your mind," Bascom laughed. "I'll be there at 7 and up fifteen minutes later."

XXXII

The sun bakes southern Arizona for more than 300 days a year, but for some of its residents, seeing the golden orb day after day was boring and they longed for a change. They got their wish on a dreary day in November when a late monsoon flooded dry riverbeds. The downpour stranded campers and turned modified Jeeps, which could climb boulders with ease, into clunky, unmanageable river craft.

On that day Bascom sat in his office lamenting his second anniversary in Whitney when Helen dropped the *Times* on his desk.

"Good news for a change," she said. "You should frame this article."

Bascom jumped out of his chair after reading the headline.

WCH Accused of Welfare Overcharges (he read)

"State Comptroller Robert Maury today accused the Whitney Community Hospital of 30 percent unjustified ER charges.

"Testifying before the McBurney Commission looking into fraud and waste in the government, he described the 14-year-old welfare program as a fiscal 'debacle.' Maury said he checked 255 claims for ER services covering a 4-month period.

"He found that doctors billed for their services at higher than approved codes and performed unneeded services. Medical consultants discovered doctors making cases more complicated and expensive than their patients' symptoms suggested.

"The report could lead to investigations of other parts of the hospital," Maury stated. "Thirty percent is normal when we find over billing. It's never 5 or 10 percent."

The news elated Bascom. Whether it was his or Charlie Flemming's articles that had lured the commission into reviewing Davidson's hospital was irrelevant. It was his first victory and he celebrated it that night at *Il Pappagallo* with Donna.

Two months after the *Times* reported the Comptroller's findings, wintry winds, whipping dust tunnels high into a dark Arizona sky, blew Charlie Flemming into Bascom's office. The storm had knocked over the green, hairy tepees of his Mohawk haircut, and he straightened them with his hands after he plopped into the chair in front of the desk.

"This details the state's ER investigation we published in November," he explained, waving a letter he took from his inside jacket pocket. "It found the overall care of patients in the ER was correct except for one doctor whose histories and physical examinations were substandard. They also state he rarely needed all the laboratory and X-ray studies he ordered, based on the patient's symptoms."

Bascom leaned over his desk and took the letter. "That's Evans. How about the overcharging?" he asked, skimming the document.

"They reduced reimbursement for reasons that went from 'service not indicated by patient need,' to 'inadequate documentation to support claim for payment.' Bottom line: WCH must return $24,130 of the $217,500 it billed the State."

"That's all?" he asked, returning the letter. "One million bucks a year is closer to what they rip-off."

"I know," Flemming replied as he folded it and put it into his pocket. "You're not going to like my next article."

"Why not?"

"The guy who gave me this told me the charges made by a Whitney doctor, 'not officially identified,' didn't check out."

"What are you talking about, Charlie?" Bascom asked, slamming his fist on the desk. "How can he agree and disagree with me at the same time? Especially after you already reported in the *Times*, and your letter confirms again, that I was right?"

"Donno. Maybe someone received a cash bonus for re-reviewing the charts," he replied cynically as he stood from his chair. "It wouldn't be the first time in this town. Whatever the reason, I have to include his statement in my next article."

Bascom nodded gloomily as the reporter left his office. He rued that Davidson had somehow managed to circumvent the Comptroller's findings and had tarnished his reputation even further.

In Flemming's article the next day, Cohen said: "we were not without fault, but we did not deliberately overcharge our patients." He also stated his ER billed $3,000,000 a year and since the alleged overcharges represented less than 1 percent of the total, the state would not be seeking further refunds.

"Damn these lying bastards!" Bascom shouted as he threw the newspaper across his office. "Sure $24,000 is less than one percent of $3 million, but it's over 10% of the charges which were actually reviewed!"

I'll never beat these people, Bascom thought as he retrieved the newspaper and added the article to the growing "Ripley's File of Medical Oddities" folder in his bottom desk drawer.

XXXIII

After repeated pleas from its new chairman, Bascom reluctantly agreed to attend the Health and Consumer Affairs Board meeting in April. The only news he had to report was Maury's ambiguous investigation into Davidson's machinations, and he doubted the committee would find it useful in its alleged fight against corrupt hospital practices, especially if Adelsohn was still in charge.

On the morning of the meeting a cylindrical package arrived from Lizzano in Belvedere, a village of 600 feisty souls nestled in the Apennines north of Bologna. He extracted a poster from the mailing tube, unrolled it on the kitchen table, and grinned from ear to ear. It was a photograph of his *baita* buried under two feet of snow on a gloriously sunny day. A thin man standing on a path tunneled to the door, Cristina's father, Enrico, was waving him into the picture. In its bottom right corner was shakily scrawled, "*Ci manchi, Roberto. Torna presto, Babbo,* 'We miss you, Robert. Return soon, Dad'."

The picture brought him back to the day he was skiing down a *piste nere* at the Corno alla Scala, a resort not far up the mountain from Lizzano, when a woman crashed into him. He was sitting on the snow, berating her skiing abilities when she pulled off her ski mask. He was dumbstruck by the beautiful flaxen haired, blue-eyed imp who would soon become his wife.

It also called to memory the day when he, Lance, and Enrico had trudged ahead of Cris' black hearse up the snow covered, cobblestoned *Via Tre Novembre*, the town's main street. Despite the howling winds and numbing cold, the entire population of the hamlet had joined the *corteo* to mourn the passing of one of its favorite citizens.

He remembered how, at the path leading to the cemetery, eight of the town's youths had pulled Cris' casket from the hearse, carried it cautiously down the slippery grade to her family's tomb and had lifted it into its cubicle in the wall. The granite block that would seal the young woman from the world of the living stood upright on the marble altar. Her picture in a silver frame, the mate to the one sitting on his night table, was affixed above her name in the middle of the slab.

He also remembered how, after a brief ceremony, the townspeople left him, Lance, and Enrico shivering silently in front of the altar. After a long silence, her father had tightened the belt of his green loden and with tears in his eyes, murmured, "She loved you so much, *Americano*."

"And I her," he had replied as the old man turned and exited the tomb.

"We're both lost," Bascom recalled saying as he had watched Cristina's father fade into the whirling snow.

"We'll all miss her," Lance had replied before they pulled up the hoods of their parkas and trekked up the hill to his *baita* with their breaths condensing in the frigid air.

Two days later, he, Lance, and a real estate agent had stood in the waiting room of a small office.

"Is this ok, *Dottore*?" the agent had asked.

"It'll do," Bascom had replied unenthusiastically.

"Cristina asked me to find you an office by the *Delùbro*," he had said, pointing out the window to the

1,000 year-old stone monument from the Byzantine Empire. "She thought it would bring you luck."

"It didn't bring her luck, Paolo."

"It did; she found love there," he had corrected. "I'll draw up the contract, *Dottore*."

"Thanks."

"It's settled then," Lance had added. "Now let's look for furniture. What's the name of that town down the hill?"

"Silla. Nice people, good prices, too."

A few days after that, Bascom had driven Lance to Bologna for his flight to the States, stopping to buy a case of grappa on his return to Lizzano. Ten days later he had opened the medical office he and Cristina had so carefully planned.

His practice had grown rapidly but his reliance on alcohol to ease the pain of her death grew even faster. He was drinking himself to sleep at night and "topping up" during the day. His nervous system rebelled and his hands shook so much he could no longer hold his stethoscope to a patient's chest.

Three months later he had put a note on his office door and walked away, knowing word of its closure would spread rapidly through the small community.

As he studied the poster, Bascom remembered the night Lance had convinced him to accept the task of "straightening out the bastards" in Whitney. He had doubted he was the man for the job and had repeatedly refused the offer. In the end he had accepted it because he had hoped his new responsibilities would force him to cast off his alcoholic shackles and begin a new life.

Now he was in Whitney, no longer drinking to excess but entrenched in a battle far worse than what he and Lance had fought years ago. And it was one he was certain he would lose at great personal expense

.

He tacked the poster to his bedroom wall and then grabbed an apple from a bowl on the kitchen counter before leaving for the meeting.

An hour later, as he settled into his same seat at the table in the old hospital's conference room, Emily Stone, a young WCH secretary, sat next to him.

"W-What are you doing here?" he stuttered.

"Dr. Davidson asked me to record this meeting," she replied curtly as she set up a tape recorder in front of him.

He was indignant the Board had not told him of this turn of events, since he could face significant legal problems if Emily's boss played his tape for others to hear, which he was certain he would do. He was wondering if he should leave when another participant approached him.

"Dr. Bascom," the studious type with thick glasses said, "I read your article about overcharging for blood panels. Our hospital is doing the same."

"Really?" he answered halfheartedly, still distracted by Davidson's microphone that was aimed at his face like a gun barrel. He wanted to run from the room, but then thought if he chose his words carefully, avoiding comments that could the panel could consider a personal attack against the San Franciscan, perhaps he could still testify and not be sued.

A few minutes later Marvin Adelsohn waddled into the room chomping on a cigar and wearing a pinstripe suit. He frowned at Bascom before plopping down in a chair directly across from him.

As the remaining panelists assumed their places, Dr. Kirnan introduced himself as the new chairman. The tall, thin doctor acknowledged Bascom with a nod.

"What news do you bring us from Whitney, Doctor?"

he queried in a distinctly British accent.

"Before I begin," Bascom said, "I want to protest the hospital's recording of my testimony. I think it shameful that you did not notify me beforehand that Davidson would be recording this meeting. If problems arise, I will hold you responsible."

"Your comments are noted," the chairman responded politely.

"Since our last meeting," Bascom continued, "the Comptroller has uncovered unnecessary testing, poor care, and overcharging at WCH. Even though the hospital has admitted its billing errors, the State dropped its investigation. It ignored the likelihood that the hospital had overcharged on all of the bills it submitted, and not just those pertaining to the few charts its Comptroller reviewed.

"As a taxpayer I feel the investigation should continue and the hospital should return all money the State overpaid it."

"Dr. Bascom," a young man with a persistent tic of his left eyelid asked, "why did they stop the investigation."

"I don't know," he replied with a shrug.

Dr. Kirnan agreed. "Maybe we should investigate further. Please continue," he said.

"Before I do, I would like the WCH recorder turned off," Bascom said.

"Why?"

"Because I intend to name the doctor I believe the Comptroller singled out, and I would like it to remain confidential."

"It should stay on," Adelsohn rebuffed, "unless you are afraid of repercussions from false accusations."

Bascom's eyes narrowed at his pinstriped adversary. Davidson was like *la piovra* 'an octopus' that latches his tentacles onto the easily corruptible, and then propped them up in front of him as a defense against all adversaries.

"Dr. Adelsohn, your remark underscores obvious bias," Bascom replied coolly.

"If I guarantee you immunity," Kirnan interrupted, "would you consent to leaving the recorder on?"

"Yes, since I'm certain Dr. Davidson will receive a full account of this meeting from sources other than his tape recorder," he replied.

"Excuse me?" he asked, confused by the reply.

"The Comptroller," Bascom continued, "found one doctor making cases more complicated and expensive than his patients' symptoms suggested. Dr. Albert Evans is that doctor. I personally believe he's a threat to his patients and a disgrace to the profession."

"Those are mighty powerful charges," Adelsohn interrupted, resting his stubby cigar in an ashtray. "Can you corroborate them?"

"The State already has," he replied curtly.

"Since therapy is opinion," Adelsohn replied heatedly, "no one can prove Dr. Evans performed unnecessary tests."

"Maybe not," the man with the tic disagreed. "If the Comptroller found he did things that were wrong, then therapy might not be just simple opinion. I still think we should review the report."

Dr. Kirnan struck his gavel on the table. "I agree." Adelsohn fumed silently.

"Do you have any further comments, Doctor?" Dr. Kirnan asked.

"No,"

"Then thank you for coming tonight."

Bascom bid good-bye to the panel and left the room. His crusade was over. He had met his duty and then some.

A week later while Bascom was filling in an Italian

crossword puzzle, Helen put a large brown envelope on his desk. It bore no return address.

"I think you should X-ray this before you open it," she said lightly.

"Can't fight destiny," he laughed, "but I'll wait until you're back in your office before I do."

After she was gone, he tore open the envelope and extracted a copy of the minutes of the HCAB session he had attended. From the document he learned that after he had left the meeting a WCH doctor had testified that, "Dr. Bascom is a troublemaker who does not appreciate what Dr. Davidson has done for the community. He resigned during a difficult period and has had no direct contact with the staff or the hospital since then. Everything is working smoothly since Dr. Davidson took over."

In another paragraph Dr. Adelsohn stated, "Dr. Bascom, as always, has presented unfounded complaints unsupported by evidence." In its final paragraph it reported the committee had voted unanimously against requesting a follow-up audit of the hospital by the Comptroller's Office.

The day will come when HCAB members won't have to turn over rocks to look for vermin. A glance around the table will suffice.

Bascom tossed the missive onto his desk and returned to his crossword puzzle.

XXXIV

Bascom was reading the newspaper in his office the next day when his telephone rang. He dropped the paper, picked up the receiver, and said, "Pronto!"

"Hi, Bob. Do you get it yet?" Ben asked tiredly.

"Get what, Ben?"

"I had to hire a nutritionist," he said, ignoring the question. "I did my best in the kitchen, but Ev wouldn't even look at the meals I prepared for her, never mind eat them."

"Where did you learn to cook?"

"From the hospital chef," he laughed. "I also hired physical and respiratory therapists and converted our den into a hospital room. I don't know how he found out what I was doing, but Davidson insisted on sending over his own people to run it. I told him I wouldn't object as long as I could send you over to run his hospital."

"Only you would say that, Ben," Bascom roared as tears of laughter came to his eyes.

"I wanted to kick his scrawny butt. Ev and I have decided we don't want that drug we talked about. I won't expose her to a pill that guarantees only side effects. Could you prescribe something for her muscle spasms?"

"Sure. I'll call it in to the pharmacy and have them deliver it."

"Thanks. Ev promises she'll invite you to dinner as

soon as she's well."

"I'll be there. Should I come see her now?"

"No. She's waiting for me to help her dress so we can get out before it gets too hot. She looks forward to her trips to the park to watch the kids chase the ducks around the pond. She also wonders when I'll drive her car into a tree or onto a park bench."

"That might liven up this dead town. How are you doing, Ben?"

"As I've always said, 'if I can stand and pee in the morning, it'll be a good day.' So far I'm good, even if I'm having trouble with both."

"You have an unbeatable outlook on life," Bascom laughed.

"It might seem silly, but you can imagine how miserable I would be on the morning I couldn't do one of those two things? No matter. As long as I devote every minute to Ev, I don't have the time, or need, to think about myself.

"Ev is calling. Gotta go."

After the phone call, Bascom sat deep in thought, searching his mind for something, anything, he could do to help his friends beat Evelyn's illness, but could think of nothing.

Bascom had promised himself he would withdraw from his battle against Davidson after the Health and Consumer Affairs meeting, but he returned to the fray a few weeks later when a teary-eyed farm worker lamented he could not pay $30,000 for the appendectomy Joe Thompson had performed on him. Lawyers had pounced on his only asset, a dilapidated 50 year-old singlewide mobile home. Without it his wife and their five children would be living on the street.

Bascom suggested he demand the hospital reduce its

bill to $5,000. If not, he should send his bills to the Comptroller's Office and request an investigation into the overcharging their prior investigation was supposed to have stopped. He told the man to return after hours and he would help him write the letter.

A few days later Davidson's lawyers dropped the case against the farm worker, decreasing his bill to $8,000. Two weeks after that, his patient's "David against Goliath" victory made the headlines in the *Times*, the *Globe*, and the *Guardian*.

Bascom smugly added the articles to his Ripley's folder, wondering when Davidson's counter blow would arrive.

He had only to wait 24 hours.

"Charlie Flemming's here to see you, Doctor," Helen announced from the doorway.

"Tell him I'm busy," Bascom replied, trying to remember the 15-letter word to describe Gertrude in Alessandro Manzoni's famous novel, *I Promessi Sposi*.

"You should see him," she insisted. "It's important."

La Monaca di Monza! He smiled as he penciled the letters into his crossword puzzle and then looked up. His secretary was shaking her head in warning.

"Show him in," he ordered.

Moments later the bald reporter with a camera strung over his shoulder entered Bascom's *Piccola Repubblica*.

"What's up, Charlie?" Bascom asked, tossing his crossword book onto his desk. "And what happened to your colorful Mohawk haircut and earrings?"

"I'll tell you later. Right now I'd like to hear about the lawsuit," he said, placing his camera on the edge of the desk. He took a red pad from his shirt pocket and sat down.

"What lawsuit?"

"The one the hospital filed against you in Superior Court yesterday."

"I have no idea what you're talking about."

"Seriously?"

"Seriously. Enlighten me."

"Dr. Davidson says you owe him $100,000 because you resigned before your contract expired."

"That's a lie!" Bascom replied irately. "His representative and I agreed he would cancel my contract if his *ad hoc* investigation into ER abuses turned out to be a whitewash, as it did. Besides, he broke the contract when he stopped paying my rent."

"Who agreed?" Flemming asked, clicking the button on his pen.

"Henry Rutledge. Dr. Thompson arranged the meeting and George Cohen was there," Bascom said. He walked to his file cabinet, retrieved a copy of the letter he had sent to Davidson's lawyer, and handed it to the reporter.

"This details the meeting."

"Can I have it?" he asked after skimming the missive.

"I'll make you a copy," Bascom replied. He retook the letter and went to his photocopier and placed it on the glass.

"I'm curious to know if a jury would condemn me for trying to protect my patients from incompetent medical care and price gouging," he mused as the machine whirred softly.

"Will you countersue?" Flemming asked.

"Sure. Davidson owes me rent. I want it, plus interest." He took the copy the machine spat out and handed it to Flemming. The reporter folded it into his pad as Bascom returned to his chair.

"It could be an interesting trial," Charlie said as he lifted his camera from the desk. "Mind if I take your picture for my article?"

"Why not?" he replied as a light flashed.

"Thanks," the reporter said. "I'll send you a copy of tomorrow's paper."

"Ok. Now, about your hair?" he asked, standing from his chair.

"This will be my last article for the *Times*," he explained, running a hand over his bald head. "I've accepted a job in San Diego and had to get rid of the Mohawk and the ear piercings for the interview. It'll grow back."

"I'm sorry to see you go," he said as he shook the reporter's hand. "Good luck in your new venture."

"You'll need more luck than I will. Call me when the trial's scheduled," Charlie replied, walking to the door. "I don't want to miss it."

"I will."

Helen reentered his office moments later. "I heard," she said with a worried look. "What will you do?"

"Nothing. This is a rumor. I don't believe Davidson wants his schemes on record. He's trying to intimidate me."

The next day the news of the Whitney Community Hospital vs. Robert Bascom, MD, lawsuit filled the front page of the *Times*. Helen's hand shook as she handed Bascom the newspaper.

"You won't like this," she said delicately. "Remember your blood pressure."

"I'll try, Doctor Sylva," he replied with a smile.

According to the article, the hospital argued it did not owe him rent, but Flemming wrote that Cohen had given him a copy of his letter of resignation stamped, "received December 6." Since his contract had expired in November, it was written proof he had fulfilled his agreement. Davidson, however, had not paid him his rent for the last two months of that agreement, and if anyone was in breech of contract, it was he.

As for the meeting itself, Rutledge denied agreeing to his resignation and Cohen did not remember attending it. “Damn tape recorder!” he cursed. He could feel his blood pressure rising.

In the last paragraph of the article, Joe Thompson was quoted as saying; "I remember Dr. Bascom promising to stop writing negative articles about the hospital if Dr. Davidson would tear up his contract."

Bascom leaped out of his chair with his blood thundering in his ears, yelled, "son of a syphilitic whore!" He slammed his fist on the desk. "Rutledge offered to tear up my contract if I would stop execrating his boss. That bastard Thompson reversed our agreement to make me look like a blackmailer. Damn him to hell!"

"What will you do, Bob?" Helen asked.

"'Tell the truth, but keep one foot in the stirrup,' is an ancient Arabian proverb my mother taught me as a child. I should have returned to Italy after Perkins let a man die because of the color of his skin, or fled Whitney's medical cabal when Norman Jefferies offered me a job in Phoenix. Now it's too late. Thompson's statement has ruined my reputation, I'm almost bankrupt, and a lawsuit would guarantee I remain in Davidson's debt for years to come.

"So what will I do, you ask? Nothing. There is nothing I can do. I'm trapped here," he lamented. He sat down and rested his head on his desk. "People believe the first thing they hear or read. Nothing I could say now would change their minds," he mumbled. "Thompson only hinted at blackmail in the press. Even if he recanted his statement, they would print the retraction under an ad for tractors on the last page. No one would see it or believe it."

"I'm sorry, Bob. Can I help?"

"No. Go to your office and shut my door on the way

out. And cancel my appointments for today. How many do we have, by the way?"

"Three."

"Big fu…, big deal."

Within a week of the article Bascom's work had decreased even further, and he learned the reason from one of his patients:

"Rod and I read about the lawsuit," the retired shopkeeper explained. "We're sorry the hospital has to sue you to get its money back. And what Dr. Thompson said you tried to do to Dr. Davidson, well, we just didn't think you were like that."

"Do you think I'm a thief and a blackmailer, Mrs. Phelps?" he asked irately.

"We'll pray you'll do what's right."

He could not know if Davidson had expected this result from his lawsuit, but to the religious zealots in town, the mere fact that Whitney's largest employer was suing him was proof enough of his guilt.

"Take two of these a day, Mrs. Phelps, and you'll be well in a week," he said, handing her a prescription. *And I hope you choke on them.*

He was still fuming when he exited the room and bumped into his meager staff in the hallway. "I've got to decrease your hours, Helen," he said. "Our work has slowed too much to keep the present schedule."

"Fran has something to tell you," she replied excitedly.

"Hal and I are getting back together, and we're moving to San Diego where he has a good job," the pretty nurse explained. She was smiling as if she had just won the super lotto. "Helen says she can take over my duties as long as you'll run the lab."

"I'm happy for you," he replied, "and I wish you many exciting Tuesdays."

Fran blushed and looked at Helen, who smiled and shook her shoulders. "Thanks, and the same to you," she grinned now that he knew her secret. She kissed him on the cheek, gave Helen a hug, and left the office.

"Oh, I forgot to tell you," Helen said when they were alone, "Cohen is now assistant administrator with a Los Angeles hospital. Gossip has it Davidson fired him because he balked at a new rip-off. And you thought he didn't have a conscience."

"One down, but it's like chopping heads off a Hydra," he replied sarcastically. "Ninety-nine more to go."

A week after the *Times*' article, Bascom was beginning to think Davidson's lawsuit was pure fantasy until a court officer in his official gray garb arrived in his office.

"Dr. Bascom?" he asked.

"You've been my patient since I arrived here, John," he replied, "and you still don't know if I'm Dr. Bascom?"

"Sorry," he said, handing him a large brown envelope. "It's the law. We have to verify the identity of the person we give these documents to."

"I see. Then thanks, I guess."

After the officer left, he opened the envelope and skimmed its thick document. Its legal boilerplate and causes of action made only moderate sense to him. He put the complaint in his desk and searched the phone book for an attorney in Phoenix, since he doubted he could trust a local one.

The first lawyer he called asked if he was the doctor who had been the subject of repeated scandals in the newspapers.

"Yes, I am."

"Hold the line, please."

Minutes later the squeaky voice said, "sorry. My associates and I are busy for the next year." Bascom was still laughing when the line went dead.

The next one asked if he had $20,000 for his retainer. When he said no, the lawyer replied, "ethics aren't worth bankruptcy. Beg Davidson for forgiveness and back off. Crow doesn't taste so bad if it saves $100,000."

"Thanks anyway," Bascom replied as he hung up.

The next two lawyers gave him similar advice, but the fifth, Frank Helleman, set up an appointment for him the next day.

XXXV

The next morning Bascom drove to Frank Helleman's office in Phoenix, an elegant Victorian mansion on Central Avenue north of the bustle of the city. The restored gingerbread building sat in the middle of a manicured lawn surrounded by pine and mesquite trees.

He parked his SUV at the side of the building and entered it through its stained glass door. A sloe-eyed, red-haired woman guarding the portal to the Hobbes & Helleman law offices directed him to Frank's office.

"Through that door then straight to the end. Last door on the left," she said with a smile.

"Thanks," he answered, repeating the directions in Italian.

He knocked on the door and a husky voice drowning out Beethoven's *Ninth Symphony* invited him into a spacious room. Floor to ceiling bookcases with wire mesh doors and filled with leather bound texts lined its walls.

"Have a seat," the bespectacled, 40-year old lawyer said, pointing to the captain's chair in front of his Birdseye maple writing table. He rested his unlit meerschaum pipe in a silver ashtray and closed the book he was reading.

Bascom sat down and rested his leather briefcase on his lap.

"You're on time," he said, checking his watch. "Unusual for doctors. You told me a hospital is suing you. Do you have the complaint and your agreement?"

"Yes," Bascom answered. He took them from his brief-case and handed them to Helleman who perused them, pausing often to write brief notes on a yellow pad. When he finished he removed his horn-rimmed glasses and set them on the documents.

"Why did you leave?" he questioned, looking Bascom in the eye.

"To protect my patients," he replied. For the next thirty minutes he summarized the events leading to the complaint and then concluded, "the committee investigation was a farce and I resigned, as per my agreement with Rutledge."

"Did anyone hear him agree to let you resign?"

"The administrator and Dr. Thompson, but they have forgotten they even attended the meeting."

"Your deal won't count without witnesses to support his oral modifications of the written agreement," he continued, clasping his hands together on the desk. "Do you still talk to Davidson?"

"Through the press," he replied, handing Helleman his newspaper articles. The lawyer scanned the titles and then dropped them on his desk.

"What would you like me to do for you?"

"Get me justice, and my back rent plus interest."

"How much is that?"

"$4,800."

"That's not much for all you've been through. How about a $1 million reimbursement for defamation of character and sexual impotency resulting from stress?"

Bascom laughed. "No. I just want you to prove I was right to leave when I did, and to get me my back rent."

"I'm glad you didn't ask me to file a frivolous cross complaint," he replied. "I would have refused. I might be able to get you your rent, but I can't promise you justice."

"Mr. Helleman," Bascom explained, tapping on his briefcase, "as long as WCH fulfilled my needs, I would have admitted my patients there. But when the level of care fell and costs went through the ceiling, I had no choice but to consider my patients' welfare and resign."

"Has anyone else commented on the problems?" Helleman asked, rubbing the back of his index finger with his thumb. He winced as he touched a spot and then scraped it.

"Sure, but they'll deny it."

"Damn cactus spines." He scratched it loose with his thumbnail and then brought it to his eye for closer examination.

"So no one will testify for you?" Helleman asked. He brushed his nail on his blotter and then made a notation on his pad.

"Probably not. But I had no choice but to correct the problems."

"Why?"

"As the ER director I had to make sure patients got proper care."

"I've never heard anything like this before," he said, circling a word on his pad. "You walked away from a good contract knowing you would have to repay everything the hospital gave you if you voided it, just to protect your patients? And all you want is $4,800 back rent?"

"Plus interest."

"Which will be pennies, since you'll get legal, not bank interest. Do you have their $100,000 and another $10,000 for me to defend you, win or lose?"

"No," he responded. "But I'll find the money. I always pay my bills."

The lawyer picked up his pipe, rose from his chair, and walked to the window in the rear of his office. The man was well over 6 feet tall.

"Nice day," he mumbled, sucking the stem of his empty pipe. "But when isn't it in Arizona? Have you thought of rejoining the hospital staff? I'm sure Davidson would like to settle this amicably."

"NEVER!" Bascom replied heatedly, jumping from his chair. "And I would quit medicine if a judge forced me to!"

"Calm down, Doctor. Lose your temper on the stand and you lose your case," Helleman explained, returning to his desk. Bascom dropped back into his chair.

"Lawyers usually don't want to know if their clients are guilty, but is everything you just told me true?"

"I wouldn't be here if it weren't."

"Um. Well, we have a few defenses here. One, the hospital breached the contract when it failed to pay your rent, allowing you to leave legally. But I'll need proof you were on staff until December. Davidson may say he stopped paying because you verbally resigned in September but you just didn't submit your written resignation until later."

"I operated on a patient in November," Bascom interrupted. "And I wouldn't have resigned before the meeting in December since I had hoped it would resolve our differences. Had I resigned in September, there would have been no surgery and no investigation."

"The surgery is ok, but December's still shaky. They can say you resigned right after the surgery, and then, only after their pleading and apologizing, you returned on staff to try to resolve the issue."

"Whose side are you on?" Bascom demanded.

"Yours, but I want you to understand how difficult they can make this case if they want to. Anyway, write down what you told me: the article where the hospital admitted over billing but refused to reimburse its patients, the Comptroller's audit, and the 'Treatment Permission for Minors' letter. Have I forgotten anything?" the lawyer asked.

"The Lavabo Laboratory scheme," Bascom continued after a moment, "plus the hospital's billing blood panels as individual tests to increase the costs tenfold."

"Ok. Next there is the agreement between you and Rutledge. It won't stand even if people get their memories back since they've already denied it ever happened, so we can forget it.

"Last, and this is pure legal fantasy, we'll say the hospital breached an implied warranty to provide high quality care at a fair price, which formed the underlying basis for your agreement to enter the contract."

"Finally!" Bascom exclaimed, smacking his hand on his briefcase. "Someone understands! But why is that defense a fantasy."

"Because it doesn't exist in law. We can defend their lawsuit without it, but it will give Davidson's lawyer something to worry about," he continued, leaning back in his chair. "If you intend to expose the hospital, which will be costly, time-consuming, and probably unsuccessful, this may be the knife that cuts the deepest."

"What do you think of its chances?"

"Harrumph," he grunted with a shrug if his broad shoulders. "Not much, but it might work if we're not thrown out of the courtroom by a blockhead judge. We'll need the records the committee audited, and then we'll have to convince a doctor with credentials to counter WCH's hired 'specialists' who'll testify the records are correct and that your disagreement with them is an example of '20-20 hindsight and subjective judgment.' WCH will pay them big bucks to make you look like a bungling, blabbering, troublemaking idiot."

"That'll be easy," Bascom chuckled. "But will the jury buy it?"

"Maybe," Helleman replied, holding his eyeglasses up to the light. He took a handkerchief from his pants' pocket, exhaled warm vapor on his lenses, and then wiped them clean before replacing them. "They like certificates. As long as a witness owns a parchment with a raised seal, they're happy. It makes no difference if he makes his living as a highly paid, professional expert witness; they'll always favor the specialist over the generalist.

"Are you specialized in emergency medicine?"

"No, but I was the ER director at WCH," Bascom replied. He was incredulous at how the judicial system worked. "Would a jury find for Davidson simply because I'm not a specialist?"

"Don't overestimate its intelligence," the lawyer explained, "since it's made up of people not smart enough to come up with reasons to be excused from duty."

Bascom laughed. "Encouraging. How do you intend to convince Davidson to turn over some damning records?"

"I don't know yet. He'll pressure you into giving up your case before we get to trial by filing a flurry of absurd delays and appeals that will cost you thousands to counter. North will do everything in his power to prevent a judge and jury from hearing this story."

"Do you have any thoughts about the trial?"

"No. The problem right now is the judge at what we call 'law and motion proceedings.' Most would not understand the real basis of this case and that would swing opinion in favor of the hospital, especially when it comes to discovery that involves confidential patient records.

"Anyway, I'll file an answer to their lawsuit and cross-complain for the rent they failed to pay."

"Plus interest," Bascom interrupted.

"Plus interest. Boy, you're a bulldog."

"It's my strongest trait."

"We'll see," Helleman laughed. "I'll also file a cause of action in the cross-complaint for interference with business relations, which is a claim for the business you lost because of such practices as redirecting patients and telling them you've left town." The lawyer leaned back and rubbed a finger over his lips.

"While it's not yet clear who might be the proper individual or governmental plaintiff," he added after a while, "there is the possibility of a class action suit on behalf of all WCH's patients, brought against the hospital for the total amount of the over billings and its other questionable practices.

"I'll alert the various governmental agencies that might enforce these claims, and I'll try to generate enough interest on their part to conduct a more thorough investigation into WCH's practices."

"That's it?" Bascom asked innocently, "No bombing and strafing the hospital?"

The lawyer laughed again. "Not today."

"I'll hear from you?" he asked, clasping his briefcase and standing from his chair.

"You will," Helleman agreed.

They shook hands, and Bascom left the office smiling.

XXXVI

The next evening Ben Wiggins sat with Bascom in his living room. He had called in sick for the first time since his arrival in Whitney, and Helen had asked the old physician to make a house call on her employer.

"How do you feel?" Ben asked as he wiggled the arms of his chair. He wiggled them again and added, "You should tighten the arms of this chair before it collapses."

"I'm better, and I will," Bascom replied, lying on his couch. He closed his robe over his hairy legs and studied his feet. "Just a little fever and cough, a simple cold. You didn't need to come over."

"Helen was worried and we need to keep our women happy," Ben replied. "How's the lawsuit coming along? It's the talk of the town."

"So my patients tell me. I found a lawyer yesterday. He thinks we've got a good chance of winning, and even though he didn't mention it specifically, he thinks I'm on the moral high road."

"Ha!" Ben said. "Morality won't get you far. You're like the soldier who refuses to kill an unarmed civilian, and is then executed for disobeying orders.

"I warned you your colleagues would cut you to pieces, and they're not finished yet," Ben explained. He shook the arms of the chair again and said. "There's only one ass in town big enough to do this – Thompson's."

Bascom laughed. "You don't miss anything, do you?"

"I never miss the obvious," he replied. "Usually I'm optimistic, but I know these people. They will do their darnedest to destroy you."

"Why?"

"Because you're a danger to them and they want you dead or gone from here. In fact if you left tomorrow, Davidson's lawyers would not even come after you."

"Are you kidding?" Bascom asked, sitting up on the couch. "How can a recluse like me be dangerous?"

"You know thc truth and aren't afraid to follow it where it takes you. Our corrupt, incapable colleagues know you see through them and their pathetic ploys to squeeze money out of our migrant 'stones.' You've already exposed the hospital and Evans, and they want to stop you before you expose them personally."

"Are you afraid of me too?" Bascom wondered. He coughed a few times and then blew his nose into a tissue.

"Of course not, and I never was. I knew who you were and what you would do here as soon as Donna told me about the incident with Perkins in the ER.

"Why not return to Italy and forget this place? Reopen that clinic on the mountain you told me about," Ben asked.

"I might someday if I ever find the money. But I can't leave here until the lawsuit is resolved, and more importantly, until you have no further need of my help with Evelyn."

"Suppose she lives another 40 years like Professor Hawking? Will you stay that long?" he asked, massaging his earlobe between his fingers.

Bascom shook his head. "Why not ask me something easy, Ben, like 'do I get it yet'?"

"Because you don't and might never. It doesn't surprise

me though, since few people ever do. But you need to think about your future. I'll take care of Evelyn, who, by the way, reads about you in the newspapers. She's worried and upset by what they're doing to you."

Bascom lay back on the couch. He coughed a few times and then pressed the back of his hand to his forehead.

"Want me to kiss it for you," Ben volunteered. "My mother always kissed mine when she wanted to know if I had a fever."

Bascom laughed. "Thanks, but you're not my type. Tell Ev not to worry. I'm just a foolish person who attacks windmills. Once I accept the fact the real problem is the wind and not the mill, I'll be ok."

"Very perceptive," Ben laughed. "By the way, how is Donna?"

"Busy. I call her now and then, but it's hard to get to see her. Been a while."

"I know. She calls Ev every day to check on her, sometimes more than once. They're like sisters, or mother and daughter, and gab forever. It does Ev good to get her calls. They keep her spirits up."

"Does she ever mention me?"

"Among others," he replied cryptically. "Well, it's time to return to Evelyn. I need to hold her. Should I send my inflated bill for this visit here or to your office?"

"Here," he laughed as he rose from the couch and escorted his friend to the door.

After work a few days later, Bascom stopped by the local western shop to buy a new pair of jeans, a couple of piped cowboy shirts with pearl buttons, a Stetson Catera hat, boots, and a black belt with a silver buckle. As a result of his running several times a week for months, he had lost the weight he had gained since Cristina's death, and needed a new wardrobe.

Helen was bending over her keyboard, her gray hair covering her face like a diaphanous curtain, when he knocked on her Dutch door dressed in his new garb the following morning. She brushed her hair from her face and after her shock at seeing the new Bascom, exclaimed, "You look different, Cowboy! Are you on drugs?"

"Nope," he responded lightly.

"You sure could have fooled me," she said with a smile. "You've got eight patients this afternoon, including Evelyn. A record for us," she said. "But your landlord is increasing your rent 15 percent starting next month."

Bascom paled. "If he raises it again," he replied with a click of his tongue, "we'll convert an ice cream truck into a mobile office and ride up and down the streets ringing our bell and offering free rectal exams with each frozen fudgecicle."

"You're sure you're not on drugs?" she repeated.

"Nope. I mean 'yup.' That's what cowboys say, ain't it?" he asked before going to his desk. He put his feet up and dialed a number. On the second ring a male voice answered.

"Hi, Jonas, this is Bob Bascom. Just calling to hear how Carl is doing."

"This is Carl, Dr. Bascom, and I'm doing fine," the boy replied.

"Carl! I didn't recognize your voice. How's your therapy coming along?"

"I can walk ok, but my right leg and arm are still a little stiff. My mom says I'm lucky to be alive, so I shouldn't complain."

"You'll be fine. How are your parents?"

"They're ok. Dad's working and mom's shopping."

"Say hello to them and keep up the good work."

"Ok, Dr. Bascom, and thanks for everything."
Bascom hung up and went to see his favorite patient.

XXXVII

On a Saturday afternoon a few weeks later, Bascom was doing push-ups on his living room rug when his telephone rang. *If Friedrich Nietzsche had disliked postmen, he would have hated cellphones,* he thought as he wiped the sweat off his brow with the sleeve of his sweatshirt. He flipped open his cellphone and said, "Yep."

"Hi, Bob," Helleman replied. "The good news is that it's a beautiful day. The bad news is that North refuses to give us the *ad hoc* records."

"Merda! Did you expect anything different?" Bascom asked.

"No, but even if we were to get them, releasing medical records to the public evokes concern. I'm sure the court will allow WCH to delete the names from the records."

"That doesn't bother me. As long as they don't change Evans' orders and notes, we're still ok," he assured his lawyer.

"That won't happen. By now I'm sure you realize this procedural gimmickry will consume considerable time and money, since WCH intends to appeal any adverse orders requiring the production of documents."

"Frank, I don't mind waiting, but keep it to a minimum, ok?"

"I'll try."

Bascom snapped shut his phone and returned to his push-ups.

Lawyers are like women; you can't live with them and you can't live without them.

On the night of December 15, two weeks before his first hearing and after a harrowing drive though a blinding sandstorm that had reduced visibility to a few feet on Route 10, Bascom entered Helleman's office in his new cowboy shirt, jeans and Stetson hat.

"Ciao," he said, sitting in front of the desk.

"Ciao. I've never seen an Italian cowboy before," the casually clad lawyer said as he turned off Bach's Fugue.

"Would you like to see my spaghetti western imitation of Clint Eastwood in *per un Pugno di Dollari*?"

"Try it and I'll double my fees," he laughed. "Well, since WCH won't voluntarily produce the ER records," he continued, "I've asked the court to order them released. I've also sought expenses because it refused to surrender them without substantial justification."

"What does North think about that?"

"Not much," he shrugged. "He's asking the court for $2,500 to journey from San Francisco to defend what he calls our 'absurd affirmative defense of an implied warranty.'"

"It doesn't seem absurd to me."

"I didn't think it would. He's also filed a motion for summary judgment to strike it because he says there's no legal basis or contractual provision supporting it," Helleman replied, doodling on his yellow pad. "He says it contradicts the agreement you signed and he wants the judge to throw it out."

"Wow! That's unfriendly. Could the judge do that?"

"Sure he can. Bob, I don't think you understand the difficulty of this defense. If you win with it, you win a measly five thousand in back rent, since you refused to let me file the interference with business relations cause of action in your cross complaint. That won't even cover my bill. If you lose, it could cost you $100,000 plus.

"You need to swap your idealism for realism," Frank continued thoughtfully. "You know your colleagues will never support you on this. They need the 'Medical Grail,' the money they rob from their patients to pay for the big house, the Mercedes Benz, and the expensive Ivy League colleges for their spoiled kids. You got in their way and they are punishing you by stealing your patients and trashing your name. Davidson is the icing on your bankruptcy.

"I'd like you to use WCH's breach of contract to win your case and forget all the rest. I'm sure North knows the wisest thing Davidson could do would be to pay you your rent and quietly drop his suit."

"If I continue with this implied warranty defense, what do you think he'll do?" Bascom asked, trying to calculate his odds.

"He'll try to eliminate it. Even if a judge should agree with us now, it would have little impact on your case. We'd still have to convince him and a jury that WCH provided poor, overpriced care to its patients. If we fail, he won't allow us to try to prove a doctor under contract can insist his continued employment be conditioned on the hospital's keeping certain standards. After all, the hospital's services and prices are its business and not yours," Helleman explained.

"That's what I keep hearing," Bascom replied. "Still I don't believe patients should be economically mauled by tricky billing schemes or be physically maimed by incompetent physicians."

"Noble, indeed, but North feels the hospital's billing

and competency standards aren't relevant to this case."

"According to his philosophy," Bascom said after a moment's reflection, "theft and murder were acceptable until God inscribed on a stone tablet they weren't. Violation of written law is illegal, but ethics are unimportant in the overall scheme of things." His knuckles whitened on the brim of his ten beaver Stetson. He was angry that Davidson's lawsuit and the principles fueling it were skinning away his onion of beliefs one thin layer at a time.

"Damn it, Frank," he continued, "I'm not the first to demand a hospital respond to the reasonable requests of its physicians. Hammurabi did it few thousand years ago, and with great success. Of course he chopped off fingers and gouged out eyes when a physician screwed up, but he got his point across."

"We need a more recent and less violent example," Helleman laughed, scratching his head. "I've searched and couldn't find a case on point that has been appealed and thus would give us reliable precedent."

"So you're saying Davidson has no duty to maintain a minimal code of behavior. But even if that were the case, does he believe he can force me to admit my patients to his organization that kills and bankrupts my patients with immunity? Alice in her travels through the Looking Glass had it easy by comparison," he concluded with despair.

"Maybe she did," Helleman agreed. "Anyway he's asking the court to strike our defense, and he'll pull it off if one of our more thickheaded judges gets the case. So, my friend, do we continue on Frost's 'road less traveled,' or not?"

Bascom laughed.

"What's so funny?"

"I've been on that road my entire life and am trying to get off it."

"Now's your chance. Just sue for your back rent. They'll lose, you'll get a few bucks, which you'll turn over to me as partial payment of my fee, and you'll be off the road. So what will it be?"

"I need to think about it," Bascom replied. He stood from his chair, waved his hat in the air, and left the office.

XXXVIII

Six days before Christmas, to Bascom's great enjoyment and wonder, a once in a century snowfall dusted the cacti in his yard. It was a far cry from amount of snow the blizzards regularly dumped on his *baita* in the Italian Apennines, but insignificant as it was, it would turn out to be his emotional highlight of the day.

Evelyn was one of three patients waiting to see him that chilly morning. The frail woman's thin skin hugged the curves and crevices of her face as if sucked in by a vacuum. She wore a child-sized blue dress over her frail frame, and sat forlornly in her wheelchair, oblivious to her surroundings.

"She's much weaker and laughs and cries for no reason," Wiggins said disconsolately, holding her wasted hand in his. "She rarely talks to me, and there are times she doesn't even know I'm around." Food stains again covered the bald physician's jacket, and he had aged a year and lost a pound for every month of Evelyn's relentlessly progressive illness.

"Unfortunately that's usual behavior with this disease, Ben. How's her appetite?"

"Poor, but she still swallows ok."

Bascom knew that during the final stages of her disease, Evelyn would be able to chew her food, but because of muscle paralysis, would not be able to swallow it. Liquids, unable to pass at all, would exit uncomfortably through her nose.

"Let's see how she's doing," he offered before examining her in her wheelchair.

"Not bad," he said a few minutes later. As he returned to his desk, he thought, *Imbecile! She can barely lift her arms above her waist, a feat she could easily do at her last visit, and you say, "not bad"?*

"Does she still take her medications, Ben?" he asked while writing a note on a chart.

"Yes, but they don't help anymore," he replied softly as he stroked Evelyn's hair with a shaking hand. The woman stared vacantly at her hands in her lap, ignoring his caresses.

"How are you doing?" he asked, turning to his friend.

"I pass the night reading to Ev or combing her hair. I can't sleep because I'm afraid I won't hear her if she calls me," he explained. "I couldn't live knowing I had slept through my last chance to tell her I love her.

"It's ironic how the wheel of life turns," he continued sadly. "I've gone from doctor to nurse, and Ev from nurse to patient. It would have been nicer if our wheels were the size of those on a mammoth dump truck rather than a Mini Cooper, but even so, I'm grateful for the time we've had together."

"Would you like me to admit her to a nursing home?"

"No, Bob," Ben said emphatically. "Ev stays at home. She would do the same for me. But I am looking for a nurse to help so I can get a few hours sleep."

"Maybe Donna could come down from Phoenix part-time," Bascom offered.

Wiggins brightened when he heard her name. "Are you two dating?"

"Occasionally," Bascom said. "Well, keep up the great job you're doing and phone if you need me."

"Thanks. We'll see you again soon," he said. With a "Vroom, vroom," that now sounded more like a sputtering Model-T than the roaring Ferrari it once was, Ben limped slowly out of the room, pushing the wheelchair ahead of him. The playing cards clipped to its frame clicked slowly, almost mournfully against the wheels' spokes as it traveled down the hallway.

After his friends left Bascom recalled the adage of a long deceased colleague: "A physician's job is to cure those he can, assist those he can't, and console all." He could not measure the effect of his consolation on the Wiggins' lives, but to him it seemed a small offering.

According to his records' review at his desk later that day, he had seen 50 percent fewer patients that month than the same month a year earlier. He had eliminated every luxury to meet expenses, but unless his practice picked up, he would soon be unable to pay his bills. Yet when Helen put a patient in his X-ray room, he rarely performed an X-ray or a laboratory study. "I won't compromise my standards just because Davidson is suing me," he remembered once telling her.

"Are you going to charge Evelyn today?" Helen asked from his doorway.

"No."

"Have you finished revising the billing schedule as you promised?"

"I changed my mind. Our patients have enough trouble paying our regular charges," he replied.

"Um, you're right about that, just like we have trouble paying our bills. But why not charge Ev? She has insurance and we need the money."

"It's an honor when a colleague chooses me over another to care for him or his family. That's payment enough."

"But it won't pay your rent," she chided. "Bob, you delayed my last paycheck a week, so I know you're in trouble. Why don't you leave this crummy town before you go bankrupt?"

"I'm not sure if my wallet or my reputation has taken more of a beating, but I can't leave until I've vindicated the latter."

"What do you get out of all this?" Helen asked, scratching her head.

Bascom leaned back in his chair. It had been many years since a friend had asked him that same question. Now, as then, why anyone who knew him would need to, puzzled him.

"During my residency," he explained, bending one arm of a paper clip into a metal comma, "I was president of the house staff. Married residents earned twice as much as single ones, and weekend duty meant working 56 hours straight, which was exhausting and risked patients' lives. I unionized the house staff and corrected the problems, but I became the target for every poisoned arrow the administration could fire at me," he explained. He threw the bent clip into the wastepaper basket beside his desk.

"A colleague who had worked closely with me to form the union asked me the same question you just did. He refused to believe I had acted altruistically and deridingly nicknamed me, 'DQS,' 'Don Quixote in Scrubs.' The title stuck and another friend still calls me that just to tick me off.

"So now you ask what I get out of this? Nothing but an empty waiting room. And when it's all over, win or lose, I'll be a pariah. But why I have to do what I'm doing and why I would do it all again is the question you want to ask. It's the one I'd like to know the answer to also.

"Don't give up, Helen, I need your support to get through the final stages of this battle," he continued. "Even if Davidson beats us, it won't be important as long as we haven't compromised our principles."

"Oh, Bob, I'll try. But don't be upset if I falter now and then," she said before returning to her office.

XXXIX

Gunmetal clouds threatened a downpour in Arizona's capital on the morning of January 2nd as Robert Bascom parked in a 30-minute green zone in front of Phoenix's stately glass and steel courthouse. A $50 fine awaited those who stayed longer, but Frank Helleman had assured him his hearing would last no longer than 20 minutes.

He exited his SUV and strolled around the building's flagstone patio, stopping once to snap a small branch from a powder blue spruce. It was Cristina's favorite tree. He sniffed its fragrant pine aroma and then slipped it into his jacket pocket as Frank Helleman pulled up in a restored Jaguar XKE in British racing green. The smartly dressed lawyer stepped from the car holding a leather briefcase. Smiling broadly, he waved to Bascom.

"Where's your cowboy outfit?" he asked as he approached his client.

"Rin Tin Tin is guarding it at home," Bascom replied.

"Ha!" he laughed.

Once inside the courthouse, the men climbed the stairs to an oak-paneled room on the second floor and walked up its center aisle. Bascom sat in the front row on the right as his lawyer continued into the bullpen and placed his briefcase on the table. Helleman nodded to the Asian stenographer setting up her machine below the witness-box and sat down.

At 8:15 a.m., a tall man in a black robe emerged from a door in the front of the courtroom and strode to the bench. His chiseled face looked as if it would crack if he smiled.

"All please rise," the bailiff announced, "for the Honorable Judge Montfort."

The judge glanced around the courtroom and sat at the bench. "Be seated," he commanded gruffly before asking the only lawyer present if he was ready to begin.

"I am, your Honor," Frank replied, rising and buttoning his hound's-tooth jacket.

"Bailiff," he asked, "where is plaintiff's counsel?"

"I don't know, your Honor," the young man replied. "He was aware of this hearing."

"Very well, we'll wait a few minutes." The judge drummed his fingers on the bench.

Ten minutes later a young man in a three-piece pinstriped suit and wingtip shoes strode through the gate held open for him by the bailiff. He walked to his table and placed his alligator skin briefcase on it.

"Mr. North?" Judge Montfort inquired.

"Yes, your Honor. I was here at eight, but in the wrong room. I'm sorry for the delay."

Montfort rubbed his chin and said to his stenographer, "let the record reflect that please." He then glanced at Bascom and added, "let the record also reflect the defendant is personally present and accompanied by his counsel, Mr. Frank Helleman."

He squinted at the lawyer through his gold-rimmed glasses. "Your full name, sir?" he asked.

"William Rodney North, your Honor," he replied, tugging a shirt cuff over his gold watch.

Montfort skimmed a document and then said, "Whitney Community Hospital versus Robert A. Bascom, MD.

Motion number eleven is Mr. Helleman's request for the production of documents and number fourteen is Mr. North's request for summary judgment as to defendant's third affirmative defense. This states the Hospital has an implied warranty to provide good care at fair prices to the people of Whitney.

"Because the production of documents is tied in with motion number fourteen, which is Mr. North's contention that the contract contains no such warranty and that the terms of the contract negate any such warranty, I think I will hear motion eleven now.

"Mr. Helleman," he said, leaning forward, "Mr. North describes this as a 'creative affirmative defense.' Your position on this implied warranty is creative, isn't it?"

Helleman stood from his chair. "Not at all, your Honor. I believe it's a sound and equitable principle of law we should apply in this case. If I could take a few minutes of the court's time, I'll explain why."

The judge glanced at North who was arranging documents on his table. "Continue," he ordered.

"What we have," Helleman said, pointing to Bascom, "is a doctor who went to work for a hospital under a standard employment contract: 'you work for us, and we'll pay your relocation and start up expenses. If you leave before your contract term is up, you return all the money we gave you.'

"The doctor agrees," he continued, "but the hospital is sold six months later and changes are made he could not accept. He airs his concerns to the administration and to the community, but the hospital does not correct them. In fact, it compounds them to the detriment of its patients.

"The doctor says, 'I can't accept what's happening in your ER, and the State of Arizona says you're overcharging and providing substandard medical care.'"

"Was the doctor in the emergency room?" Montfort interrupted.

"He was its director and had primary responsibility for, and intimate knowledge of, everything that went on there."

Montfort nodded. "I see," he said. "Continue."

"The hospital then says: 'Ok, we'll have a committee examine patients' ER records during a certain period of time. It'll tell us whether we're fulfilling our responsibilities.'

"So as the committee's doctors are discussing their findings, my client leafs through the charts and sees classic examples of what he considers to be the problem. His colleagues say everything is fine, but my client says, 'You're covering this up.'"

"So he resigns from the hospital," Helleman said, "and its owner sues him for $100,000 he claims he gave him. The doctor says, 'you can't make me work under a contract with an implied warranty that says you're going to provide quality medical care at reasonable prices to my patients if you don't provide it.'

"Your Honor, in his 'Declaration for Summary Judgment,' Mr. North says no implied warranty should be imposed on the basic terms of the agreement. I'm saying there should be and that I have the right to produce evidence at trial to show it was clearly and repeatedly breached by the hospital before the doctor's resignation and departure.

"If I fail," he explained, "then Mr. North will prevail at least as to this specific defense. He'll also be entitled to seek summary judgment to say 'the warranty doesn't exist because it isn't written in the contract, or cannot be reasonably implied,' but this court must decide if his position conforms to the equitable standards this court is willing to impose."

Helleman sat at his table as Judge Montfort said, "that's

why I wanted to hear this motion, Mr. North. I realize I asked him to speak first even though it was your motion, but I was curious about this. Go ahead, please."

"Your Honor," North began, standing and smoothing his vest, "the question is not 'what did the doctor discover after the hospital hired him.' The question is, 'what did he contemplate when he signed the contract, and was it reasonable under all circumstances'? We hired a doctor to care for patients, not a physician administrator or an expert on billing practices to tell us how to run the hospital. If you allow an implied warranty in this professional services contract, you give Dr. Bascom and doctors in general *carte blanche* to say, 'I disagree with your billing practices or competency standards, and I'm walking out.'"

North put a hand in his pocket and walked in front of his table. "According to counsel's argument, his client can imply anything he wants in his contract that will let him walk if he doesn't like the way the hospital conducts its business, leaving it no recourse against him.

"Your Honor," he continued, "in his declaration the doctor says nothing about what he expected at the time he signed the contract. If he wanted veto authority over how the hospital billed its patients, he should have requested it be written into the contract.

"He negotiated a contract that provided him with a high compensation. I don't think he should be allowed to present evidence about things he doesn't like as an excuse to get out of it. I think it's clearly a question of law. There is no implied warranty in a contract such as this."

Montfort turned his gavel in his hand. "Mr. North," he mused, "suppose a law firm hired you, as a lawyer, under a contract similar to the doctor's, and then you learned the firm overcharged its clients, engaged in questionable and unethical practices, and mishandled cases. After being there several months you think, 'my gosh, I've got myself and my reputation on the line. I've got myself open to malpractice suits, possible disbarment, and perhaps criminal liability. I can't work under these circumstances and I'm going to leave.' Is that a breach of the contract?"

"Er, I believe it is, your Honor," he responded feebly.

"Can you raise these matters as defenses to a breach of contract action filed by the law firm?"

"The hospital did not engaged in criminal activity."

"Overcharging clients and providing substandard care may not be criminal, but such practices may well be unscrupulous or unethical, might they not?"

North hesitated. "Mr. Helleman would like us to believe the hospital... I don't even think this third defense says..."

"Someplace I read it," Montfort interrupted.

"This defense says the hospital would provide acceptable care and reasonably priced services," the lawyer replied. "According to whom? According to the doctor?"

"He doesn't have or want veto power," Montfort corrected. "He's just saying, 'I don't want to work there anymore.' He's not saying, 'I want to run the hospital.'"

"Well, if you're talking about a small hospital," North continued, "he might have veto power because he can say, 'I don't like the way you're managing the hospital. Therefore, I'm entitled to walk.' He can force a small hospital to say, 'we have no choice. We can't get a doctor to replace you and we'll have to do whatever you demand.'"

"I see," Montfort said, turning to Helleman. North returned to his chair and shuffled his papers, clearly relieved to be out of the line of fire.

"Mr. Helleman, isn't this like the trial of the Chicago Seven years ago where everything was dragged in, the legality of the Vietnam War and all the rest of it? Aren't you doing that in this case?"

"No, sir, I'm not. I have a doctor," he stated firmly, pointing at Bascom, "who came to this court to explain why, as a concerned physician, he could not allow the hospital to mistreat, misdiagnose, or overcharge his patients; it was and is morally and ethically reprehensible to him. If he is wrong on this point and the rest of his defenses, the court will award judgment for the plaintiff.

"If defendant is right, the court will say the hospital breached the contract and he was right in leaving. That is all we want."

Montfort drummed his fingers on the bench. "Tell me about these patients' records you want to drag around my courtroom."

"It's our allegation the hospital and its doctors ran these patients through unnecessary and then overcharged for them," Helleman explained. "We are certain a record review will confirm it."

Montfort nodded. "Mr. North," he said, "please proceed to your second argument." The lawyer's chair scraped the floor as he rose to his feet.

"I don't want to put my hospital in jeopardy of being sued or prosecuted because we're making available confidential records without the consent of the patient, your Honor," he said. "We cannot be put in a position where a patient asks, 'what right does the hospital have to make my personal and privileged medical records available to Dr. Bascom or to anybody else who is not treating me?'

"'This is not an insurance claim,'" North quoted the fictional patient as saying. "'This is not a malpractice case. This is nothing but a third-party wanting to look at my file.' As I read the law, either we get a court order requiring the disclosure or we get an authorization from the patient. Still there is the confidential nature of these records. The law is clear that these patients cannot be identified. Without either I don't think the hospital can be compelled to place itself in jeopardy."

"I agree with your coming to court, Mr. North," Montfort said thoughtfully, "because if I order you to turn over the documents, you are insulated. Nevertheless, there is much we could do *in camera,* all kinds of protections we could work with. I don't relish the idea, even if I were to grant Mr. Helleman's motion, of going through all these files and striking names and so forth. How many files are we talking about?"

"The doctor says he walked into the audit, picked up four files at random and said 'this is a whitewash.' Does he want to review just those files? I'd be surprised if he can remember what they are," he said with a hint of sarcasm.

Montfort looked troubled. "Maybe...."

"Your Honor, there are 2,000 files," Helleman interrupted, "and they exist as the remnants of this audit. We're willing to decide which are of evidentiary value and which are not, and I can't imagine there will be 2,000 separate lawsuits going on here."

Montfort looked at Bascom. "Is your doctor – he hasn't filed a cross-complaint, has he?"

"Yes, but it's not relevant to this motion."

"It's for $4,800 for rent supposedly not paid to him," North volunteered.

"Something not connected with this?"

"Your Honor," Helleman answered, "we're not coming in here, pie in the sky, inflated damages. This is a straightforward breach of contract claim, but we need to access hospital records to prove our defense. That is all we want."

"I see," the judge nodded. "Mr. North, do you wish to add anything?"

"Your Honor, if we're talking about 2,000 files, and if

at some point you decide the evidence is admissible, then both sides would have to examine them.

"Their experts are going to say, 'this obviously reflects substandard care or over billing.' My experts will say, 'no, this is not substandard care or over billing.' I'm looking for a practical solution to this, but I don't believe having patients' files bantered around the courtroom, whether they are four or 2,000, is it.

"At some point somebody will need to ask, 'was this patient over billed? Did this patient receive substandard care?' I might need to contact the patient to find out if he did get substandard care or was over billed. Was there a later credit or refund that might not be reflected in the file? I can see this growing to where we have 2,000 patients as potential witnesses running around the courtroom."

Helleman rose from his chair. "The Comptroller of State of Arizona has already examined Whitney's ER files, your Honor," he explained, "and he found, and it has been published in Whitney's newspaper, there was 30 percent over billing, substandard care, and other violations. And he did this without talking to one person. We would like the same opportunity.

"I don't care if this lawsuit is going to be inconvenient for the hospital. The court doesn't make a distinction on the merits of the litigation based on how much time or money the parties are going to have to spend. They have sued my client for $100,000, a sum that will force him into bankruptcy if he loses. As a matter of law and equity, the defendant has the right, and I and the court the duty, to allow him to present facts relevant to the meritorious defenses he has raised."

Judge Montfort sighed. "I came in here with the opinion that your motion to get rid of this third affirmative defense might be a good one, Mr. North. I'm not sure now, but I haven't made up my mind and I'm not about to allow a simple breach of contract claim to turn this court into a three-ring circus.

"There being no further comment from counsel, the matter is submitted," he said, banging his gavel on the bench. The judge gathered his notes, wrapped and picked up his robe, and left the courtroom as quickly as he had entered it.

Helleman stuffed his documents into his briefcase, spoke briefly to his adversary, and then went to Bascom.

"Well," he said cheerily, "round one is over."

"Do you think we'll get the records, Frank?"

"Donno. We need to hope Montfort is interested enough in our allegations to give you your day in court."

Helleman left for another hearing and Bascom drove home to Whitney after taking the parking ticket from under his windshield wiper.

XL

Several weeks after the hearing, Bascom's cellphone clapped its annoying sound and flashed Frank Helleman's name across its tiny screen.

"We won, Bob," Helleman reported laconically. "Judge Montfort has compelled WCH to give us the records, provided they're already grouped and the patients' identities are not disclosed. He wasn't as convinced as North was about the liberties hospitals could take with their patients' health and wallets.

"That should pick up your spirits."

"He said, 'provided they're already grouped,' correct?" Bascom asked.

"WCH says they're not any longer."

"I figured as much. I'll bet they burned them to bypass the order," Bascom groused.

"I don't doubt it," Helleman agreed. "We might be able to get around the obstacle if you're willing to compromise."

"How?"

"Halve your request and share the costs of reproducing the charts."

"Ok, but I want all the charts from 1 September to 15 October, consecutively numbered. I don't want Davidson to skip the records he wants to hide."

"I'll relay your message," Frank said.

Six weeks later Bascom's cellphone rang while he was working in his garden. It was early March, and although in the northeast cars were up to their hubcaps in dirty snow, weeds were popping through the gravel of his xeriscaped yard. He dropped his hoe and flipped open his insufferable companion.

"I died and went to heaven," he said. "Leave a message and my guardian angel will get back to you."

"Bob," Helleman asked, "are you off your medications again?"

"I hate cellphones, especially when I see people driving, smoking, eating, putting on make-up and talking into them at the same time. What's up?"

"North says the judge misunderstood the number of files involved. At the hearing he insists we were concerned with fewer than 100."

"Damn him!" Bascom yelled. "Montfort knows there are 2,000 files."

"I know," Frank agreed. "He wrote to the judge directly about this, violating protocol. Sending me a copy doesn't excuse the breach."

"What'd he say?"

"He wrote, wait a minute," he said, shuffling papers. Over the phone they sounded like wood popping in a fire.

"Ok. He wrote, 'the guidance I'm seeking arises from a dispute as to whether the production of these records is required. The hospital has found the files requested are not grouped together and the cost for pulling them, which number nearly 2,000, is prohibitive. Dr. Bascom's attorney has suggested we limit the number to 1,000 and divide the costs between our clients. However, my client feels the production of this many records is not what the court had in mind when it issued its order.

"'Part of the confusion,'" Frank read, "'stems from a misconception on my part as to how many files we were dealing with when the motion came before you. Then I understood Dr. Bascom was seeking to inspect fewer than 100 files. It appears he meant fewer than 100 files reviewed by the audit committee reflected the improper billing and unnecessary procedures he is complaining of in this litigation.'"

"What is he talking about?" Bascom demanded, scraping the ground with his hoe. "He invents the number 100 and then has the cheek to say I said it? Montfort won't buy that, will he?"

"I doubt it," Helleman answered. "Do you want to hear the rest, or is your pressure high enough for today?"

"My ears aren't ringing yet, so please continue."

Frank laughed. "He ends his epistle with, 'Bascom claims a review of the 2,000 patient charts at issue will confirm his allegations. The hospital disputes this.

"'Rather than moving for a protective order or being faced with an enforcement order, I believe we both would benefit from a modification of your order. Might I suggest Dr. Bascom be allowed access to a random selection of the files, perhaps no more than 200, and he be required to reimburse the hospital for the extraordinary costs for gathering them?'"

"No! No! NO!" Bascom shouted. "I know what they mean by 'random' and I can imagine the costs they'll put on the copying. I now want all the charts, the full three months' worth. I will not face another whitewash. *Capisci*?"

"Calm down, Bob. North has hurt himself with the lies in this letter. I'm going to suggest to Montfort he read the court reporter's transcript of the hearing. The number 2,000 appears there several times. Next, I'll point out that although the hospital alleges the records are no longer bundled, his ruling clearly recognizes their relevancy. Finally, the records are consecutively numbered and dated and to say they're not bundled is disingenuous. The court's order does not require they be in a neat stack with a bow around it."

"Will they comply, Frank?"

"Not right away. They'll further irritate the court first. Anyway, it's clear Davidson doesn't want anyone to see those records. He knows if we prove what we have alleged, the damage to his own reputation and to WCH's, would be far greater than any judgment he might be awarded if we lose."

"Thanks. Keep me informed," Bascom fumed as he snapped shut his phone.

He phoned Donna a few minutes later and she agreed to dine with him at a sushi bar in Phoenix that evening.

At 7 p.m., Bascom knocked on her apartment door dressed in a blue blazer, sport shirt, jeans, and cowboy boots. His Stetson hat covered his long, carefully brushed hair.

Donna opened it midway through his second series of knocks. Her black tailored silk suit and white blouse stunningly hugged her flawless shape, and her long auburn hair flowed loosely to her shoulders, framing the soft, mesmerizing features of a perfect face.

"You're beautiful," he said.

"You always give the nicest compliments, Robby," she laughed.

"I mean it. Shall we go?"

She shut her door and then put her arm through his as they walked to his SUV.

The sushi bar was one of a chain of restaurants that served entry-level Japanese food in the northern part of the city. A gray, feather-rock waterfall welcomed guests into its small dining room where two chefs, their heads wrapped with colorful blue and gray bandannas, sliced fish behind a glass topped counter. Bascom and Donna went to a booth being cleaned by a young Asian girl. She picked up her tray of dirty dishes and backed away as they slipped onto the benches. Bascom put his Stetson on the seat next to him.

"So how's work?" he asked, reaching for the menus at the end of the table. He gave Donna one and kept one for himself.

"Great, Robby," she replied, opening her menu. "I love my job at the U of P. I'm glad I left Whitney and I'll never set foot in that dumpy town again."

"I wish I could say the same."

"Any plans to join me and Dr. Jefferies?"

"Maybe when my battle is over."

The waitress reappeared and they ordered ice teas and *maguro*, *ebi*, *unagi*, *uni*, and *tako*.

"Tuna, prawns, eel, sea urchin, and octopus," he said after she left. "They beat my home-cooked, often inedible meals."

Donna laughed. "You never learned to cook in Italy?"

"Cris taught me how to make tortellini and tortelloni, but mostly I just learned to eat."

"Clown. Have you seen Evelyn recently?"

"Yes."

"How's she doing?"

"Not well. Ben calls daily for advice, but he knows more about the disease than I do. The guy is brokenhearted; he even cries during the calls. All I can do is listen and offer encouragement."

"I called her yesterday," Donna said. "Ben said she was sleeping and didn't want to disturb her. She never called back. How's the court case coming along?"

"Davidson intends to bankrupt me before we get to

trial. I wish I'd never complained about the mess at WCH. My contract would be up already, and I'd be gone from here."

"You couldn't let the abuses continue. I knew that when we first met in the ER. Considering all they've done to you in that town, it must be tough for you to continue to stand up for what you believe is right."

The waitress arrived with their iced teas, said their food would be along shortly, and left.

"People fight for what they believe in despite the obstacles," Bascom said as Donna stirred a pouch of synthetic sugar into her tea. "'Tough' doesn't enter their minds."

"Why'd you become a doctor?" she wondered.

Bascom shrugged. "Damned if I know. There's never been one in the family and I didn't even know one until I graduated med school, so I have no idea."

"Predestination?"

"I don't subscribe to theories that destroy man's will to decide for himself," Bascom said, reaching for a green-capped bottle of soy sauce at the end of the table. He rolled it in his hands. "Low salt," he mumbled before swapping it for the red-capped bottle he placed in front of him.

"What did your parents do?" Donna asked.

"My mother kept our family together in hard times and my father was a holier-than-thou Puritan who ran a grocery store. He was so rigid he even refused to sell chewing gum since he believed it was bad for your teeth. It was one of his many bizarre rules I had to follow or get my lumps. I think they invented child abuse laws with him in mind."

The waitress returned and Donna opened her napkin on her lap as she placed the trays of sushi on the table. The woman bowed and backed away.

"Did you enjoy medical school?" Donna asked, peeling the chopsticks from their wrapper. She picked up a large dollop of green wasabi from her plate with the wooden utensils and stirred it into a small dish of soy sauce. The black liquid turned dark brown.

"Sure," he said as he watched her soak the *uni* in the potent mixture and then bite into it. Tears immediately welled up in her eyes and she started to blow and cough. "Wow!" she said catching her breath. "Guess I used too much wasabi."

"It does get your attention, doesn't it?" Bascom laughed. "But, yes," he said, chewing a small piece of octopus, "I enjoyed med school. Living in a medieval city and exploring Italy's castles on my breaks was exhilarating. Oral examinations in Italian, however, were harrowing. At the finals professors asked us three questions from anywhere in the text they used to teach the course. Miss one and you had to wait months to retake the exam. Under that system some students took years to graduate.

"We had to know everything about the disease in question, even absurd theories long disproved. At first it seemed useless and impossible, but it forced me to consider all aspects of a patient's illness and taught me how to avoid the traps specialists fall into.

"For example if you have chest pain, a cardiologist might say you have heart disease and a gastroenterologist might diagnose an ulcer. Each would run a battery of expensive niche tests to prove he was right, sometimes even over reading their results to make a diagnosis where none exists. But they'd both be wrong if it were a pulled muscle, which is only the beginning of the tragedy. It psychologically destroys the healthy patient misdiagnosed with heart disease.

"That was the good side of what they taught at Bologna. The bad side was that a professor could fail you for any absurd reason that entered his mind, such as your

...style. If he didn't like it, no matter how well you answered his questions, he could toss you out of the exam room. Since an oral exam doesn't leave a paper trail, it was his word against yours, and you had no recourse.

"It sounds absurd, but it happened to a friend of mine who wore a Beatles' haircut. Because the professor hated their music, he made him retake the dermatology exam three times. The last time a different examiner quizzed him, and he passed with a perfect score. He's now practicing dermatology in a small town in Pennsylvania."

"I could never have survived in a system like that," Donna said. She tried to pick up a piece of tuna but could not hold it between her chopsticks. After several tries she picked up her fork and impaled the fish on its tines.

"I think you're smart enough to survive it if you wanted to," Bascom said.

"If you were to start over and had your choice of going to Harvard or to Bologna, which would you pick?"

"Bologna. There I learned what good food is, what true friends are, and what life is about, all wrapped in a cocoon of art, architecture, history, and music. It's why I readily agreed to return to Italy when Cris suggested it. We had everything money could buy here, but nothing of what it couldn't. I was starved intellectually and culturally and needed to return home.

"But if I had a choice, I'd have gone to work in my father's store. Sure it was a dead-end job working with a bigot that made Archie Bunker from 'All in the Family' look like Mother Teresa, but my idealism in this imperfect profession has become an impossible burden for me."

"Maybe you need to reevaluate your beliefs," she replied.

"I do, I know I do," he repeated softly. "I hope I will someday."

XLI

Donna had promised Bascom she would never again work in the Whitncy Community Hospital. She was not alone. No capable nurse would work there once she learned Doctor Albert Evans would blame her for his frequent and predictable diagnostic and treatment errors.

Those in the medical community knew he spent hours in the gym training for a "Mr. Doctor" title and used illegal anabolic steroids to sculpt his physique. Many believed the drug had decreased his intelligence, although the most cynical felt it had raised it to that of an idiot.

Donna would never forgive Cohen for firing her for calling Evans incompetent, but in exchange for a profuse apology from Sid Josephs, the hospital's new administrator, and a wage double that of the inexperienced nurses she would be coddling, she agreed to moonlight for one 12-hour shift in his ER.

She parked her yellow Jeep in the employee's lot on the cool, windy evening of March 25th and entered the emergency room. Besides the drunken Mexicans and Indians asleep in the waiting room, there was a young boy sitting with his mother on a corner bench. He was pale and breathing rapidly. She quickly crossed the room and knelt in front of him. The listless child was about 6 years old and had a bloodstained bandage wrapped around his neck.

"Hi, I'm Donna. What happened?" she asked the mother.

"Tommy's brother accidentally shot him with his pellet gun," she said, pulling her son to her breast.

"How long have you been waiting?"

"Over an hour."

"Let's go." She picked up the boy and quickly carried him into the trauma room. A young nurse arrived to help her as she lay him on a stretcher.

"What's your name," Donna asked the blond, pimply-faced girl.

"Kathy," she replied uneasily.

"I'm Donna. Is this your first night on the job?"

"Yes," she said. "I graduated last week."

"You'll do fine. Just ask me before you do anything you're unsure of. I want full vitals, an IV, and blood for labs on this boy. Can you do that?"

"Yes."

"Good. Who's on tonight?"

"Dr. Evans. He's in his office."

"Ok," Donna frowned, ruing her agreement to work that night. "And put an oxygen mask on him."

Kathy nodded as Donna went to the doctor's lounge where Evans was at his desk eating a sandwich and reading the comic page of his newspaper. A blue mask was resting on his forehead.

"I need you to see a critically ill patient, Dr. Evans," she said sternly, amazed he could chew and read at the same time.

"Hi, Donna. Longtime no see. I will as soon as I finish eating," he mumbled before taking a bite of his sandwich.

"Now!"

"Jeez," he pleaded, looking up. "I've been working hard for the last hour."

"That's what you're paid to do. Get in there now! I won't ask you again!"

The muscular doctor grunted and put down his sandwich before popping his mask onto his face. He strutted to the boy's stretcher, stopping three feet in front of it.

Donna went behind it and put her hand on Tommy's brow. The boy grimaced with every breath and held his tiny hand to his chest.

"What are his vitals, Kathy?" she asked as she caressed the child's forehead.

"Pressure 110/50, pulse 115."

Turning to Evans, Donna asked, "Did you hear that, Doctor? He's lost more blood than the bandage shows."

"But, but, that's all that came out," the mother protested.

"Don't worry. Doctor Evans knows what to do," she replied, resting her hand on the woman's. She knew he did not, but hoped he had understood the boy's abnormal vital signs meant he was bleeding internally.

She turned back to Evans who was ogling Tommy's attractive young mother. "Your patient is over here, Doctor," she said, impatiently tapping her ring on the stretcher's metal railing.

"Yes, of course," he said. "What is the problem?"

"Tommy's brother shot him in the neck with a BB gun and he's short of breath now," his worried mother explained.

"Where does it hurt, Timmy?" Evans asked.

The boy pointed to his chest. "I'm… Tommy," he said between gasps.

"Does your head hurt?"

He shook his head slowly.

"Belly?"

He shook his head again.

"Well," Evans concluded without touching the boy, "we need some tests. We can't be too careful." He ambled to the nurses' station ahead of his staff.

"Get a skull X-ray and an abdominal series, Kathy," he said as he wrote on the chart, "and a chest X-ray."

"But he said his head and stomach didn't hurt," she protested.

"Don't contradict me!" he ordered. "Do as I say! I also want a blood count, liver studies, a urine test and an EKG. Can't be too careful. And change the dressing on his neck," he said, handing the chart to the inexperienced nurse. Her hand shook as she reached for it.

"Yes, Doctor," she said dutifully. "His pressure is now 100/40 and his pulse is 125. They're worse than when he arrived."

"Just turn up the IV. I'll worry about his vitals."

"Yes, Doctor," she replied weakly as he returned to his office.

"Don't leave Tommy for a second," Donna cautioned. "Let me know immediately if there are any further changes in his vital signs."

"I will," she promised.

An hour later the nurses were waiting by Tommy's stretcher when Dr. Evans arrived. "His B/P is 90/50 and his pulse is 130," Donna said gravely. "I've started another IV in case you want to transfuse him."

"His tests are back," Evans said through his mask, ignoring the nurse's suggestion. "His blood count and hemoglobin are low. That means he's anemic. He probably eats too much junk food and needs iron. Now let's take a look at these X-rays," he continued. He carefully avoided contact with the boy's stretcher as he went to hang the films on a view box on the wall behind it.

"His skull looks ok, belly ok, and chest.... Hmm, this film is crummy. Looky here," he said, pointing to the base of the left lung. "It's all white on the bottom. It should be black, like the other side. This film stinks," he said. "Terrible technique." He tossed it into the trashcan and then turned to Tommy.

"I see the nurse has changed your dressing. There's no more bleeding. You were lucky."

"Are you sure he's ok, Doctor?" his mother asked apprehensively. "What about the pellet? Shouldn't you take it out? And he's pale and not breathing right."

"Ma'am, from the small amount of blood he had on his bandage, the pellet just nicked the skin. His color will come back with the iron pills and his breathing will return to normal once he calms down. Everyone gets nervous in here."

As he rebuked the mother's protests, a voice over the loud speaker called Donna to the intensive care unit.

"I'll be right back," she whispered to Kathy. "Don't do anything to this boy without asking me first. Understand?"

The nurse nodded as Evans continued to reassure Tommy's mother her son would be fine.

When Donna returned to the ER thirty minutes later, Tommy was gone. She asked Kathy if he was in the operating room.

"No, Dr. Evans pulled the IVs and sent him home with a prescription for iron."

"Iron?" she recoiled in horror. "The boy is bleeding internally and he sent him home with a prescription? Where is that idiot?"

Just then paramedics burst into the ER pushing Tommy on their stretcher. The boy was pale and gasping for air like a dying fish.

"Code blue!" Donna yelled. The other nurse on duty

rushed over to help as the ward clerk announced the emergency over the intercom. Evans, who was standing three feet away from a patient when the alert sounded, ran to the exit in the rear of the room.

"Damn you, Evans! Get back here!" Donna shouted as he disappeared through the door.

"John," she hollered to the clerk, "get Thompson in here, *stat*!" She helped lift Tommy onto the stretcher and cut off his clothes while Kathy pumped up a blood pressure cuff around his thin arm.

"Zero!" she called out in panic. "I can't get a blood pressure!"

"Calm down and listen to me," Donna ordered. "Start an IV with the largest catheter you can and hang a liter of saline. You did it before and you can do it again," she said evenly as the EMT picked up a laryngoscope from the crash cart and began to intubate the boy.

"I can't find a vein," she protested running her hands over the boy's arms. "They're all flat."

"I can't find any either," the other nurse said.

The EMT agreed. "We couldn't find any in the ambulance. He needs a cut-down, and only a doctor can do that."

"Keep looking," Donna ordered. Since Tommy would die without desperately needed fluids, she took a scalpel and a curved clamp from the crash cart and quickly sliced through the skin above his ankle. She dug deep into the tissue until she found a vein and slipped the clamp under it. Slitting it with the scalpel, she slipped a large plastic catheter into the opening. *All they can do is pull my license for exceeding my privileges,* she thought as she connected it to a bag of clear solution.

As she stitched the skin around the catheter, she ordered a technician to bring all the O-negative blood he had. Only a doctor could order blood, but a Mexican had died the last time she had waited for one to do so. It had taken her months to get over the events in the ER the night she first met Bascom, but at least Perkins was a doctor, sometimes. Evans was far worse.

"What else would Robby do?" she asked as she put a gauze pad over the stitches. "ABC, ABC," he always said. "Airway. Breathing. Circulation. Ok. We've done it all. Now what? Oh, why aren't you here, Robby? I need you!"

"Christ, don't let this boy die!" she pleaded as a nurse pasted the monitor leads on Tommy's chest. Then she cursed, "Damn it Thompson, where are you?"

At that moment the monitor pitcously screeched its dreaded news; Tommy's heart had stopped beating.

"Noooo!" she yelled, smashing her fist on the boy's chest. "Beat!" she ordered. She scrambled onto the stretcher, hiked up her skirt and straddled the boy's abdomen and began pumping rhythmically on his chest.

She continued relentlessly, perspiration beading on her face and running down her back, until she felt Joe Thompson's meaty hand on her shoulder.

Tommy was dead and he was asking her to stop the resuscitation.

Donna put her head on his shoulder and wept. As she sobbed over her failure to save the boy, Thompson put his beefy hands on her back, patted it gently, then slid it down her side onto the inside of her naked thigh.

XLII

Bascom had not seen a single patient for two days when Helen entered his office.

"Did you forget to pay the electric bill, Bob? They sent a second notice," she asked, holding up a letter in her right hand. In her left was a rolled up newspaper.

"I guess I forgot," he shrugged. "After they shut off all our utilities and we're forced to work by candlelight, I'll dress in buckskins and show our patients what frontier medicine was like."

"Funny," Helen laughed. "I'd rather not show you this," she added, handing him the *Times*, "but you'd find out anyway. Try not to shout your usual Italian expletives while you're reading it. They make the African Violets on my desk cover their purple flowers with their leaves and weep," she said wryly before returning to her office.

"Get back on your mood elevators, Helen," he yelled after her. She laughed from the hallway as he read the front-page article about Tommy's ordeal in the local ER. A minute later he tossed the newspaper on his desk. "It had to happen," he said as he telephoned a WCH X-ray technician.

"It's been the number one topic around here for the last two days," he said. "Dr. Muscles threw the boy's chest X-ray into the garbage because he said it was unreadable. Dr. Compton had me pull it out of the can the next morning and he said it showed a pellet lodged in the kid's neck and massive bleeding into the left chest from the artery it nicked. Evans was too dumb to know the white area he called 'bad technique' was blood.

"Our administrator said the boy had been admitted at 5:00 p.m. and died at 9:00 p.m. He never mentioned the kid sat an hour in the waiting room and that Evans discharged him at 7:30 p.m. with a script for iron pills. He was almost dead when paramedics brought him back an hour later. According to Donna Franklyn, Evans split when she called a code on the boy."

"Donna was there?" Bascom asked. W*hy hasn't she called me about this?*

"Yeah. She was the best nurse we ever had here. Josephs pleaded with her to work because he's desperate for help. No one wants to work with Evans. From what I hear, she called him an incompetent, egotistical bastard with less knowledge than a first year medical student. She said if Davidson and the others had listened to your warnings, the boy would still be alive.

"Someone called Davidson after the boy died. He pulled Evans and made Thompson work the rest of the night."

"Joe must have loved that," Bascom said.

"He bitched the whole time and especially the next morning. Someone saw him fondle Donna after the code and put nails or spikes or something behind the rear wheels of his Mercedes. When he backed out of his spot in the morning, bam! bam! Two flat tires. Took him hours to get them fixed and made him miss his surgery in Phoenix. I thought the fat bastard was going to have a heart attack.

"Did you read the mother's statement?"

"Where she said 'incompetence and bad care killed her child'?"

"Yeah. Her husband's a big wheel in town. I'll wager a month's salary this place will cough up millions to settle this one."

"Maybe," Bascom agreed, "but they've got a dead child and a 12-year-old son who'll be stigmatized for life as his brother's killer. An incompetent doctor destroyed that family, and money won't put it back together again, no matter how much WCH pays them."

"It's a tragedy," the technician agreed.

"Well, thanks," he said. As he was hanging up, Helen brought him a list of people who had called to ask his opinion about the accident.

"I'm not the coroner," he answered bitterly, saddened it had taken a tragedy to awaken the community to the dangers of their local ER.

He telephoned the Health and Consumer Affairs Board's most gallant representative.

"Hello, Dr. Adelsohn?"

"Yeah?"

"This is Dr. Bascom from Whitney. Do you remember me?"

"Whaddaya want?"

"Have you heard about the death of the boy they treated in the Whitney ER?"

"I read about it."

"Since you're concerned with the quality of the care in this state, I wanted to know if you intend to look into this case. Especially since it involves the doctor I complained to you and your Board about. You remember him, the one the state also accused of inventing symptoms and performing unnecessary tests."

"That's not my job, Bascom," Adelsohn growled. "But you'll hear from us. A doctor shouldn't discuss these matters with the press."

"I haven't spoken to the media yet, but I'm sure they'll contact me and then I will," he replied before slamming down his receiver. It startled Helen who was leaning against his desk and listening to the conversation.

"As long as his supply of bananas remains constant, Arizonans can feel safe knowing he's on the job," he said, bringing the article to his copy machine. He placed it on its glass, pushed a button, and waited until the machine spit out a duplicate.

"Send this to Helleman," he said, handing his secretary the copy.

Two days later Bascom read the article in *Times* entitled "Emergency Room Change Eyed." It reported that Davidson had summarily fired Evans and the doctor who had falsely testified against Bascom at the HACAB meeting.

It's too little too late, Davidson. I'll bet you're worried that a 'not officially identified,' local physician will testify for the distraught parents of a child who would still be alive had he received the proper care in your ER.

You should be, because he will.

He stapled the article to the one reporting Tommy's death and added it to a second, already bulging "Ripley's File of Medical Oddities" folder in his bottom desk drawer.

XLIII

A week after Tommy's death, Bascom sat in his office mulling over Evelyn's worsening condition. He had become emotionally involved in her care, and although his professional judgment remained unclouded, their friendship made his inability to cure her personal and painful.

He was wondering how difficult her last days would be for all of them when his phone rang. "We've won, Bob, we've won!" Helleman exclaimed jubilantly in his ear.

"We've won what?"

"North says Davidson will drop his lawsuit if you'll drop yours," the lawyer yelled in a sentence that sounded like one long word. Bascom rested his head on the back of his chair and closed his eyes.

"He can drop his if he wishes," he replied after a while, "but I won't drop mine unless he pays my back rent with interest, all attorney fees and costs, and prints an apology in our local rag."

"Wha... what.... Are you serious?" he stuttered. "You have no legal right to any of that."

"Maybe not, but it's what I want. Davidson knows he'll lose his case if we go to court. He's trying to bribe me to prevent that from happening. At the same time he's hoping I won't testify for the family of the kid who died in his ER. He can't buy me, and I will testify. Tell North to go fu..., to take a hike."

"But it'll cost you $100,000 plus if we lose," Frank protested. "Against our $5,000 claim, what you're asking doesn't make sense."

"This isn't about money, Frank. It never was."

"You know he could dismiss his lawsuit, Bob."

"Then why doesn't he?"

"I don't know. Maybe he thinks it'll look better in the press if he can say you agreed together to drop his lawsuit. If he does it alone, it'll look like you beat him. Bad for his ego.

"Whatever his reason, will you at least think over his offer?" he asked.

Bascom could hear the disappointment in his voice. "I already have," he said.

"Ok, but you'd better be ready for my bill."

"I will be."

"You know, Bob," he continued in a conciliatory tone, "most of my clients would accept this offer. It takes brass balls to battle a wealthy plaintiff like Davidson. I can't guarantee I'll win this, but if I do, I promise it'll be on your terms."

"I can't ask for more," Bascom replied. "Now back to our problem; I want those records. Davidson knows when we bring up the pellet gun episode at trial and I tell the jury I had warned him Evans was incompetent, the malpractice attorneys will pounce on him like hungry hyenas. That might even open this case to punitive damages his insurance won't cover."

"My firm's ahead of you there, Bob. We have top malpractice attorneys here, and Tommy's parents retained them today. They want your testimony as well as that of a nurse named Donna Franklyn."

"How poetic."

"I knew you'd like that. But North says if you don't accept the offer, we're going back to court."

"When?"

"The end of June."

"That's three months away!"

"Sorry, jammed schedule."

"If I made you wait that long for an appointment, you'd be ticked off, wouldn't you?"

"Sure, but that's life in my world."

Bascom sighed. "Okay. I just hope North is the most expensive lawyer in the land and that his billing schemes are as innovative as his client's."

That night Bascom drove to Phoenix to hear Donna's version of the pellet shooting incident.

When he arrived at her front door, he could hear John Coltrane playing "Blue Moon" on her stereo. He rang her bell, the music stopped, and a minute later she opened the door.

"Hi, Robby. It's a beautiful night, why don't we enjoy it?" she asked, quickly closing the door behind her. She pulled her sweater tightly around her shoulders and held it with crossed arms.

"Well, er, sure," he said, surprised she did not invite him into her house. They walked the path to the sidewalk and then towards the lights of a shopping mall.

"You said you won your case against Davidson?" she asked. Two boys on skateboards roared past them, forcing them into the street.

"He wants to drop the case," he replied as they returned to the sidewalk. "He hopes I'll appreciate his magnanimity and won't testify against Evans for his misdiagnosis of the boy who died from the pellet wound. By the way, why didn't you call me about that as soon it happened?"

"I thought about it," she shrugged, "but then decided not to add to your problems with Davidson. It was a bad scene though. I get nightmares trying to save that kid's life."

"You're a fine nurse and you did more than any other would have done," Bascom said. "You did much more than Evans did. You couldn't prevent his death, so don't crucify yourself over it."

"I don't have to; others will do it for me. The nursing board is looking into the case since Evans filed a complaint against me. He alleges he never heard the code and the boy died because I performed an illegal cut-down on his leg. It supposedly caused a pulmonary embolus that killed him."

"The son-of-a-bitch is incompetent <u>and</u> delusional," Bascom replied, shaking his head at the absurdity. "The autopsy will prove the boy died from an internal hemorrhage caused by the severed artery in his neck. His parents filed a malpractice suit against Evans and the hospital, and we'll testify for the family. Norm Jefferies threw Evans out of his residency program because he was incompetent, and I'm sure he'd testify for you and against Evans if he's called as a witness."

Donna rubbed a tear from her eye. "Thanks," she said, "but it'll only cause you more grief if you get involved in this case." They reached the end of the block and turned around.

"No it won't," Bascom protested. "Davidson will throw Evans to the wolves. Don't forget he pulled him off duty that night and fired him a few days later. He can't say he did that to reward him for the excellent care he gave Tommy. Davidson knew his revenue-generating troglodyte was incompetent because I told him so. Anyway, I won't let you face this alone."

"Thank you," Donna replied. She put her hand briefly

on Bascom's arm before crossing it in front of her again.

"Something funny happened after that boy died," she laughed. "While I cried my heart out on Thompson's shoulder, he was trying to feel me up."

"I heard about that. Slimy bastard! What did he actually do?" Bascom asked as he turned to face her.

"He put his hand on my thigh while I was still sitting on the ER table. When I realized what he was doing, I smacked the daylights out of him. A technician who hates that fat bastard saw what he was doing and put some nails or something behind his tires. Wrecked two of them when he tried to back out of the lot the next morning.

"It served him right."

"The man is a pig," Bascom said as they turned onto the path leading to her house.

When they reached the front door, he heard strains of Willy Nelson's, "Always on My Mind" coming from the living room.

"Didn't you turn off your stereo before you left the house?" Bascom asked.

"Er, I thought I did, but sometimes the control sticks and the records continue to drop," Donna explained, turning away from him. She took a key from her sweater pocket and inserted it in the lock.

"But Willy Nelson? I thought you hated Country and Western music."

"People's tastes change," she offered unconvincingly. "I'd invite you in, Robby, but I have a headache tonight. Maybe some other time, ok?"

"Sure, D, whatever you say," Bascom replied before returning to his SUV.

XLIV

In the middle of June, Ben Wiggins telephoned Bascom with news he had been dreading for months. "Ev's having trouble swallowing, Bob," he lamented. His sad words knocked against a door that would never reopen.

"I'll be over as soon as I finish with a patient."

"Thanks," Ben replied.

Twenty minutes later, Bascom pulled up in front of the Wiggins' Santa Fe home in its private cul-de-sac. Each of the three cubes of the stately stucco structure was offset from the one to its right and painted a different hue of brown. It was similar to villas he had seen on his trips through Tuscany.

He walked the winding flagstone path around an eight-foot tall blue yucca, between velvet mesquite trees and strawberry hedgehogs, and up to the porticoed entrance. The intricate, hand-wrought iron and glass doors were open and Ben was standing in the entryway. He was not waving his handkerchief as he had on the day they first met, nor was he wearing his toupee. Grief deeply lined his once cheerful expression, and the liveliest thing about the once vibrant man was the colorful Hawaiian shirt hanging loosely from his emaciated frame.

"Hi, Ben," Bascom sang out with an outstretched hand. "How are you today?"

"Ok," he replied dully. "Thanks for coming, Bob. Evelyn will be glad to see you."

The old physician stepped aside, allowing Bascom to enter a long, wide hallway that extended the full-length of the home. He paused to admire the carved wooden statues of Hotei, the Laughing Buddha, and Zocho, one of the four guardians who protect the world from demon attack, guarded the archway to a large living room. Hand stripped Vega logs and wood planking covered its 12-foot high ceiling.

Colorful handmade Indian rugs covered its Saltillo tile floor, and intricate bark paintings hung from its ocher walls. Brilliantly upholstered, hand-hewn log chairs and a huge sofa sat in the center the room. The glass rear wall opened onto a covered patio and a Pebble Tec pool. Water bubbled over a red sandstone waterfall.

"Ev's down the here," Ben said, as they walked past ships in glass display cases. A four-foot long model with a white and black hull caught Bascom's eye, and he stopped to examine it. "Built by Ben Wiggins for his Beautiful Consort, 1980," was inscribed in Gothic letters on a brass plaque under the ship's bow.

"Did you build this, Ben?" he asked. "It's beautiful."

"Yes. She's the *Amerigo Vespucci.* I built her and many others too. I had to quit modeling when my hands shook so much I couldn't string the rigging."

Rachmaninoff's *Piano Concerto no. 2* was playing on the stereo when they entered the large room at the end of the hallway. Leather-bound tomes, rolled manuscripts, exotic ceramic sculptures and photographs in antique frames filled the floor to ceiling cherry wood bookcases. A desk and captain's chair on wheels sat in a corner with a computer, an open medical textbook, and a lit Tiffany lamp on its leather top.

Evelyn lay with her head on two pillows on a new hospital bed with shiny chrome side rails in the middle of the room. She was gazing out the bay window at the pool's waterfall.

A middle-aged nurse pulled a sheet over her as Bascom approached, but not before he saw the yellowed, wrinkled skin covering her thin abdomen. After Ben's introduction, the nurse stepped away from the bed.

"This is the most luxurious patient room I've ever seen, Ben," Bascom said. He passed his hand over the dials of a new respirator by the bedside. "The surroundings, the view, the music, the equipment, and especially the care," he said, nodding to the nurse, "are gracious."

"Pulmonary and physical therapists come in three times a day," he explained. "Thanks to nurses who work around the clock, I sleep in my own bed at night. For a little while anyway. I'm usually back here with Evelyn after 30 minutes of tossing and turning. I can't bear to be away from her even for that long.

"A full-time nutritionist is preparing lunch, but Ev won't eat much of it. I don't know how to get food into her."

"No one could do more for her than you have," Bascom said, gently squeezing Ben's shoulder. "Don't ever doubt it."

"Thanks," Ben replied. "I just want you to make sure I don't make any mistakes."

"You won't, but I'll keep a careful watch anyway," Bascom assured him before turning to his ashen patient.

"Hi, Ev," he said, picking up her skeletonized hand. She silently moved her lips and continued to gaze out the window. He palpated her abdomen under her sheet and then performed a brief neurological exam. He wondered if it was at that moment a physician realizes his ministrations had passed from the sublime to the ridiculous. Evelyn was dying. She had no more than a few months to live, and his superficial examination would do nothing to prevent it. She and Ben knew it also, and they would never believe him if he told them otherwise.

He put his hand on Evelyn's. "I'm still waiting for that meal you promised," he said as he gently brushed a lock of hair from her pinched face. She stared vacantly at him before returning to the bubbling waterfall.

"Do you have time for a chat, Ben?" he asked his friend.

"Sure," he replied. Bascom bid good-bye to Evelyn and the nurse before they reentered the hallway and walked to the door.

"Is Ev still against the feeding tube?"

"Yes."

"Then we need to change her medications and begin intravenous feeding, since she hasn't objected to that. If we can get her out of her depression and get some nourishment into her, her life will be more meaningful for both of you."

"That would be great!" Ben said brightening at the thought. "What would you suggest?"

"I'll need to check for something that won't hurt her. I'll have the pharmacy deliver it today."

"Thanks, Bob. I appreciate it. Oh, by the way," Ben added, opening the front door, "you've never sent us a bill."

"It'll arrive. Keep checking your mail."

"I'm sure," he said knowingly. "Meanwhile, I'd like to stress how grateful we are for all the help you've given us. You can't know how much it has meant."

They hugged and then Bascom walked to his SUV.

XLV

On June 29, Frank Helleman, wearing a blue pinstriped suit and red collegiate tie, stood behind his table in the bullpen of the oak-paneled room of the Superior Court building in Phoenix for the second time. Bascom, dressed in a cowboy shirt and jeans with his Stetson resting on his lap, sat directly behind him in the first row. He had accused Frank of treachery in the parking lot when he saw him wearing Davidson's team uniform, and it took several minutes for his lawyer to calm him. Once Frank understood the cause of his client's tirade, he apologized for appearing to have joined the enemy, and promised he would never again wear anything striped. Not even pajamas.

Judge Montfort sat at the bench, impatiently drumming his fingers while glaring at Helleman through gold-rimmed glasses.

"Where is Mr. North?" he demanded.

"I can't say, your Honor," Frank responded.

"I'm interrupting a murder trial to give you people an opportunity to clarify my order about the production of records. Why must I always wait for Mr. North?"

"Your Honor, this matter was set at his convenience and properly noticed."

"Harrumph," Montfort replied.

Frank doodled on a yellow pad until Davidson's lawyer

arrived. "You're thirty minutes late, Mr. North," Montfort reprimanded the dapper figure.

"I apologize, your Honor," he said simply as he walked to his table.

"Your tardiness has prevented us from hearing your presentation," the judge growled. "Please go to the clerk's pool to coordinate a new date at the court's and Mr. Helleman's convenience."

The attorneys exited the courtroom with Bascom following. He slipped out a side door as soon as they entered the hallway.

Two weeks later Bascom, twirling his thumbs in his front row seat, Helleman, tapping his pen on his table, and Judge Montfort, impatiently drumming ten fingers on the bench, again sat in the courtroom waiting for Davidson's attorney. Although tardiness had been his rule, this time North did not appear at all, and the judge underscored his displeasure in his ruling:

> "The matter having come regularly on the calendar in department six of the Phoenix County Superior Court, the Honorable Ernest Montfort, Judge presiding, upon the stipulation for rehearing previously entered into by counsel, defendant and cross-defendant appearing himself and through his attorney Frank Helleman and there being no appearance by plaintiff and cross-defendant or counsel, and upon consideration of the entire file, pleadings, and argument, it is hereby ordered, adjudged, and decreed as follows:
>
> "That the records previously ordered to be produced by plaintiff and cross-defendant be produced,

"That the issue of the responsibility for the cost of the production of these records be specifically reserved by the court, and,

"That pursuant to motion duly filed and noticed, sanctions of $1,500 are hereby awarded against plaintiff and cross-defendant in favor of defendant and cross-complainant."

Legalese had become Bascom's fourth language after English, Italian, and Medicalese. He could not know if Davidson was aware of the job his society lawyer was doing for him, but he translated the ruling into English and sent it to the Whitney *Times* for publication, identifying both the plaintiff and defendant by name.

On November 23, eleven months after Judge Montfort's original order, a courier delivered the emergency room records in two large, duct-taped boxes to Frank Helleman's office.

Bascom's long sought and hard fought victory came shortly after his 5th anniversary in dusty Whitney. He celebrated it alone in front of his river rock fireplace, the poster of his snow covered *baita* with a glass of fine Barolo wine.

XLVI

At 3:30 a.m. Christmas morning, Bascom's phone jarred him awake. "Pronto!" he mumbled an Italian hello. "Cris? *Pronto*."

"Bob?" the shaky, tearful voice asked after a deep, convulsive cough.

"Ben? Sorry. I was dreaming."

"Evelyn is (cough) dying. Will you...?"

"I'm on my way."

"The door's unlocked."

Evelyn had developed pneumonia and had been in a coma for several days. Her life now was being measured in hours, but yesterday only in minutes until Ben convinced Bascom to intubate her. She was starving to death and he could not bear to see her suffocating as well. The old physician knew the love of his life would soon be gone, but he would not give her up quietly.

During the last weeks of her illness, he had hobbled on his weak, arthritic legs to his desktop computer to search online medical journals for new cures for Lou Gehrig's disease as well as every life-sustaining procedure imaginable. Unfortunately his attention span was brief and his grief even greater. After a few minutes he would abandon his search and would return to Evelyn's bedside to hold her hand and pray.

Bascom did not try to convince him they had done everything possible for the dying woman, since that would destroy his firm belief he could still save her. Instead he stood by discreetly, ready to help his friends at any moment.

Ben also had developed pneumonia for which he refused all treatment. He had looked like a withered cactus melting slowly into the desert when they were together just a few hours earlier.

Bascom dressed quickly, raced to his SUV. Minutes later he screeched into the Wiggins' driveway. Apart from the carriage lights on the sides of the garages, the majestic home was dark. As he ran to its stately entrance, motion detectors sensed his presence and lit his way.

He entered the home, waved to Hotei and Zocho who guarded the entrance to the living room, and looked to the glow at the end of the hallway.

"Ben?" he called. He could hear Evelyn's respirator rhythmically interrupting Beethoven's "Fűr Eliza," the same piano concerto that was playing on the radio in his office the night Cristina died. It gave him a chill.

"I'm here, Bob," he said after a deep, rattling cough.

"Coming," Bascom replied. He passed the *Amerigo Vespucci* in its glass case and entered her room. Ben, in his food-stained pajamas, was holding a red catheter in one hand, and with the other, was clumsily trying to separate the plastic tubes taped together in the corner of Evelyn's mouth.

"She's full of mucus. I can't suction her," he said before a racking cough shook his frail frame. He dropped the catheter on the bed and held his chest until the spasm passed.

"Let me," Bascom said. He separated the tubes, inserted the catheter into the endotracheal tube, and sucked out the obstructing mucus. He then reconnected the tubes and turned to check the respirator's settings. When he turned back, Ben was struggling breathlessly to climb onto the bed.

"Where are your nurses?" he asked as he helped his old friend onto the raised mattress.

"I sent them home," Ben replied as he crawled under the covers and stretched out next to his skeletal wife. "Death is too personal to share with strangers. Thanks for coming."

"I wouldn't have forgiven you had you not called me," Bascom replied. "Ben, please let me treat your pneumonia."

"There's no (cough) need now," he replied as he lifted Evelyn's head onto his shoulder. He coughed until he was blue before catching his breath. He then moved a few gray hairs from his dying wife's face and kissed her temple.

"Ronald's in Africa on a photo safari and is flying back for the funerals," he explained weakly, exhausted from his relentless cough. "Since he won't make it tonight, I'd like you to call the number on the kitchen table before you leave. They'll know what to do."

He again pressed his lips against his wife's head and tenderly caressed her face with his trembling hand. "Evelyn and I thank you from the bottom of our hearts for the friendship and kindness you've always shown us, especially during this time of trials," he said. "She was the most wonderful thing that ever happened to me, and even if our time together as husband and wife was short and plagued with suffering, being with her gave me more happiness than all my years without her.

"Ev and I followed your struggles, Bob. One day you'll be proud to know you had the courage to hold to the truth as you saw it. Not many can say that. We wish you success and happiness in the adventures life has in store for you, though I still think you could serve people best (cough) by running a not-for-profit clinic on some Italian mountaintop.

"In the kitchen," he explained between gasps, "you'll find things we feel only you would appreciate. I'm also returning your wonderful book. I didn't want it to fall into less worthy hands."

"But, Ben," Bascom interrupted.

"Please." His trembling hand whitened as he pressed Evelyn's head to his chest. "This life has nothing left to offer us," he said softly. "We'll soon be on another journey. If we can take our memories, you'll be with us."

Bascom rested his hand on Ben's bony shoulder. "You're not…," he insisted.

The old physician held up a blue-tinged hand. "Remember, no matter how long you may live, life's too short to learn on your deathbed you chose the wrong path, fought the wrong battles, or worshiped the wrong gods. After almost 85 years on this earth, the only man I ever met whom I think understood that was swaying on the gate of a lunatic asylum. To each passerby he sang out contentedly, 'I'm free and you're not.'"

Ben coughed and after a brief pause added, "I learned almost too late I couldn't change the world, but I could enrich the lives of those few people who wanted my assistance and love, and 'that has made all the difference,' to reinterpret Frost. Now push the respirator over to me, Bob."

Bascom moved the machine to the side of the bed and Ben switched it off. When Evelyn made no effort to breathe, he kissed her forehead. "Good-bye, my love," he said tearfully, caressing her face with his bony hand. "Don't stray far. I'll be right with you." He turned to Bascom and with a smile, said, "thanks for all you've done for us, Bishop. I'm grateful to have known you, but now I must go. Evelyn's waiting."

"But, Ben," Bascom said tearfully, "you can't…"

"I must. Do you get it yet, Bittle?" he asked before kissing his wife's forehead. Bascom thought for a moment, and then a light went on in his head.

"I finally get it, Ben! I do!" he exclaimed to his dying friend. "Alpha-Omega, the beginning and the end. Life and death." It was a simple idea, but at last he had realized he needed something between the extremes of his being to give his existence meaning.

Seeing Ben and Evelyn lying together made him understand there was more to life than fighting Davidson, incompetent physicians, and injustice. Altruistic knights-errant had a moral duty to defend those unable to fend for themselves, but he now realized he had to fight those battles, not with bitterness and self-righteousness as he always had, but with love, both for himself and for those who cared about him.

As his shoulders molted his rusty burden, a smile appeared on his lips.

Ben looked into Bascom's eyes. "Yes, Dr. Bascom, I think you do finally get it. Congratulations," he said, extending a tremulous hand. Bascom took it and held it between his own. "But will you do anything with your new knowledge?"

"Why do you always ask me these tough questions? 'Do you get it yet?' And now, 'What will I do with my new knowledge?' I don't know what I'll do with it."

"Good luck anyway, Robert. Now I'll be on my way. Vroom." He squeezed his friend's hand and closed his eyes. His breathing slowed and after a minute, ceased.

"Ben, Ben. I'll miss you. The world will miss you," Bascom said as tears streamed down his cheeks. He held the old physician's hand for a long moment before placing it on his wife's shoulder in a lover's embrace. He then removed the tube from Evelyn's throat and repositioned her head next to Ben's. He hoped their journey, wherever it would lead, would be together.

He went to the kitchen and turned on the light. There in the middle of a beautiful hand-carved table painted with colorful scenes of exotic birds, was a scrapbook, a shoebox, and Evelyn's bowling statue. He picked up the statue and rotated it slowly at eye level, studying the offensive award George Cohen had given her for her years of faithful service in his stucco shack.

"What in Hades will I do with this brass bomb?" he wondered.

No answer came to mind, and he replaced it on the table and then picked up the shoebox. He slit the tape on its lid with the small Swiss army knife on his key chain and opened it. In it were the *Religio Medici* he had given to Ben as a wedding gift, a blue envelope, and a wrapped object with a red bow on top. He removed the latter, carefully pealed away its tissue paper, and then roared with laughter until tears ran down his cheeks.

"I can't believe you left me this, Ben," he howled. Still laughing, he replaced it in the shoebox and picked up the envelope with his name and the sentence, "Please contact my attorney, Peter Henry, in Phoenix," was shakily scrawled on the front. He opened it.

"Dear Bob, (it said)

"We've taken care of Ronald, but could think of no better investment in the future than you. We're sure you'll find a way to care for the unfortunate that need your help. You're one of the best physicians we've ever known during our decades in medicine.

"Good luck and long life.

"With great affection,
"Ben and Evelyn"

"Thank you," Bascom said. He carefully replaced everything in the shoebox and opened the scrapbook and read the history, in browned, friable newspaper articles, letters and photos, of Dr. Eric Leighton's battles against medical corruption in Whitney from the early 1930s to the 1950s. Following his story were Ben's own struggles.

He skimmed the scrapbook's collection of documents until one article caught his eye: "Hospital Accused of not Serving Patients." Then another, "Hospital Urges Investigation," and still another, "Let's Investigate Hospital Emergency Room Costs."

Bascom was incredulous as he continued to flip through the pages of the worn album. Ben had saved every article he had ever written, or had ever been written about him, since his arrival in Whitney, and had added them to his scrapbook of war stories. A shaky question mark was scrawled across the page after the last article. The rest of the book was blank. It was as if Ben had considered the scrapbook a caduceus to pass on from warrior to warrior, both to document the battles of their predecessors, and to offer hope for the future.

The stories in the scrapbook were a *vade mecum* of battles not to fight, since the physicians in the loosely bound tome had lost theirs. But it began to make sense as Ben's last words echoed though Bascom's head: "life's too short to learn on your deathbed you chose the wrong path, fought the wrong battles, worshiped the wrong gods."

I will miss you, Ben.

He closed the scrapbook, picked up the slip of paper

from the table, and called the number scrawled there. It was the local mortuary, and the man who answered said he would be over to "collect the bodies."

"Bodies" to you; ethereal spirits to me.

Bascom hung up and returned to the den. He squeezed his friends' hands in a silent good-bye, pulled a sheet over their heads, and returned to the kitchen to pack up his inheritance.

He turned off the light and left the Wiggins' stately home for the last time.

XLVII

That Christmas afternoon Bascom sat alone in his living room listening to carols on the radio and reading Thomas Coar's 1822 edition of *The Aphorisms of Hippocrates*, a book he had brought with him from Italy. It had been his favorite holiday since his childhood years, even when Santa had been too poor to bring him a gift, but he had not celebrated it since Cristina's death. Because of Ben's and Evelyn's deaths, he would not celebrate it this year either.

He called Donna that evening to tell her about the double tragedy.

"You mean he willed himself to die?" she asked incredulously.

"Yes. Ben's is only the second case I've ever seen. The first was when I was an intern. A nurse called me to help an 80 year-old unconscious patient lying on the floor in his bathroom. When I put my hand on his chest, he opened his eyes, looked squarely into mine, said, 'I'm dead. Leave me alone,' and closed his eyes again.

"He had come back from the dead to tell me he was dead. So I left him alone."

"Are you kidding me?" Donna asked.

"Nope. I get goose bumps every time I think about it."

"I've never heard of such a thing, but if you say it's

true, I'll believe it," she replied. "I'll be at the funerals. Meanwhile have a Merry Christmas."

"I'll do my best," he replied before hanging up.

He was sipping orange juice and listening to Stan Getz' "Autumn Leaves" when the doorbell rang 30 minutes later. He ignored it since he did not relish letting anyone see how miserably he was passing the holiday, but when the staccato ring insisted, he reluctantly rose from the couch and opened the door.

"Merry Christmas," the Price trio sang out in imperfect harmony. He laughed and stepped back to let Jonas, wearing a red and white Santa's cap, enter his home.

"Merry Christmas, Dr. Bascom," he said as he passed him.

"And a Merry Christmas to you," Bascom replied, "but I don't…"

"Martha insisted we bring you dinner before going to my mother's," Jonas interrupted. "We felt it time we made a call at your house after all the ones you made to ours.

"And it's ready to eat," Martha said in her red and white candy cane scarf and black boots. She held a covered plate up to his nose as she entered the house. "Where's your kitchen?" she asked. He smelled the hearty aroma of roasted turkey as she followed his pointing finger.

Carl, a pointy nosed elf in curly-toed shoes and carrying a red box with a gold bow on top, limped in behind his mother. "This is for you, Dr. Bascom," he said. His right arm shook slightly as he handed up the gift.

"How nice, Carl," Bascom said, pleased by the unexpected present.

"Open it," he said excitedly.

"Ok, give me a minute."

He sat on the couch and carefully and teasingly slit the

tape on the wrapping.

"Come ON, Dr. Bascom," Carl pleaded. "Hurry! Open it!"

"Ok, hang on," he grinned as he peeled away the paper and opened the box. He removed a large-scale model of a red 250, short wheelbase, Berlinetta Ferrari and held it up for all to see. One decal was off center and a dab of glue marred a seam, but otherwise it was perfect. Bascom knew the boy's tremor would be permanent and had often wondered how he would react to being different from his peers. Now he sensed Carl had accepted his disability. He thought it might just be the impetus to drive him to greatness.

"It's beautiful, Carl," he said. "Thank you."

"My hand shook as I was putting on the decal, but I'm learning how to control it."

Bascom put the model on the coffee table and hugged the boy tightly.

"You're doing great, Carl. If I had a son, I'd want him to be as brave as you are."

"We need to be on our way," Jonas said. "We're late for dinner and my mother isn't the most patient person in the world."

"She's a real bitch," Martha mumbled.

"That's the Christmas spirit," Jonas chided.

Bascom hugged each of the Prices, and after they left, picked up Carl's masterpiece from the table and studied it carefully.

"Hippocrates was a smart guy," he said as he admired the model's detailed interior through the driver's window.

XLVIII

Four days after Christmas, twin hearses carrying Ben's and Evelyn's polished caskets drove up to a remote, wind ravaged knoll in Whitney's World War II cemetery. It was overgrown with weeds and lightning had split a tree, leaving one of its branches resting on a headstone next to the Wiggins' burial plots. It was a lonely and desolate place, but Ben had wanted to be buried next to comrades who had fought with him in the Great War.

It was cold and drizzling when Bascom, Helen, and Donna joined the hundreds of Whitnians paying homage to a couple that for decades had brought solace to a populace sorely in need.

"So, you're the woman my boss told me about," Helen said as they followed the crowd to the gravesites. "You're different, though. He told me you were overweight and homely."

"What?" Donna said, glaring at Bascom through narrowed lids.

"Only kidding," she answered, pulling up the hood of her parka.

When all the mourners had arrived at the rim of the gravesites, Father Hartnet spoke. "Friends," he began, "Ben asked me to hold an Indian style ceremony instead of the usual stodgy, open coffin, 'doesn't he look great,' one. So I would like you to circle the caskets now and to join hands."

After the gathering had formed concentric circles around the graves, he said, "Ben practiced medicine in this community for more than half a century. Some of you he brought into the world, others he 'snatched from the jaws of death' as he liked to say. 'Thank you' was often payment enough for this special human being who dearly loved us and especially Evelyn, his wife and equal for too short a time. I wish them Godspeed on their journey, and know they will unite in everlasting happiness.

"Are there any among us who would like to recall a special memory?"

Ronald, Evelyn's son, and an elderly man leaning on a cane were standing in front of the caskets. The old man rubbed his red-rimmed eyes with his handkerchief. Hartnet looked at them. "Peter, Ronald?" he asked.

The man mouthed, "I, I can't." Ronald shook his head and burst into tears.

A thin, stooped man in a brown overcoat spoke. "I have cerebral palsy," he said, taking his hat off and resting it over his heart, "but thanks to Ben, I've been your mayor for years. In my darkest moments he made me understand my humanity and spirit were far more important than my physical appearance. He convinced me I could do anything I put my mind to, so I ran for office and he got me votes. I'll be forever grateful to him."

An overweight middle-aged woman leaning on a gaunt man stepped forward. "Ben and Evelyn took turns sitting by our Ricky's bedside for three days and nights after he got meningitis. They left only after he was ok. We were destitute and Ben never asked us for a cent. If there's a list of great doctors and nurses somewhere, they should be at the top. There'll never be others like them, especially in this town," she said tearfully. Her husband put his arm around her shoulder and kissed her on the cheek.

When it was Bascom's turn, he said simply, "If Ben is watching us now, I'm sure he'd be pleased to hear those he most loved appreciated his life's work." Donna squeezed his hand, signaling her esteem for the great man.

The eulogies continued until a downpour ended the services. Father Hartnet held his worn bible over his head as he said his final words. He tossed a handful of mud onto the coffins, and then scurried to his car behind Bascom and the other mourners.

"Ben was more than a just doctor to me," Helen said in the SUV on the way to the office. "He was a humble hero of medicine. The 'physicians' he left behind in this town can't hold a candle to him."

"He couldn't have been gentler with his patients," Donna added. "He always asked me to take care of them. I'm only a nurse, but I don't think he ever made a mistake."

"'Only a nurse'? You're more competent than many doctors in this town," Bascom interrupted. "But since a person doesn't die until the last person who remembers him does, Ben will live for decades to come."

Bascom dropped off Donna at her yellow Jeep before parking his SUV behind his office.

"Did you decide what do with Evelyn's statue yet?" Helen asked him as they entered the building.

"No. That ugly thing is still sitting on a shelf in my bookcase," he answered. "I should melt it down and be rid of it."

They crossed the waiting room and she entered her office through its Dutch door. Bascom leaned on its ledge while she doffed her wet parka and hung it on a clothes tree in a corner of the small room.

"By the way," he said, "I've finished my review of the ER records."

"And?" she wondered as she pulled a few charts from the file cabinets.

"Albert Evans, the masked doctor who refuses to touch a patient, is worse than an incompetent shaman. The records don't show Davidson's innovative billing schemes, but that'll be our next step."

"What does Frank think about your chances of beating him?" she asked. She frowned as she put six files in a metal rack by her phone. "This used to overflow with charts. Today we have only a handful of patients. I guess I shouldn't complain though. Recently we've had only one or two a day."

"Business will pick up again, Helen. Just be patient. As for Davidson, Frank is waiting for my review before he'll comment. Norm Jefferies, Donna's boss, said he'd testify for me if he agrees with my findings, so I'm optimistic."

"Testify like fat Thompson did at the District Board meeting?" she asked contemptuously.

"I doubt it. There are still some good doctors out there."

"Fewer than you think."

"And Davidson called me cynical."

"I'm not cynical, Bob," she retaliated. "I've seen how shabbily they treated you simply because you wanted the best care for the people in this town. I don't know how you survived the stress and humiliation."

"I almost didn't," he replied. "Well, it's time to document the bad news," he said before going into his *Piccola Repubblica* to audit his books.

It took him only 30 minutes to realize he had seen an average of nine patients a day that year, down from thirty when he first arrived in town, and was in a severe financial bind. He was rechecking the numbers when Helen knocked on his door.

"What do the books show?" she asked. She leaned against the jamb and crossed one foot over the other.

"We're down a bit," he replied as he shut the ledger and sat back in his chair.

"'A bit'? That's the understatement of the year. Did you forget I run this place?" she asked irately, rubbing her neck.

"If Davidson would stop importing doctors into this town," he answered, "we and the farm workers would be better off. A doctor's Mercedes and his ex-wives eat up a lot of his income, which comes only from what he charges his patients. When many doctors share a small patient pie, they increase the number of examinations they order, striking fear into unsuspecting patients by threatening them with a health disaster if they don't undergo immediate investigation by the most expensive technology.

"We're being hurt even more because the once popular 'Dr. Bascom has left town' is now, 'Dr. Bascom can't treat your runny nose. Go to Dr. Plank, our newly arrived ENT specialist who can.' ER docs refer patients, especially ours, to doctors who are on the hospital staff. If you're not a member of the club, you don't get referrals."

"Don't use the word, 'colleagues,' please," Helen rebuked. "They're not worthy of the title. Anyway, excuses and explanations can't hide the fact we're in deep trouble," she said softly. "You need to do something."

"I have," he said with a smile. "I bought two lottery tickets yesterday."

"Darn it, Bob! How can I make you understand the trouble you're in?"

"I know how bad it is, Helen. I know."

XLIX

On an evening three months later, as a blustery winter storm filled the air with dust and the spores of the Valley Fever fungus, Frank Helleman knocked on Bascom's door.

"Am I late?" he sneezed as the door opened.

"Nope," Bascom answered. "Neither is Norm Jefferies. He's right behind you."

He showed the men into his living room and offered them a tray of homemade *hors d'oeuvres*. Frank took a cheese cracker before sitting in Thompson's chair with its shaky arms. Jefferies sat on the couch. He had gained a few pounds since they last met, but kept his distinguished air.

"Well, Bob, what did you find?" Norm asked.

Bascom handed him a pile of patient charts from the coffee table and sat next to him. "Bad care, unnecessary testing, falsified patient statements, all thanks to your old friend, Albert Evans," he said as Jefferies read the top chart.

"He can't defend these records in court, Norm," he continued, "no matter whom Davidson pays to testify on his behalf. In the case you're looking at now, Evans admitted the patient to the hospital with pneumonia, but his X-ray, blood tests and vital signs were all normal. He might have had a cold, but that was all.

"The next describes an injury to a patient's 'anterior

calf,' wherever that is," he added sarcastically. "This ambulatory patient had X-rays of both legs and hips, all of which were normal, as was his unnecessary urinalysis. Evans' diagnosis? Carpal tunnel syndrome. I guess he didn't know his diagnosis was for wrist and hand pain."

Jefferies shook his head. "Are they all like this?"

"Some are ethically worse. All the patients in those charts who had head CT scans specifically denied head injuries or loss of consciousness at the time of their minor automobile accidents. He added the words 'possible head trauma,' or 'suspected loss of consciousness,' on each chart and then ordered the scans."

"My god, that's terrible!" he exclaimed, clucking his tongue.

"It is, but worse than the imposition of nonexistent symptoms, is his misdiagnosis of injuries and diseases that were present," Bascom said, retaking the first and handing Jefferies a second pile of charts.

"After X-ray, he diagnosed all of these injuries as sprains. The radiologist diagnosed a fracture in every case.

""He ordered unnecessary tests both for nonexistent illnesses and for legitimate ones. In either case, he misdiagnosed his patients. Four out of in his ER are pawns in his expensive game, but since they usually recover on their own, if he doesn't kill them with dangerous medications or procedures, his misdiagnoses are meaningless.

"If a patient does need emergency care at WCH, like the kid who died after his brother shot him in the neck with a pellet gun, or the Mexican who bled to death because his skin was the wrong color, he loses. A different doctor was involved in that case, but it shows what's been going on in that place."

"This is far worse than I imagined," Norm said, placing the records on the table. "No wonder you're upset. Any competent doctor would be."

"Dr. Jefferies," Frank interrupted, "are you saying Bob's observations correct?"

"Yes. Evans was incompetent when I knew him. I was certain he'd get into trouble someday."

"You know him? Is he specialized in ER medicine?"

"He might be, but I don't know for sure. I threw him out of my program after six months. He was the worst resident I ever had. He would have done well in a weight lifting contest, though. He was the perfect dumbbell."

Frank laughed. "Would you be willing to testify that these records reveal serious deficiencies in regards to the medical expertise of this doctor?"

"Certainly. This guy shouldn't work in an ER where you need to make a life-or-death decision in a split second. He shouldn't practice, period."

"Would you list your qualifications, please?"

"Excuse me?" Norm replied, visibly startled by the unexpected question.

"Witnesses with the most weight have the most influence," Frank explained.

"I should do fine, then," he replied, patting his belly. He listed his credentials and then, rising from the sofa, said, "I'm sorry I have to break up the party, but I've got to return to the hospital to check on a patient."

After Bascom saw his guest to the door, he returned to the couch.

"What do you think, Frank?"

"He's at the top of his specialty, and that's a big plus for us. Add the fact he dropped Evans from his program, and it doesn't get much better. How many charts do you have for me?" he asked as he took a piece of blue-veined *Gorgonzola* cheese from the tray on the table and ate it in one bite.

"About ninety," Bascom replied, handing him a handwritten list of the charts and their errors. Frank wiped his fingers on a napkin and scanned the list.

"After my secretary translates this into English," he grinned, "I'll send out a request for admissions. We'll see what Mr. North has to say about our findings."

"How long will that take?"

"A while. Don't expect answers the first time around."

"I know, the wheels of justice turn slowly but I'd rather not win this case posthumously."

"Let's just win it," he said.

"Ok," Bascom answered. They walked to the door and after a handshake, Helleman exited into the still blustery night.

A month passed before Bascom received a copy of the 85 questions Frank wanted Dr. Davidson to answer about Evans' work, as well as a letter from North that specified the date they would take depositions in Phoenix. He would have to pay North's time and travel from San Francisco, but he was willing to do so since the suit had been dragging on for two years and he did not know how much longer he could survive in his almost patient-less office. He dreaded losing his battle with Davidson simply because he could not afford to fight it.

North's succinct answer to Frank's request arrived a week later. "In answering these interrogatories," he wrote, "Whitney Community Hospital objects because they are not calculated to lead to the discovery of admissible evidence. Interrogatories one though eighty-five: Objection."

They don't waste words in San Francisco, Bascom thought as he flipped open his cell phone and dialed a number. "Frank," he said when the lawyer came on the line, "I'm calm, my pressure is down, but TELL ME WHAT IS

GOING ON."

"Ouch!" he replied.

"Sorry. I forgot to count to one."

"Lawyers love to play games," he continued. "It prolongs their client's agony and makes them more money than if they were to quickly resolve his litigation. Are you ready for the depositions?"

"Yes."

"Ok. I'll call you to confirm."

"I'll be waiting without food or water until I hear from you."

The next time Bascom spoke to Frank was the evening before the scheduled depositions. "Bob," the lawyer said apologetically, "we have to cancel the depositions."

"Why, Oh Learned One?"

"Davidson has jury duty and Rutledge is never free on Wednesdays."

"Frank," he said angrily after counting to one, "do you expect me to believe these people make the date for a Wednesday and then realize at the last minute one of them is NEVER free on Wednesdays, and the other has only one day's notice before having to appear for jury duty? My father called me many names while I was growing up, but stupid was never one of them. I'm fed up with those bozos. I want a trial and I want it now, so schedule it!"

"It doesn't work that way, Bob."

"Davidson sues me and I'm fighting to get him into court! What the hell kind of a system is this? You schedule it or I will!"

"I'll try."

"Don't try, just do!"

"Let me check with the court, and I'll give you an answer."

"I'll be waiting," Bascom said abruptly before hanging up. He understood why North did not want to revisit Judge Montfort; however, it made him no less irate. WCH had done more than wear on his nerves and his pocketbook; it had deliberately destroyed his reputation and his practice. He had become impatient to see them both restored.

Frank's letter to North resulted in an agreement to an August 9th trial date and a new set of answers to his interrogatories. "The X-ray," North wrote regarding a patient injured in an automobile accident "shows a compression fracture of the fifth cervical vertebra. The ER doctor interpreted the X-ray as not showing a fracture."

Bascom thought it was kind of Dr. Davidson to admit his famously incompetent doctor had misdiagnosed a broken neck, but his other answers were evasive and useless. He tossed the letter aside and called Norm Jefferies. He had to know if his only witness had changed sides, and his anxiety built as he waited for his secretary to connect them.

"Norm, this is Bob Bascom in Wacky Whitney. How are you?"

"Fine," he answered. "How's the political climate down there?"

"It's ok as long as you don't hold Aces and Eights. Are you still willing to testify for me?"

"Certainly," he replied energetically.

"Great! Do you know another unimpeachable physician I could consult about these charts?"

"I have a friend who's a program director in Flagstaff. He's as angry as we are with the mess in ERs. Tell him I said he'd better be nice to you."

"Thanks," Bascom said, jotting down his number. "I'll keep in touch."

He called the physician and spoke with a cooperative,

understanding voice that after a ten-minute conversation replied, "I'll be pleased to testify. Subject to a review of the files, of course."

The odds of victory still favor the hospital, *but I'm making headway*, Bascom thought as he hung up his phone.

L

Two weeks before his trial was to begin, Bascom was completing an Italian crossword puzzle at his desk in his empty *Piccola Repubblica* when Helen stuck her head into his office.

"Mr. Flannery is on the phone," she said.

"Who is he?" he asked without looking up.

"WCH's third administrator in two years."

"What's he want?"

"He won't tell me. He says it's personal. See that button?" she asked, pointing to the blinking light at the base of his telephone. "Push it, pick up the receiver, and you'll get your answer."

The idea of speaking with someone from the hospital had long ago become repulsive, but he did as ordered.

"Dr. Bascom speaking," he said formally.

"Hello, Doctor, I'm John Flannery, the new hospital administrator. How are you today?"

"I'm listening," he answered coolly.

"Er, yes. Do you think we could meet?"

"Why?"

"To talk."

"About what?"

"Things."

"I doubt it, but if I decide to, I'll call you back."

"That'll be fine, Doctor. Good-bye for now," he said. Bascom heard the click that had accompanied all the phone calls from Davidson's administrators since his meeting with Henry Rutledge. Even though recording telephone conversations without permission was illegal, Davidson's administration was taping his calls.

"What did he want?" Helen asked as he replaced the receiver in its cradle.

"A powwow," he replied, tapping a tooth with a fingernail as he thought about the call.

Bascom and Donna had dinner in a Mexican diner on the outskirts Phoenix that night. After finishing their enchiladas, rice and beans, he talked about Flannery's enigmatic request.

"He knows WCH will be in trouble if I can convince a jury I'm right," he explained, slowly spinning his glass of iced tea between his hands. "But so far I've convinced only one lawyer, two out-of-town doctors, Helen and you, that I'm right. Everyone else in town thinks I'm wacko, a troublemaker, have moved, or am incompetent compared to the new arrivals."

"That's untrue, Bob," she offered. She folded her napkin and placed it by her dish. "There are people who believe in you, but most have their own problems and don't want to get into the middle of someone else's fight. Others are too lazy or just too stupid to understand what you're doing for them. Accept it."

"That's not easy to do. Not one person in this town has written a letter to the editor in my favor, although some have written against me," he continued bitterly. "And most of those who criticize me don't know me and have never spoken to me."

"Again, accept it. Will you meet with Flannery?"

"I don't know. I thought a trial would bring Davidson's corruption into the open and solve some problems here, but I realize now that even if I convince a jury Evans killed Tommy, nothing will happen to him since he's not on trial.

"They say the truth will set you free," he continued sarcastically as he doodled on the tablecloth with a finger. "Well, that's bullshit. In this case it'll set free the guilty and get me sued for slander.

"Anyway Davidson knew his pet rock was a loser, but he'll say his qualified staff physicians had investigated Evans at my request and had found his work to be flawless, which is exactly what they did. He'll explain, maybe with a tear in his eye, that he had no reason to disbelieve them, which is false, but as soon as he learned the 'truth,' he fired him.

"The same goes for his so-called 'billing errors.' He'll claim he knew nothing about them, but corrected them as soon as I exposed them in the local press. He won't mention that every time I shut down one scam, he found a new way to screw patients.

"This is a Pyrrhic victory," he added, rubbing a hand over his chin. "If I win, I owe Frank $10,000 in attorney's fees and they go free. If I lose, I pay the hospital and its lawyer $100,000 plus, pay Frank $10,000, and they still go free. I can't afford to win or lose this case."

Donna frowned and bit her lower lip. He disliked seeing her features distorted by worry, especially if he were the cause. "A penny for your thoughts," he offered.

"Bob, Flannery's call means you've won," she said as she reached across the table and clasped his hand in hers, "but Davidson hasn't lost."

Her incongruous statement puzzled him, but he said nothing as she traced his lifeline in his palm with a polished nail.

"You're an idealist," she explained, "and you expect Davidson to obey your moral and ethical beliefs. He can't. They're so high no one I know could. You're not a major problem for him; you're simply an annoyance, like a flat tire on the highway. It'll stop him momentarily, but he'll call AAA to change it for him and be on his way again. He'll never get his hands dirty doing menial tasks.

"To save face and his bank account, Davidson has offered to drop his lawsuit if you'd quit hounding him for your rent. You've refused and he'll never understand why, but he thinks he's beaten you. No matter how this ends, you'll never convince him otherwise."

Donna let go of Bascom's hand and took a sip of her tea before continuing.

"You want to help people, but face the facts. There are over 6 billion people on this planet; many are victims of disease, malnutrition, wars and natural disasters. Has your battle against WCH helped any of them?"

"No," he replied. "But..."

"But, but what?" she continued, her voice cracking. "You're the best physician I've ever worked with, even better than Ben. No matter what the crisis, when you walked into the ER trauma room, everyone knew you could fix it. Unfortunately your idealistic view of the world clashes with the reality of life. You keep hoping that some goody-two-shoes will descend on a winged horse, pat you on the head, tell you you're right, and then punish all the bad guys.

"Well I'm here to tell you it ain't gonna happen.

"You can't save the world because the profiteers won't let you, but you can help those who need you. So I'd like you to think about ending this and getting back to being a doctor before you're no good to your patients or to you."

"The trial's still two weeks away," he replied as she sipped her tea again. "I'll think about it, but I don't think I can do as you ask."

"Damn it Robby," she said angrily, slamming down her glass. The tea sloshed onto the table and she mopped it up with her napkin. "You're like a worker bee who sees a flower on the other side of a pane of glass but doesn't realize he'll never get to it. He just keeps pounding his head against the glass until he dies of brain injuries or someone swats him. You can't change the world!"

"I don't want to change the world, Donna," Bascom protested. "I just want my patients to get good care."

"You want a hell of a lot more than that!" she said loudly. Other diners looked over to Bascom, making him feel uncomfortable in the limelight.

"Please keep your voice down," he pleaded with a downward patting movement of his hands.

"Sorry about the outburst," she apologized. "Now it'll make it tougher to tell you I'm getting married"

"Married?" asked, shocked by the bombshell news.

"In two months. I met a doctor in Phoenix. He's not half as good as you are and hasn't your courage, but he dotes on my every whim, something I don't think you could ever do. I'm no Evelyn. She adored Ben and would follow him to hell and back. She put up with his lifelong fights against the establishment, but I couldn't. I need peace in my life, at least at home, and you'd be bringing your fight even into the bedroom. Besides there is room on the pedestal for only one of us, and that's you."

"What pedestal?"

"The one in every town square, where the rabble honor the hero who did wonders for them before they stood by and watched him being drawn and quartered by the ruling gentry. They shine his brass balls, I mean his bronze helmet and shield, as long as his effigy continues to bring in the tourists. Eventually they'll be nothing left of him except a corroding mound of brass covered in pigeon droppings and graffiti spray-painted by high school dropouts who could care less about whom you were or what you did.

"The world needs people like you to slow down its inexorable degradation, but you don't need us mere mortals. You can live on beans in a shack without running water on a freezing mountaintop. And you can trudge through six-feet of snow in pajamas and sandals, but I can't. Sure, we could get along for a while, especially because the sex is great, but eventually we'd go our separate ways. It would hurt much more then than it does now."

Bascom started to speak, then paused and knitted his brows. "First Ben, now you chastise me," he said, tapping the tip of his knife on the table. "It hurts to admit it, but you're right. I loved Cris more than anything in the world, but I think if she were here today, she'd applaud you.

"I pretended there weren't any, but now I'm sure the cracks in our marriage were because of my battles against everything. I'll bet she wanted so desperately to return to Italy to save us.

"Lizzano is a small town on the side of a mountain, but it's where I practiced medicine as I believed it should be practiced and had no battles to fight." He dropped his knife and ran his hand though his long hair, bunching it in his hand behind his neck. He had often thought of wearing it in a ponytail, common among Whitney's farm workers, but then he would have to get tattoos to match. He had abandoned the idea immediately.

"I find no pleasure in doing what I'm doing, Donna. Public speaking gives me sweaty palms; lawyers give me hives; and threats give me sleepless nights. I don't want statues, honors or even tidy newspaper articles written about me. I fight my battles to do what I think is right and not for any reward. Still…."

"'Still' what?" she asked impatiently. He could see his father standing in front of him. His arms were crossed and he was tapping his foot. "Well, you Communist failure, when the hell are you going to grow up and act like a man!" he was yelling.

Bascom bit his lip. "Emotional and psychological torment, and bankruptcy seem like a high price to pay for simply asking my colleagues to give patients good, honest, inexpensive, care," he said, shaking the repugnant image from his head. "No wonder people smarter than I grumble about what's wrong with the world and then do nothing. It's a lot safer.

"Well, Donna, it's been great knowing you," Bascom concluded with a weak smile. "I wish you luck, fortune and happiness with your new husband. If you ever need my help, just call."

"I will," Donna replied, stroking her nose. "Now please take me home before I start to cry."

Bascom paid the bill and they left the restaurant. They drove in awkward silence until he pulled up in front of Donna's home. Before the SUV rolled to a stop, she jumped out and ran up to her house.

As he watched her enter her home, he heard Ben scolding him. "I thought you got it, Bob," he said, "but I was wrong." He had understood Donna's lecture but he still believed it was cowardice to retreat from a battle before clear victory or defeat. He was not yet ready to blend grays into his black and white world, even if it had cost him a future with Donna and meant facing Ben's wrath from the heavens.

After a week of agonizing soul-searching, Bascom called the WCH administrator and agreed to meet for lunch the same day. It was a decision not easily reached, but it won over his stubborn adherence to his romantic and unrealistic vision of his role in a good profession but a bad business.

John Flannery, a carrot-topped man in his mid-thirties with freckles and crooked teeth, was waiting in front of the shabby Mexican restaurant west of Whitney when Bascom arrived five minutes late for their appointment.

"Hello, Doctor," he said, offering a thin hand with manicured nails.

"Hello, Mr. Flannery. Shall we go in?" Without waiting for an answer, Bascom passed several men in overalls arguing heatedly in Spanish and entered the restaurant. He slid into a booth whose torn seating had been repaired with duct tape. Flannery sat across from him.

"What's good here?" he asked.

"Nothing, but I usually have a combination platter."

"I'll have the same," he told the waitress who had arrived to take their orders.

After she left they stiltedly discussed automobiles, rodeos, and desert dust until their food arrived. When it did, Bascom absently forked the refried beans around his plate.

"How can we settle our differences, Doctor?" Flannery asked cautiously while cutting his enchilada.

"We should get a few things straight first," he responded, resting his fork on his plate. "Your boss is trying to gouge as much money as possible from this community, while ignoring the human suffering he is causing its citizens.

Flannery put his utensils on his plate, straddled it with his elbows, and closed one hand over the other as he listened.

"Since his lawsuit is simply retaliation for my interference in his schemes, for him to settle this, I want him to pay me my back rent, with bank, not legal, interest, and all my legal fees and costs.

"Then I want an apology in the *Times*, acceptable to me, explaining how he has dismissed his lawsuit and reached a financial settlement with me. I also want him to credit me with the professional competence I deserve. I will accept nothing less.

"Finally, I want the remaining records from the *ad hoc* audit copied at your expense. Evans is incompetent and I want his license." Bascom tried to push his warm plate away from him, but it stuck to the plastic tablecloth.

"I can't answer for Dr. Davidson," Flannery said, putting his hands in his lap. "But I will tell him about your proposal and get back to you with an answer."

"I will have no further contact with you. Your lawyer can call mine," Bascom responded, remembering the unpleasant results of the meeting with Henry Rutledge, Davidson's last emissary.

"Fine," he replied. He shook Bascom's hand and picked up the tab before leaving the booth.

Bascom was in his deserted *Piccola Repubblica* an hour later, boots on the desk and a newspaper in hand, when Helen announced over the intercom that Helleman was on the line. He put down the paper and picked up his phone.

"We've won!" Frank exclaimed as soon as he said "*pronto*." "WE HAVE WON! North told me Davidson has authorized him to give you everything you want. Well almost everything. He can't guarantee Evans will lose his license. What happened there today?"

After Bascom summarized the meeting with the administrator, Frank said excitedly, "this is great! You're as stubborn as a mule, and it worked out."

"I'm a real Ripley's character," he replied self-mockingly. "How long will it take to wrap up this mess?"

"Probably a couple of weeks to copy the records and draw up the settlement documents. I'll make sure the *Times* publishes the apology even if we have to pay to get it in a part of the paper where readers might see it."

"That'll be before the personal advertisements offering sexual gratification with sheep."

"Cynical right to the end, eh, Bob?"

"Sorry, Frank, you're right. You did a great job. I'll talk to you later."

He hung up and called Helen into his office. "It's over," he said as she stepped though the doorway.

"I TOLD you we'd win!" she said, running around the desk and giving him a hug. "I knew Frank could do the job!"

"At times your help was more important to me than his. But now you need to take a letter," he said.

After dictating the missive, he handed her a magazine from his desk. "The address is in this journal. Go home when you're done typing it. No sense both of us hanging around an empty office."

"Right, Boss," she said. She turned to leave but not before he saw tears in her eyes.

As he leaned back in his chair, his eyes fell on Evelyn's retirement statue in his bookcase. "Ben's gifts!" he said before retrieving the shoebox and the bowling trophy with its middle finger transformed into a Bronx salute.

Evelyn was worth much more than this. He shook his head and put the statue on his desk before removing the blue envelope from the shoebox. Ben's instructions scrawled across its front said, "Please contact my attorney, Peter Henry, in Phoenix."

He sat at his desk and dialed the lawyer's number. A secretary answered the phone, and seconds later a friendly voice came on the line.

"Hello, Dr. Bascom. I've been waiting for your call."

"I'm sorry about the delay, Mr. Henry. How can I help you?"

"How can I help you? Ben and I grew up together and I was privileged to be his friend and counsel. He was more than a good man and a fine physician; he was also an astute businessman of significant worth."

"So this is about Ben's estate?" Bascom asked.

"The Evelyn and Benjamin Wiggins' Trust, to be precise. He established it to provide free medical services to the needy. We will administer it here, but aid may be provided anywhere in the world. There are three trustees. I'll focus on its legal aspects, Mr. Bill Tillman on investments and financial, and you on medical aid and services.

"In addition, Ben specifically requested you be an employee of the trust. It now generates $50,000 a month. As we refine its assets, you should have $75,000 a month to divide between services and personal income, as you see fit."

"You mean $75,000 a year," Bascom corrected.

"A month."

Bascom was incredulous. Because of his penchant for giving free care to the poor and not running useless tests on his patients, it was far more than he grossed in a year.

"How much did Ben give to this trust?"

"$10,000,000," Henry responded, "although when we settle the estate, additional funds will pour into it. I'd like to meet with you and Bill to go over the specifics."

"Maybe in a week. Would that be Ok?"

"That'll be fine, Doctor. I'll await your call."

Bascom hung up and called Lance Berkford. After a half a dozen rings, a grumpy voice answered, "Go away."

"What are you doing in bed in the middle of the afternoon, Lance?"

"I had a terrible night in the pit. What's up?"

"I won."

"I said you would," he yawned.

"I feel I sold out by not going to court."

"You did more than you needed to do, but if you think it wasn't enough, wear your hair shirt for a week. Is it still hanging in your closet?"

"Yes," he laughed. "The damn Jesuits taught me how to think, but not how to survive in a vicious world. They also instilled in me a constant sense of guilt. It's terrible when you always feel you've done something wrong, even when you know you haven't. Anyway, I'm tired of watching a few greedy souls destroy other people's lives in their struggle for the 'medical grail,' as Frank calls it," he said. "So I intend to take Ben's suggestions on how to be an idealist and keep your sanity at the same time, even if your colleagues think you're nuts."

"You must have liked the guy. You always speak about him," Lance interrupted.

"They'll never be another like him," Bascom replied.

"That's a real compliment coming from a nit-picking pain-in-the-ass like you."

"Thanks," he laughed. "I'm returning to Lizzano, where men doffed their caps when I passed them on the street and women left plucked chickens outside my door in appreciation for care I gave their families. It was the way folks there showed their respect to another human being for his worth, and not for what he thought his title or riches deserved."

"What'll you do there, Bob?"

"Open a clinic. The government sends disadvantaged kids there every summer to play tennis in a smog-free environment. I'll make sure they get special medical assistance when needed. I'm concerned about how they'll receive me though, since I failed them after Cris' death."

"They'll welcome you back," Lance replied. "I don't think they've forgotten how good you are. Where will you get the money?"

"I get $900,000 a year from Ben's trust to use as I see fit."

"$900,000?"

"Yup."

"Wow! Did you win!"

"I didn't win," Bascom replied. "I'll never win. People like me fight with our wooden swords and end mocked and maimed for our efforts. Ironically, even though we know what awaits us, we still fight our losing battles."

"That's why Fred named you 'DQS,' 'Don Quixote in Scrubs,'"

"Please don't call me that again, Lance. It makes me feel like a fool."

"If it weren't for fools like you, this planet would be much worse off."

"I doubt it."

"'Thick headed,' doesn't begin to describe you. Will you take Donna with you?"

"We broke up."

"Are you some failed lab experiment, Bascom?" Lance sighed.

"It's likely, but I hear there's a home frontal lobotomy kit on the market. One little hole in my skull, and I'll be happy even sitting on Davidson's lap."

"Don't forget to castrate yourself first. I wouldn't want a stray erection to confuse you," Lance replied cynically.

"I told you the Jesuits screwed with my head," he answered. "But that's over. I'm giving up living my life based on some religious dogma. And while I'm on the mountain I'm going to expand my old newspaper articles into a book in my spare time. I've even thought of a catchy title."

"What's that?"

"How to Be a Patient and Live to Tell the Tale!"

"The establishment will trash it," Lance laughed.

"Maybe. King Hammurabi decreed in 1700 B.C. that doctors guilty of malpractice would have their fingers cut off. It was better justice than today's oversight by trial lawyers looking for their share of juicy malpractice verdicts, but patients need a more practical guide to survive what's happening in medicine today."

Lance laughed again. "How do you come up with this stuff?"

"Bedtime reading."

"Do you think anyone will publish it?"

"No, but it'll give me something to do when I'm not seeing patients, skiing the *Corno,* or hiking in the forests around the town."

"I'll never understand you, Bascom."

"That makes two of us. What are you up to?"

"I'm accepting a position with the Indian Health Service in New Mexico."

"Will Rachael go along?"

"Nah. We broke up too," he explained. "Beauty is only skin-deep, and in her case, beneath the skin was just more skin. Maybe I'll find a Squaw."

"I could use help in the clinic. Since your Spanish is first-rate, you'd learn Italian in six months."

"Maybe someday," Lance replied, "but now I have to run."

LI

The next morning Bascom dropped off Evelyn's repugnant bowling trophy at his mechanic's garage and then drove to his office where Dr. Chang was awaiting him. After a brief meeting, the young doctor handed Bascom an envelope and left.

He then bundled Evans' ER records with the newspaper article reporting Tommy's pellet gun death and left for Phoenix. There he joined Peter Henry and Bill Tillman, co-trustees of the Wiggins' trust, in a productive 2-hour meeting. Afterward he drove to Marvin Adelsohn's building.

He entered the Health and Consumer Affairs Board member's empty office at the lunch hour with the documents tucked under his arm. A green-eyed secretary typing with one finger, looked up as he approached her desk.

"I'd like to speak to Dr. Adelsohn," he said firmly. "I'm Dr. Bascom."

"One moment, please," she replied, picking up the telephone. She spoke briefly and then hung up the receiver.

"I'm sorry. Doctor says you'll have to return when you have an appointment," she said primly.

"Sure thing," he said, walking towards a door marked "Private."

"Wait! You can't go in there!" she protested, standing from her chair.

"It'll take only two minutes," he responded, flinging open the door. Adelsohn was eating a sandwich at his desk, and his head jerked up as his door crashed into the wall.

"See here, Bascom," he spluttered, "you can't come in here like…"

"Sit down," he growled at the obese figure. "I won't take much of your time." He strode across the room and dropped the records on the desk, knocking over a Styrofoam cup. Its dark contents raced across the desk and spilled onto Adelsohn's lap.

Bascom put his fists on the desk and leaned toward Adelsohn who was brushing the liquid off his pants.

"You said you wanted proof, fat man? Here it is," he snarled, rapping the back of his hand on the files. "There's also an article in here reporting the tragic story of a boy who would be alive today had he received even basic care in our local ER. I called you about him after he died, but you said it wasn't your job to care. Well now it is."

"Lis…" came the pathetic interruption to the diatribe.

"Zitto! Shut up!" he commanded as his opponent paled. "I want you to remember this boy, Adelsohn," he continued, wagging a menacing finger in his face. "Had it not been for you, Evans would have been off the ER staff and that boy would still be alive!

"Your proof is in these charts," he jeered. He picked up a few of them and flung them one at a time like floppy Frisbees at Adelsohn. "I doubt you'll ever read them, or if you did, you'd have the brains to understand them or the guts to act on them. But no matter what you do, I want you to remember the boy! Every time you look at your kids, every time you see your fat, stupid face in the mirror, I want you to remember the boy you killed and the job you failed to do!

"By the way," Bascom continued in a more conciliatory tone, "as an incentive for you to begin a real investigation, my attorney has a copy of these records. Should you do nothing, in one month he will release my final article to the Phoenix papers, indicting your lazy, incompetent ass. Then the community can judge the job you and your group have been doing." He glared at the ashen figure a moment longer before turning. As he did, Adelsohn yelled out behind him.

"This is intimidation! I'll sue! I'll have your license for this! I, I'll..." he sputtered lamely.

Bascom wheeled. His anger was at its peak and he wanted to pull Adelsohn from his chair and pound him into a greasy hamburger.

"If you're smart you'll cover your ass with a real investigation," he growled contemptuously. "But if you prefer to sue me, go right ahead. I'd love to take you on." He again turned and walked towards Adelsohn's secretary. The young woman was pressing herself against the door in an attempt to blend into the paint.

"He wasn't so busy," he said gently to the terrorized woman. She smiled nervously as he brushed past her.

When he arrived back in Whitney, he dropped off his SUV at his mechanic's garage and walked the few blocks to his office. He saw three patients that afternoon and then returned to the garage. His truck was in the lot, and after verifying the newly installed shelf was level with the base of its rear window, he entered the office.

"Nice job on the SUV, Fred," he said. "How about the statue?" The mechanic took the trophy from a shelf and shook it. "Perfect," Bascom said sinisterly. He paid his bill and left with the bronze figure as Fred shook his head in awe.

Bascom drove home, whistling all the way. He had not

felt so good in many years. He felt even better two days later when he read the article in Sunday's Whitney *Times*:

"To Whom It May Concern: (it said)

"Whitney Community Hospital and Robert Bascom, M.D., have announced they have reached a settlement in the litigation initiated by the hospital. WCH has dismissed its complaint with prejudice and will pay Dr. Bascom an undisclosed amount in settlement of all current and future claims he may have, including all attorney's fees and costs.

"The hospital would like to thank Dr. Bascom for his most professional assistance to WCH during his term as its Emergency Room director.

"John Flannery,
"Hospital Administrator"

On Monday morning patients and well-wishers flooded his office with phone calls. He refused to speak with any of them except Jonas Price.

"Congratulations, Doc," he said. "I knew you'd win, even if most of the town didn't think so."

"It's over, Jonas. That's all that counts."

"Not yet it isn't!" he disagreed. "Some important people and I will be filing a class action suit against Davidson and his hospital as soon as we can find the right lawyer. Will you help?"

"No. I'm returning to Italy, but Frank Helleman is your man."

"Italy?"

"My adopted land. Someday you might send Carl over

to spend a summer with me," he added. "I can show him the country and, if he's interested, help him apply to my alma mater, the University of Bologna Medical School."

"You'd do that?"

"Of course. Someone has to carry the caduceus," he replied, recalling Ben's scrapbook.

"What's that?"

"It's not important, Jonas. Helen will give you my new address. Give my love to Martha and Carl."

"But..."

"I have to go. Stay well and good luck," he said, before hanging up. He leaned back in his chair and put his boots up on his desk, wondering whether Jonas and his friends would stand up to Davidson. People do rebel as the French aristocracy learned to its dismay during a popular uprising a couple of hundred years earlier. Whether the Whitnians would find the strength and courage to fight medical corruption in their town was no longer his problem.

Helen was bubbling with excitement when she entered his office. "The phone's been ringing off the hook all morning, Bob. I've been hearing comments from 'we knew you were right,' to 'you're a great doctor,' to 'we were rooting for you all along.' We have more patients scheduled for tomorrow than we've had since you opened," she said enthusiastically, her eyes sparking as they did when they first met. "Old patients are making appointments for physicals for weeks from now, and new ones want you as their doctor."

"Dr. Chang will be pleased to know he has such a busy schedule ahead of him," Bascom said as the doctor entered his office. Dr. Chang smiled at the news, stopping just inside the door.

"He's your new commander-in-chief."

"You won't stay?" she pleaded tearfully.

"No. I'm returning to Italy. Helen, you stuck with me

through it all, and I'll never forget you for it," he said. As he rose from his chair he picked up an envelope from his desk with a $25,000 check in it. He walked over and hugged her.

"This is for the increases and bonuses you never received, thanks in part to Dr. Chang," he explained, handing her the envelope.

"Bob, I don't..."

"No need to say anything," he said. He then took Ben's shoebox and scrapbook from his desk, shook Dr. Chang's hand, wished him luck, and left without looking back.

He drove home and packed his suitcases but left the poster of his snow-covered *baita* on the living room wall. He fetched the bottles of Armando Manni's olive oil and Pedroni's *Cesare* balsamic from the cabinet over the sink where he had stored them after Joe Thompson had unceremoniously emptied them onto his salad, and dropped them into the garbage.

Time for new memories. He picked up his suitcases, returned to his SUV, and tossed them into the rear of the truck.

He took Evelyn's modified bowling trophy from the passenger seat, unscrewed the wing nut from its base and then screwed it onto the shelf in the back of the vehicle so it could be seen from the rear window.

Now for the piece de resistance. He climbed into the driver's seat and took Ben's toupee from the shoebox. He laughed as he put it on his head and checked it in his rearview mirror.

Satisfied he had tilted it just as Ben would have worn it, he started the SUV and drove away. In his rearview mirror he could see the female figure in her bowling poise with her right arm extended with a thermometer growing out of the middle finger of her hand. Every time the SUV bounced or braked, her arm would swing up and down in an unmistakably obscene gesture. It resembled, in a profane way, the bobblehead dolls in the rear windows of the classic Chevrolets and Fords that paraded Whitney's main street on Saturday nights.

He drove past doctors' offices and down Navajo Trail, Whitney's ritzy neighborhood, tapping his brakes when he passed people so they too could enjoy the statue's one-armed salute. He was sure Wiggins was somewhere up there saying, "Atta boy, Bathtub."

As he drove past the hospital, Simon Davidson and Joe Thompson were talking together on the sidewalk. He pulled up in front of them and rolled down his window.

"Hi, Joe," he said. "I thought I'd say good-bye to you and your loser friend."

"Loser?" Davidson roared like a male lion. "You're the loser, not me."

Bascom, looking straight into his eyes, replied, "Davidson, when I was growing up there was a kid in the neighborhood who thought he could do whatever he wanted because he had money. He was wrong. The other kids hated him and regularly kicked his ass until his mother paid them off.

"Rather than kick your puny ass," he growled contemptuously as Thompson backed away from the curb, "I'm leaving you and your hospital to a pack of wolves and their lawyers.

"And as for you, Joe, say hello to your son for me," he said to the obese surgeon.

"I, I don't have a son," he stuttered lamely.

"You sure do. You remember Helen, don't you? You've got her picture in your office. Her son has inherited your congenitally dimpled earlobe, but not your pathetic personality. It's never too late to redeem yourself," he said before quickly adding, "I take that back. In your case it might be.

"Ciao," he concluded as he pulled his SUV a few feet forward. When he was sure they could see Evelyn's statue, he tapped the horn and then the brakes. He watched her arm swing up and down in his rearview mirror and then sang out, "I'm free and you're not," before driving away.

He was humming "*Vincerò*," "I shall win," from Giacomo Puccini's unfinished operatic masterpiece *Turandot*, when he arrived at Sky Harbor airport an hour later. He parked in the lot, where a friend of Donna's would pick up the truck that evening, and then rode the passenger bus to the terminal. After checking his bags he sat in the waiting room until his plane boarded.

Almost six years after first setting foot in Arizona's beautiful Sonoran desert, Bascom began the long return trip to his adopted homeland, eager and curious, but most of all, confident about the real contribution he would now make to the profession he loved.

***

Telephone lines in Whitney hummed with rumors and regrets the next day after the news services reported the crash of a British airline into the North Atlantic, 300 miles off the European coast. The pilot of British Airways flight 506 from Phoenix to London had reported engine trouble before ditching into the ocean. Ships and planes were continuing to scour the frigid waters for survivors, but so far had found none.

The Whitney *Times*' front-page article stated that Robert Bascom, M.D., a passenger on the flight, had been a frequent subject of its articles over the years. It quoted Dr. Simon Davidson as saying, "even though we disagreed on a few matters, I always respected his views and his concern for his patients. I'm sure all who knew the man will miss him."

*** FINE ***

The Author

Raymond C. Andrews is an American born physician who graduated from the University of Bologna Medical School in Italy in 1970. After training in general surgery, neurosurgery, and aerospace medicine, he accepted the position as an emergency room director in a New Jersey hospital.

In the late 1970s he entered private practice in California and later wrote a popular series of articles on health care for the Bakersfield *Californian*. Other articles and comments of his have appeared in the *New England Journal of Medicine*, the *Bergen Record*, and *Private Practice*. While in practice he developed "Drop-in-Laboratory Services" to make access to medical care easier and less costly for the migrant workers that were a large portion of his patients.

Lured back to Italy by medieval castles and the opera at *La Scala* in 1984, Dr. Andrews worked ten years for the state health system. He was the first physician to participate in the then newly established Italian emergency hot line system.

After twenty-five years of medical practice on two continents, and with the regrettable certainty that patient care has taken a backseat to bureaucracy and to the questionable tactics of some of his colleagues both here and abroad, in 1995 he accepted a position with the United States Public Health Service and was a director of a Navajo clinic on their reservation in northeastern Arizona. He was also director of the clinic's Emergency Medical Services, and a director of the National Native American Emergency Medical Services Association.

Dr. Andrews is retired and passes his time writing, building model ships, and driving his modified Jeep and camper in the Arizona desert with his wife, Jennifer.

He has published Dr. Bascom's book, *How to Be a Patient and Live to Tell the Tale!*

Books by Raymond C. Andrews, MD

The Life and Times of Benjamin Wiggins, MD
Medical Grail
Medical Grail Unabridged Edition
How to Be a Patient and Live to Tell the Tale!
Driving the Great Western Trail in Arizona

All books are available on Kindle and in a soft cover, printed version through Amazon, many online retailers, and at the author's website:

www.medicalgrail.com.

Made in the USA
San Bernardino, CA
22 October 2012